Magic, mystery, and high fashion— this is not *your typical honeymoon!*

"Thief!" Lady Sylvia's voice was unmistakable. "Stop, thief!"

Lady Sylvia must have issued a more magical command as well, for someone uttered a wild cry of surprise and dismay that made the little hairs on the nape of my neck bristle. Glass broke. Then came silence, followed by the inevitable sounds of a household rousing in the dead of night.

I tried to see over Thomas's shoulder as we peered into Lady Sylvia's bedchamber.

"Mother!" Thomas was alarmed. "Are you all right?"

"Yes, dear. Quite all right. I'm afraid he escaped, drat the man."

"Who was it?" Cecy demanded, her curiosity unquenchable as ever. She and James were behind us.

"My dear, I have no idea." Lady Sylvia brandished a man's slipper. "He left only this. Do you think we should send a footman out with this on a velvet cushion to see whom it fits?"

The
GRAND

*being a revelation of matters of
High Confidentiality and
Greatest Importance, including
extracts from the intimate diary
of a Noblewoman and the sworn
testimony of a Lady of Quality*

Patricia C. Wrede
and Caroline Stevermer

TOUR

or THE PURLOINED
CORONATION
REGALIA

Magic Carpet Books
Harcourt, Inc.
Orlando Austin New York San Diego Toronto London

www.HarcourtBooks.com

First Magic Carpet Books edition 2006

Magic Carpet Books is a trademark of Harcourt, Inc.,
registered in the United States of America and/or other jurisdictions.

The Library of Congress has cataloged the hardcover edition as follows:
Wrede, Patricia C., 1953–
The Grand Tour: being a revelation of matters of high
confidentiality and greatest importance, including extracts from
the intimate diary of a noblewoman and the sworn testimony of
a lady of quality/Patricia C. Wrede and Caroline Stevermer.
p. cm.
Summary: In 1817, two English cousins take a honeymoon "Grand
Tour of the Continent" with their new husbands and become entangled
in a mysterious plot to create a magical Emperor of Europe.
[1. Cousins—Fiction. 2. Honeymoons—Fiction. 3. Supernatural—
Fiction. 4. Diaries—Fiction. 5. Europe—Social life and customs—
19th century—Fiction.] I. Stevermer, Caroline. II. Title.
PZ7.W915Gr 2004
[Fic]—dc22 2004001120
ISBN-13: 978-0-15-204616-3 ISBN-10: 0-15-204616-X
ISBN-13: 978-0-15-205556-1 pb ISBN-10: 0-15-205556-8 pb

Map created by Patricia Isaacs

Text set in Fournier
Designed by Lydia D'moch

A C E G H F D B

Printed in the United States of America

ACKNOWLEDGMENTS

Deepest gratitude to Chris Bell,
Charlotte Boynton, Anna Feruglio Dal Dan,
Diana Wynne Jones, Anna Mazzoldi, Delia Sherman,
Sherwood Smith, and Eve Sweetser, who helped
to catch the mistakes we made in this book.
Any fresh errors are, of course, our own.

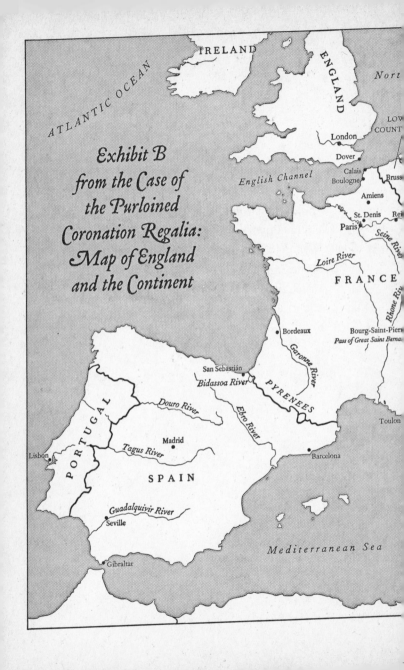

Exhibit B from the Case of the Purloined Coronation Regalia: Map of England and the Continent

ENGLAND

I suppose that if I were going to blame our involvement on anyone (which I see no reason to do), I would be compelled to say that it was all Aunt Charlotte's fault. If she had not been in such a dreadful temper over Kate's marriage, Kate and Thomas would not have decided to take their wedding journey on the Continent in preference to remaining in England, and James and I would not have gone with them. And then very likely we would never have known anything about any of it.

Kate is my cousin, and now that she is married she is a Marchioness, which is what put our Aunt Charlotte's nose so dreadfully out of joint. Admittedly, Kate said some awful things to Aunt Charlotte, but after the way Aunt Charlotte treated Kate, she deserved every one of them. She made matters worse by hinting that I ought to be as put out as she, because Kate was going to be Lady Schofield and I was only going to be Mrs. Tarleton. So it is her own fault that none of us wished to stay and listen to her nagging.

At first James was dubious about our joining Kate and Thomas on their wedding journey, though he and Thomas are nearly as great friends as Kate and I. I felt compelled to point out that even if we did not accompany them, they would have Lady Sylvia traveling with them at least until they reached Paris. "And if Kate does not object to having her mama-at-law with them, you ought not to be such a high stickler about our going as well. Besides, she and Thomas invited us."

"You mean you cooked up the idea and talked Kate into it, and she persuaded Thomas," James said. "Sometimes you go too far, Cecy."

"I did not!" I said hotly. Which is not to say that I would not have done so if I had thought of it, but I saw no reason to mention that to James. "Kate came to me, I promise you, and it was Thomas's idea, not hers."

"Thomas wants us on his wedding journey?"

"It's our wedding journey, too," I pointed out, feeling rather annoyed. "And I believe he thinks he is doing us a favor."

"A favor?"

"Aunt Charlotte," I said succinctly.

"I am perfectly capable of handling—" James broke off suddenly, looking rather thoughtful. "You're right," he said after a moment. "That does sound like Thomas."

"If you are quite determined, I can tell Kate to tell Thomas that we have other plans," I said. "But since he already knows perfectly well that we haven't—"

"No, no, I'll talk to him," James said hastily. He turned away, muttering something about keeping me out of it, which I chose not to hear.

So James went off to see Thomas, and they ended up in some gaming hell or other and were *odiously* drunk. (Or so my brother, Oliver, informed me. He was quite scathing about it, until I inquired very sweetly how he had happened to be there to see.) And when I saw James late the next day, he had agreed that when Kate and Thomas and Lady Sylvia left London, we would go along with them.

James made a point of asking who was making the arrangements, and he seemed quite relieved to hear that Lady Sylvia was managing it all. I gather that he does not entirely trust Thomas's skills in that regard.

Naturally, Aunt Charlotte made a number of shocked and uncomplimentary remarks when she discovered what we were planning. As it was none of her affair, James and I ignored her. After all, Aunt Elizabeth did not see anything amiss about it, and she is at least as high a stickler as Aunt Charlotte. (Well, actually, what Aunt Elizabeth said was that if going on a wedding journey together was the oddest thing the four of us ever did, Aunt Charlotte should be grateful.) Papa, of course, was delighted, and gave Kate and me each a long list of antiquities that he said we must see (most of them quite unsuitable, but I dare say that didn't occur to him).

The wedding was rather small, as we held it barely three weeks after the announcements appeared, but it was most elegant. James and Thomas stood up for each other, and Kate and I were each other's maids of honor, and Papa gave both of us away, since Kate's Papa has been dead these five years. I must confess that at the time I somewhat regretted the haste and the quietness of the ceremony, but I would have gone to much greater lengths in order to be married along with dear Kate. Upon reflection, however, I see that it was a very good thing we were so quick about matters. If we had waited, Aunt Charlotte would probably have unbent and begun speaking to Kate again, and then she would certainly have tried to bully Kate into wearing a wedding gown identical to mine (which was Brussels lace over cream satin), and it would not have done at all. Kate is far too short to look well in the styles I wear, but she was perfectly *stunning* in the white silk brocade that she and I and Lady Sylvia picked out.

Kate was a little nervous before the ceremony started; I believe she was afraid she would trip while she was walking up the aisle, or become entangled in her veil, or tear the hem out of her gown. Nothing of the sort happened, and I am quite sure she forgot to worry as soon as she saw Thomas waiting for her. She looked very happy indeed, and positively *floated* down the aisle. I am afraid I didn't pay too much attention to Kate after that, because it was my turn to walk up the aisle and I was looking at James.

The wedding breakfast afterward was a sumptuous affair. Neither my brother, Oliver, nor Aunt Charlotte could find anything to turn up their noses about, but none of us wished to linger. Finally, a footman came to say that the carriages were at the door, and we said our good-byes. Aunt

Elizabeth hugged us both and gave us each a pair of pearl earrings, which she had enchanted so that they would never fall out or get lost. Papa (who was beginning to look vaguely rumpled already) gave me a bottle of brandy (in case any of us should be carriage-sick) and another list of antiquities he had forgotten to include the first time. Oliver, to my complete astonishment, gave me a hug that did severe damage to his cravat and promised James and me one of Thunder's foals. Aunt Charlotte sniffed and said she hoped none of us would regret it, and then presented Kate and me with identical boxes of starched linen handkerchiefs. Kate immediately found a use for one; her sister, Georgina (who has always been something of a watering pot), had already soaked her own handkerchief, and Kate was too kind to let her continue dabbing at her eyelashes with a soggy ball.

We escaped at last, climbed into our carriages, and started off. Lady Sylvia travels in the first style of elegance. She had a carriage for herself (I thought it was out of kindness, to keep from invading the privacy of the newlyweds, but Kate told me later that her carriage is specially sprung), one for each couple, two more for the servants, and a sixth that was completely filled with baggage (most of it Lady Sylvia's, as Kate and I had not had sufficient time to assemble much in the way of bride-clothes). Most of the servants were Lady Sylvia's, too. James had brought his valet and Thomas had brought a man named Piers, who he said filled the same office, but neither Kate nor I had had the opportunity to engage a maid. Lady Sylvia seemed to think that we would do far better to wait until we reached Paris to replenish our wardrobes and hire personal servants, and we saw no reason whatever to disagree with her.

Lady Sylvia was eager to return to France, so instead of taking the journey in easy stages, we went straight to Dover. Despite all her planning, we were not able to board a packet that night; the winds were against us, and no boats could cross the Channel until they changed. So we spent the night at a small inn in Dover. (Kate was quite thoroughly taken aback when the proprietor addressed her as "Lady Schofield.")

The following morning the wind had changed, so after Thomas and James finished arguing about who was to settle up at the inn (each of them insisted on paying the whole himself), we all went down to the docks. It was cloudy and looked as if it might rain at any moment, but there was a good stiff breeze blowing and the captain of the packet assured us that we would have a quick and easy passage to Calais.

If what we had was a quick and easy passage, I am not at all sure that I wish to return to England until someone invents a spell to whisk people across the Channel without benefit of boats. We were barely under way when I began to feel a bit peculiar. I decided to go and lie down in our cabin, but it did not answer; I was most vilely unwell for nearly the whole of the crossing.

James came in at least once, looking worried, but of

course there was nothing he could do. I heard him a few moments later, talking to Thomas outside the cabin.

"Don't fret," Thomas told him, in what I thought was a most unfeeling tone. "Nobody ever dies of seasickness; they only wish they would."

Kate came by just then and made them go away. A little later she returned with a cup half full of something dark and strong-smelling. "Lady Sylvia made this," she told me. "She says it will do you good."

"If you have any friendship for me at all, you will not even speak to me of swallowing anything," I replied.

"If I have to take it away, I shall probably spill it, and someone will slip in it and break a leg," Kate declared. "You had better drink it."

"You haven't spilt anything in ages," I told her. "Not since you and Thomas finally settled things between you." But I drank it anyway, because Kate can be very persistent. It was not nearly as nasty as it looked, and it did help. On her way out of the cabin, Kate tripped over the doorsill, just to prove I was wrong about her spilling things.

Lady Sylvia's potion sent me off to sleep, and when I woke up the boat did not seem to be tossing about quite so much. I was just wondering whether perhaps I might dare to try standing up, when the door of the cabin opened and James came in.

"We've arrived," he told me. "Are you feeling well enough to come ashore?"

"For solid ground under my feet, I can do anything," I said fervently, and swung my feet out of the bunk. My head swam a little, but not enough to stop me. It was only when I reached the deck that I realized my ordeal was not yet over. Despite the multitude of travelers coming to France of late, no one had yet built docks in Calais suitable for receiving them. Instead, the packet stopped some way out from land, and we disembarked into smaller boats to be rowed ashore.

A crowd of workingmen waited on the beach. I thought they meant to carry our luggage, but when I mentioned this, Lady Sylvia said, "They will do that, certainly, but their first duty is to carry us."

"What?" Kate said, alarmed, but just then the boat must have reached some crucial point, for the men surged forward into the sea. They surrounded the rowing boat, shouting incomprehensibly. Having made the crossing many times before, Lady Sylvia rose immediately, stepped up on the seat of the rowboat, and with considerable aplomb seated herself on the shoulders of two of the men. She was borne off immediately, and the rest of us did our best to follow her example, with varying degrees of success. Soon we were deposited onshore, most of us only slightly damp from the sea spray and none the worse for wear (though Kate had somehow contrived to become soaked to the waist, despite Thomas's care in selecting two of the huskiest porters to carry her ashore). The sun was shining out of a clear, blue sky. We were in France.

Inscribed upon the flyleaf of the commonplace book of
the Most Honorable the Marchioness of Schofield

This book was given to me as a wedding gift by my uncle, Arthur Rushton. In it, I am to record my experiences and impressions. Uncle Arthur made a fine speech of presentation in which he admonished me to remember that the thoughts that we record today will become the treasured historical documents of the future. If this is so, I feel sorry for the future. Every other attempt I have made to keep a commonplace book rapidly degenerated into a list of what happened to my pocket money. This time I will try to do better. I intend to write an account of our wedding journey. But I will be astonished if anyone ever considers it a document of historical interest.

From the commonplace book of Lady Schofield

> *10 August 1817*
> *Written aboard the packet, en route from Dover to Calais*

If I live to be one hundred, I will never forget my astonishment the first time I heard my title used. The five of us, Thomas and James, Lady Sylvia, Cecy, and I, were at the Black Swan in Dover, where we were to spend the night before catching the packet boat to Calais. When our rooms were prepared, the innkeeper asked if we found them satisfactory.

"And you, Lady Schofield?" he asked. I glanced at Lady Sylvia. She was regarding me with a very faint smile, and paid no attention to the innkeeper. Puzzled, I turned to Cecy, who watched me, eyes dancing. "Oh!" I said. "Ah, er—perfectly satisfactory, thank you."

The innkeeper looked relieved and left us. Lady Sylvia waited at the door while I took a look out of the window and Cecelia inspected the mattress on the bed. "I feel a complete goose," I remarked.

"You'll get used to it," said Cecy. "'Mrs. Tarleton' sounds just as odd to me." She sat down on the bed with a flounce that made the feather bed puff softly under the coverlet. "I think marriage will agree with me."

Lady Sylvia closed the door gently. "Since the subject has arisen," she said, "I think it might be well to discuss it a little." She loosened the ribbons of her hat and crossed to stand before the looking glass to take it off. "You do know what tonight entails? I think it only fair to Thomas that I inquire. And to dear James, of course."

Cecy looked appalled. "We certainly do," she exclaimed. "How could anyone grow up in the country without noticing—" She broke off in some confusion, coloring slightly. Cecy blushes beautifully, with pure rose rushing up to her cheeks. It is a pity so very few things provoke it.

"Do you, Kate?" asked Lady Sylvia gently.

I felt myself blush to the roots of my hair. I blush dreadfully, a hot scarlet like a cooked lobster. "Aunt Charlotte explained things to me once," I said.

Cecy and Lady Sylvia exchanged a look of horror. Cecy sprang up off the bed. "I'll just go see if James is finished downstairs," she said hastily.

"Yes, do," said Lady Sylvia. "And if you find Thomas, contrive to keep him with you for a few more minutes, won't you? I'd rather we weren't interrupted just now."

"I should think not!" exclaimed Cecy, and left us.

N.B. Sixpence to innkeeper's daughter for putting a nosegay of lavender and rosemary in my room.

Lady Sylvia's explanation was much more plausible than Aunt Charlotte's. Nevertheless, when I was alone with Thomas in my room that evening, he told me, "There's no need to look so stricken."

I couldn't think of anything to say. Did I look stricken? I was trying so hard not to.

"There's nothing to be afraid of. No need for haste."

I tried to reassure Thomas, the way Thomas was trying to reassure me. "I'm not afraid. Not exactly. But I've spent my whole life being clumsy, and this seems to offer more scope for embarrassing myself than anything I've done yet."

For a moment, Thomas looked quite fierce. Then he demanded, "What's wrong with the way you dance?"

"Nothing." What did dancing have to do with it?

"Of course not," Thomas said. "If you can dance, you don't have a thing to be concerned about. Just stop worrying."

"I can't help it."

"Yes, you can. Stop thinking about yourself," Thomas ordered. "Think about me, instead."

The odious Mr. Strangle told me once that he thought I must be passionate because I had that kind of mouth. Given how carefully Aunt Charlotte always watched me during my Season in London, it seems odd that the most ill-bred person I met was in her company. Mr. Strangle was supposed to tutor young gentlemen in behavior as well as scholarship. I would not trust him to tutor a dog's behavior. I was terribly put about by his remark, not merely because Mr. Strangle was detestable, but because I have always feared my own feelings. Mouth or no mouth, Mr. Strangle or no Mr. Strangle, I suspect I am passionate. When I want something, I want it with all my heart. When I hate someone, such as Mr. Strangle, I hate them with all my heart. Prayers and repentance for such strong feelings aside, I want passionately, I hate passionately. When I love someone . . .

I don't know why I love Thomas. On occasion he has angered me more thoroughly than Mr. Strangle did. He is bossy and devious and obstinate. He's not above middling height, and he stubbornly refuses to admit he is not tall. It has taken me our entire acquaintance to convince him that I have a perfectly good brain in my head and a perfectly strong body to go with it. He treats me as if I am made of spun sugar, of cut glass, of Chinese porcelain—until he forgets and treats me as his absolute equal in everything. He is the soul of consideration and generosity, inviting James and

Cecy and even Lady Sylvia to accompany us on this wedding journey, so that I would feel more comfortable as I venture out in the great and fashionable world for the first time.

I tried not to worry anymore. Not about embarrassing myself by being too passionate. Not about anything.

I thought entirely of Thomas, and it was all far more wonderful than even Lady Sylvia had led me to expect. Lest Uncle Arthur ever set eyes on these pages, I will reserve the details. After all, if I live to be one hundred, I will never forget that night.

The waves seem to be increasing in violence. My spirits are unimpaired, though poor Cecy is sadly ill, yet the motion of the ship is making it difficult to write. I will stop now, lest I blot the page or spill the ink.

CALAIS

From the commonplace book of Lady Schofield

> 10 August 1817
> Calais
> At Dessein's Hotel
> After dinner

N.B. Two francs to small boy at quay for catching my bonnet when the wind sailed it along the pier and nearly into the water. He called me "Madame" when he thanked me. I almost looked behind me to see whom he was addressing.

N.B. What is stain on pink dress? Ask Lady S. what was in that seasickness potion. Any hope of removal?

This afternoon we reached Calais. I have quite dried out now. Thomas has sent a card around to Mr. Brummell inviting him to join us all for dinner here at Dessein's tomorrow evening. Such dinners are part of a practice called Calais blackmail. It is the custom for all English travelers who arrive here en route to Paris (or anywhere else in France). It allows them to sustain any acquaintances they meet in reduced circumstances here—and there are a great many English exiles leaving on means of the slenderest—by tipping them or entertaining them to a square meal.

It is Lady Sylvia's invariable habit to dine with her old friend at every opportunity. As loyalty is one of Thomas's lovable traits, he keeps this custom eagerly. I was grateful that he sent Piers to arrange the bill of fare with the chef. I have ordered meals at home on occasion, but this sort of thing is quite beyond me.

N.B. Dinner with Beau Brummell tomorrow!!! What to wear??? Ask Lady S.

At dinner tonight, James told Cecy, "Thomas thinks we would do better to rest a few days before we set off."

That remark gave Thomas the expression he has when he is savoring something. "I like that. As though my reasons have anything to do with it. In the first place, James won't let us go on because he wants you to have time to recover from your, er, indisposition."

"It's fairly common among journeyman sorcerers," put in Lady Sylvia. "There seems to be something deeply disturbing to a magician's system in crossing water. If you work on your orisons and invocations while you are traveling, you should be far enough along that you won't experience it on the return voyage. You needn't fear a relapse."

"And in the second place," Thomas continued, "we always have dinner with the Beau when we are in Calais. And in the third place," Thomas added, with a glance at me, "we have no particular need for haste."

I couldn't help it. I blushed like a cooked lobster all over again.

From the deposition of Mrs. James Tarleton, &c.

The day following our arrival in Calais was quite busy. Busy for everyone but me, that is. Although I felt perfectly well now that we were on dry land, James insisted that I spend the morning resting in our rooms. He was in nearly as much of a fuss as Aunt Elizabeth at her worst, but his fussing did not bother me nearly so much as hers has always done. I was so surprised to realize this that I inadvertently agreed to do as he suggested, and so I was left behind.

Lady Sylvia and James went off to confirm the arrangements for the coaches and horses that were to take us to Paris, for although Lady Sylvia had sent detailed instructions from London, she wished to change a few things relating to the servants and baggage, which were following us. James accompanied her because he places no dependence on the French getting anything right. Thomas had been struck with the notion of showing Kate the scene of some exploit of his involving a French staff officer on leave and a great many chickens. I spent the morning in bed.

I had intended to spend my time with the book of

orisons and invocations to which Lady Sylvia had directed me, for I was determined that our return journey across the Channel would be a more comfortable experience for me than our recent crossing. Still, even though I felt quite well, I had missed considerable sleep, and I decided it would do no harm to take a brief nap before settling down with the book.

I was more tired than I had thought. Nearly two hours later, I was awakened by a discreet tap at the door. When I opened it, the concierge was standing in the hall outside.

"I am desolated to disturb you, Madame," he said. "But there is a lady below who requires most urgently to speak with la Marquise de Schofield."

"She has gone out," I said.

The concierge nodded. "*Oui,* Madame. I have told her. But Madame is of a temperament very stubborn, and says that if la Marquise has gone out, she will follow her, or wait here until she returns."

"I will speak to her myself," I said. Kate has no more acquaintance in France than I. The only females I could imagine applying to her here would be those who knew Thomas. And after hearing a few of James's stories about Thomas's exploits . . . well, I wanted some idea who this person was before promising to relay any messages.

The concierge ushered me downstairs, to the private room where the lady was waiting. Somewhat to my surprise, she *was* a lady, about fifty, in a prodigiously elegant

China blue morning dress. She was pacing up and down in the most agitated manner, and did not notice me at once, but turned with a start at the sound of the door closing behind me.

"You are not Milady Schofield," she said in English with only a slight trace of accent.

"She has gone out, Madame," I said. "But I will be happy to tell her your name and direction when she returns."

"Mademoiselle, I do not——"

"Madame," I corrected her. "Madame Tarleton. My husband and I are traveling with the Schofields."

"Tarleton?" the woman said. "Ah, yes. That would be Ernest Tarleton?"

"My husband's given name is James," I said stiffly. "I am not aware that he has any relations named Ernest. Perhaps you are thinking of someone else."

"No," the woman said with a brilliant smile. "Forgive me, but I had to be certain. But the wife of Monsieur Tarleton is without doubt to be relied upon." She pulled a small packet from her reticule and handed it to me. "I cannot stay longer. Pray give this to the Marchioness as soon as she returns, and convey my respect and congratulations to your husband."

"And whose are those, Madame?"

She smiled again. "Tell him, the Lady in Blue. He will remember, I think. Good wishes to you, Madame." And before

I could say anything more, she whisked out the door and was gone. I collected myself and followed, barely in time to see her climb into a hired coach that had been waiting outside the inn's door. The coach pulled away immediately, and I withdrew to my rooms before I could attract notice.

My first action, when I was private once more, was to examine the packet. It was about the size of my fist, wrapped in brown paper tied with a thin silver ribbon, and every flap and join of ribbon was sealed with drips of red wax. Through the paper, I could feel hard corners, like those of a box. On top was written, in a shaky, spidery hand, "Mme. S. Schofield."

I blinked, and then realized what had happened. Obviously, the news of Thomas's marriage had not yet reached the Continent, and so the mysterious woman had asked the concierge for "the Marchioness of Schofield," meaning Lady Sylvia, when she ought to have asked for the Dowager Marchioness.

Her references to James, however, still puzzled me, and I resolved to ask him about them when he and Lady Sylvia returned. Not that I had much hope of an explanation. It is a curious thing, but James does not like any discussion of his activities during the French wars, and, indeed, avoids it at every turn. Thomas, on the other hand, downplays his exploits (which, to hear James tell it, were positively hairraising) by speaking of them in his most elliptical and offhand manner. They are a most provoking pair.

From the commonplace book of Lady Schofield

> *11 August 1817*
> *Calais*
> *At Dessein's Hotel*

I am absolutely *not* to go downstairs before the clock strikes the hour. It would be rude to do so, as it would imply that Piers and the staff are not perfectly capable of running such a simple thing as a dinner. I will stay right here and write in my commonplace book until it is time to go downstairs. If I am very careful, I won't get ink on myself, either.

Remember to mention tactfully to Cecy that Thomas was talking about *moules,* not *poules,* and that he entertained that French staff officer with a great many mussels, not a great many chickens.

N.B. Where is best petticoat? Didn't leave at the Black Swan because I noticed mud on hem when aboard the ship.

N.B. Item on Uncle's list: Amiens—manor house garden ruins, probable remains of Roman temple to Minerva Anthrax. Ask C. to check Uncle's handwriting before I write home with description. He would be upset if I got name wrong and Minerva Anthrax seems most unlikely.

N.B. Is not the word poule *sometimes used as a synonym for an improper young woman? Remember just to ask T. tactfully if this is so and if I might possibly have confused things, my ear for accent being what it is. If T. changes subject, ask James same.*

Thomas and I returned from our walk along the shore rather later, and rather wetter, than we had intended. Lady Sylvia and James arrived back just as we did, and there was much confusion of muddy boots and damp pelisses before we were all comfortably disposed in a private parlor. I don't know if James detected Cecy's agitation sooner than I did, but I know he remarked upon it before I could.

James asked, "Cecy, do you wish to speak to me privately?" Eyes wide, Cecy shook her head. The signs of her excitement were not easy to identify, but to anyone who knew her well they were unmistakable. The thought that James knew her so thoroughly cost me a tiny pang, half joy at her good fortune in a husband, half regret at his sharing my knowledge of her. "No, it's something we must all discuss."

Lady Sylvia looked distinctly intrigued. "My dear, has something happened while we were out?"

"Yes. You had a caller. Only there was a small muddle . . ." Cecy told us the story of the woman in blue and the mysterious parcel she'd left for Lady Sylvia. When she brought it forth, we leaned close to watch as Lady Sylvia undid the wrapper with painstaking care.

It was not, as I had supposed from the parcel's shape, a

box of any kind. Freed of its wrappings, it was a squarish little flask of a curious glassy substance, translucent white with streaks of brown shot through it. The flat stopper was made of gold. With great caution, Lady Sylvia opened the flask. It held perhaps an ounce of a clear, oily substance. She rubbed a drop between thumb and forefinger and a pleasantly flowery aroma filled the small salon.

Thomas looked pained. "Scent? Someone went to the trouble to be so mysterious about a bottle of scent? It's not unpleasant, I grant you. But it seems a bit—"

"The stopper is made of gold and ivory," said James. "The flask is alabaster. Very old work, that. Whatever the scent is, it must be something quite out of the ordinary."

"It isn't scent," said Lady Sylvia. "Too oily. Yet it isn't a heavy oil. By no means. And it is nearly empty." She stoppered the flask and wrapped it loosely in the brown paper again, then placed it in her reticule. "I think we should keep this news among ourselves until we learn a little more. Now, Cecy, tell me again precisely what her parting words were."

"'Pray give this to the Marchioness as soon as she returns, and convey my respect and congratulations to your husband.' Then I asked her who she was, and she said she was the Lady in Blue. She said she thought James would remember." Cecy turned to her husband, all confidence. "James?"

But James was staring at the salon door, where Piers stood in unobtrusive silence. "How long have you been standing there? Well, man?"

Piers's astonishment was plain. "A moment only, Sir. The door was open. The cook wishes to know if the ragout of lamb is to be served as a remove."

"You deal with him, Thomas," said Lady Sylvia. "After all, you found him. Kate, Cecy, I think it is long past time we set about making our own preparations. Will you accompany me?" Though she phrased it as a question, it was plain even to me that she meant it as an order, so Cecy and I came upstairs with her to change for dinner. And here, for these last interminable minutes until the hour strikes, we remain.

From the deposition of Mrs. James Tarleton, &c.

I confess that when I went up to dress for dinner, I felt just a little annoyed with Lady Sylvia. It was, after all, owing to her advice that Kate and I had come away from London without taking time to arrange for proper wardrobes or maids, and now, on only our second evening in France, before we had had any time to remedy the situation, she expected us to dine with Beau Brummell! And while it is quite true that Mr. Brummell was no longer an intimate of the Prince of Wales, nor the unquestioned arbiter of fashion in London, it had been only a year since he was all these things and more. It was a good thing I had been so well occupied for much of the afternoon, or I might have fretted enough to get into what Mrs. Everslee at home refers to as "A State."

Lady Sylvia did, however, make some helpful suggestions as to which of the gowns in our rather limited wardrobes would be suitable. On her advice, I chose a green silk with a single flounce, quite simple, with Mama's little gold locket for jewelry. She chose a deep rose taffeta for Kate, which set off her figure to perfection—I think it must have been one of the gowns that the two of them bought just before I came up to London, for it was certainly nothing that my Aunt Charlotte would have picked for Kate. One of Kate's trunks appeared to have gone missing during the voyage, so Lady Sylvia loaned her a petticoat, and I, a clean pair of gloves. (I would have been perfectly happy to have provided the petticoat as well, but it would not have done; I am too tall.)

Kate finished dressing first, and sat writing in the little book Papa gave her until Lady Sylvia and I were ready and it was time to go down. Lady Sylvia wore black, as is her custom—Kate told me once that she never put off mourning after her husband and eldest son died years ago.

James and Thomas were waiting in the private parlor, and Mr. Brummell was announced practically on our heels. At first glance, he did not appear particularly formidable. He was a man of medium height and middle years, with wide, intelligent gray eyes. He neither looked nor acted like a gentleman in the grip of pecuniary difficulties; his dark coat was exquisitely cut, and he bowed over Lady Sylvia's hand with a considerable air. "It is remarkably pleasant to see you again, Lady Sylvia."

"I might say the same to you," Lady Sylvia replied. "And how is your gout?"

Brummell's lips quirked. "Oh, I should not mind so much, but it is in my favorite leg."

Lady Sylvia laughed and turned to us. "I believe you have not yet made the acquaintance of my daughter-at-law, Lady Schofield, and her dear friend and cousin, Mrs. Tarleton. You are already acquainted with my son and Mr. Tarleton."

"I am," Mr. Brummell said, bowing to everyone. "And it is an honor to meet two such brave and clever ladies, for clever you must certainly be to have persuaded my friends here to matrimony, and as for brave"—he shrugged—"one has only to look at the pair of them to recognize your courage in taking them on."

I could feel Kate's anxiety yield to annoyance, and I was not sure whether to be angry or amused myself. Fortunately, James laughed. "You have not changed a hair, Beau," he said. "But though I quarrel with your reasoning, your conclusions are more accurate than you think."

"Far more accurate," Thomas said, taking Kate's arm.

The Beau raised his eyebrows expressively and looked from James to Thomas and back. "Indeed? How fortunate; you may tell me the tale over dinner, and the discussion will be both interesting and unexceptionable—a combination that seems beyond the ability of far too many people in these unfortunate times."

"After dinner," Lady Sylvia said firmly, with a brief but meaningful glance at the French servants who were setting out the dinner.

Mr. Brummell's smile had a peculiar edge to it. "Oh, you need not be concerned about them. I stayed at this hotel when I . . . first arrived in France, and though I gave my instructions with great care in the French language, they were always misconstruing me. If they could not understand their own tongue, I hardly think they will manage better with English."

"Which is, no doubt, why you have chosen to rent rooms from Monsieur Quillac instead of remaining here," Lady Sylvia said in a dry tone. A quick look passed between her and Mr. Brummell, and then she went on, "We shall entertain you with London gossip, instead. Had you heard that Prinny speaks of leaving off his stays?"

"It would be a singularly foolish thing for him to do," Mr. Brummell replied, taking her arm to lead her to the table. "I therefore confidently predict that he will have done so by the beginning of next Season."

We sat down to dinner and talked in an amiable and frivolous fashion throughout the first course. The soup was excellent, and I resolved to engage a French cook as soon as we returned home, though I was sure Aunt Charlotte would claim it extravagant.

French cuisine may be excellent, but French domestic architecture sometimes leaves much to be desired. Just as the fish course was served, a large chunk of plaster parted company with the rest of the ceiling and landed in our dinner.

"Damme!" said Mr. Brummell.

Kate looked as if she wished the earth would swallow her. James's amusement seemed about to break loose, and I gave him a glance of warning. Thomas gave Kate a little nod of encouragement and she squared her shoulders. I recognized the expression on her face, and found myself hoping fervently that she was not about to tell one of her outrageous tales to *Mr. Brummell*. I was not at all sure I could answer for my own reaction should she do so, and I was quite certain that James would burst out laughing.

From the commonplace book of Lady Schofield

12 August 1817
Calais
At Dessein's Hotel

I was a model of genteel deportment. I forced myself not to come downstairs until the clock had struck six. The others were in the parlor before me. Thomas and James bantered cheerfully between themselves. Lady Sylvia looked rested and refreshed. Cecy's customary high spirits had returned, and there was nothing wrong with me but my usual dread of social discomfiture.

Cecy tucked my hair up at the back, made me turn slowly to inspect my buttonholes and hemline, and pronounced me neat as a pin.

Thomas chaffed me gently about my skittishness and reviewed the protocol of the situation with me. I was to be the hostess, and, therefore, Mr. Brummell was my honored guest. He would be on my right. Thomas would be at the other end of the table, to be sure, but it was not a very large table, just the six of us. If I did anything dreadful, everyone there was related to me except Mr. Brummell, and he had better manners than all the rest of us put together. Therefore, I had nothing to fear.

"After all," Thomas finished, "it's only dinner. What can go wrong?"

I felt we all looked rather nice as we went in to dinner. Elegant, but not ostentatious. It seemed terribly odd to take precedence over Lady Sylvia but I braced myself for the ordeal. Mr. Brummell made it plain that he knew Thomas and James, as well as Lady Sylvia, quite well. His table talk was divided evenly among us. The soup course yielded to the fish and I began to relax. Perhaps Thomas had been right all along. Perhaps playing my role in Society would come to me as I went on. Perhaps a bit of practice was truly all I required.

As the fish course began, I heard a soft creak overhead. I glanced up in time to see a piece of the plaster ceiling the size of a wagon wheel bid farewell to its grip on the laths above and crash down on the table. Soup tureen, candelabra, glasses, and plates alike were cast into chaos.

"Dear me," said Mr. Brummell.

The servants left the room. In the distance, I could hear the innkeeper's bay of alarm. Close at hand, I could hear soup dripping to the floor, a not-unmusical trickle.

I put down my spoon and looked around the table. Opposite me, Thomas was as expressionless as I have ever seen him. I worried what his honest response to this catastrophe might be, that such impassivity was needed. Cecy's eyes were wide with astonishment. Lady Sylvia used her napkin to extinguish a sprig of the floral arrangement where a fallen candle was trying to smolder into flame. I think James was trying not to laugh. With all the aplomb I'd learned telling fibs as a girl, I turned to our guest. "Mr. Brummell, with such fine weather, we thought it might amuse you to take the rest of the meal in the classical fashion, *al fresco* in the garden. I hope you will accompany me?" My conscience intruded. More honestly, I went on. "It may take some time for the table to be laid—indeed, there may not be a table at all."

"But the menu is worth the wait, I promise," Thomas added. He was still straight-faced, but I could see now what he'd striven so hard to hide from me. Amusement. I would not have thought it possible, but I felt my affection for Thomas increase. He probably thought it would have wounded my feelings had he laughed aloud.

"Not only that, the open air can sometimes be more private," said Lady Sylvia with a smile.

I only wish that everyone I ever told a bouncer to could be as willing to be deceived as Mr. Brummell. He was courtesy itself as he offered me his arm. "Then by all means, Lady Schofield, let us enjoy a *fête champêtre*. I believe there is to be a particularly fine moon tonight."

From the deposition of Mrs. James Tarleton, &c.

There was a delay while the staff constructed a trestle table in the garden. Once it was covered with the tablecloth, and the chairs were moved outdoors for us, it looked well enough. The fish course was lost, unfortunately, but the rest of the menu made its way forth from the kitchens in good order.

At the end of the meal, we left the gentlemen to their port, but they did not linger long, and joined us in the private parlor upstairs after a very few minutes. (James explained to me later that Mr. Brummell preferred to limit his indulgence, as port tended to aggravate his gout.)

As the door closed behind Piers, leaving the six of us entirely to ourselves at last, Mr. Brummell settled into a chair and said, "I notice, Lady Sylvia, that amid your amiable reminiscences over dinner there was no mention of the Royal College of Wizards. Ought I to attach some significance to this omission, or have they merely been even duller than usual these past few months?"

"You always were a clever one," Lady Sylvia said. "In

fact, I am a little surprised you hadn't heard already. The expulsion of Sir Hilary Bedrick from the Royal College, barely three months after his investiture, created quite a scandal."

Mr. Brummell lowered his eyelids a trifle; his expression bore a strong resemblance to the one the Vicar's cat used to assume when she was pretending not to be interested in something so as to lure it close enough to pounce on. "Indeed it did," he replied. "It is, however, a scandal peculiarly devoid of details. Normally, the reasons behind such an abrupt departure are bandied about in the most common fashion imaginable. Nor have I had the pleasure of dining with him recently, though it is usual for persons who are, ah, under a cloud to take refuge on the Continent until some new scandal permits their return to Society. Which, no doubt, accounts for the distressing lack of style exhibited by so many English persons in France—present company, of course, most thoroughly excepted."

"I don't think Sir Hilary will want to dine with you, cloud or not, once he hears you have recently supped with us," Thomas said.

"I am much obliged for the warning," Mr. Brummell said earnestly. "I must certainly see to it that he hears no such thing."

I shivered a little, remembering the strange little cloistered garden where James and I had spent a night as Sir Hilary's prisoners. "You don't really think he'll come to France when the Royal College has finished with him, do you?"

"Finishes with him?" Mr. Brummell's eyebrows rose. "Do you know, I was under the impression that they had finished with him already. That is normally what expulsion means."

"Not in this case," James said grimly. "And never fear, we do intend to tell you the whole. But it will make more sense if we tell it in order. You remember that chocolate pot of Thomas's?"

"The blue one? Quite well; I tried several times to get someone to duplicate the shade for one of my snuffboxes, but I never quite managed it."

"Yes," said Thomas, sounding a trifle put out. "That one. It . . . inadvertently became the focus for my magic."

"Inadvertently?" The Beau looked amused. "My dear Sir!"

"These things do happen," Lady Sylvia said, frowning both Thomas and James to silence. She then proceeded to give an admirably succinct summary of the events leading up to Sir Hilary's expulsion from the Royal College: his conspiracy with Miranda Tanistry Griscomb and their various attempts to enchant Thomas into marrying Miranda's stepdaughter (which Kate foiled quite neatly) or to drain Thomas's magic through the stolen chocolate pot (which ended when I deliberately smashed the pot to smithereens); Miranda's attempt to steal Kate's youth (which backfired fatally, thanks to Lady Sylvia); and, finally, Sir Hilary's attempt to murder James and my foolish brother, Oliver, and to drain me until I lost my wits (frustrated by the timely arrival of my Aunt Elizabeth and my magic tutor, Mr. Wrexton).

"Under the circumstances, the Royal College of Wizards felt that expulsion was not enough," Lady Sylvia finished. "By no means. No, they wisely decided to strip Sir Hilary of his magical abilities before exiling him from England. The process is somewhat lengthy, which is no doubt why he has not yet passed this way."

"Unless he has chosen to go to the Low Countries," Mr. Brummell said in a thoughtful tone. "I am much obliged for your information."

"Then perhaps you will be willing to advise me in return," Lady Sylvia said, and to my surprise she drew the little alabaster bottle from her reticule and passed it to Mr. Brummell. "This was delivered to me under rather mysterious circumstances this afternoon. What do you make of it?"

Mr. Brummell's face went quite expressionless. He fingered the bottle for a moment, then, holding the stopper carefully in place, he turned it over and made a brief examination of the underside. "Ah," he said in a satisfied tone, and returned it to Lady Sylvia.

"'Ah'?" said Thomas. "I could have said that much myself."

"You just did," James told him.

Mr. Brummell ignored them both and looked at Lady Sylvia. "I believe the rather blurred mark on the base of the flask is the seal of the Archbishops of Notre-Dame in Paris. As you might reasonably be assumed to be traveling to

Paris, I suspect you were meant to take the flask there." He paused, considering. "Under the present circumstances, I am not at all sure that would be wise."

"I thought the last Archbishop of Notre-Dame was executed years ago, during the Terror," Kate said.

"He was," Mr. Brummell replied. "Archbishops are, however, replaceable . . . very careless of the French revolutionaries not to have thought of that when they were going about executing people. Though I am quite sure it was not the new Archbishop who set his seal on your flask."

"I see." Lady Sylvia studied the flask for a moment, then replaced it in her reticule. "And where would it be wise to take this interesting acquisition?"

"I do not know," Mr. Brummell said, frowning. "But I can say with certainty that there are at least two other places you ought not to take it."

"And those are?"

"Vienna." Mr. Brummell paused. "And the island of St. Helena."

I stared at Mr. Brummell in considerable astonishment, as did Thomas, James, and Kate. Lady Sylvia was the only one of us to keep her countenance unmoved. The significance of St. Helena was immediately obvious—that was where Napoleon Bonaparte had been sent after his defeat at Waterloo and where he was still imprisoned. Vienna, however . . .

Then Kate frowned and said, "But what possible connection is there between a flask of sweet oil and Napoleon

Bonaparte or his wife?" and I recalled that Bonaparte's second wife, Marie Louise, had been an Austrian archduchess, and that she had returned home with their son following his exile.

"There is, quite probably, no connection at all," Mr. Brummell replied with unimpaired calm. "In which case, it would be advisable for things to remain that way. I must also caution you to be circumspect in whatever letters you may happen to write. The *cabinet noir* is as active as ever, and while it is nothing like as sophisticated as it once was, nor as much heeded, it might still cause you a certain... inconvenience."

"What is the black cabinet?" Kate demanded.

"The black *chamber* is a department of the French government devoted primarily to opening people's mail," Thomas replied. "And, of course, reading it once it has been opened."

"They have an official department to read people's private mail?" I said, outraged.

"Not exactly," Thomas said. "Reading private mail is, after all, illegal, even in France—at least, the Legislative Assembly declared it so after they deposed Louis XVI. So did the Constituent Assembly a few years later. That's why the *cabinet noir* is a secret department, not an official one."

"It can't be all that secret," Kate said, "or you wouldn't know so much about it."

"That," said Thomas smugly, "is due to the fact that I am not French."

"It is due to the fact that you can't resist poking your nose into whatever happens along, any more than Cecy can," James said with some severity.

I opened my mouth to make a stinging retort, then closed it firmly. One ought not to make a scene in company, and though I confess that such considerations have not always restrained me in the past, I simply could not do so when the company in question was Mr. Brummell.

Lady Sylvia gave me an approving nod, and turned a quelling frown on James. "I must thank you for the information, Mr. Brummell," she said when it was clear that James had subsided once more. "I am not fond of inconvenience."

"I had suspected it," Mr. Brummell replied gravely. "Speaking of which, I should mention that your old acquaintance Lord Elting was here with his wife two days ago; you only just managed to miss them."

"How fortunate," Lady Sylvia murmured. "Do you happen to know where they planned to travel next? And who else is likely to be in Paris at present?"

I was far more interested in learning more about the flask and its contents, and the reason why Mr. Brummell thought it ought not to come near Napoleon Bonaparte or his unfortunate wife, but it was quite clear that neither he nor Lady Sylvia intended to discuss the matter further. They passed quickly from discussion of acquaintances who might be in Paris to reminiscing about those they had known in the past. At length, Mr. Brummell rose to take his leave. As he made his adieux, he murmured something in a low voice to Thomas, and then departed. Thomas looked after him with a very curious expression on his face.

"What was that about?" James asked at last.

Thomas turned, looking thoughtful. "More advice."

"And shall you take it?" Kate asked in the tone that means she does not consider the answer adequate but prefers not to make a fuss about it just at present.

"Very possibly." Thomas hesitated, then sighed. "He advised me to create a new focus as soon as may be."

"Quite a good suggestion, I think," Lady Sylvia said.

James eyed the door pensively. "A good suggestion, perhaps—but not exactly a reassuring one," he said, and on that note, the evening ended.

From the commonplace book of Lady Schofield

> *12 August 1817*
> *Calais*
> *At Dessein's Hotel*

N.B. Consult with Lady S. about engaging a suitable maid. I have never done such a thing in English. Doing so in French much worse.

N.B. Mend hem in second-best petticoat.

Thomas had a word with the innkeeper after our dinner guest had departed. He made it abundantly clear why we would be leaving the next day, reasons that owed nothing to the fact that Lady Sylvia had arranged rooms for us in Amiens.

Piers was not to be found when we retired to our chamber. Thomas had a few more words to say. He finished off with, "Can't think where the fellow gets to."

"Never mind." With much tugging on my part, and a little more swearing on Thomas's part, I helped Thomas out of his coat, which was all we wanted Piers for, anyway. "He does know we're leaving tomorrow, doesn't he?"

Thomas plucked at the knot under his chin until the starched linen came loose. "With plaster in the soup, I should hope he knows we're leaving."

I couldn't help saying, "Plaster in the fish."

"You're not going to take up contradiction as a hobby, are you?" Thomas finished unwinding his neckcloth and draped it over a chair for Piers to deal with.

I felt dismayed. "Oh, dear. Do you think I'm taking after Aunt Charlotte?"

Thomas put his arms around me. "Don't look so stricken. I didn't mean it. After all, you were right. It was in the fish."

"It was everywhere." I let my cheek rest against his shoulder. "What must he have thought?"

"Oh, hang Brummell. It's over and done with now. I was proud of you."

"You were? Truly?"

"Truly. Never saw a woman to match you for sangfroid." Thomas gave me a little shake.

"Oh. Thank you, Thomas." I hid my smile. Flowery, Thomas's sentiments were not, but no one could doubt his sincerity. "Are you going to give some thought to Mr. Brummell's advice on creating a new focus?"

"Of course. He's right. I need to take care of that. Think of something for me, will you? Something crafty and brilliant?"

"Not a chocolate pot?"

"*Not* a chocolate pot," Thomas agreed wholeheartedly. "Never quite left off feeling silly about making a pig's ear of it that time. This time it's going to be something clever."

"That's good. What will it be this time?"

"I don't know. That's why I'm leaving it to you. I want it to be perfect."

"Oh, Thomas—"

"What?"

Any words I could muster seemed foolishly small in comparison to my feelings. There I was, with my own true love, who trusted me as I trusted him, and we were in each other's arms, and the rest of the world was far away. "Nothing."

Thomas seemed to understand me despite my tongue-tied muttering. "Never mind. I haven't finished telling you how much I admire your sangfroid."

We were both sleeping soundly when the alarm was given in the small hours of the night.

"Thief!" Lady Sylvia's voice was unmistakable. "Stop, thief!"

Lady Sylvia must have issued a more magical command as well, for someone uttered a wild cry of surprise and dismay that made the little hairs on the nape of my neck bristle. Glass broke. Then came silence, followed by the inevitable sounds of a household rousing in the dead of night.

I followed Thomas out of our room in all haste.

"What is it? Is it a fire?" The innkeeper emerged from his quarters in slippers and nightshirt. No one knew what was happening, so no one attempted to answer him.

I tried to see over Thomas's shoulder as we peered into Lady Sylvia's bedchamber.

"Mother!" Thomas was alarmed. "Are you all right?"

"Yes, dear. Quite all right. I'm afraid he escaped, drat the man." Someone had managed to light a lamp, and the shadows danced in Lady Sylvia's room. She was sitting up in her bed, looking displeased with herself.

"Who was it?" Cecy demanded, her curiosity unquenchable as ever. She and James were behind us. Cecy was as bundled up in her dressing gown as I was in mine. James wore a garment similar in style to Thomas's dressing gown, vivid scarlet picked out with black and gold embroidery. Neither of them seemed to have been asleep at all.

"My dear, I have no idea." Lady Sylvia brandished a man's slipper. "He left only this. Do you think we should send a footman out with this on a velvet cushion to see whom it fits?"

"Perhaps not just this minute," said James. He took the slipper from her and turned it over in his hands. "Hmm. Well-made of good leather. See the peaked instep? Turkish fashion."

"Made popular by that infernal cad Byron," countered Lady Sylvia. "Anyone might own such a pair of slippers."

"Anyone who follows fashion," said Cecy. "But who would come into your bedchamber in the dead of night? And why? Is anything missing?"

"I have not yet had time to check," said Lady Sylvia. "Perhaps we should do so now."

James and Cecy and I began assisting her to go through her things. The first place we checked was Lady Sylvia's jewelry box. The alabaster flask was safe. Thomas spoke softly to the innkeeper, who took himself off. Thomas himself slipped away soon after, leaving us with Lady Sylvia. In a quarter of an hour, perhaps less, he returned, just as we finished our task.

"Nothing seems to be gone," James told Thomas. "Whatever he came for, he didn't get it."

"Good," said Thomas. "I'll tell you another good thing. We've found Piers. Apparently he has been drugged, tied up, and locked in the scullery for the past five hours."

"Dear me. Is he all right?" I asked.

Thomas seemed indifferent to the state of his valet's health. "He has a headache, well-earned, I suspect. It seems he'd been flirting with a personable young woman since his arrival. He holds her responsible for his misfortune."

"Who? Where is she?" asked Cecy.

"She told him her name was Eve-Marie, and led him to believe she was a local resident, helping at the inn during our stay. In fact, no one here knows her, and unless the search the innkeeper is conducting proves unexpectedly successful, she's nowhere to be found."

James frowned. "How could Piers allow himself to be fooled so?"

Thomas chose his words with care. "Piers is convinced it is all our fault. The general air of, er, matrimonial bliss seems to have affected his judgment."

"Eve, indeed," said Lady Sylvia. "My intruder was no woman. I trust the innkeeper has someone searching for him, too."

"He has," Thomas said. "But no further trace of him has been found, either. I fear there's no chance of picking up his trail until daybreak."

From the deposition of Mrs. James Tarleton, &c.

Despite the stirring events of the night, James and I woke early the following morning. One of Lady Sylvia's maids had pressed my gray lustring carriage dress. She helped me into it while James's man shaved James, and so we were ready for breakfast much sooner than I had expected.

Breakfast had been laid out in a side parlor, which, though tiny, appeared to have a very secure ceiling. Early as we were,

Lady Sylvia was there before us. She looked up from *La Mode Illustrée,* greeted us in a perfectly normal fashion, and recommended the cheese to James's particular attention. As we began filling our plates, Kate and Thomas arrived.

"Ah, Kate, there you are!" said Lady Sylvia, who looked none the worse for the previous night's interrupted sleep. "Good morning, Thomas."

"Good morning, Mother," said Thomas. "You've certainly had a busy time this morning. Don't you ever rest?"

"A busy time?" I said. "Have you discovered anything new about that intruder last night?"

Kate shook her head. "Thomas is put out because when he went to order the coaches, he found that Lady Sylvia had already done so."

"Just so," said Lady Sylvia. "You had best sit down, both of you; there's just time for you to eat before we start for Amiens."

I frowned. "But shouldn't we make some push to discover who was poking about in your bedroom, before we leave Calais?"

"Whoever it was is long gone by this time," James said, giving me a look plainly meant to be quelling.

"Perhaps," said Thomas. "Though he may not have gone far, with only one slipper."

James turned his frown toward Thomas, but before he could speak, Kate said, "He can't have needed to go far. Isn't that why you didn't hunt for him last night?"

"There, you see?" Thomas said to James.

"How do you know the thief didn't have far to go?" James asked Kate in a tone halfway between horror and fascination.

"Well, I hardly think anyone would wear Turkish slippers if he knew he'd have to run miles through the streets afterward," Kate said.

"Nor would an ordinary thief wear Byronic fashions," I put in. "So Lady Sylvia's intruder was very likely someone staying at this hotel."

"Which is precisely why I wish to leave it as soon as possible," Lady Sylvia said. "Drink your tea."

"Surely you don't mean us to go on to Amiens just as if nothing had happened!" I said.

"Not exactly," said Lady Sylvia. "But I most certainly do mean to leave for Amiens as soon as possible. Calais has been far too full of events for comfort."

Unorthodox parcel deliveries, unstable ceilings, mysterious housemaids, midnight intruders—yes, I could see her point. "But nearly everything that has happened has happened to you," I said slowly. "Well, except for the ceiling, but, really, I don't see how that could have been limited. If you go on, and James and I remain here another day to investigate—"

"Absolutely not," James said.

"It would be far too obvious," Thomas put in smoothly. "No, I'll leave Piers behind, on the strength of his aching head. He can watch out for anything of interest while he recuperates, and report back when he catches up."

Kate and I exchanged glances. It was obvious to both of us that our husbands did not wish either of us involved in looking into the matter of Lady Sylvia's intruder. Still, Thomas had a point. All of the travel arrangements between here and Paris had been made for five; it would look very odd if the party split so abruptly without a reason. If I had thought of it sooner, I might have pretended to be still recovering from my seasickness, and too unwell to travel. After the hearty meal I had eaten last night (and much of it in the garden, where anyone might have observed my appetite), such dissembling was unlikely to be convincing. I did not place any dependence on Piers's investigative abilities, but there really was no other choice.

"Oh, very well," I said. "But do at least get a list of the other guests from the innkeeper, James. It may tell us something useful. Try not to let him know why you want it."

"I did that last night," Thomas said.

"Nicely done, dear," said Lady Sylvia. "And I look forward to discussing it with you all—after we are out of Calais."

With these important matters settled, we applied ourselves to our meal. Lady Sylvia had instructed her servants as to packing and loading the trunks, so that by the time we finished eating, we had nothing more to do but settle our bill, distribute the vails, and climb into the coaches.

I soon realized one of the reasons Lady Sylvia had been so insistent on such a speedy, early start. The roads in France are *far* worse than those in England. I suppose it was only to be expected in a country that had been at war so recently, and for so long, but it slowed our progress noticeably. The coaches lurched so dreadfully that even thinking was difficult, and I had the greatest concern that we would break a wheel or an axle. We changed horses at a posting inn and forged on. Near Boulogne, the roads improved somewhat, but they deteriorated again as soon as we were away from the city, and so it was quite late by the time we arrived in Amiens.

AMIENS

12 August 1817
Amiens
At the Coq d'Or

The road from Calais to Amiens is long. Even if it weren't, the condition of the road would have made it seem so. Most travelers make the journey in easy stages, with a stop in Boulogne, but Lady Sylvia had arranged only a change of horses there, and so we forged onward and made the journey in a single weary day.

By the time we arrived at the Coq d'Or, we were all somewhat fatigued. Cecy took the journey in good part, and James hardly seemed to notice any discomfort. Lady Sylvia and Thomas, unfortunately, seemed to be thoroughly tired of each other's company. Thomas was interested in discussing the list of names the innkeeper had given him. Lady Sylvia kept her counsel with such firmness that eventually even Thomas noticed. A distinct chill was evident between them as we settled in at the Coq d'Or.

I was grateful to gain the quiet chamber allotted me. After the jolting of the coach, the bed seemed to offer irresistible solace. With a sigh of heartfelt thanksgiving, I took off my half boots and stretched out atop the coverlet.

Thomas came to sit beside me. "We really must see about finding you a maid."

"I'll be fine. Lady Sylvia will loan me Aubert until we reach Paris." There, I knew, my doom would come upon me. There, I would be drawn into the details of interviewing and engaging a properly trained Parisian lady's maid. The prospect alarmed me. I knew it would take a true lady's maid only moments to judge my crumpled gown and snagged stockings—and to despise me. "You are doing without Piers, after all."

"No sacrifice there," said Thomas, as he started to pluck his neckcloth into submission. "The fellow wouldn't know a waterfall from Waterloo."

"Does it matter so greatly?" I asked. Thomas never followed fashion any great distance, and his neckcloth usually owed more to his mood when tying it than to any deliberate design.

"That's what I pay a valet for, so I don't have to know myself. I leave that sort of thing to fellows like your clunch of a cousin." Thomas gave up on his neckcloth and lay beside me. After a thoughtful moment, he observed, "Plaster seems fine here. I think we're safe to stay, don't you?"

I stopped thinking how warm and pleasant it was to lie nestled against Thomas, sharing the same pillow. Instead, I peered up at the ceiling. It was clean and in good repair, but not perfect. "There's a crack."

"Only a little one. Looks old, too. It's probably been there for ages." Thomas studied the ceiling intently. "It looks like the harbor at Genoa."

"No, it looks like Aunt Charlotte's profile. See, there's her mouth—"

Thomas caught my hand as I pointed. "Stop that. Think of Genoa, please. I don't fancy seeing your aunt under any conditions, least of all these." Thomas removed my glove and held my hand in his. "We definitely need to see about a maid for you. I can't always be here, you know, and you're always dressing and undressing, buttoning and unbuttoning..." Thomas trailed off as he concentrated on the palm of my hand.

I enjoyed the sensation he created very much. Whiskers (and by the end of a long day, Thomas definitely displayed signs of incipient whiskers) created an interesting contrast with the warm softness of his lips against my palm. I spoke dreamily, almost at random. "Are we going to Genoa?"

"Only if we take ship to Italy, which Heaven forfend, given Cecy's reaction to the Channel crossing. I have every intention of showing you Venice, at least, but I think we'd be wise to cross overland instead."

"Through the Alps, like Hannibal," I said. "Uncle Arthur will be so happy."

Thomas pushed himself up on one elbow to take a better look at me. "Are you homesick, Kate?"

I stared at him. "Of course not. I might have complained about the road, but I am having a lovely time. What gave you that idea?"

"Just that you keep talking of your family: Aunt Charlotte, Uncle Arthur, and Oliver."

"You mentioned Oliver, not I."

"So I did. Well, I wondered, that's all. Do you miss them?"

I thought it over. "No, not really. It sounds dreadful, but I was counting the hours until I could get away. Oh, that's not what I mean. It's just that I was so eager to have the ceremony over with and to be safely married to you—"

"I know what you mean." From the warmth in his voice, I think Thomas really did understand what I was trying, in my muddled way, to express.

"Since then, of course, we have scarcely had a moment to ourselves," I finished.

"Didn't you know? That's what all marriages are like. Never a dull moment. Dressing, undressing." Dexterously, Thomas removed my other glove. "Though I should like to insist on keeping duties like this to myself."

I knew he was joking, but his touch was so sweet, so deft, and so gentle, I said, "I wish you could. I don't want a maid. She'll disapprove of me."

"Disapprove?" Thomas put his arms around me, an embrace that belied his growl. "Why? Whatever for?"

"Spoiling my clothes. Losing things. Mussing the coverlet—"

Thomas interrupted me with a kiss. When we were both breathless, he said, "I refuse to have anyone who disapproves of you in our employ. Therefore, I forbid you to engage anyone you are intimidated by. No sophistry, now. You are not to use my mother's opinions as an excuse, though she'd never permit you to be such a goose. Nor would Cecy. You must face up to it, Kate, and engage the lady's maid you want. Anything less is shirking your duty."

Thomas so seldom attempts to be stern. I found the contrast between his dignified tone and his undignified position endearing. He cheered me.

"Yes, Thomas," I said.

Thomas eyed me with suspicion. "I expected you to argue."

I was meekness personified. "No, Thomas."

"'Yes, Thomas'? 'No, Thomas'?" he echoed, incredulous. "Is that you, Kate?"

I widened my eyes and nodded.

He sprang to his feet and made for the door. "Whoever you are, you're not the woman I married."

No one could resist such temptation. I said, "Whatever you say, Thomas."

"Stop that at once!" he said, and went to see about dinner.

I lay back against my pillow in a state of pure contentment. Matrimony is a highly agreeable state.

13 August 1817
Amiens
At the Coq d'Or

I think rest was just what we needed. I know we all feel the better for our unbroken night of sleep. At breakfast this morning, Lady Sylvia received a reply to an urgent message she had sent on our arrival in Amiens. With satisfaction, she informed us we would be taking tea with the Bishop at four o'clock. "We will leave here together promptly at a quarter to the hour. I have letters to write, so I'll be here all day. However you plan to divert yourselves today, do be back here on time." After making quite sure that we heard and would obey, she excused herself. That left the four of us to decide precisely how we would amuse ourselves.

"James and I are visiting the Roman ruins," said Cecy. "Won't you come with us? Papa will be so pleased when we write to tell him how studious we are, he won't notice if we never see another antiquity the entire trip."

I said, "I don't mind antiquities, but I wonder if this might not be a good time to see about investing Thomas's magic?"

Cecy's eyes are one of her finest features. At times they can seem positively enormous. "Oh, that sounds much more interesting than Roman ruins."

"Thomas might care to perform that little task in decent privacy," said James. "The fewer distractions, the better."

"Have you thought of an object for me to use for the investment?" Before I could reply, Thomas held up a hand to silence me. "Don't tell me what it is. Not just yet. Let it be like a birthday wish."

I remembered that we were at breakfast in a well-frequented inn. No matter how sturdy the ceilings, the walls could well have ears. "I've been thinking about it since you asked me to help. You need something small, or at least portable, don't you?"

"Something unobtrusive, certainly," said James.

Cecy looked more intrigued than ever. "Yet you can do magic without it, can't you? After all, when Sir Hilary had the chocolate pot, you could still perform magic."

Thomas said, "I work far better with a focus. It can be nearby, but I'd prefer something I could carry with me."

"You won't want anything noticeable," said Cecy thoughtfully, "in case you must disguise yourself."

"Why on earth would Thomas wish to disguise himself?" James asked. Before anyone could reply, he added, "Not that I haven't seen him disguised on more than one occasion."

"Viper," Thomas said to James. "You'd be as enthusiastic as Cecy if you were only better at it."

I leaned close and murmured in Thomas's ear. "I thought perhaps—a ring."

Thomas considered a moment, then murmured back, "I only wear one ring—" Beneath the breakfast table, he took my left hand in his, so that our wedding rings touched. "Rather ostentatious, wearing a ring if I do have to disguise myself. I suppose in a pinch I could put it on a chain, wear it around my neck."

"I thought," I whispered, "*my* wedding ring. If it's true that it can be nearby and still work for you."

Rather loudly, James said to Cecy, "Do you know, I get the oddest feeling that we're not wanted here. Would you care to accompany me to the ruins of the Temple of Minerva Victrix?"

"Oh, is that what it's called?" Cecy looked relieved. "Papa's handwriting can be quite deceptive at times."

"Seems perfectly clear to me," James said. "Temple of Minerva Victrix, Cathedral of Ink Pot, Chapel of the Kippered Herring, and so on. Come, before Thomas invites himself along."

"I thought they'd never leave," said Thomas, quite audibly. When we were alone with the remains of breakfast, he added, "I think your idea will serve very well. I'll need a few items for the ritual, but they won't be much bother. I should be ready to perform the investiture before lunch."

In fact, Thomas's supplies took a bit longer to procure than he'd anticipated. Such a ritual required a clean, quiet place, which our bedchamber provided, a pitcher of spring-water, which Thomas insisted on fetching himself, a basin, a great many candles, a chicken feather, a broom, and a pound of salt, all of which the innkeeper provided without betraying the slightest curiosity. The ways of the English, it seemed, had long ceased to interest him.

Thomas rolled back the carpet and swept the chamber floor twice, once to get the floor clean and once to go with his soft incantation. He made a ring of salt on the bare floor and spaced the candles carefully about the ring. He put me in the center of the circle, cross-legged before the basin, and lit the candles. He poured springwater as I washed my hands. When that was done, I took the feather he handed me and held it over the basin.

Thomas said some words, and I repeated what he said. I tried to capture not only his pronunciation but his pitch and intonation as well. The words might have been Chinese for all I knew. Despite my ignorance, I could tell that each word had its own music, a tone below the sound, low notes I strove to echo.

"Fiat," said Thomas. Even if I hadn't known that must be his final command, the curious sensation the word provoked would have alerted me. As he finished the ritual chant, the ring on my finger pulsed with a cool energy, which rippled away to stillness.

I stared at Thomas. Thomas nodded encouragingly to prompt me. *"Fiat,"* I said. The ring pulsed again, and this time Thomas stared at me, mouth ajar.

Silence hung between us for a long time. At last, Thomas swallowed audibly, cleared his throat, and said, "Just hand me the feather and stay where you are. I'll tidy up."

With utter serenity, I watched as Thomas took the feather from me and set about with deftness and care to remove every trace of the ritual from the chamber. At last, when all was cleared away, he drew me to my feet.

"I'd forgotten what it's like to be properly focused," Thomas said. "Quite a powerful sensation."

"It worked." I had no doubts at all.

Thomas rolled the carpet back into place. "You felt it, too?"

"I felt—a sort of throb. When you said that last word." I thought it might be wise not to say *fiat* aloud for fear of setting the ring to pulsing again.

"And when you said—that last word?" Thomas looked first at the ring on my finger, then into my eyes. "What did you feel then?"

"The same, except—" I put my hand over his heart. "I think that time, I felt you feel it, too."

From the deposition of Mrs. James Tarleton, &c.

The morning after we reached Amiens was clear and sunny—the perfect day for visiting some of Papa's antiquities. Lady Sylvia had arrangements of her own, and Kate and Thomas elected to take the opportunity to re-create a focus for Thomas's magic, so in the end it was only James and me. Although I would have enjoyed assisting Thomas, or even watching the spell casting, I was not unpleased by this outcome. Dearly as I love Kate, I expected to enjoy having James to myself for a few hours.

I should have known better. The first thing he said once we were alone in the hack was, "Cecy, you are *not* to badger Kate into telling you what Thomas has decided to use as his new focus."

"I had no intention of doing any such thing," I said indignantly. "And even if I had, Kate wouldn't tell me."

James gave me a skeptical look. "Kate follows your lead."

"Not where Thomas is concerned," I pointed out. "And, in any case, there is no point whatever in badgering her. If she doesn't want to explain something, she simply fobs people off with some tale."

"Thomas did mention something of the sort," James said. "I thought he was exaggerating. He does that, you know."

I blinked. My own experience of Thomas might be limited, but Kate had written me quite detailed reports of her acquaintance with him, and I think I can safely say that *exaggerating* is not a word that either of us would ever use in connection with him. I quite saw that he might well behave differently when he was with James, but I had never thought that the difference might be so extreme. "Whatever he told you, he wasn't exaggerating about Kate. She can make the most outrageous bouncers sound utterly convincing. Once she persuaded the Reverend Fitzwilliam that the reason Aunt Charlotte hadn't come to tea was that she was at home taking wine for her gout."

James frowned. "Wine isn't good for the gout; on the contrary."

"Aunt Charlotte doesn't *have* the gout," I explained patiently. "And she doesn't even drink ratafia. But Reverend Fitz believed every word."

"Well, if you weren't planning on badgering Kate, what were you planning?" James demanded, returning to the original subject. "And don't try to fob me off. I know that expression. You were planning something."

"Planning something?" I was quite bewildered. "I wasn't planning anything. It was just that Kate and Thomas going on like that at breakfast made me think—"

"I knew it!"

"—about what I should use as *my* magic focus."

James looked at me in some alarm. "Cecy! You aren't to attempt that until a qualified magician says you are ready. Look at all the trouble that came of Thomas's first try—and he'd spent years studying."

"He didn't have trouble with the spell," I pointed out. "He had trouble with Sir Hilary, afterward. That's the sort of thing that could happen to anyone—well, to anyone who crossed Sir Hilary. I had trouble with him myself, and so did you, though of course nothing to compare with Thomas's."

"So you don't know quite everything," James said. "If you want the whole story, ask Thomas sometime when he's in a forthcoming mood. Meanwhile, I want your promise that you won't try creating a focus until someone else says you're ready. Someone qualified. And don't pretend to think I don't know what I'm talking about. I learned as much of the basics as any other Oxford student who wasn't specializing."

"I don't think——" Fortunately, the hack chose that moment to arrive, so I was able to avoid either extending the argument or making promises that might be inconvenient later. We found ourselves standing in front of a large manor house in the rather ornate style favored by the French nobility of the last century. Half a dozen grubby schoolboys burst from the doors and pelted toward us; from what little of their French I could make out, they were offering their services as guides.

I looked at James. "This *cannot* be the right place," I said.

The hack driver overheard me. "Madame wished to view the Temple of Minerva Victrix, yes?" he said. His French was rather good—much easier to understand than most of the people we had so far encountered. "The temple is in the gardens behind the house. See, you are not the only visitors." He pointed at a large diligence and a smart but mud-spattered traveling carriage drawn up a little farther down the drive.

"Yes!" one of the schoolboys cried. "To the rear of the school. I will show Monsieur and Madame l'Anglais; two francs!"

"One franc!" another boy cried, and they fell to arguing over what price would be appropriate for their services. The hack driver grinned. James nodded, and took my arm, and we slipped around the boys and off into the gardens.

The Temple of Minerva Victrix proved to be a small, rather unimpressive ruin on a low hill about a quarter of a mile from the house. We could see a small group of ladies and gentlemen strolling along ahead of us, about halfway to the ruins, presumably the occupants of the diligence and the traveling carriage. As they were strolling, and we were walking briskly (in case the schoolboys should return), we reached the shrine only a little after they did. We paused at the foot of the hill, not wishing to add to the crowd. Voices floated down to us from above.

"But, Rupert, you said we would have fun!" a female voice whined in French-accented English. "Old rocks are not at all fun."

"Hush, Jeannette, *ma belle*," a rather young-sounding man replied. "Old Toothpick Legs is always dragging poor Theo off and lecturing him about something or other; I think Theo's father is paying extra for it. They're bound to head off in a minute—yes, there, see? Now, we'll just slip off this way . . ."

The voice faded, and I caught a glimpse of a dark coat and a shocking dress in a gaudy yellow color fleeing toward the woods off to the left. I frowned and shook my head.

James looked at me a trifle uncertainly. "I would offer to fetch them back, but I doubt that my interference would be welcomed. If you are concerned for the lady's virtue . . ."

"I don't think that young woman has any virtue left to be endangered," I said.

"I suspect you are right," James said, relaxing. "What were you shaking your head over, then?"

"That gown." I saw that James did not understand, and

I sighed. "If one is going to go sneaking about in the woods, it is the height of foolishness to wear bright yellow. It shows up *miles* away."

"I suppose you are speaking from personal experience?" James sounded amused.

"As a matter of fact, yes," I told him. "The first time I tried to follow Oliver when he sneaked away from one of Aunt Charlotte's picnics, I was caught almost immediately for just that reason. I was about nine."

"I can see that I shall have to have a long talk with your brother when we get back to England," James said. "In the meantime, Mrs. Tarleton, shall we proceed to this temple? The crowd seems to be thinning rapidly."

Sure enough, by the time we reached the hilltop, there was only one couple visible. The young man looked about sixteen; his companion was at least twice his age, and seemed just the sort of female Aunt Charlotte was always warning Oliver about. They took one look at James and me and fled. This time, it was James who frowned.

"Those boys can't be here alone. Whoever is bear-leading them isn't doing his job." His frown deepened. "I've half a mind to have a word with him."

"He's probably around somewhere with 'poor Theo,'" I said. "If we see him, you can tell him what you think. Meanwhile, we really should look at this temple. Papa will be terribly disappointed if I don't send him a proper description."

The temple appeared, originally, to have consisted of a long, thin building with an altar at one end and a small, round room behind the altar. The roof and most of the walls of the main building were gone, and grass grew around the base of the broken pillars that had held up the center beam. The altar had sunk on one side, and tilted crazily. The little room behind it seemed intact, though its stone walls looked even older and more worn than the altar.

"Your father actually recommended this?" James said, looking at the fallen pillars.

"Oh, yes," I said. "Papa hasn't much regard for appearances. He's only interested in history. I think this place had something to do with the ancient Frankish chieftains, before the Romans came and took it over. I suppose I had better look at all of it."

We strolled down the edge of the building, toward the skewed altar stone. The opening to the little room behind it was dark and doorless; there were no windows in the near walls, and evidently there were none on the far side, either. I thought it must have been some sort of storeroom, but as we came closer, I heard the muffled murmur of voices.

Puzzled, I let go of James's arm and peered through the low doorway. The room inside was quite dark, except for one corner that seemed lit from below. "James!" I said. "There's some sort of cellar!"

"I suppose you want to investigate," James said.

"It's where the voices are coming from, and you did say you wanted a word with the boys' tutor," I said. "Besides, I promised Papa."

James rolled his eyes, but he did not object. Carefully,

we made our way inside and down a short, narrow flight of stairs. As we did, the voices grew louder.

"—left their offerings for the chieftainship rite," a man said in a pedantic tone. "Just to the right, there, under the statue."

"Gold?" a younger voice said with interest.

"No, it had to be personal. Something the man had made himself, representing his skills and abilities. A hunter would leave a claw or tooth from his kill; a warrior, the ears of an enemy. A lover"—the tone dropped and became almost lascivious—"some *personal* token from his lady. Then they touched the statue for luck, said their prayers, and left."

James stopped short at the foot of the stairs, and I peered over his shoulder. We had come out into a round, cavelike room. The walls seemed to be carved from stone, and the air felt damp. A tall, thin man in rather shabby clerical dress stood a little in front of us, holding a lantern in one hand; by its light, we could see a niche about three feet high carved into the far wall. The right side of the niche had been extended and deepened to make a sort of bowl. The left side held a statue. Its nose had broken off long ago, the features were worn, and its stone robes covered it from neck to heel so that it was impossible to tell whether the figure had been intended as a man or a woman. Except for its feet, the statue was rough-carved; the feet had been polished to a glossy smoothness, probably by centuries of visitors touching them "for luck."

A young man, about sixteen, stood in front of the statue.

His hair was dark, and his expression was very serious. "Do you think I might—"

"There's no harm in it; go on," the thin man said. A trick of the light made him seem for a moment like some bird of prey, an effect heightened by the fact that his nose had plainly been broken at some time in the past, though he was clearly not the sort of person one would expect to indulge in fisticuffs.

As the youth leaned forward, the thin man made a surreptitious gesture with his free hand toward the niche, and I saw something drop from his fingers into the bowl beside the statue. The student did not seem to notice. His hand touched the statue's feet, and he shivered. I felt a frisson of magic ripple through the air, and caught my breath in surprise.

The older man turned and saw us. His eyes narrowed. "Ah, more visitors to the shrine of Mithras," he said with a sort of oily, insincere politeness.

"Mithras?" I could hear the skepticism in James's tone; it was clear that he had taken the man in instant dislike. "The Temple of Minerva Victrix seems an odd place to find a Mithraeum."

"You are a scholar, Sir?" the boy said eagerly, turning.

"Of a desultory sort only," James said. "I cannot claim more than the most rudimentary knowledge."

"Yes, quite so," the thin man said patronizingly. "Make your bow, Theodore; it is time we were going."

The young man drew himself up. "Theodore Daventer, at your service, Sir, Madam."

"It is a pleasure to make your acquaintance," James replied automatically. "My name is Tarleton, and this is my wife."

He drew me forward, forcing Theodore and the thin gentleman to move aside. There was a moment of shuffling around the small space, and I found myself next to the niche. James and Theodore continued exchanging polite small talk under the tutor's increasingly disapproving eye; no one was paying the least heed to me. Turning slightly to hide what I was doing, I felt behind me until my fingers found the rough bowl-shape carved into the wall. There was something in it; it felt round and rough, like a walnut shell, but very light. I scooped it up, along with what felt like a few pebbles, and hid my hand in my skirt.

"I think that you have taken enough of Mr. Tarleton's time, Theodore," the thin man said.

"Oh, there's no harm in it," James said. He looked at the man and added pointedly, "Not compared to the things he *could* be doing."

The thin man gave him a sharp look. "Nevertheless, it is time we rejoined the others."

"High time," James muttered, quite audibly.

The thin man's expression turned sour, and he looked at James with dislike, but all he said was, "Master Theodore."

The boy turned to me. "Mrs. Tarleton? Have you seen enough? I suppose we could leave you the lantern, but—"

"I am quite satisfied," I declared quickly, and made my way to the stairs. James shoved in behind me, and to my surprise, the boy and his tutor followed directly. Above, they took themselves off in search of their vanished companions; James suggested helpfully that they search the east wood.

"Now, Cecy," James said when they had gone, "what were you up to down there?"

"I'm not sure," I said. "Something magical happened when that boy touched the statue; I felt it. It wasn't like any other spell I've sensed, though. And that tutor dropped something beside the statue just before. What was his name?"

"He never said." James looked after the vanished pair with another frown. "I suppose you expect me to go and re-trieve your mysterious object."

"No need; I picked it up while you were distracting Theodore and what's-his-name." I pulled my hand out and opened it. I held two rather damp stones and a tightly crumpled wad of paper. I dropped the stones and uncrumpled the page. James and I stared at it in surprise. It was written in neat Latin, all but the signature: Theodore Daventer.

"James—"

"It's an essay on the Druids, as described by Caesar and Strabo," James replied after a moment of concentration. "Apart from the subject matter, it's a fairly typical schoolboy composition." He grinned suddenly. "Right down to the phrases that are unexceptionable when properly translated, but that sound thoroughly vulgar if one simply reads the Latin aloud. Clever lad; he doesn't even seem to have reached hard for them."

"What phrases?"

James looked at me with an expression of exaggerated shock. "Cecy! Do you really expect me to sully my wife's ears with vulgarities?"

I widened my eyes at him. "But the exact Latin might be of great magical importance."

"Very true; I'll have to show it to Thomas." He reached for the page, but I snatched it away just in time and stuffed it into my reticule.

"I think that I should show it to Lady Sylvia," I said. "I'm sure she'll know even better than Thomas what to make of it. Unless you wish to change your mind about explaining it to me?"

"I should never have mentioned it," James said.

We argued amicably over the subject all the way back to the hotel.

From the commonplace book of Lady Schofield

> *13 August 1817*
> *Amiens*
> *At the Coq d'Or*

Later

We were, amazingly enough, prompt and presentable on arrival at the Bishop's palace. His Excellency was a round man of advanced years. He set aside what looked remarkably like a skein of yarn and welcomed us cordially.

When Lady Sylvia introduced me, he said, "I knew your father well. A very brave man, indeed."

I said, "You knew my father?"

"We were engaged in an enterprise of great importance."

Soon we were served a beautiful repast. The Bishop's idea of tea included not merely tea, but a selection of tempting herb tisanes, and brandy for the gentlemen. When the sandwiches were served, the discussion turned from the generalities of the weather for the time of year.

"You wished to show me something, Lady Sylvia?" the Bishop said.

Lady Sylvia gave him a smile of approval. "You have made a study of the church treasures scattered during the Terror, I believe?" She dealt with her bread and butter and took a sip of tea.

"I've asked for scholarly help where appropriate to reconstruct the inventory of treasures and furniture here in Amiens," said the Bishop. "Much was lost for all time, but we do our best to restore what we can, and to protect what we were able to recover."

"May I ask if you have made provision for the safety of the treasures in your care?" asked Lady Sylvia.

"I have, I assure you."

The rest of us munched our sandwiches and waited for Lady Sylvia to frame her next careful question.

"Take me there," she said.

We all, even the Bishop, put down our teacups at that.

The succession of startled chirps of porcelain on porcelain made a pleasantly musical effect.

"It is a matter of the gravest urgency," said Lady Sylvia.

"You alone?" asked the Bishop. Without enthusiasm, he added, "Or your young people as well?"

"All of us," said Thomas firmly.

"That would be best," said Lady Sylvia.

"Very well." The Bishop rose and led us from the palace, across the fountain court, and into the cathedral. Lady Sylvia walked beside him, but the rest of us trailed along like ducklings.

In the well-secured treasure room of the cathedral, the Bishop turned to us, hands outspread. "It would be best, I think, to close the door."

"I'll keep watch out here," said Thomas, and closed himself out in the corridor. The rest of us looked at one another. The room was low-ceilinged, lined with shelves. Even without Thomas it was crowded, and the air seemed cool and close.

"Here is the treasure of our blessed Savior." The Bishop gestured to the shelves. "Books, principally, as you can see. The chests hold the records that remain, parchment scrolls, and some of the more fragile of the bound documents. The reliquaries you see for yourself. A small collection, given the treasures we once possessed, but a fine one, if you recall the devastation of those years."

"It is not so very long ago. Certainly it does not seem

nearly twenty-five years," said Lady Sylvia. "I remember." She reached into her reticule and drew forth our flask. "May I ask if you are able to identify this, Your Excellency?"

The Bishop took the small container and turned it this way and that in his soft hands. Lovingly, he inspected the polished stone vessel. "May I open it?"

"You will be careful?" said Cecy.

"Indeed I shall." With precision, the Bishop removed the stopper and sniffed at the neck of the flask. The scent of the oil filled the room and we all found ourselves smiling a little for no real reason.

The Bishop restoppered the flask. "How have you come by this?"

Lady Sylvia held out her hand. "We were given it in trust."

The Bishop's eyebrows lifted. "Sylvie, what have you been doing?"

"I cannot say just yet. But my beliefs have not altered. Have yours?"

With reluctance, the Bishop returned the flask to her. "I am loyal to the League of the Pimpernel and all it stands for."

Lady Sylvia smiled at him, warmth unrestrained. "Don't look so worried, Your Excellency."

The smile he gave her in return was most reluctant. "I never worry. It's bad for the digestion. But if I allowed myself the luxury, this would be worth considerable concern. You have come into possession of the Sainte Ampoule—

how, I do not inquire, please note—that is to say, of the royal holy chrism. It is used to confirm the coronation of the true kings of France. Of old it was kept in the royal treasury in Paris. When that was looted in the Terror, all the coronation regalia stored there was lost. The survival of this flask must surely be miraculous."

"Not a great deal of it did survive," said Lady Sylvia. "And I have diminished it still further by trying a drop or two when I opened it."

"Indeed." The Bishop looked troubled. "Yet enough remains to cause considerable trouble. There is enough for one more coronation. Just."

"Can't someone make more?" asked Cecy. "If it's holy chrism, surely more could be blessed."

"This is not merely holy chrism," said the Bishop. "Precious as that is, this is far more rare. The ancient magic that created it exists no more. To crown a king is to acknowledge his temporal sway. To mark his brow with this is no mere blessing. With the proper rituals, it renders him the true king indeed, makes him a ruler by divine right."

James looked intrigued. "Who, precisely? Who would it make into a king? Lady Sylvia seems unscathed."

"Without the proper rituals, it will do nothing. Yet with the correct procedure—any of the pretenders who come forth so regularly to grasp for power."

"Bonaparte?" breathed Cecy. "Would it have made him the true king?"

The Bishop smiled bitterly. "What, the Little Emperor?

Quite a diminution of his powers, from emperor to mere king. But, yes, it would have rendered even the little Corsican into the rightful king."

"No wonder the Lady in Blue was so agitated," said Cecy. "And no wonder she was so concerned about delivering the parcel."

"No wonder we shouldn't take it to Paris," said James. "Even with Bonaparte in exile, there will be those who search for this."

"If they know of its existence," I said. "As long as it's a secret—"

"It's not a secret," said Cecy. "Think of our caller in Calais."

"If that was what he was after," countered James thoughtfully, "why did he leave without it?"

Lady Sylvia restored the flask to her reticule and drew the strings taut. "I am not entirely helpless. Thank you, Your Excellency, for satisfying my curiosity. I think we must take mercy on Thomas now and rejoin him. Kate, you may tell him all this at the earliest opportunity, but you must do so in perfect privacy. Do you understand?"

I must have looked nettled, for she added, more gently, "Of course you do. Still, secrecy is imperative."

I agreed and promised to wait until I could share our news with Thomas safely.

"Now, perhaps we should return to my parlor," said the Bishop. "I will ring for fresh tea and we can turn our attention to the pastries. Then I have something to show you that I hope may prove useful."

Thomas was most restrained when we rejoined him. We were all subdued as we resumed our interrupted refreshment. The pastries were worthy of our undivided attention. When nothing was left but crumbs and those had been cleared away, the Bishop took up the skein of yarn he'd set aside as he greeted us.

"You may recall this, Lady Sylvia," he said, "but I suspect it may prove a novelty to your young people." With deft fingers he shook out the skein and it became evident that it was no mere skein of yarn. Rather, it was a soft, shadowy piece of knitting, still on the needles, about the size of his two palms together. Crafted of dark sheep's wool, undyed and loosely spun, it was as insubstantial as a bit of storm cloud. "Look closely, please."

In turn, we inspected the knitting, careful not to let the needles slide a stitch free. Upon closer examination, it became clear that there was no pattern to the knitting. In places several stitches had been dropped at once. Elsewhere the yarn had been allowed to snarl or to snag small oddments. I found a willow leaf, hardly wilted, and a glossy, dark feather no bigger than my thumbnail.

"Heavens," said Lady Sylvia, when she held it at last. "How this takes me back." Gently, she smoothed the knitting flat on her lap and grazed it with her fingertips here and there. "Let me see. *Seven weeks since . . .* a visit? Is this feather from a cockerel? Possibly there's a pun on a name there. Hmm. *I send my regrets that I cannot attend in person.* Is that something like what your message says?" When she looked up at the Bishop, she seemed slightly pink-cheeked.

The Bishop was gratified almost beyond the power of speech. "You remembered."

Thomas and I exchanged a puzzled glance. It hardly seemed possible that anyone could find anything more than a tangled skein in the unfinished knitting.

"Is it a kind of code?" James asked, just as Cecy exclaimed, "You can read that?"

"Well, not all of it. Yes, it is a code, of sorts. But I think my rustiness may be excused. It has been some time," Lady Sylvia answered.

The Bishop took the knitting back and tucked it carefully away. "The message is incomplete, of course. That hinders you in reading the meaning, naturally. But if you recall the old system, we might use it as a means of communication again."

"Excellent notion," said Lady Sylvia. "However, I'll go over the system with you in full, if it is not inconvenient. I may recall the most elementary codes, but the subtleties I've long forgotten."

"I would be delighted to review the codes with you. It will take some time, of course. I have made a few refinements of my own, in addition to the system we used in the old days." Almost as an afterthought, the Bishop added, "I trust you will all be able to stay for dinner?"

"I think that would be delightful," said Lady Sylvia. "We will all benefit from the lesson. Particularly Thomas. He's never been patient with handwork."

"I resent that," said Thomas. "I've never had a knitting lesson in my life, but I'm a devil with a darning needle."

I couldn't help the chuckle that escaped me. Thomas looked reproachful, and James added, "He's quite right. Modest, even. I wouldn't have had a stocking to my name back in the Peninsula if it hadn't been for Thomas."

"That's extremely fortunate," said Cecy, "because when it comes to needles, Kate's a positive menace."

"I'm afraid I am," I confessed.

"Nonsense," said Thomas. "You simply haven't had a good reason to concentrate on it until now. I'll teach you."

"But you don't know how to knit any more than I do," I reminded him.

"Details," said Thomas, and our lessons began.

From the deposition of Mrs. James Tarleton, &c.

Both James and Kate had great difficulty in mastering the art of sending messages in knitting, though Kate at least found it easy to decipher the messages—it was the knitting itself that caused her problems. Every time she dropped a stitch, it changed what she was saying. Thomas was surprisingly adept, and I did not find it as confusing as I had expected. Still, the lessons took a good while longer than we had anticipated. The Bishop's curate peeked in several times, but the Bishop sent him away. I took it as a measure of his concern over the situation.

I was somewhat distracted in my knitting efforts by my thoughts. If the mysterious Lady in Blue had given Lady Sylvia *one* of the missing pieces of the French kings' coronation regalia, did she have the other pieces? Where had she come by it, or them? If our midnight caller in Calais had been seeking it, what was his reason? Was he a Royalist hoping to keep it out of English hands, or a Bonapartist hoping to reinstate Napoleon, or perhaps a Republican hoping to destroy it utterly? Or perhaps he was something else entirely. I found myself wishing that Papa had been less interested in antiquities, and more in politics, for the past ten years; I could not see that knowing about the Temple of Minerva Victrix would do me the least good in the current situation; whereas it might have been a great deal of help to know more about the various factions in France.

Unfortunately, none of my questions had an obvious answer, and Lady Sylvia seemed very reluctant to discuss the matter except in the safest of venues. I wondered suddenly if perhaps she had reason to know that we were being magically spied upon. Upon reflection, I decided that this was unlikely; if she had actually detected a scrying spell, I was sure that she would have found some way to warn us.

Eventually we finished our lessons and departed for the Coq d'Or. Though I was extremely curious as to what Lady Sylvia intended to do with the chrism, now that we knew what it was, I refrained from asking about it. Instead, James and I recounted our visit to the temple, and then I brought out Theodore's essay on Druids for Lady Sylvia to look at.

Thomas craned his neck to catch a glimpse of it as she read, and she obligingly laid it on the table for him. He read through it and chuckled, just as James had. "Cheeky young devil. I think you're tilting at windmills, Cecy; there's nothing magical in this essay."

"You are half correct, my dear," Lady Sylvia said. "There is nothing magical about the *writing*."

Thomas gave her a startled look, then frowned at the wrinkled page. "Ah—yes, I see. It's an odd harmonic."

"*What* is an odd harmonic?" James asked. "The rest of us would like an explanation. When you are quite finished enjoying yourself."

"He means, when you are quite finished being mysterious," Kate told Thomas.

"Oh, we both know that's what he meant," said Thomas. "Most enjoyable it is, too."

"That will do," Lady Sylvia said. "Thomas is referring to the residue of the spell in which this little essay was used."

"I *knew* I felt something in that temple!" I said.

"I am a little surprised that you did," Lady Sylvia said. "You must be quite sensitive to it. Can you describe it more particularly?"

I was forced to admit that I could not; a general sensation of magic was the best I could do.

"It is a pity that you have not progressed further in your studies," Lady Sylvia said. "I should like to have some idea what this spell was intended to accomplish. It is, as Thomas said, an exceedingly odd harmonic, quite apart from the unusual nature of the setting and the ingredients. Well, it cannot be helped." She smoothed the essay, folded it, and placed it in her reticule.

Our discussion turned to inconsequentials, such as whether it was possible to reach Paris in a single day with the roads in the condition they were. Thomas held that it was; James considered it inadvisable. Lady Sylvia at last informed them that she, at least, did not propose to spend another night on the road if it was possible to spend it in her own *hôtel* in Paris, and that settled the matter. Shortly after, we retired to our respective rooms.

I spent the evening studying the book of orisons and invocations that Lady Sylvia had given me. At first, I was rather disappointed, for it was quickly plain that none of the incantations *did* anything, but after a short while I realized that they were like the five-finger exercises that our governess used to make me and Kate and Georgy practice on the pianoforte. The scales were not intended to make music, but to accustom the fingers to their proper positions on the keys; the incantations in Lady Sylvia's book were, similarly, intended to accustom the would-be wizard to channeling and controlling magical power, so that when one finally attempted a spell, one would not need to concentrate on anything but what the spell was supposed to accomplish.

The following morning, as we climbed into the coach, I asked Lady Sylvia if my insight was correct. She looked quite pleased, and nodded. I would have liked to discuss the matter more thoroughly on the journey, but I settled for requesting a private conference with her later. I could not feel that Thomas or James would welcome a review of what must to them be quite basic information, and Kate had never expressed more than polite interest in the technical details of magic.

The talk was not lively, as Lady Sylvia had been quite firm about getting an early start. Due to some mix-up, we had only the one carriage, but it was quite large and not at all uncomfortable, even with five of us inside. Lady Sylvia set the difficulty down to Thomas's account, and warned him that if it happened again, she would leave him behind to follow along with the servants and the baggage, but I do not think that even Kate believed she would actually do such a thing.

We made good time despite the roads, which seemed to grow worse instead of better the nearer we came to Paris. By midafternoon we had reached Sevran and our final change of horses. It appeared that we would arrive in Paris with daylight to spare, but shortly after we rattled away from the coaching station, I began to feel slightly unwell.

I am not accustomed to being carriage-sick, no matter how poor the roads, and I was determined not to cause a delay, especially as Lady Sylvia had been so adamant about reaching Paris by evening, so I leaned back and closed my eyes. James and Thomas were arguing about some obscure point of military strategy during the Peninsular War, so I could safely ignore them and concentrate on retaining my lunch.

The unpleasant sensation in my stomach grew worse, and I was just wondering whether I would have to say something after all, when Kate said, "Lady Sylvia, are you unwell? Should we stop the coach?"

"No," Lady Sylvia said in a voice that sounded decidedly weak. "No. This is . . . this is . . ."

"Cecy, wake up!" James said in my ear.

"I'm awake," I managed with some effort. I forced my eyes open. Lady Sylvia was leaning back against the squabs, looking pale. "I just feel exceedingly peculiar."

"I should have warned you not to have the fish," James said.

"I hardly think it can have been the fish," Kate said. "Lady Sylvia barely touched it, and Thomas didn't have any at all."

"Thomas?" James said, frowning in evident puzzlement.

"I'm in excellent health," Thomas said in a strangled voice. "Never better."

"You are not," Kate said flatly. "And it's very odd that of the five of us, it's the three wizards who are suddenly feeling not the thing."

Before James or Thomas could respond, the coach lurched violently. I heard incoherent shouts outside and then a muffled crack. We stopped moving, but I felt no better.

Then the coach door was flung open, and a man thrust his head—and a large pistol—into the coach and said something in incomprehensible French.

James looked quite fierce for a moment, but then he glanced at Lady Sylvia and me. His lips tightened. "We had better do as he says," he said.

"What did he say?"

"We're being held up," Kate said much too calmly. "We're to get out of the coach. James, will you help Lady Sylvia? I think Cecy and I can manage together, and I'm sure Thomas will do quite well on his own. Since he is feeling so perfectly well."

"Held up?" I said as James followed Thomas out. My stomach seemed to be settling at last, but my head still felt very fuzzy. "On the main road to Paris?"

"It does seem rather unusual," Kate said. She was a little pale, but she had the intent look on her face that meant she was thinking very hard. It is the oddest thing—Kate can be positively terrified by balls and the theater and other ordinary social events, but in any real crisis, she is quite composed and coolheaded. I suppose it is because she is much better at improvising than at remembering rules, and highwaymen are unlikely to care much about faux pas.

We climbed out after Lady Sylvia. An extremely scruffy man with a faded muffler wrapped around his face sat on horseback, pointing a rusty shotgun at the coachman. Another horseman, similarly muffled, held a pair of pistols aimed at James and Thomas, while a third man went through their pockets. James looked ready to commit murder, and he kept his eyes fixed on the men with the firearms. Thomas looked more saturnine than usual, that was all, but Kate watched him with a faint worry line between her brows.

The footpad collected Lady Sylvia's reticule and necklace and delivered them to the man with the shotgun, then came to me. James stopped watching the men with the guns and gave me a warning look, which was quite unnecessary. I am not foolish enough to think myself invulnerable to firearms. I let the fellow relieve me of my jewelry and reticule. He delivered them to the leader in similar fashion, and then he turned to Kate. Having possessed himself of her reticule and earrings, he reached for her left hand to strip off her wedding ring as well. And Thomas went mad.

I had not set Thomas down as such a romantic, and evidently neither had anyone else. His charge was so unexpected and thorough that the thieves were caught quite by surprise. The one who was mishandling Kate was knocked off his feet and landed quite ten feet away. The horses shied. James ran at the horseman with the pistols, while Thomas snatched at the boot and lower leg of the man with the shotgun, levering him up to throw him off balance and dislodge him from his saddle.

The shotgun discharged, fortunately over the head of our coachman. The blast set the coach horses rearing and plunging in their traces. The gunman struck out at Thomas and wrenched his horse around. *"Filons!"* he shouted, and galloped off. Kate picked up a large rock and began advancing with a purposeful air toward the highwayman Thomas had downed, who scrambled to his feet and fled. The remaining horseman saw Thomas coming to assist James, and raised his pistols.

Thomas saw the motion and dodged, but James had just put a hand to the horse's reins. The guns went off; the horse reared; James fell backward on the verge. The highwayman set spurs to his mount and followed his companion.

I stumbled forward to kneel beside James. He lay on his side, gasping as if the wind had been knocked out of him, and his coat was already wet with blood.

I do not perfectly recall the next few minutes. The ball appeared to have gone in under his arm, toward the back, and there seemed to be a great deal of blood. I remember Thomas making some comment about stopping the bleeding, and stripping off his cravat for me to use as padding. (It is the greatest piece of folly for romantic novels to advise ladies to rip up their petticoats in such an emergency. Without scissors, even muslin is exceedingly difficult to begin tearing; linen and silk are quite impossible.)

By the time we had the bleeding under control, the coachman had quieted the horses. After some discussion, Thomas and the coachman lifted James into the carriage (despite his protests; he was apparently under the delusion that he was perfectly capable of walking, though the ball was still lodged). Kate and Lady Sylvia and I crowded together on the opposite seat, while Thomas rode outside with the coachman.

The remainder of the journey seemed interminable, though we had agreed to travel only as far as the next inn. It was easy to see that James was in considerable pain. The coachman drove slowly, so as to minimize any jostling, but shortly before sunset, the coach wheels rattled against the cobbles of a paved town street. Quite soon after, we came to a stop in an inn yard, and I heard Thomas shouting directions.

Men came running from the inn, full of questions but willing to help. As they lifted James out of the carriage, I heard Kate ask, "Where are we?"

"St. Denis," Thomas told her.

ST. DENIS

From the commonplace book of Lady Schofield

> 15 August 1817
> St. Denis
> At the Lion d'Or

If I try to set my thoughts down in order, perhaps they will make some kind of sense. At the very least, I will be out of the way here. The room James and Cecy are in is next to this one. If anyone should need me, I will be able to hear the call. The walls are none too thick. I hear all too much as it is.

Now. Orderly thoughts.

It is a great disadvantage to spend one's time worrying about what may go wrong. When things do go wrong, one would think that worry would've prepared one in some way. This is not the case. Instead, the senseless disorder of one's thoughts grows more and more uncontrollable as one rehearses the events that befell, to no good effect since nothing can undo the damage, no amount of muddled thinking can ever result in any other outcome.

Magic is confusing. Before I met Thomas, when I felt ill,

I felt ill, and that was that. Now I cannot be sure when I truly feel ill or not.

I think the moment of empathy the two of us shared when Thomas focused his magic in my ring must have returned in the coach. When Thomas fell prey to the malaise that overcame Lady Sylvia and, to a lesser extent, Cecy, I felt it, too. I felt his discomfort sharply enough to know when he played the fool by lying to us about it. Yet that discomfort faded before the dreadful apprehension we all felt when James was hurt.

Cecy has been a miracle of calm and common sense throughout. Thomas and Lady Sylvia issued orders, but it was Cecy who supervised James's arrival at the Lion d'Or. It was Cecy who saw him disposed as comfortably as possible. It was Cecy who looked the local physician in the eye and made it plain without a word spoken in any language whatsoever that she would be the final arbiter of what would be done for James.

Lady Sylvia was willing to send for physicians from the city, as it was scarcely more than seven miles away, but the local man seemed well trained and capable. I did not attend at the bedside during the surgical procedure that removed the pistol ball from James's side.

Instead, I was sitting on the staircase with my head in my hands wondering if the cold, unsteady sensation in my midsection was my own nausea or something Thomas was feeling as he held James still so the physician could do his work.

Again and again I rehearsed the disastrous events. Again and again I reached the inescapable conclusion that it is all my fault. I am to blame for the fact that James was injured. My folly is to blame, for I persuaded Thomas to invest his magic in my ring. My pride is to blame, for I hesitated after handing over my reticule and taking off my earrings. I could have handed the villain the ring myself and spared James. I could have prevented the terrible gasping sounds that James made as he tried to stifle his pain. I could have prevented the stricken look in Cecy's eyes when she fell to her knees beside her husband.

The sounds from behind the bedroom door ceased at last. The silence lasted a long time before the door opened. Thomas came out to sit beside me on the splintery wooden stair. He'd taken off his coat, his shirtsleeves were rolled up past his elbows, and his shirt buttons were undone halfway to his waistcoat. His breeches were spattered with mud and blood, not all of it dry. There were smudges of fatigue under his eyes and his whiskers were beginning to show, a dark shadow that made him seem all the paler.

I looked up at him in silence. I simply couldn't think of anything to say.

Thomas let out a long breath of pure weariness as he took my left hand in his right, touching my wedding ring. His hand was cold, and when I glanced down I could see his fingers were rosy red, he'd scrubbed so hard. I knew he must have been washing blood away. My stomach lurched at the thought. Thomas tightened his clasp and gave my hand a heartening little shake. "He'll be fine."

I rested my forehead on his shoulder. "Oh, Thomas."

"I know. But the doctor says he's going to be right as a trivet. Back on his feet in a few weeks." Thomas let out another, shorter breath that might, under better circumstances, have been a faint chuckle. "A very few weeks, if I know James. Now, in another two minutes, there's going to be more work to do. Fetching and carrying and scrubbing, basins and trays and buckets up and down. You don't want to interfere, do you?"

"Of course not."

"Then you'll have to move. The servants are using the back stair for the moment, but you're considerably in the way here. Come along and wash your face." Thomas pulled me to my feet. "We're going to have a council of war."

It was a very small council we convened. Cecy was with James, naturally, so it was just Lady Sylvia, Thomas, and me seated around the fire in Lady Sylvia's room. Lady Sylvia had a rug over her knees for warmth, but in every other way she was looking much more herself. She was knitting one of her bird's-nest messages as she sat beside the fire. When I asked after her health, she fixed me with a reproving look. "I am perfectly well. Thank you for asking. Really, Kate, I have seen you in difficult circumstances before, but I never realized you were so self-regarding."

"Mother!" Thomas looked shocked.

"Then you know," I said. My throat was so tight, the words came out as if I were being strangled.

"Thomas told me a little and I guessed the rest. Your fault, is it?" Lady Sylvia was relentless. "All your fault and no one else's?"

I clasped my hands in my lap and tried to will the tears back before they overflowed and disgraced me. "Yes."

"Gammon," said Lady Sylvia. "Thomas had to invest something with his magic. It was not your fault the ring attracted unfriendly attention. Nor was it your fault that he behaved so impulsively when it was threatened. He could have done the sensible thing and let it go to be recovered later."

"Oh, no, I couldn't," Thomas retorted. "I'm not losing my focus twice."

"Perhaps you couldn't." Lady Sylvia seemed amused by Thomas's vehemence. "Perhaps it wasn't your fault, either, dear boy. Perhaps the blame belongs to the thieves who waylaid us."

Thomas agreed readily. "Of course it was their fault. Mighty bold thieves they were, too, striking in broad daylight on the main road. Clever of them to incapacitate us first."

"Extremely clever." Lady Sylvia looked thoughtful. "Not really what one expects of thieves, however bold. I wonder whom they consulted? Or, more realistically, who consulted them."

"You think someone hired them?" It was Thomas's turn to look thoughtful.

"I do." Lady Sylvia put a few more loose stitches into the knitting in her lap. "When we discover who sent them, we will know who is truly to blame for this misfortune. Until then, Kate, I want no more of your breast-beating mea culpas, do you understand me?" She eyed me sternly.

I nodded and sniffed. Fortunately, I had one of Aunt Charlotte's handkerchiefs ready to hand, and I used it. "How will we find out who they were?"

"I intended to enlist help the moment we reached Paris," Lady Sylvia replied. She held up the knitting. "I'll have to send a message, that's all. It's unfortunate that word of the recovery of the Sainte Ampoule must be accompanied by word of its subsequent loss, but so it must be. Things might have been much worse." She held up another object, almost as shapeless as her knitting. It was a black woolen cap. "Our footpad was careless enough to leave this behind when he took to his heels to escape you, Kate. I have handled it as little as possible. The friends I intend to send this to should be able to determine a great many things from their study of it. Possibly some of that information may be of use to us."

Thomas looked grim. "Indeed, things might have been a great deal worse. While we wait for your friends to reply, what shall we do?"

Lady Sylvia looked from Thomas to me. "We must do precisely as we have done. Protect James. Help Cecy. Behave as if we are all as blameless and bewildered as we actually are. Above all, be very, very careful."

From the deposition of Mrs. James Tarleton, &c.

As might be expected, James was the worst patient imaginable. The French medical man was, fortunately, quite competent, but the ball had lodged against bone, and extracting it was a difficult business. It was not at all surprising that James came down with some slight fever the following day due to having been "pulled about" (as he put it), but he refused to acknowledge it and put considerable effort into attempting to demonstrate his alleged fitness for duty. Eventually I convinced him that his only duty was to remain abed, but I was much relieved when his valet arrived, late in the day, to reinforce my efforts.

The weather, too, cooperated. "Not even you can think it advisable to travel in a cold downpour," I told him when he began complaining again on the second day. "And there's nothing else to do here, so you may as well stay in bed."

"Nonsense," James said. "You act as if I've never been shot before."

"You haven't been shot in front of me before," I pointed out. "And if you dare try to say, 'It's just a scratch,' I warn you, I shall have strong hysterics. I saw what that surgeon had to do, remember?"

"Cecy—" James tried to sit up, and winced involuntarily.

"There, you see?" I moved one of the pillows to make him more comfortable.

"You shouldn't have been there," he said fretfully.

"When the surgeon dug the ball out, you mean? I most certainly should. If you are going to continue making a habit of getting shot—which, I own, I would rather you didn't—then I think it only sensible for me to learn what is best to do under such circumstances."

"I don't make a habit of it," James said.

"Don't you?" I was not altogether sure I ought to argue with him; the physician had (so far as I understood his French) stressed the importance of keeping James calm. However, as long as he was arguing, he was unlikely to do anything utterly cockle-headed, such as attempt to get up.

"Of course not!" His tone lacked conviction, and he looked decidedly uncomfortable—and, I thought, not only because he had recently had a ball dug out of him.

"James," I said, "just how many times *have* you been shot?"

"That has nothing to do with the matter!"

"Very well, if you insist on being mulish, I shall ask Thomas."

James glared at me. I returned my sweetest smile, and made as if to rise from the chair. "Four," he growled.

"Counting this one?"

"All right, five. But three of them were in battles. Being

aide-de-camp to the Duke of Wellington was no sinecure—
they don't call him the Iron Duke for nothing. And the other
time was Thomas's fault, too."

"Really?" I sat back down in the chair, all polite attention. "And how did that happen? It can't have been anybody
being unpleasant to Kate. She'd have told me, and, anyway,
you were at Tarleton Hall the whole time she was in London
meeting Thomas."

James stared at me for a moment, then laughed ruefully.
"You've done it again, haven't you?"

"Done what?"

He shook his head. "Never mind. It's a pity old
Carmichael couldn't have put you on the secret payroll
when we were in Spain. You'd have collected more information than any six of the fellows he did have. With the possible exception of Thomas, of course."

"You were going to tell me about Thomas," I reminded
him.

"The things I could tell you about Thomas . . . ," James
murmured.

I frowned. It wasn't like James to lose the thread of a
discussion. "Perhaps you ought to rest now. We'll have
plenty of time to talk later."

"What?" James looked at me and shook his head. "No,
no, it's all right, Cecy. I was trying to tease you, that's all."

"In that case, about Thomas . . . ?"

"Bulldogs aren't in it," James muttered. "All right, about
Thomas. He was one of Carmichael's fellows, and quite

good at it—kept being told off for 'long reconnaissance,' and everyone knew what that meant."

"Well, I don't."

"Slipping into French-held territory to find out where Soult's men were and, more important, where Napoleon had told them to turn up next. It wasn't too difficult when we were in Spain—the Spaniards hated the French. They used to ambush couriers just for fun, and send us Napoleon's dispatches. Sometimes it seemed as if we knew more about what the French were supposed to be doing than their generals did."

"That sounds useful," I said.

"It was. Sometimes we needed to know more, though, and then we sent out people like Thomas to fill in the gaps. He'd get himself up in some unlikely fashion and vanish, then turn up a few days later with just the information we needed. Until San Sebastián."

"San Sebastián?"

James didn't seem to hear me. "After we took the port, Soult retreated into the Pyrenees. Thomas went off for a look at the defenses of the star fort on the Bidassoa River, by the Pass of Vera. He was gone nearly two weeks. Then a fellow showed up—a thoroughly disreputable-looking cutthroat of a Spaniard—claiming to be a courier from Thomas. With a lot of information and a note saying the French had taken him for a local and pressed him into their army, but that—"

"—nobody was to worry, he would manage it all himself," I finished. James gave me a startled look. "Kate has told me all about Thomas's appalling tendency to overconfidence."

James snorted. "It's not overconfidence, my girl; it's a dislike of making fusses. And of being caught at a disadvantage."

"Yes, that does sound like him," I said, nodding. "And knowing that, of course you went after him."

"Somebody had to," James said. "As soon as he left the French army, they'd consider him a deserter, and they shot deserters on sight. So I waxed persuasive and got leave to track him down.

"It was easier than I'd expected. He'd dropped enough hints, one way and another. He'd gone to ground with a supposedly respectable French widow in Bayonne. I'd thought she was a friend of his mother's, so I was expecting someone older and . . . more sedate. But I hadn't met Lady Sylvia then, of course."

"The Lady in Blue!" I said. "That's who it was, wasn't it?"

James nodded. "I never did find out her real name. She didn't tell me then, of course, in case the Frenchies caught us on the way back. She'd managed to hide Thomas, but she was low on funds. Naturally, Thomas had had to abandon most of what he'd taken with him when he realized he was about to be caught in the press sweep. I gave her most of what I'd brought, and slipped Thomas out the back ahead of the search party, so she could safely let them search the house and wax indignant over their suspicions."

"James, are you telling me that you managed to sneak past the French?" I demanded. For James is *terrible* at sneaking; I've seen him try.

"Not exactly." James looked embarrassed. "I, er,

borrowed a coat from a French officer we'd taken prisoner. I thought nobody would question a wounded officer with a dispatch case, so I put my left arm in a sling. And limped. Well, when I remembered. I think that's what gave us away in the end, actually."

"You should have put a pebble in your boot," I said severely. "Then you wouldn't have forgotten to limp, and you wouldn't have been shot."

"Oh, that wasn't when I was shot," James said with revolting cheerfulness. "That was just when Thomas and I had to run for it. I didn't get shot until we were back in Spain. I was still wearing the officer's coat, and with Thomas in tow . . . well, a Spanish guerrilla took me for just what I'd been playing, a French courier escorting a prisoner, and he took a couple of potshots at us. We rode for it, but I took a ball in the thigh. Nearly spent, fortunately; it didn't take much to dig it out. But it was three weeks before the sawbones would certify me fit for duty, and I missed taking the fort at the Bidassoa."

Men are extremely odd. I hope I am properly conscious of my duty to my country, but I do not think that in similar circumstances I would have been at all sorry to have missed the chance of being shot at for several hours together.

"And it was all Thomas's fault," James finished, smothering a yawn.

"Are you too tired to continue talking?" I asked carefully.

"What?"

"If you aren't too tired, I have a few questions," I said.

"I follow the general outline of your adventure, but there are a few gaps..."

"Cecy, I—" An enormous yawn interrupted him. He blinked at me, frowning slightly. Then his expression cleared. "Yes, I think I could do with a nap."

"I'll be here if you want something," I assured him.

James smiled, lay back, and closed his eyes. It was not many minutes before his pretense of sleep became the real thing. I stayed where I was until his breathing deepened and I was quite sure he would not awake; then I slipped out. Direct tactics are not always the most effective with James.

From the commonplace book of Lady Schofield

17 August 1817
St. Denis
At the Lion d'Or

Things have been quiet, blessedly quiet. We have had two solid days of rain, but we are comfortable enough here at the Lion d'Or. Two days of utter quiet have done wonders for James. James's improvement has done wonders for Cecy, who permitted herself an unbroken rest only after James spent an entire night in undisturbed slumber.

This morning the weather improved. At breakfast, the day looked as if it would be fair and fine. I was glad of Thomas's suggestion that I accompany him to the Basilica of

St. Denis. After all, it is one of the ancient sites Uncle Arthur will be sure to ask us about. Hundreds of years of history have accumulated there, century upon century, kings and queens drifting in like leaves in autumn.

Very suited to my mood it turned out to be, too, since the whole place was wrecked during the Revolution. Fifty-seven royal tombs have been desecrated, the stained-glass windows broken, even the leading torn from the roof. Hard work in the years since had made a start at putting the ruin back to rights, but to me it seemed a dreadful place—gloomy, chill, and damp despite the fine weather outside.

Only one place in St. Denis seemed free of the despair of the past. Someone has displayed good common sense and converted the old buildings of the abbey into a free school. We were told it is for the daughters of officers of the Legion of Honor. The signs of school life make a welcome contrast to the maimed old abbey church. There is hope for the future if more such outworn monuments of antiquity could be put to good use.

21 August 1817
St. Denis
At the Lion d'Or

The physician has pronounced James fit to rise from his bed. I suspect James may have been doing a bit of rising on his own, but certainly today was the first time he was officially up and around. Not that he did much. Cecy was at his side to prevent any untoward exertion. She is looking a thousand times better.

So it was that our second council of war took place in the rooms James and Cecy shared, and this time it was James who had a rug over his knees as he sat beside the fire.

The five of us made ourselves comfortable in close quarters, and Lady Sylvia began. "First I must ask a very simple question. Given the circumstances, do you wish to change your plans and return home?"

"Home?" Cecy was seated on a footstool beside James's chair. This permitted her to lean against James's knee. "We can't go home. We haven't even reached Paris yet. How will we ever find out what this is all about if we go home now?"

"Lady Sylvia is offering us an alternative," James answered. He let one fingertip touch Cecy's shoulder, as if to reassure himself that she was safely within his reach. "We need to be very clear about things if we choose to go on."

"Fine. I'm very clear. I want to go on. Don't you?" Cecy's customary air of decision was firmly in place.

James smiled at her.

"Before anyone else answers," Lady Sylvia said, "I must clarify matters. I have enlisted help from friends in Paris. I intend to stay there and make inquiries, whether you stay or go. So you needn't feel that going home now will deprive you of the eventual solution to this mystery. We will find out what this is all about, I promise."

Thomas met my eyes and nodded slightly. I said, "If you're staying, we're staying."

James said, "We're all staying. Or to be more precise, we're all going with you to Paris. Moreover, we'll all work together to puzzle this out."

"Good." I could tell Lady Sylvia was pleased, even though she immediately turned a severe gaze upon Thomas. "But we will have no more foolhardy tricks, is that clear?"

For a wonder, Thomas only nodded meekly and made no other reply at all.

"Very good. Then we may turn our attention to the matter at hand." From her reticule, Lady Sylvia produced an untidy bit of knitting done in gray yarn. "I have received a reply to the message I sent ahead to Paris along with an article of clothing discarded by one of our attackers. This tells me there is more news for us than can be conveyed in this fashion. In addition, my friends wish to show me something that may be of particular interest to you, Thomas."

"I trust your friends will have no objection if we join you?" Thomas asked.

"They will not object in the least." Lady Sylvia showed us the gray knitting. "But see? The last four stitches are purled, meaning time is of the essence. Do you think you will feel well enough to travel tomorrow, James?"

"Of course." James seemed to have no doubts at all, but Cecy looked concerned.

"How far will we need to travel?" Cecy asked. "It's only

a few miles to Paris, but I have always understood Paris to be a rather large city."

"We go just to my house in the Rue des Capucines," Lady Sylvia replied. "As soon as we're settled comfortably there, I'll send for my friends. We'll see just what they have to tell us."

"To Paris, then," said James. "At last."

PARIS

23 August 1817
Paris
At Lady Sylvia's house

We took our time about leaving the Lion d'Or yesterday.
James was in fine spirits and in as good health as might be
expected, but since the journey was to be so short, we made
it a very leisurely one. Even so, by the end of the afternoon
I was very glad to be settled at last in Lady Sylvia's Paris
house. It is an elegant place of considerable age, not far
from the Madeleine, the new church they're building to look
like a Greek temple. However noble the architectural history that went into its design, Uncle Arthur would still be
scandalized by the sight. Its stone is raw and glaringly new.
In fact, everything about it looks new. Even when it is finished, I expect it will keep that jarring effect. I would not
have thought I had an opinion in the matter, but I find I am
not in any doubt. A Greek temple should not look new.

Lady Sylvia was as good as her word. At dinner, we
were joined by her friends, Mr. Lennox and Mr. Reardon.
Both men are far closer in age to Thomas and James than to

any of Lady Sylvia's friends we've met so far. Initially, I assumed from their names that Mr. Lennox was Scottish and Mr. Reardon was Irish, but there was nothing in their speech or manner to betray any provincial origin at all. Mr. Lennox is more wiry than Mr. Reardon, but they are of a height and share similarly nondescript coloring. Indeed, I had a difficult time remembering which was which. I finally settled myself to remember that Mr. Reardon's neckcloth was a thought more elegant. Heaven help me when I meet them again. They will have changed clothes. I'll have to start all over.

Both the short notice of the invitation and the state of James's health—although he made light of the exertions of the day's travel—made informality desirable. After dinner, we all repaired to the drawing room, where Lady Sylvia and Thomas made sure that our meeting was protected from all other eyes and ears.

When the protection spell was set, Mr. Lennox and Mr. Reardon brought forth a map of Paris and a sheaf of papers, all of which they deposited on the mahogany table in front of Lady Sylvia.

"We used the cap you sent us, Lady Sylvia," Mr. Lennox said, "and for the first three days it worked very well."

"Simple directional spell," Mr. Reardon added. "Good thing it was an old cap. Plenty of sympathetic vibrations to work with."

"By the third day we had located the owner of the cap to within a few hundred yards, at a lodging house in a down-at-heels part of town. It didn't seem wise to press matters

further. We just kept an eye on things at that distance."
Mr. Lennox tapped the map. "That night there was a disturbance."

"Quite an embarrassment," said Mr. Reardon. "We should have realized we weren't the only ones keeping a watch on the place."

"We did our best with limited resources," Mr. Lennox told him. It sounded to me as if they'd had the same discussion several times before. "We did what we could."

Mr. Reardon gave Mr. Lennox a small shrug that might have been agreement.

Mr. Lennox continued. "We lost all sympathetic vibrations through the cap. Fortunately, the owner of the place raised a hue and cry when he discovered the disturbance. We rushed in but it was too late. The man who owned the cap was dead. The intruders, whoever they were, got away."

"On the floor beside our man was another corpse, a gentleman of considerable means, to judge from his clothing." Mr. Reardon selected a sheet of paper from the sheaf on the table and held it out to Thomas. "This was in his pocket."

Thomas took the sheet. As he read it, his jaw tightened and his eyes grew cold. "My God. Is this genuine? Do you have anything to corroborate the identification?"

Mr. Lennox looked regretful. "He'd been robbed, of course. If he had letters of credit with him, or anything else that would have identified him beyond a doubt, they were gone by the time we got there."

Thomas held out the paper to Lady Sylvia. "It's a letter

to Sir Hilary Bedrick." While Lady Sylvia read the letter, Thomas turned back to Lennox and Reardon. "I want to see the body."

Mr. Reardon winced. "Ah. I thought you might. Unfortunately, the weather has been rather warm for the time of year. Both bodies were buried Friday. We've encountered similar situations and have found that it sometimes helps to sketch the victim as well as the crime scene. I am no hand with a pencil, but I did the best likeness I could under the circumstances." Mr. Reardon handed Thomas another sheet of paper.

We all craned forward to see. I perceived Mr. Reardon had underestimated his artistic abilities. Though rough, the unfinished likeness was unmistakably that of Sir Hilary. A grim silence fell over the room as we absorbed this news.

Sir Hilary Bedrick had caused Lady Sylvia and Thomas great grief. He had intended further misdeeds. He'd planned to murder James and to send Cecy mad. He was a man of ability, authority, strength, and learning. He had misused all of that in every possible way. Because he was stripped of his magic and sent into exile, perhaps it was inevitable he would come to a bad end. Still, that made it no less shocking to be presented with evidence of his involvement in our current puzzle.

Cecy was the first to break the silence. "How on earth did Sir Hilary reach Paris so quickly? Mr. Brummell said he hadn't arrived in Calais."

"There are other Channel ports." Lady Sylvia folded the letter and put it back. "Sir Hilary's correspondent, who signs his letter most discreetly with the mere letter X, promises help in a project of Sir Hilary's, and urges him to make haste to the room he'd hired for him. A room where he met our attacker, presumably. I assume the address is the same?"

Mr. Lennox nodded. "No one remembers who engaged the room. It's the sort of place no one remembers anything unless they are compelled to."

"Not that we didn't try to compel them." Mr. Reardon unfolded his sketch of the crime scene. "The table had been overturned, but from the number of broken mugs and the position of the freshest stains on the table, four men sat around having drinks."

"How do you know they were men?" Cecy asked.

Slowly Mr. Reardon's ears turned a deep yet delicate shade of pink. "I . . . I . . ."

Mr. Lennox attempted a rescue. "We surmise that they were men, as the nature of the place makes it unlikely that any of the women who might frequent the premises would be invited to—" Confronted by Cecy's expression of candid interest, Mr. Lennox cleared his throat and fell silent.

"They are fallen women, you mean? Soiled doves?" Cecy prompted. "I know *just* what you mean—"

James had mercy on Mr. Lennox and interrupted her. "He means, I gather, that it is most likely to have been a man who sat at that table to talk on terms of equality with Sir Hilary and our subject."

"More likely, perhaps—" Cecy broke off. "James, you look so tired. Are you quite sure you are not—"

James was gentle, yet firm. "I am entirely positive. I'm quite all right."

Cecy subsided.

"Neatly phrased, James, but Sir Hilary never deemed anyone to be on terms of equality with him," said Thomas. "If we accept this reading of the situation, it wasn't a straightforward attack, was it?"

"By no means," Mr. Lennox answered. "More likely a case of thieves falling out. From the injuries inflicted on our subject, we believe that Sir Hilary had a knife. Someone else had a blunt instrument, but he took it away with him once he used it on Sir Hilary."

"Four men, you said." James looked thoughtful. "Sir Hilary killed our footpad, possibly in self-defense. Someone else killed Sir Hilary. What of the fourth?"

"From the nature of Sir Hilary's injuries," said Mr. Lennox, "the fourth man was involved in rendering him immobile."

"One held him down," Mr. Reardon summed up, "while the other killed him."

The blunt words rendered us all silent for some time. I would not dare to guess what was going through anyone else's mind. To me, however, it seemed not unjust that Sir Hilary, who had sacrificed so many to his thirst for power, had died like an animal in the slaughterhouse.

Mr. Lennox broke the mood at last. "By the time we arrived, there were no valuables of any kind at the scene. The Sainte Ampoule was gone."

"If it was ever there to begin with," said Cecy.

"Oh, I think it was." Lady Sylvia wore her most thoughtful look. "I think it must have been. That is why the thieves fell out, I think."

"You think Sir Hilary was the one to hire the men who attacked us?" Thomas asked. "But how could he have known we had the chrism?"

"He couldn't have known." Lady Sylvia looked as stern as I have ever seen her. "He had been stripped of his magic. He blamed us for that, quite rightly, I'm pleased to say. In his impotent rage, he hired footpads. I think the project Sir Hilary enlisted X's help with must have been the attack upon us."

"That would explain the illness that incapacitated the three of us," said Cecy. "Sir Hilary would have known he couldn't send footpads to attack wizards without doing something about the wizards first."

"Sir Hilary could not have cast that spell, nor any other," I said. "Not if he'd been stripped of his power."

"X seems mighty confident he could help Sir Hilary in his project," said Thomas. "Perhaps we have X to thank for that nasty bit of magic."

"To be quite sure of that, first we must find X," said Cecy.

"But how?" James sounded fatigued by the very thought of the search for such a needle in a haystack, and I could not help but sympathize.

Cecy unfolded the letter and offered it to Lady Sylvia.

"How odd are the harmonics in *this*, I wonder? It may be able to tell us something about X."

Lady Sylvia took the letter and looked at it appraisingly, then held it out to Lennox and Reardon. "Gentlemen? Will you work with us on this matter?"

Mr. Reardon merely nodded, but Mr. Lennox said, "It will be our pleasure, only I must warn you, the process will take some time."

"That's good," said Cecy, "because we will need to stay here in Paris for some time. Now that we're finally here, we have several important things to do. But the most important thing right now is to prevent James from overexerting himself. May we meet again tomorrow? First thing in the morning, perhaps?"

Mr. Lennox seemed amused by James's faint air of discomfiture. "By all means. For now, we shall adjourn. Lady Sylvia, I'll leave the documents in your care."

24 August 1817
Paris
At Lady Sylvia's house

Yesterday morning I left Thomas sleeping and came down to breakfast at the same time Cecy did. I tried to think how long it had been since the two of us had been given the chance of a quiet moment together. It seemed like years.

"How is James?" I asked, as soon as we'd been brought our breakfast and left to ourselves.

"Much better. He made his valet sharpen the razor twice when he was being shaved this morning. He's much more like himself." Cecy stirred sugar into her tea, buttered half her croissant, and set to with a will. You'd never guess it from her trim figure, but Cecy heartily appreciates her meals. "I think Paris agrees with him."

I said, "It's lovely to be settled for a bit. We can all use the rest."

Cecy's mouth was full, so she just nodded. As soon she could, she said, "It is lovely here. But we won't have a chance to rest long. We have things to do. For one thing, we must find maids. We can't go on borrowing Lady Sylvia's servants forever and ever."

Maids. My heart sank at the thought. "Oh, dear. I suppose so."

"And we simply *must* do some shopping. We can't pay calls and collect gossip wearing London modes—not in *Paris!* And in the matter of gossip, have Mr. Reardon and Mr. Lennox called yet?"

Sometimes I forget that I was the one who had a London Season, not Cecy. "Of course not. It's hours and hours until anyone would dream of calling on us here."

Cecy looked puzzled. "Mr. Lennox did say first thing in the morning, didn't he?"

"You and I are used to first thing in the morning in the

country. First thing in the morning in the city is a very different pair of shoes," I explained. "That's one reason we're having breakfast by ourselves."

"Indeed? I thought it a trifle odd." Cecy finished her tea. "I hope they don't waste half the day getting here. Though they did leave the letter with Lady Sylvia. That might be lucky. I suppose if they're dreadfully late, we could start without them."

"I don't know how much useful information they'll be able to get out of an anonymous letter." I poured us each another cup.

"Of course you don't. Neither do I. But Lady Sylvia's experienced in these matters, and she seemed to think it was well worth a try. Mr. Lennox and Mr. Reardon did very well with that cap."

"They seem quite young to be friends of Lady Sylvia's," I observed.

"They do, don't they? Perhaps they're related to someone she knew in her youth, back when she and the Bishop of Amiens were having adventures." Cecy helped herself to another croissant. "Do you suppose it will seem as peculiar to our children, years from now, to think of us having adventures?"

I thought it over. "It doesn't seem at all peculiar that Lady Sylvia had adventures in her youth. She's having them now, after all. But I admit I don't see how it could possibly seem as peculiar as the idea that the Bishop of Amiens had adventures in his youth."

Cecy laughed. "It's hard to imagine the youth, let alone the adventures. But I'm sure we'll seem just as sedate and dignified in years to come, when we're having breakfast with children as old as we are now."

I thought of my parents, long dead, and of Cecy's Mama, whom she scarcely remembered, and I wondered what it would be like to sit at breakfast with them. I couldn't imagine it. "I'm sure you'll seem sedate and dignified to them. I doubt anyone will ever find me either one."

"Oh, Kate. Don't be so sure. After all, there will be Thomas's influence at work." Cecy's eyes danced as she said this, for Thomas had entered the room as I was speaking.

"What's this about my influence?" Thomas asked as he was served with coffee and croissants. "Ever a force for good, I assure you."

"We were just wondering if we'd ever seem as sedate and dignified as the Bishop of Amiens," I explained.

Thomas gave a great crack of laughter. "Don't let the odor of sanctity deceive you. I think there's a good bit of mischief left in the old boy yet. If anyone can bring it out, it will be Mother. I wonder how many more of the League we'll meet before we're done? Probably a good many of them are still right here in the city."

Cecy said, "I thought the League of the Pimpernel existed only to save victims from the guillotine during the Terror."

"That's how it began," said Thomas. "Once the Terror was over, the members were able to rest in safety. Yet the need to defend the innocent never ends. There will always be work for those of us who wish to use our wits against the enemy."

"Napoleon Bonaparte, I take it, was the most recent enemy?" I inquired.

"One of many," Thomas replied. "As the shape of the world has changed, the demands upon the League changed, too. There isn't always agreement among the members concerning who the enemy is. But there is always an enemy somewhere."

"Do Mr. Reardon and Mr. Lennox have any connection to the League?" I asked. "I was wondering how your Mother came to call upon them for help."

"Mother's social circle has always been wide." Thomas went through his first croissant with as much speed and enthusiasm as Cecy. "She keeps her eyes open for competency, particularly in magic."

"Will they be back soon, do you think?" asked Cecy. "They did say first thing in the morning."

"Oh, they've been and gone already," said Thomas.

Cecy gave me a look and I felt my fine air of sophistication about my London Season droop and fade. I felt slightly better when Thomas continued.

"Unaccountable, coming around so early. Mother said she didn't think they'd been to bed at all. She dealt with them and sent them on their way before I was up. Don't worry. They'll be back. This will be a long process." Thomas handed me a note. "Mr. Reardon left this for you, Kate.

Mother mentioned you were hoping to engage a maid while you were here. It seems Mr. Reardon has a cousin."

I read the note while Thomas demolished his second croissant. It was from someone named Emily Reardon, who begged me for the privilege of calling upon me to apply for a position as my maid. I felt my spirits sink. "Oh, dear."

Thomas patted my hand. "Take heart, my tea cake. She speaks perfect French, Mr. Reardon says, but she was born in Gloucestershire. You won't need to speak anything but English to her."

Cecy looked horrified. "Kate, you can't. You simply cannot travel all the way to Paris to engage a maid from Gloucestershire. It won't do."

"Kate must do precisely as she pleases," Thomas reminded Cecy, as he divided the last croissant with her.

Cecy said, "Well, of course she must. But it's such a waste. Do pass the butter."

25 August 1817
Paris
At Lady Sylvia's house

Miss Emily Reardon called upon me yesterday. She is a few years older than I, a young woman of the most reserved demeanor. According to her cousin Mr. Reardon, her father (that is, Mr. Reardon's uncle) was under the authority of Monsieur Champollion when that distinguished scholar was in Egypt to record and study the cryptic inscriptions of the ancients. Unfortunately, his constitution was unequal to the rigors of the Egyptian climate. He died before he could return to France. Miss Reardon has been in service ever since the small inheritance he left her was exhausted. She is, by any reckoning, an experienced lady's maid.

After the opening pleasantries had been concluded, I dared to ask, "Forgive me for my impertinence, but you seem to dress very simply yourself. Is that your preference?" Or was it financial necessity? I left the words unsaid but they hung in the air between us. I had to ask, for everything about Emily Reardon was the model of severity, from her pelisse to her unornamented gown to the slippers she wore, plain and well worn.

Miss Emily Reardon was entirely composed. "I assure you, I am expert in achieving the dress and hairstyles favored by ladies of fashion, though I do not affect such things myself."

I liked the way she looked me in the eye. She seemed not the least impressed by the grandeur of Lady Sylvia's house, though her manners were unexceptionable. It was clear that she wanted and needed the position, but she would do nothing to make it seem she was pleading for it. There was a fine stoicism about her. I found myself wishing I had a turn for stoicism myself. Perhaps it can be learned.

It seemed a tempting proposition, engaging Emily Reardon. In addition to her own qualifications, she would spare me the onerous task of meeting other prospective maids.

"When would you be able to start?" I asked.

Emily Reardon's eyes lit up. "At once, Lady Schofield."

I stated the terms of employment (bless Lady Sylvia for going over the finer points with me before I arranged the interview), and Emily Reardon consented to them with every sign of pleasure. I decided she might not be as stoic as I had assumed.

I have engaged her to start tomorrow morning, for I do not feel I can go immediately into the happy state of having a maid. I need a few hours to get used to the idea first.

When Emily Reardon was gone, I did a brief dance across the drawing room and went to find Cecy.

"I suppose it will have to do," Cecy decided, when I'd recounted my ordeal to her. "Reardon's only your first maid, after all. You can always hire a French maid next time."

"You can show me how it's done," I said, while privately promising myself I would stick to Emily Reardon even if she were as unaccountable as Thomas's man Piers.

From the deposition of Mrs. James Tarleton, &c.

As soon as I was able, I cornered Lady Sylvia regarding shopping. This was not immediately possible, as a number of business and household matters had arisen during her long absence from Paris, which required her attention. It was not until early afternoon, the day after Kate had engaged her maid, that the three of us had a chance to consult. We had just begun discussing the best time to visit the modiste, when a footman entered to announce a visitor.

"Captain Reginald Winters," the footman said.

We all rose and curtseyed acknowledgment of the sandy-haired man in his twenties, in full dress uniform including a neat military mustache, who entered on the footman's words.

"Captain," Lady Sylvia said, "I don't believe I've had the pleasure of your acquaintance."

"I am certainly the loser by it, Madam," the Captain said, bowing over her hand with stiff formality. "But I am afraid I am not here on a social call. The Duke was much disturbed to hear of your encounter; he has been at some trouble to see the roads around the city made safe. He sent me to make certain you have suffered no ill effects from your unfortunate adventure, and to assure you that everything possible is being done to apprehend the miscreants."

"His Grace is all consideration," Lady Sylvia murmured. She studied him a moment, and I thought her eyes twinkled. "No doubt you wish the particulars."

Captain Winters seemed taken aback by this forthright comment. "I do not wish to distress you, ladies," he said uncertainly.

"So you shan't," Lady Sylvia responded. "Raoul, ask the gentlemen to join us, please."

The footman bowed and left. Lady Sylvia presented Kate and me, and we resumed our seats. The Captain seemed

relieved by this return to social normality, but his relief did not last long. Lady Sylvia apparently had a large acquaintance among the Army of Occupation and the poor man was hard-pressed to keep up with her queries about the current activities of all of them.

The sitting room door swung open at last, and James and Thomas came in. The Captain rose and turned.

"Reggie!" James said. "Haven't you sold out yet?"

"Obviously not," Thomas said. "And someone appears to have had the bad taste to promote him."

"Bad taste?" Captain Winters responded with mock indignation. "No such thing! This is purely a matter of ability."

"Primarily your ability to find excellent wine for your commanding officers, even on bivouac, I expect," James said. "Don't you agree, Thomas?"

"Undoubtedly." Thomas studied Captain Winters. "Which puts me in mind of the fact that you still owe me that dozen bottles you promised after that dice game in Le Havre. And I'm sure you've been in Paris long enough to have found the best sources."

I believe they would have continued in this vein for some time had Lady Sylvia not called them to order. "While it is pleasant to observe the reunion of old friends, Captain Winters is here on business," she informed Thomas.

"Business?" James said to the Captain.

"Investigating the attack on your carriage is my responsibility, for my sins," Captain Winters said, raking a hand

through his hair. "The army has officially turned that sort of thing over to the new French government, of course, but unofficially we're still the ones everyone looks to when it's a matter of public safety. And I'm the liaison for the City of Paris and environs, which puts this squarely in my lap."

"*You* are supposed to find out who shot James?" Thomas said skeptically.

"Among other things. There's been a rash of murders down in the Rue St. Roch; bad area, mostly fallings-out among thieves, but we still have to make sure there's nothing more in it than that. There are at least two groups of Bonapartists plotting to take advantage of the split in the government—one lot seems to be preparing to assassinate the Duc de Berry; the other looks like it's trying to suborn the leader of the Estates-Generale. Someone broke into the Sainte Chapelle two nights ago. And with the London Haut Ton flocking back to Paris, I have at least three ladies a day fluttering into my office to complain about something that isn't satisfactory—the noise, the way the coach traffic was handled before their *grande soirée*, something." He gave James a fulminating look. "If you'd had the least consideration, you'd have got yourself shot just outside Amiens and dropped this in someone else's lap."

"It does sound as if you are very busy, Captain," Lady Sylvia said composedly. "And with such a variety of things, too. Murders and assassinations certainly sound much more pressing than a mere holdup or a break-in."

I did not consider the shooting of my husband to be a *mere* anything, and I was about to say so when Thomas shifted slightly. Both Kate and James stiffened in reaction, and Kate gave me a warning glance. I swallowed the remark I had been about to make, just as Thomas said, "Yes, what *was* that about the Sainte Chapelle?"

"Bonapartists, most likely," the Captain replied. "There are still plenty of people who aren't happy with the restoration, particularly the way the Bourbon has been running it, and the Sainte Chapelle used to be the royal chapel."

"Used to be?" Kate said.

"It's been used for storage since the Terror, and the new court hasn't had it cleared out yet."

"Sounds like a prime bait for thieves," James commented.

Captain Winters shrugged. "You'd think so, but all this lot did was shove some crates around and make a mess. That's why I think it was some of those—lunatics."

"A mess?" I said. "It doesn't sound as if it was very tidy to begin with. How could you tell?"

"Hah! You couldn't miss it. Ashes and wax all over everything, and that awful stale smell you get from old incense."

"Some sort of ceremony?" Lady Sylvia mused. "I trust your wizards have been over the area carefully. If the chapel was associated with the monarch, someone may have been attempting a spell to interfere with them."

"We thought of that, my lady," the Captain said. "But the wizards say there's no significant magical residue."

Thomas pounced on the phrasing. "No *significant* residue?"

Captain Winters rolled his eyes. "Oh, come, Thomas, you remember what these people are like. Most of them don't have any training—half of 'em can't even read their native tongue, let alone Latin or Greek. There are a few kitchen magicians and hedge wizards around, but the real wizards were murdered in the Terror, or left the country to escape Madame la Guillotine. The ones who are left have about as much ability as James here. They were probably *trying* to cast some sort of spell, but they didn't succeed."

"And a good thing, too, I am sure," Lady Sylvia put in. "But we must not keep you from your duties, Captain, however pleasant the discussion. I believe you wanted to know more about our little holdup?"

"If you please, my lady," Captain Winters said.

Lady Sylvia nodded and embarked on a severely edited summary of our adventure. She made no mention of the Sainte Ampoule, nor of the suspiciously convenient disability suffered by all of the wizards in our party, nor of the cap the last fleeing ruffian had left behind, nor of Sir Hilary Bedrick, nor of any of Mr. Lennox and Mr. Reardon's discoveries, and she contrived to give the impression that we had been set upon by quite ordinary highwaymen.

Captain Winters paid close attention to Lady Sylvia during this recitation, which was a very good thing. If he had glanced at Kate, he would surely have realized that he was not getting the whole story. Kate's face was a study. I don't believe she'd ever had to cope with someone *else* telling bouncers—Georgina and I always left that to her, because she is so very good at it. So Kate had never before had to listen and nod with a straight face, and she was caught completely unawares.

Fortunately, by the time Lady Sylvia finished, Kate had schooled her expression. Naturally, we all confirmed what Lady Sylvia had said, and then Thomas and James made arrangements to meet with Captain Winters the following afternoon to discuss wine and reminisce. The Captain departed at last, and we were left alone.

"I can see where Thomas gets his tendency to withhold information," James commented at last. "That was a masterful rearrangement of the facts, Lady Sylvia. I don't think I've seen a better spur-of-the-moment job."

"That's only because you haven't heard Kate when she's in top form," Thomas said. "Mother, what are you up to?"

"I should think that was obvious, Thomas. If there is any connection between the Sainte Ampoule and this incident at the Sainte Chapelle, the situation could be far more serious than your friend is capable of dealing with." Lady Sylvia tapped her fingers thoughtfully against her teacup.

"But I thought, from what Captain Winters said, that even if someone did a spell at Sainte Chapelle, it couldn't have been successful," I said. "Wouldn't the army wizards have been able to tell if it was?"

"If it was an ordinary spell, most certainly," Lady Sylvia said. "But there are some ceremonies that do not leave a normal magical residue yet still have profound consequences."

"Coronation ceremonies, for example?" Thomas said.

"That is certainly one example," Lady Sylvia replied with unimpaired calm. "I do not think a coronation was the reason for the unpleasantness at the Sainte Chapelle, however."

"Why not?" I asked. "With the Sainte Ampoule missing . . ."

"A coronation ceremony of the sort I had in mind requires considerably more than holy oil to be effective," Lady Sylvia said.

"So there would be no point in using the Sainte Ampoule alone," Thomas said.

"None whatever," Lady Sylvia answered.

"Which leaves us with the question of what the vandals were up to," I said.

"Leaves us?" James put in pointedly.

"Leaves you and Thomas, at least," Lady Sylvia said serenely. "I expect that there will be opportunities for you to discuss his job with Captain Winters tomorrow, and perhaps you can discover some additional details. It would be extremely reassuring if we could be certain that whatever occurred in the Sainte Chapelle did *not* involve the Sainte Ampoule."

"If you want an investigation, it would be better to ask

Reggie," James said, though he sounded a bit doubtful. "He is the official in charge."

Thomas shook his head. "Nonsense. Reggie Winters hasn't the slightest notion how to handle things quietly."

"And you do?"

"I have a much better notion of it than Reggie."

James frowned. "I don't like it. This should be dealt with by the proper authorities."

"I entirely agree," Lady Sylvia said. "But I doubt that Captain Winters has quite enough authority to be proper, in these circumstances."

"Who would you consider—" Thomas stopped short. "Mother, you wouldn't. Not even you—"

"Don't blither, Thomas. I am speaking of the Duke of Wellington, naturally. How fortunate that I have the custom of giving a card party whenever I return to Paris." Lady Sylvia smiled. "I shall have to sort through the invitations we have received to see which evening would be best. An unintentional conflict would never do."

"Whereas intentional conflicts are the done thing?" Thomas said.

"Only when I do them, dear."

James was looking at Lady Sylvia with a fascinated expression. "The Duke is an old friend, I presume?"

Lady Sylvia considered. "He is forty-eight," she said at last. "I do not believe I would call him old."

I caught the twinkle in her eye. "Don't tease, Lady Sylvia," I said. "How long have you known the Duke?"

"We have been acquainted since his return from the India campaign, sufficiently well that I believe I can depend on him to accept an invitation to a card party, however last-minute. Especially when he has other old acquaintances to renew." She looked at James.

"A mere former A.D.C. is unlikely to be much of a draw," James said. "I hope you won't depend on that to persuade him to come."

"Nonsense," Lady Sylvia replied. "The Duke speaks very highly of his 'family.' I'm sure he'll be pleased to see you. Especially if we can reassure him as to the events at the Sainte Chapelle."

"*Just* like Thomas," James muttered under his breath. Fortunately, neither Lady Sylvia nor Thomas chose to hear. No one raised any more objections to interrogating Captain Winters. I do not think either of them actually wished to, despite the long-suffering expressions they had assumed. The thought of having an excuse to go poking about plainly pleased them both. "But you are not to go haring off to the chapel yourself while we're with Reggie," James told me sternly.

"Of course not," I said. "I have every confidence in you and Thomas. Besides, Kate and I will be much too busy to go to Notre-Dame tomorrow."

"Busy?" James looked at me suspiciously. "With what?"

"Shopping, of course. We can hardly attend Lady Sylvia's card party in London fashions."

From the commonplace book of Lady Schofield

27 August 1817
Paris
At Lady Sylvia's house

In truth, I never thought it possible that shopping in Paris could live up to Cecy's expectations. Shopping in Heaven itself would have a hard time matching the glories of her imagination. Yet, somehow, the dressmakers and the milliners we visited with Lady Sylvia succeeded. If they did not surpass our hopes, then they matched them easily.

This is the very thing I hope to remember fondly in years to come, so I intend to set forth an account of yesterday's events in as much detail as I can muster. It was a day that began well and ended even better.

We set forth on a fine morning, Lady Sylvia, Cecy, and I, accompanied by my maid, Reardon, and Lady Sylvia's maid, Aubert, in Lady Sylvia's coach. Every detail of the city seemed spruce and clean, fresh and crisp. I hardly took my eyes off the passing streets, so fascinating were the indefinable differences in proportion, in light, in atmosphere. If I were forced to try to describe what it is that makes Paris so distinctly Parisian, I couldn't muster a word. Yet there is no doubt in my mind that no one who has once seen even a part of Paris could ever mistake it for any other place in the world. Not that it is all beautiful, by any means. On our route we saw nothing of the cramped streets, encrusted with the filth of the ages, one found in the poorest quarters. The only jarring detail on our way was on the most elegant street of all, the Champs-Élysées, a boulevard lined on either side with tree stumps.

"They cut the chestnut trees down for firewood during the war," Lady Sylvia told us. "Understandable, but most unfortunate."

"Surely they will replant the trees," said Cecy. "It would be foolish not to."

"Someday they may," said Lady Sylvia. "I find the sight even more melancholy than you do, for I remember what it was like in its glory."

Cecy and I could not really understand what had been lost. We could only try to imagine how fine that broad street must once have been. Respect for Lady Sylvia kept us silent for the rest of the short journey.

"Here we are," said Lady Sylvia, as the carriage drew up to our first port of call, a prodigiously elegant dressmaker.

"So soon?" I said. It seemed we had hardly settled ourselves in the carriage. We might easily have walked the distance from Lady Sylvia's house.

"At last!" sighed Cecy. "I've been waiting all my life for this moment."

We descended from the carriage, and then we descended upon the dressmaker. As Lady Sylvia was well known to the establishment, we were greeted with great cordiality.

"Oh, this is *just* as splendid as I thought it would be,"

Cecy murmured to me, as we were shown to a corner of the shop with a few elegant yet comfortable chairs, where we were invited to seat ourselves.

We concealed our gratification and excitement as best we could, so our descent upon Lady Sylvia's modiste was not quite so much like a ravening wolf descending upon a sheepfold as it might have been. Yet there was no point in pretending we were even mildly blasé about things. For one thing, no one could miss the glow of satisfaction in Cecy's eyes as she took her first long look around. I suspect that, like me, she was marveling at the colors and textures of the fabrics, the design and detail of the gowns, and the elegance and refinement of the workmanship.

"Oh, Kate, that rose-colored silk would suit you to perfection." With that, Cecy was off and running, aided and abetted by the modiste and her skilled assistants.

"This is only the first, remember. We have a great many more shops to visit before we are through," Lady Sylvia told us in an undertone. "We must pace ourselves."

The fine morning yielded to a stubbornly rainy afternoon. Despite the weather, our shopping campaign, under Lady Sylvia's generalship, lasted the rest of the day, with only a brief intermission for refreshments. By the time we returned to Lady Sylvia's house, we were hungry and thirsty, surprisingly leg-weary, given that all we had done was shop, and filled with a sense of righteous accomplishment. With Reardon and Aubert to help match ribbons and hold things for us, we had worked our way through our entire list of necessities and rather a lot of the luxuries. We had ordered gowns, we had chosen hats, we had purchased gloves, fans, and bottles of scent.

N.B. Bought a flask of scent to give Georgy for her birthday. She loves jasmine.

I was ready, after the day's exertions, for nothing more strenuous than a nap before dinner. Cecy's constitution really must be one of iron, for she and Lady Sylvia interviewed no fewer than three young women for the position of her maid. I did not help. Instead, I retired to my room and took off my slippers while I watched Reardon lay out the gown I would wear at dinner that evening.

It did not take long for table talk at dinner to travel from a gown-by-gown description of our shopping expedition to a detailed account of James and Thomas's interview with Reggie, a young man whom Thomas seems to hold in low regard.

After some spirited remarks from Thomas, James countered, "There's nothing wrong with Reggie's wits."

"I never meant to imply there was," Thomas said. "It's just that I never fail to be amazed by the yawning abyss between what Reggie's keen wits perceive and what he makes of it. Honestly, drop him into a vat of boiling olive oil and I've no doubt he could tell you if it was the first pressing or the second. But then he'd spend his last breath complaining that he never cared above half for olive oil and hinting that he would greatly prefer to be boiled in some other kind."

"At times he *is* rather slow to draw an inference," James conceded. "But on the other hand, he doesn't often jump to conclusions."

"James," said Thomas, in that martyred tone of voice he uses when he thinks he might like to tear his hair in frustration but it would only put him to the trouble of tidying his appearance again, "stop making excuses for Reggie. I ask it of you as a friend of long standing. No, I order you. Stop immediately."

James said nothing, but he replied as only a friend of many years would do, by launching a bread roll directly at Thomas's head. He would have made a direct hit, but Thomas ducked efficiently. Apparently, Thomas took this retaliation as a matter of course, for he went on speaking to us as if nothing had happened.

"Reggie showed us the scene of the break-in at Sainte Chapelle, and he'd made the most perfect notes: the marks on the floor, the candle wax, the fact that incense had been burned there—but he never mentioned that the incense had a very off quality to the scent, and he hadn't noticed that the marks on the floor made a pattern. Someone held a ritual of some kind on that spot, and it wasn't a small one."

"Reggie insists they detected no magical traces remaining," James said.

"That only means Reggie was told no traces had been

detected. I think someone's being a bit less than honest with him," Thomas said. "A safe enough proposition, given Reggie's fine qualities."

"You made us promise not to visit Sainte Chapelle without you," Cecy said, "so I don't think it was very fair of you to go without us."

"Oh, Reggie insisted," said James. "Once we'd begun to question him, he wished to demonstrate that he'd left no stone unturned."

"*Had* there been a stone left unturned, by any chance?" Cecy asked.

"What Reggie noticed, he recorded meticulously," Thomas conceded. "Nothing had been taken, nothing left beyond some drops of candle wax and the smell of incense. But it was rather unusual incense." Thomas produced a snuffbox from his pocket of his white waistcoat and placed it before Lady Sylvia. "Deuced peculiar, in fact."

"We scraped up what wax we could," James explained. "In one of the lumps of wax we found a bit of the unburned incense. Thomas sacrificed his supply of snuff to bring it safely back."

"Someone had cleared a circular space about eight feet across," Thomas said. "At regular intervals on the periphery of the space, seven candles were set out. Someone drew something on the floor in chalk. I think it was a seven-pointed star."

"Someone cleaned up after themselves thoroughly

enough that we can't be absolutely positive. That would be my guess, too." James narrowed his eyes.

"Was there any sign that the Sainte Ampoule was used?" Lady Sylvia asked. "Any marks that might have been chrism?"

"None we could find," Thomas replied.

"Whatever they were doing," said James, "it's an odd place to do it. Even though it was once the private chapel of the kings of France, it's just a storeroom now."

"Was that where the coronations were held?" Cecy asked.

"No. The coronations were at Reims," Lady Sylvia replied. "No one would contemplate holding a coronation in Sainte Chapelle."

"Indeed not," said Thomas. "It would be like staging *Hamlet* in a hatbox."

We had finished our dinner when word came to Thomas that Piers had arrived and was asking to see him at the earliest opportunity.

"The prodigal valet? I don't believe it," James said. "It took him long enough to find his way here from Calais, didn't it?"

Thomas looked at me. I can't describe the precise mixture of elements in that look. There was something of guilt, a little reluctance, but most of all resolution, a brave and honest look that meant to tell the truth and hazard the consequences. I looked back inquiringly, and Thomas gave a little nod, as if he'd come to some decision. "I think this interview is one we must conduct in company. Mother, may we speak to him in the green room?"

"By all means," said Lady Sylvia. "I'm pleased to hear that we'll be included in the conversation. Raoul, please have Piers join us in the Salon Vert."

The five of us were seated in the drawing room when Piers was shown in. The poor man, never very prepossessing, showed signs of a long journey in bad weather. He looked exhausted, in dire need of a bath and a shave. His clothing was rain-soaked and his boots squelched with every step he took.

Piers looked startled as he glanced from Thomas to all the rest of us in the room, but he stood before Thomas with his shoulders back and his chin up, with the calm resolution of a man confronted by a firing squad. "Thank you for seeing me, my lord."

"We're eager to hear your report," Thomas said. "Too eager to wait until morning. Please tell us what you've been doing since we left you in Calais."

"As you requested, I've been investigating the identity of the intruder at Dessein's," Piers said carefully. "I found the owner of the Turkish slipper. It belonged to Lord William Mountjoy."

"William Mountjoy?" Lady Sylvia looked thoughtful. "I knew his uncle. The son was killed at Waterloo, and Mountjoy inherited quite unexpectedly. Very sad story."

"For everyone but Mountjoy," said James.

Cecy glanced sharply at James, as if his tartness surprised her.

Piers went on. "Unfortunately, identifying the owner of the slipper did not necessarily identify the intruder. It seems someone took the trouble to steal the man's slippers and dressing gown as a disguise. When he heard of the incident, he discovered that his possessions were missing and reported the loss to the authorities. Very indignant he was, having his things worn by an intruder pretending to be him."

"Was he?" This time there was no ignoring the edge in James's voice.

"If you're wondering whether the gentleman wore his own slippers, it can't be proven, for his valet says they were together at the time," Piers said.

"Then we're looking for someone who stole into the inn and helped himself to Mountjoy's things. Whoever he is, he's a man of iron nerve, I collect," said James. "Did the intruder take anything else?"

"No one reported anything stolen," Piers answered. "That doesn't mean much, I know, but it is all I could ascertain."

"You spoke to Mountjoy's valet?" Thomas asked. "Did he have any idea how someone could have gained entry to Mountjoy's room to steal the dressing gown and slippers?"

"I spoke with Mountjoy and his manservant Rupert together at first. Neither had any idea how the thief got in."

Piers looked pleased with himself. "I took the trouble to get Rupert on his own later. He admitted that he let himself be deceived by the same young person who tricked me and locked me in a cupboard. She had him so thoroughly in his cups, he can't be sure who might have been in or out of Mountjoy's room."

"Most unfortunate," said Thomas in a tone that caused Piers's complacency to evaporate completely.

"Rupert found the other slipper and the dressing gown out in the garden, soaked with dew. Mountjoy refused to give up the slippers once the pair was reunited, and he insisted on keeping the dressing gown, too." Piers was all business. "He had it made to measure in Venice."

"So we can't ask Mr. Lennox and Mr. Reardon for their help," I said.

"Alas, no," said Lady Sylvia. "I wish I'd thought to try it myself in Calais, even if it had only led us to the slipper's owner."

Piers continued. "Mountjoy has been on the Continent for a year or more, doing the Grand Tour. He was glad to be going home at last. He postponed his sailing for England, he was so annoyed by the theft. Lucky for me he did, or I would have missed the chance to question him."

"This young person of yours, Piers," said Thomas, "have you any idea where she went? Or, for that matter, where she came from?"

"I do not." Piers stiffened under Thomas's scrutiny. "If

she took ship for Dover, she could have disappeared no more thoroughly."

"Could she have?" Cecy asked. "Taken ship for Dover, I mean?"

"She could have," said Piers. "But she was not an English young person. I think, though I could not swear to it, that Eve-Marie was genuinely French. For her to choose to go to England would amaze me. She had little respect for the British. Highly unlikely she would go there by choice."

"Unless she was up to something," said Cecy thoughtfully.

"As you say, Ma'am." Piers fixed his attention on Thomas but said nothing more.

Thomas returned him look for look. "Is there anything else, Piers?"

"Just this. Of the guests at the inn that night, all could account for their whereabouts within minutes of the intruder's discovery. I think it unlikely another guest perpetrated the masquerade."

"What about servants?" James asked.

"Same goes for them."

"So your Eve-Marie assisted whoever it was in gaining access to the inn from outside," said Thomas.

Piers looked pained. "She is not *my* young person in particular. However, that is, in essence, my surmise, my lord."

"Next time remember her perfidy and see if you can be a bit more careful," said Thomas. He shifted his attention from

Piers to the rest of us, but Piers remained standing as stiffly as if he were at attention. "Mother, is this room protected?"

"Of course it is, my dear. As is the entire house." Lady Sylvia was tranquil. "Have you something in particular to tell us?"

"You know me too well," said Thomas. "I must make a confession. I hired Piers here to serve as my valet, but he has no previous experience in that role."

"Hardly news, that," said James. "I've seen you turned out better in some of those disguises you dug up to wear back in our days on the Peninsula."

Thomas paid him no heed. "When we planned this journey, I had no idea we were going to find it half so eventful. I did think it might be a good idea to be prepared for the unexpected, however, so I asked a few old friends to recommend someone capable, someone experienced. In short, someone useful in an emergency." Thomas was looking right at me now, and that oddly mixed expression of his was back. On anyone else, it might have been apologetic. "They recommended Piers to me."

Something in Thomas's expression must have seemed more familiar to Lady Sylvia than it did to me, for her expression lightened suddenly and she spoke. "You hired Piers as your valet, despite his lack of previous experience. May we inquire then, of just what your manservant's previous experience consists?"

Thomas looked pained. "He's a bodyguard."

James gaped and then grinned. "Thomas, you can't be serious. You don't need a bodyguard."

"Of course he doesn't," said Lady Sylvia. "Not for himself."

"Well, James and I don't need a bodyguard, and you certainly don't, Lady Sylvia. So who—" Cecy broke off abruptly. "Oh, dear."

I didn't spare any of them a glance. I couldn't take my eyes off Thomas. "You felt I needed a bodyguard?" Given recent events, it seemed a logical idea to have someone capable along on our journey. Yet Thomas had made this arrangement before we ever left London. Thomas had made all sorts of arrangements without consulting me, and I blessed him for it. But I felt cross with him for taking the initiative on this arrangement. He might have at least mentioned it to me. "Am I that clumsy?"

"Lord, no!" Thomas said. "I never meant that. Never crossed my mind. No, it's just that I can't be everywhere, Kate. I know it. There are going to be times when you need someone to watch out for you and I won't be able to do it all myself. I meant to be serious and responsible and thoughtful. I was trying to plan ahead. In a way, it's fortunate I did, because I never dreamt we'd walk into anything like the mess we have."

"*Fortunate,*" I said, but I couldn't get out another word. I didn't trust my voice.

Piers spoke then, still standing rigidly at attention. "My

lady, I was hired to see to your safety. His lordship made it plain that was the only thing that mattered to him."

"Quite unusually prescient behavior for Thomas," said Lady Sylvia. "Quite responsible of him, too."

"Good idea," said James. "Wish I'd thought of it."

"I beg your pardon?" Cecy's indignation was plain.

I just looked at Thomas.

"Kate, I should have told you all about it at the start," said Thomas. "For that mistake, I apologize. But I don't apologize for hiring him to help me take care of you. The world is a very big place. I think we've all seen that it can be a dangerous place, too."

I looked at him in silence for a moment longer. Thomas's eyes said even more than his words did. When I was very sure that I could keep my voice level, I said, "Very well. Thank you for your help, Piers. Please excuse me now." I started for the door.

"That will be all, Piers," said Thomas, then added to the room at large, "Good night." He reached the door before I did and held it open for me as I passed.

"You needn't," I said to him, under my breath.

"I must," said Thomas.

"I have Reardon now," I said. "I can manage perfectly well alone."

"I can't," said Thomas. So he came upstairs with me.

I let Thomas persuade me of his good intentions before I accepted his apology. At the expression on my face, he drew back. "Kate? What is it?" With sudden suspicion, he added, "Why are you smiling?"

I poked him gently. "You could have told me about Piers, but you didn't. Instead, you had the complete gall to complain to me about his incompetence as a valet."

"He *is* an incompetent valet. After that performance in Calais, I'm none too confident of his skills as a bodyguard, either. I would have told you, but I didn't want to worry you. Don't change the subject. You haven't answered my question. Why are you smiling?"

"I could tell you." I thought it over. "But I wouldn't want to worry you."

Thomas made it clear that he wanted me to answer his question.

"Oh, do stop. I surrender." I caught my breath and pushed the hair out of my eyes. "I'm smiling because not only do I accept your gracious apology, I believe your motives are pure. You hired Piers to protect me from outsiders and not from my own clumsiness. But now you must forgive me, please."

"What for?" Thomas demanded.

"I *was* hurt at first," I confessed. "I did think you were making allowances for your clumsy wife. But Sir Hilary's presence in Paris proves you had good reason to hire Piers. It wasn't kind, nor even honest of me to let you go on thinking I was overset. I apologize."

For once in my life, I had the utter satisfaction of seeing Thomas caught by surprise. He stared at me a moment, eyes wide, mouth slightly agape. It was an endearing expression, one of fuddled, innocent astonishment. I almost regret that I will, in all likelihood, never see it again.

"Kate—" Thomas's voice scarcely attained a whisper. "You were roasting me? The whole time?"

"Not the whole time. For the first few seconds, I was quite distressed. But after that—" Thomas didn't let me finish what I meant to say. Yet I have reason to be certain that, eventually, he forgave me.

28 August 1817
Paris
At Lady Sylvia's house

During the past few days, I have seen far less of Cecy than I have of the seamstress sent by the modiste to do the final fitting on my gowns. While I have Reardon safely ensconced in my service to help bring order out of the chaos of my personal appearance on a daily basis, Cecy still has not engaged a maid of her own. Lady Sylvia's maids help her, of course, but a great deal of Cecy's time is taken up with the interviews and the checking of references. I find it lowering to see how much time and attention the task of hiring a servant requires when it is done properly. Still, this does not prevent me from frequent bouts of exultation that in engaging Reardon, I have escaped the task.

Reardon's adjustment to the household has been effortless, though I'm sure it must have cost her some pains to make it seem that way to me. The other members of the staff accepted her and she dealt with them in kind. Of necessity, she sees a great deal of Piers. He seems only to benefit from her calm example of service. Thomas's clothing has returned to its customary state of order and refinement (which means that it is just as neat as James's but somehow not as staid). Thomas himself has taken to early morning rides with Cecy in the Bois de Boulogne, as James is still recuperating, though he refuses to admit it. I am often pressed to join them, but given my relative lack of skill in the saddle, I prefer to make it my custom to lie in and begin the morning with a sleepy cup of tea or chocolate. An hour or two of sleep while Thomas is off galloping about somewhere makes a world of difference to my outlook on the day.

29 August 1817
Paris
At Lady Sylvia's house

This morning James and I were present when Mr. Lennox and Mr. Reardon paid a call on Lady Sylvia. Thomas was off riding with Cecy, so it was just the five of us. Mr. Reardon wore his neckcloth in a new style, but I was glad to discover it made no difference. I could still tell him from Mr. Lennox. They both looked rather sheepish, as if they expected a good scolding from Lady Sylvia.

"I'm afraid we may have exceeded our authority." Mr. Lennox held out his hand. Nestled in the palm were Cecy's pearl earrings, stolen by the highwaymen.

"Good heavens, where did you find these?" Lady Sylvia asked, as Mr. Lennox gave her the earrings. James and I stared wordlessly.

"To be exact," Mr. Reardon replied, "on a velvet cushion on the counter of a pawnshop in the Rue d'Horloge."

Lady Sylvia asked, "In what way do you fear you may have exceeded your authority?"

"We pursued a variant of the location spell," said Mr. Reardon, "using a few of the objects we found discarded at the scene of Sir Hilary Bedrick's murder. A clay pipe proved unexpectedly rewarding. We followed the trace to the pawnshop. The trace was extremely clear. We assumed the clarity owed something to the strength of the link."

"We don't know that it didn't." Mr. Lennox gave the distinct impression this was a point they had already discussed at length.

"Be that as it may," Reardon continued with patience and precision, "the clarity of the trace came from the recent presence of the man we traced. Extremely recent, as it turned out."

"We were questioning the proprietor," Lennox said, "when we discovered the owner of the pipe was actually still on the premises. When he overheard our questions, he fled."

"We pursued him, but he eluded us." From the blandness of Reardon's tone, I think it safe to assume that much more had happened, but that we weren't going to hear any of it.

"Eventually we returned to the proprietor. He turned the earrings over to us after only a minimal amount of persuasion," Lennox said.

"Yet it was regrettable. Whoever the man who pawned the earrings was, he must have heard us. If he had sufficient wit, he now knows someone is taking an interest in Bedrick's murder and your robbery. It won't require much research to identify you through us. We apologize for our ill-timed interrogation," Reardon concluded.

"It can't be helped." Lady Sylvia gazed at the pearl eardrops in her hand. "If someone realizes we are taking an interest in this matter, there's nothing we can do to remedy it. Whatever we've stumbled into, it may prove to be a good thing, if our interest puts them off."

"It may merely make them more cautious," I said. "Whoever they are."

James said, "The man who pawned Cecy's earrings may have had nothing whatever to do with the robbery. He may know nothing at all. In that case, even if he overheard you asking about him, he has no reason to connect us to the incident at all. And no one to tell if he did."

"That adds up to a great many ifs," said Mr. Reardon, "a word I have always held in considerable distaste."

Lady Sylvia gave the earrings to James and closed his hand over them gently. "You shall be the one to return these to their owner."

I said, "Now we know Aunt Elizabeth's charm really did work. Cecy couldn't lose those even when they were stolen from her."

Lady Sylvia looked thoughtful. "Even the simplest of spells may have unlooked-for consequences. Who can say what part that little charm played in these matters?"

From the deposition of Mrs. James Tarleton, &c.

The Bois de Boulogne is quite a pleasant place for a ride, and I was looking forward to the day when James would be well enough to join me. In the meantime, Thomas made quite an acceptable substitute, particularly as he had no foolish notions about what constituted a suitable mount for a lady. Indeed, I was obliged at one point to decline his offer of a particularly fine and spirited gray gelding; dearly though I would have loved to try his paces, I could see that he was too strong for me, and I would not risk doing a mischief to one of Lady Sylvia's horses.

The ride to and from the Bois was nearly as pleasant as the wood itself. Paris is a city of great beauty, and the boulevards are wide and well considered. We took a different route each day. Thomas claimed it was in order to familiarize himself with the city, though I thought it was more that he wished to show off how familiar with it he already was, without the chance of embarrassing himself in front of Kate.

One morning, a little over a week after Piers's return,

we had a late start from the stables due to some unexpected difficulties with the tack. Consequently, the streets were more full and our progress both to and from the Bois was slower than usual. Thomas had chosen a particularly circuitous route, and as we turned an unfamiliar corner, I saw a small shop just ahead of us.

I reined in my horse. "Thomas, is that a bookshop?"

"That's usually what *la librairie* means," he replied. "Why?"

"Papa gave me a list of titles he has had difficulty in obtaining from his usual sources," I said. "I have not been able to look for them yet, but this appears to be a most promising possibility." The shop looked *just* like all the ones Papa has dragged Oliver and Aunt Elizabeth and me to in the past. "Would you mind if we stopped for a moment?"

"I suppose it's a sort of shopping I can tolerate," Thomas replied. "And it certainly doesn't *sound* like anything James would object to."

Taking that for assent, I rode to the door and dismounted. Thomas found an urchin who agreed to hold the horses for the princely sum of half a franc, with another to follow when we came out.

Bookshops are much the same, whatever the language. Dusty shelves reached to the ceiling, piled high with shabby literature and smelling of musty leather. The proprietor was very helpful, but he could supply only two of the volumes Papa had requested. "Me, I do not keep *les histoires*," he explained. "They do not sell here at all well. When by chance some arrive, I send them to my friend in the Rue de Rivoli. That one of which you ask"—he waved at Papa's list—"I sent to him only two days ago."

"Very well; can you give me his direction?" I said.

"It is most easy to find," the man told me. "It is near the Île de la Cité, a few turns from the bridge."

Thomas stared at the bookseller in transparent disbelief.

"The Île de la Cité?" He transferred his stare to me. "I don't believe it. *How* did you set this up?"

"Set what up?" I said. "Is there some reason— Oh." I felt very dull not to have seen instantly what Thomas was getting at. The Île de la Cité is, of course, the location of the Cathedral of Notre-Dame, and the Sainte Chapelle. The bookseller was looking anxious, so I thanked him for his information and paid for my purchases. Thomas frowned at me the entire time.

"You are not going anywhere near Sainte Chapelle," he said firmly as we left the bookstore.

"If this bookstore is nearby, I most certainly shall," I replied. "You heard the gentleman; this place has one of the books Papa *particularly* requested. If you choose not to accompany me, I am sure Lady Sylvia—"

"Absolutely not," Thomas said. "You are every bit as bad as James warned me, and he would not approve of this. Not at all." He paused a moment, thinking. "I'll take you back to the house, and then you can give me your book list and I'll retrieve your titles for you," he offered at last.

"You may have the list this very moment," I said, digging it out, "but I do not think it will serve."

"Why no— Good God, this is *writing*?" He peered at Papa's list. "*De No . . . Nobis*, or *Novum*? Or *Nocturne*?"

"Papa's handwriting is not the best," I said. "Kate and Aunt Elizabeth are the only other people I know who can make any sense of it."

Thomas favored me with an intense glare. "And I don't suppose you're willing to write out a clean copy. You *want* an excuse to go poking about Sainte Chapelle."

"I don't expect there would be much point to it, after you and James examined everything so thoroughly," I said sweetly. "Now, are we going on to the Rue de Rivoli, or shall we finish our ride? I'm sure Kate and Lady Sylvia will be happy—"

"You are not dragging Kate anywhere near the Île de la Cité," Thomas said flatly. "Not that dragging would be necessary; she's as bad as you are. Very well, we'll find this bookstore and get your father his books. How I'm going to explain this to James . . ."

"I'll explain it to him myself," I said. Thomas only rolled his eyes.

We turned our horses' heads toward the river. Thomas sulked the entire way, and left it to me to locate the bookshop. Fortunately, the proprietor's directions were quite clear, and for once someone was correct in saying a place was easy to find. It was much the same as the first in appearance, except that it had more custom. As we entered, I heard the bookseller speaking to someone near the far wall.

"Monsieur, I have said I have only Volume IV of the *Anciennes Pratiques*; I cannot magic the books out of thin air. If you wish to buy Volume IV, you may do so, but more than that, I cannot sell you."

"That is not adequate," said an unpleasantly familiar man's voice.

"If he doesn't have them, he doesn't have them," a younger voice said. "Don't make a fuss, Harry."

Although the speakers were hidden by the rows of bookcases, I was quite sure it was young Theodore Daventer and his oily tutor, whom James and I had met at the Temple of Minerva Victrix. Thomas had stopped in the doorway, still frowning ferociously. I gave him a reassuring nod and started forward.

"I sent a note around requesting the *Anciennes Pratiques*," the tutor replied. "I did not ask for Volume IV alone. If he does not have the set for sale, he should not have answered."

I came around the end of the bookcases, and the first thing I saw was Theodore Daventer, looking acutely uncomfortable. The tutor, by contrast, seemed to be positively reveling in the prospect of making as much fuss as possible. I smiled at Theodore and pretended not to notice the tutor or the distressed bookseller.

"Mr. Daventer!" I said. "How nice to run into you again."

"Good morning, Mrs. Tarleton," said Theodore Daventer, for of course it was him. "And Mr.—um." He looked over my shoulder uncertainly.

Thomas's frown could make anyone uncertain. I turned. "Lord Schofield, may I present Theodore Daventer?" I said. "And—"

"Harry Strangle," Thomas said in a soft, dangerous voice. "What are *you* doing in Paris?"

The tutor's face went white. He took a step backward, stumbled, took another step, then turned and fled. Thomas surged after him, pushing past the shopkeeper and Theodore and knocking over a stack of books in his haste. The shopkeeper's cry of distress did not slow him down in the least, but the overturned books did—enough to allow the tutor to dodge around the bookshelves and race for the door. Thomas followed.

"What is *that* about?" Theodore demanded.

"I am not perfectly sure," I replied, not altogether truthfully. Kate had told me a good deal about Mr. Strangle in the letters she wrote during her London Season. In addition to his disagreeable personality, he had been in league with Sir Hilary Bedrick's colleague Miranda—more than sufficient reason for Thomas to wish to cross-question him regarding Sir Hilary's recent demise. "Perhaps you should ask your tutor when next you see him."

Theodore looked down. "I suppose."

"I take it Mr.—Strangle?—prefers not to confide in his students," I said. "I believe it's not uncommon behavior for tutors."

"It's not that," Theodore said. He sounded just like my brother, Oliver, and I gave him my best encouraging smile. "It's just— I don't think my father would— Even if Uncle did recommend— I—I don't think I like Mr. Strangle very much. And he doesn't know nearly as much history as he pretends. His lessons are much too easy."

I blinked. Oliver and his friends did a good deal of complaining about their tutors while we were all growing up, but I had never heard any of them grumble about lessons being too easy.

My surprise must have shown more than I intended, because Theodore blushed slightly and waved at the bookcases. "I suppose it's well enough for the other fellows, but—well, you heard him going on about the *Anciennes Pratiques.*"

"He did seem quite set on getting hold of it," I said carefully.

"Yes, he wants me to read it." Theodore snorted. "I tried to tell him, I've *already* read it. Well, looked at it, enough to see that it's all secondary and tertiary sources strung together with a lot of metaphysical nonsense. But he won't listen. The only worthwhile reading he's given me is Monsieur Montier's monograph on the history of the Île de la Cité. And his 'practical applications' aren't teaching us anything, even if we *do* get to see—" He stopped short and reddened, from which I assumed he had been about to say something completely unsuitable for a lady's ears.

Despite the brevity of my acquaintance with Mr.

Strangle, it did not surprise me in the least that he would encourage his pupils in such a fashion. To avoid embarrassing Theodore further, I turned to the shopkeeper and inquired about the books Papa had requested. He was evidently a trifle deaf, for he had some trouble in understanding me, but Theodore was of considerable help in making him understand my wishes. The man did not have quite everything Papa wanted, but I crossed several more items off the list.

"Thank you," I said to Theodore when the shopkeeper had gone off to collect the titles I required. "My father will be so pleased."

"I am happy to have been of service," he said with a formal little half bow.

"Will you be in Paris long?" I said. "I'm sure my husband would be as delighted to see you again as I am."

"Only a few more days," he said. "Harry and I are heading east." He scowled. "I wish the other fellows were staying with us, but there's been some mix-up or other, so it'll just be the two of us for a while. My uncle is meeting us somewhere along the way. Milan, I think."

"What a pity," I said. "James will be sorry to miss you. But perhaps he could stop by your lodgings tomorrow, before you leave?"

Theodore brightened at the prospect, and gave me his direction, which was what I had wanted all along. I arranged for the delivery of my purchases, made my adieux, and left the shop, wondering what I would do if Thomas did not turn up soon. But he had arrived, apparently, only a moment before I did. His cravat had been somewhat disarranged by his exertions, and he looked quite grim.

"He got away," he said without preamble. "It's quite clear that he's been here some time; he knows the streets—especially the alleys—in this part of town much too well."

"That's a pity," I said as he threw me into the saddle. "Still, I expect you and James can catch up with him at the Pont du Gard Auberge tonight or tomorrow."

Thomas flipped the horse boy a franc, mounted, and looked at me with narrowed eyes. "Indeed? And why would you think that?"

"I asked young Mr. Daventer for his direction," I said. "So that James can call on him. And since Mr. Strangle is apparently bear-leading the unfortunate boy, I presume they are both to be found in the same lodgings. You'll have to go tomorrow, though; they're leaving Paris in a few days, Theodore says."

"Theodore seems to have been remarkably forthcoming."

"Theodore Daventer is a pleasant, studious young man who deserves much better than to have that dreadful man as a tutor," I said. "I can't imagine *what* his father was thinking. Though perhaps he was not in a position to turn off a man recommended by Theodore's uncle."

"You *have* been busy," Thomas said. "Very well; let us go and inform James of the arrangements you have made for his time tomorrow."

Unfortunately, by the time James and Thomas paid their call, Mr. Strangle and Theodore had departed. They cross-questioned the servants, who said that Mr. Strangle and his charge had left the city. James was willing to believe them, but Thomas insisted on continuing the investigation in the hopes of at least discovering their destination, if they had indeed left Paris.

From the commonplace book of Lady Schofield

> 5 September 1817
> Paris
> At Lady Sylvia's house

N.B. No pomegranates or figs. T. hates them. T. likes apricots and raspberries. Also marrons glacés.

> 6 September 1817
> Paris
> At Lady Sylvia's house

This morning Thomas said, "I like this chaise longue." He had been reading bits of the news aloud to me while I answered letters. "Let's purchase one for your boudoir at home."

"I like it, too." I could not help but admire the picture he made, stretched the length of chaise longue with his nose in one of the many gazettes and journals he'd accumulated around him. "Shall I truly have a boudoir when I live in your house?"

Thomas didn't look up from his reading. "Oh, I insist. I had no idea what I was missing, staying out of boudoirs. You shall have the boudoir of your dreams. Mine, too, for that matter. I quite like it here, watching you pull out your hairpins while you compose your missives."

"You'd pull more than hairpins over this one. It's to Aunt Charlotte."

Thomas shuddered elaborately and kept on reading the newspaper.

I thought it over. "I never dreamt I'd have a boudoir. It seems unlikely somehow, after all those years when my great ambition was not to share a room with Georgy."

The paper rattled as Thomas turned the page. "Lord, I don't wonder. Share your room, share any little possession she fancied, from the sound of it."

"That was at its worst when she was gaming. I'm sure she'll grow out of it, now we know she's taken after Grandfather. She's not to be permitted any gambling at all. She was always most generous with her own things before." In an effort to be fair, I added, "To do her justice, Georgy has many fine qualities. I was ill-situated to appreciate them sometimes, that's all."

"I suppose." Thomas's voice had taken on a preoccupied tone, a distinct note of inattention.

To test my analysis, I asked, "What color is my boudoir to be?"

Thomas turned the page. "Any color you please, my sweet."

Of all the absurd terms of endearment that Thomas employs, perhaps *my sweet* is the one I care for the least. I waited until I was perfectly certain he'd grown absorbed in his reading. "Puce, then. It's settled."

In a distant voice, Thomas replied, "I said any color and of course I meant it. Whatever you like, Kate." Then, in his usual crisp tone, he added, "You do realize your cousin will say puce makes you look quite twenty years older? Distinctly washed out? Perhaps even pulled down?"

"I was sure you had stopped listening."

No trace of absentmindedness lingered in Thomas's voice. He was all virtue and vigilance. "I hope I know better than that, now that I am an old married man. I hope I am awake to the perils of not listening to remarks intended to be provoking, no matter how artfully sweet the voice that utters them."

"You *are* a married man, aren't you?" I marveled all over again at this phenomenon. Thomas, a married man. And married to me at that. Incredible. "I am a married woman. How very odd."

Thomas dropped his newspaper, sprang up from the chaise longue, and came to stand behind me, his hands warm on my shoulders. "How fortunate it is we are married to each other. I couldn't bear it otherwise."

I tipped my head back to look up at him as I covered his hands with mine. "Nor could I." Aunt Charlotte's letter went unanswered that day. But it went unanswered for excellent reasons.

From the deposition of Mrs. James Tarleton, &c.

James and Thomas spent most of a week attempting to discover Mr. Strangle's whereabouts. It reached the point where Kate and I hardly ever saw either of them. I was, consequently, rather surprised when Kate and I returned from shopping to discover the pair of them ensconced in the sitting room with a lovely woman of perhaps twenty-five. Her walking-dress was plainly several seasons old, and of only middle quality even then, though her spencer had been turned and retrimmed with cheap braid in a creditable attempt to bring it up to the current mode. Her black hair had been carefully dressed in the very latest fashion, and she seemed a trifle flushed.

"Thomas?" Kate said uncertainly as we paused in the doorway.

"Ah, come in, Kate," Thomas said. "Madame Walker was just leaving."

But for the torrent of impassioned French that erupted from the visitor, I might have thought that I had imagined the faint emphasis Thomas put on the word *Madame*. She spoke very rapidly, but I could make out the words *"responsabilité," "respectable,"* and *"acte de mariage"* as she jerked at the knotted strings of her reticule.

"Yes, yes," James said. He sounded rather grim. "Come along."

"One moment," I said. "What is this about?"

"Nothing," James said in the unconvincing tone he uses when he thinks I ought not to be involved in something. Since he is invariably wrong in this regard, I persisted.

"Madame, if you would slow down a little—"

"I speak the English very well," the woman replied. "And I am a respectable person, me; I have my *acte de mariage*." She pulled a paper from her reticule and waved it at me, and I realized she meant her marriage lines.

"I'm sure you do," James said even more grimly. "Cecy, if you will just—"

"Madame Walker?" Kate said. "But surely you are French?"

"My husband was of the English," the woman said with dignity. "He was killed at Waterloo, and his family did not want to have to do with a French person. So I am in Paris."

"But why are you *here*?" I said. "James, was this Walker one of your army friends?"

"No," James said. "Cecy—"

"I came because of Monsieur Strangle," Madame Walker informed us.

"Mr. Strangle?" I said.

James rolled his eyes. "That's done it."

"What have you to do with Mr. Strangle?" Kate asked.

Madame Walker shifted uncomfortably. "I have nothing to do with him. Only, it is very hard to feed *un bébé* when one has no money, and one must be practical, no?" She glanced at James and then down at the document she clutched so tightly.

"You have a baby?" I said. "But if your husband died at Waterloo—"

"Annalise is four years old," Madame Walker said proudly. "She is at a convent school in the Loire Valley. They are very understanding, but one must pay something."

"But then why did you come here?" Kate asked.

"I heard the talk, that Milord and Monsieur were trying to find Monsieur Strangle," Madame Walker said simply. "I thought perhaps they would pay a few francs for what I knew."

"And what do you know?" Kate said, holding her eyes.

"That he has left Paris with the young gentleman," Madame replied, "to complete their circle of Europe."

"The Grand Tour, yes, we'd more or less come to that conclusion ourselves," James said.

Madame Walker shrugged. "I do not think, me, that it was any such thing. For the English do not make so much of a mystery when they come to see the statues and the paintings and the buildings in Paris."

"What mystery?" I asked.

Madame hesitated and glanced at James and Thomas again. Then her shoulders slumped. "I do not entirely know," she confessed. "But he made a great show of not allowing me to see his visitors, which was entirely foolish since I usually saw them in the street outside."

"Visitors?" Thomas said. He and James exchanged looks. "The concierge said nothing about visitors."

"But I have told you, Monsieur Strangle was very secret about them!" Madame said. "Even the one who was, I think, only *un commerçant* come to collect some bills. I know *les commerçants,*" she added darkly. "It was only the small gentleman who was truly important. I myself only saw him once. Monsieur Strangle, he pretended that the small gentleman would have to approve his hiring me, though I am quite certain that he never said anything about me to him at all."

"Mr. Strangle wanted to hire you?" I said, frowning.

James made a choking noise. Madame Walker drew herself up indignantly. "He tried, but I am not like that other woman who visited him. I am a respectable person, me. Only—" She looked down suddenly. "Only I did not tell him so all at once, you understand, because he would sometimes buy the dinner. Sometimes I thought, perhaps, for Annalise's sake . . . But he was so, so—" She waved her hands expressively and shuddered.

Suddenly I realized just what Mr. Strangle had wanted to hire her to do. "That is appalling!"

"Just so," Thomas said.

"And now he has gone," Madame said with growing intensity, "and he did not even leave the money he promised— though I did not really expect it. I shall starve, and Annalise also." She sank down on a chair and began to cry. "What am I to do? I am a respectable person, me, but the ladies, they want the references, and the dressmakers also, and even the *maîtres des hôtels* will not take on so much as a *femme de chambre* without the letters. An *acte de mariage* is not enough."

"If that is the sort of position you would like to have, Madame, the matter is quite simple," I said. "I will hire you to be my maid."

James and Thomas both looked at me as if I had run mad. Kate cocked her head to one side. "But, Cecy, do you really think it will do?" she asked.

"Will what do?" Lady Sylvia's voice said from the doorway, and she swept into the room. She studied Madame Walker's tearstained face and refurbished turnout, then glanced at Thomas and James. Her eyes settled on Kate and me, considering. She waited.

"Madame Walker finds herself in a difficult situation," I explained. "So I have just offered her a position as my maid."

"I see." Lady Sylvia reviewed us all once more. "And has Madame accepted?"

"Oh, yes, yes, yes!" Madame said, and burst into another torrent of rapid French, which even Lady Sylvia seemed to have difficulty in following for a moment.

Lady Sylvia nodded and raised a hand, cutting Madame off in midsentence. "Very good," she said. "Raoul and Aubert will see you settled in. I gather you can start at once?"

"*Oui*, Madame," she replied, and curtseyed. Lady Sylvia rang for a footman, instructed him what to do with Walker, and they left.

As the door closed behind them, James looked from me to Lady Sylvia and back. "Cecy," he said at last, "what maggot have you got in your brain this time? You can't believe that woman's story!"

"Oh, but I do," I told him. "And not just because she was so insistently waving her marriage lines, either. If she were—were—were truly not a respectable person, she would not be in such straits that she had to turn her gowns. Not with a face like that."

"Hmm," said Thomas. "You may have something there."

"Also, she may know more about Mr. Strangle's business than she's told us," I pointed out. "More, perhaps, than she realizes herself. If she can recognize those mysterious visitors of his, we may learn something really useful."

"But, Cecy, are you sure?" Kate said. "After all the work you have done—the interviews and checking references!"

"Well, it's obvious just from looking at her that she can dress hair and sew a neat seam," I said. They all looked at me. I sighed. "I couldn't just turn her out onto the street. And at least she's French."

James laughed suddenly. "My Lady Quixote! Very well; I won't tease you about your new maid any longer."

"An excellent notion," Lady Sylvia said. "Now, if one of you would explain to me just what Madame Walker has already told you of Mr. Strangle's business, everything will be quite satisfactory all around."

From the commonplace book of Lady Schofield

> *14 September 1817*
> *Paris*
> *At Lady Sylvia's house*

At last, at last, the opera season has begun. Last night we went to *The Marriage of Figaro.* I think I have never truly heard music before. Thomas has promised to take me again in a fortnight, when *The Barber of Seville* will be performed.

The evening would have been one of the highlights of my life, even without the music. We dressed in our very best clothes. My gown was made of white velvet. With it, I wore my pearls, the longest pair of white kid evening gloves I have ever seen, and white kid sandals. Best of all, I wore one of the Schofield tiaras. Two of them are so elaborate I am not yet old enough to carry them off, but the one Lady Sylvia recommended is relatively simple, and as it is set with pearls, it was quite perfect. Reardon spent hours putting my hair up properly. It is an art, wearing a tiara, Lady Sylvia says.

The five of us arrived at the opera house at exactly the right time, just tardy enough to be fashionable, yet not tardy enough to be rude. Some people make their evening's entertainment standing around outside places like the opera house, envying the fashionable world as it arrives. I would not find that a satisfactory way to spend the time. Unless Thomas were with me, of course. I feel sure he could shout very amusing things, if he were so inclined.

We survived the press of interested onlookers shouting critical remarks and gained the relative quiet of Lady Sylvia's box. There was a brief, yet excruciating, period of Being Seen, as we were ogled by the occupants of the other boxes. Much flourishing of opera glasses, much looking down noses. For once, I didn't care. I knew I was looking my best, I could tell from Thomas's expression. I concentrated on sitting up straight and doing the tiara justice.

The overture began at last, and the fashionable world fell away. I forgot all about everything, even my tiara. The music was like—oh, I can't think of anything that isn't trite. Instead, I will compare it to that day last spring when I attended the investiture at the Royal College of Wizards and stumbled across the threshold into a garden far away. Between one step and the next, I crossed into another world.

The music was like that.

When we left the opera house, it was quite a disappointment to me that we spoke ordinary words. It would have seemed more natural to sing. I wonder if that is what birds do. Lucky birds, if so.

By the time we returned to Lady Sylvia's house, the music had faded. I was in the real world again. But I hadn't been alone on that voyage. It is always difficult to deduce what tune Thomas thinks he's humming, but in this case, I recognized certain passages distinctly.

Only thirteen days until we go to the opera again. It seems an eternity!

17 September 1817
Paris
At Lady Sylvia's house

At times I had grave doubts, but I have survived Lady
Sylvia's card party. I made a cake of myself, but it was only
a small cake, and not in the usual way, for nothing whatever
was spilt, torn, or broken.

With Lady Sylvia's help and Cecy's encouragement, I
chose which of my new gowns to wear last night. It is the
color and texture of a pink rose petal, and it fits to perfection.
I wore my best pearl necklace, and when I put in the pearl
eardrops Aunt Elizabeth gave me, I remembered the charm
she cast upon them. If it worked so spectacularly upon
Cecy's, surely mine would be safe for one evening.

I haven't dared to jinx it by remarking upon it aloud, but
I've been having an extraordinarily good run of neither losing nor breaking things. I devoutly hope my luck will hold. As
I readied myself for the evening, I made all sorts of bargains
with Providence in hopes it would not give out spectacularly
while I was in the presence of the Duke of Wellington himself.

I was ready in good time, but I stayed in my room until
the last possible moment, eager to avoid any possible
mishap. Perhaps it was a mistake to spend so much time
alone thinking about it. As I waited, I grew more and more
convinced that some great piece of clumsiness would befall
me before the evening was over.

Thomas came to fetch me down and with a single glance

took in my frame of mind. "Goose." He crossed the room and took me in his arms. I rested against him, sending up a silent prayer of thanksgiving that my husband was not one to ask what was the matter or to need things explained. "It's all right, you know." He drew back a little to take a better look. "You do know, don't you?"

"I know." My words came out in a very timid way. "I'm just a coward."

Thomas made a noise expressing disagreement and disbelief. "Gammon. You're aware of the possibilities, that's all. Social acuity is an asset."

"I'm well aware of the possibilities. I'm aware that I have hardly dropped a crumb in days. What are the odds that I spill something sticky on someone important tonight?"

I could tell Thomas was thinking it over. "You're right. You haven't had anything turn awkward since you dropped that jam-side-down slice of toast in your lap at breakfast last week."

I'd forgotten that. "I was thinking of the sauce I spilt on my bodice at dinner five days ago."

"Five whole days? You're right. Steps must be taken." Thomas chose a glass on a tray left on the tea table and poured water from the accompanying carafe until it reached the rim. "Hand that to me, please."

I picked it up and the inevitable happened. An ounce or two of water spilt from the glass to the tray. Thomas took the brimming glass from me and put it back on the tray. "There. We'll see if that helps, shall we?"

I mopped up the spill with my handkerchief. Thomas took the sodden bit of fabric away from me. "Find yourself another handkerchief, my dove, and we will go down to put it to the test."

I couldn't think of anything to say that wouldn't sound like shirking or whining, so I just looked at him. He held me. "You needn't come down if you don't wish to, but I hate the thought of you alone up here, castigating yourself."

"I'm so afraid I'll do something to embarrass you." In fact, I had a strong presentiment I was doomed to. Not all the preemptive water spilling in the world would save me from my fate. "I just have a feeling I might—"

Thomas put me away from him, suddenly all decision. "I don't like the cut of this coat above half. If you feel it coming on, spill something on me. It would give me a good reason to be rid of it." Thomas put my hand on his sleeve and we left the room to proceed very slowly and very carefully down the stairs.

James looked as stylish as Thomas did, all sign of his indisposition gone. Cecy was resplendent in a green gown that did wonderful things for her eyes. Lady Sylvia, as ever, was the personification of breeding and taste. Her gown was simple to the point of severity, her jewels understated yet profoundly impressive. She leaned upon an ebony walking stick, her air one of perfect ease, ready to greet her old friends. It was her past we were meeting that night, her comrades in arms, her allies. As her guests arrived, I marveled at the army of affection she commanded, all the while I took pride in the role I played in her family.

Chicken stakes. The phrase makes wagering sound rather fun. Insignificant losses balanced against the insignificant wins and the all-important amusement of oneself and one's friends.

Perhaps my dread of embarrassment turned on itself somehow. For whatever reason, I found the prospect of playing cards for an evening held no appeal. Indeed, it filled me with misgiving. Each time I inspected my hand, I asked myself if this was how Georgy had started on her road to disgrace.

It was my social duty to play cards, to help amuse Lady Sylvia's guests. Therefore, I played cards. Yet my careful cheerfulness didn't fool Thomas, for after the first change of tables, he collected me from the group I'd been about to join and beckoned a friend over to play in my place.

"My apologies, ladies and gentlemen," Thomas said as he took my hand. "I will return her eventually. For now, duty calls."

One of the men at the table knew Thomas of old, it was clear from his mocking tone. "You're a dutiful man, Schofield. I've always said so. Don't let anyone tell you differently." We were chaffed good-naturedly, but they let us go.

Thomas escorted me out of the card room. In the small room adjacent to it, we were able to converse in an undertone.

"Kate, what is it? Do you have a headache? Have you torn your gown? I've been watching you play, and with every hand you look more and more unhappy."

"No, do I?" I felt dismayed. I'd been trying so hard to conceal my feelings.

"What's the matter?"

"Nothing. I don't object to playing cards since it is to oblige Lady Sylvia." I trailed off before Thomas's penetrating glance.

"Out with it." Thomas was stern. "You don't object to playing cards. Now that we've established that, what do you object to?"

"I'm being foolish."

"I'll be the judge of that. I am the arbiter of all things foolish, at least in this arrondissement. Ask anyone. So. Whatever it is that's making you look so sad, tell me."

"I wish I didn't have to gamble."

Thomas looked adorably confused. "What are you talking about? You aren't gambling. This isn't Watier's. It's a simple card party."

"But I am gambling. We all are."

Thomas shook his head slightly, as if to clear it. "We're playing for chicken stakes. Nothing more. That's not real gambling. Gambling is when there's a stack of guineas the size of your head riding on the turn of a card or the throw of the dice." Thomas did not seem to find this an unpleasant thought.

"Chicken stakes," I repeated. "That's how Georgy began. Soon enough she had to borrow my jewelry to cover her losses."

"She's your sister, so I will use moderate language, no matter how great the provocation." Gravely, Thomas held my gaze with his own and I could not doubt his sincerity. "Georgy is an utter peagoose. You are not."

"Georgy began by playing in a setting very like this, and she is now so hardened a gambler that she must at all costs be kept from it."

"You, my buttercup, are not your sister. For which I offer frequent prayers of gratitude to a merciful God."

At times, Thomas's choice of endearments can be distracting. I believe he does it on purpose. I let the *buttercup* go and kept to the point. "You asked me what was troubling me and I am trying to explain. Georgy takes after Grandfather. I am his grandchild just as much as she is, and I'm afraid I will take after him, too."

Thomas was much struck by this reminder. "Faro Talgarth, they called him. I'm sorry, Kate. I'd forgotten that."

"He was clever about wagers, most of the time," I conceded. "With all the practice he had, I suppose his expertise was almost inevitable."

"He made quite a name for himself at the tables, I can't deny it. I apologize. I wasn't thinking." Thomas took a quick look to be sure we were unobserved, and kissed me.

"You do that so well," I told him. "Apology accepted."

"I should apologize well. With all the practice I've had?" Thomas looked back into the card room. "They all look happy as children, even Old Hookey. You've not been missed by now, so you won't be missed in future. I can think of several ways around the problem. I'll leave it to you to choose. I could hereby forbid you to play, even for chicken stakes. I don't recommend that alternative. It would be quick and easy, but, unfortunately, it is as good as a public statement that I don't trust you not to have the family failing. Now, almost as easy, since we have an audience conveniently at hand, I could make a point of cajoling you to play cards."

"But I don't wish to play cards," I protested. "Really, I don't."

Thomas was all patience. "Yes, Kate. That's precisely what you say. As many times as necessary. Tell me you'd rather sit by me as I play my hand, smile at me with insipid sweetness, that sort of thing."

"Oh." Belatedly, I saw Thomas's point. "I suppose I could do that."

"Or you could simply say you don't know any card games and you refuse to learn. No one minds a touch of the farouche in a new bride."

I tried out an insipid smile. Thomas seemed to find no fault with it. "I'd rather sit by you and watch you play your hand."

"So you shall, then." Thomas looked a little wistful. "It's the best choice. Some other time I will come the stern husband and forbid you to do something."

"Oh, are you looking forward to that?" I asked.

"Yes, very much. Some other time you will obey me, as you vowed at the altar when we were married."

I felt a pang of pure sentiment. My affection for Thomas surpassed even my gratitude for his ready understanding and sympathy. "I shall obey you, as I love and honor you."

Something in my words seemed to touch Thomas deeply, for he looked at me with such an expression of soft and open affection that my breath caught. He said, "With my body, I do worship thee, Kate." After a moment, he murmured in my ear, so close his warm breath tickled me. "We'll have a spot of that later, if you've no objection."

"Not the least objection in the world," I assured him with heartfelt sincerity.

From the deposition of Mrs. James Tarleton, &c.

A card party sounds as if it must be the most pedestrian entertainment possible, but from the moment responses to Lady Sylvia's invitation began arriving, it was obvious that an invitation from her carried the weight of a royal command. His Grace, the Duke of Wellington, was perhaps the most illustrious of the guests, but there were sufficient lesser luminaries present that when he arrived and glanced around, he asked Lady Sylvia whether she had ambition to take the place of the late Madame de Staël as the heart of intellectual Paris.

"None whatever," Lady Sylvia replied. "If Paris wishes to have an intellectual center, she must make her own arrangements. I have quite enough to do already."

His Grace gave her a sharp look down his long nose. "Indeed?"

"Indeed," Lady Sylvia said. She made a completely unnecessary show of consulting the schedule of tables and said, "We shall be partnered later this evening. If you still wish to hear my views on Madame de Staël, you may inquire then." Firmly, she introduced him to Kate and me and sent him in to mingle with the other guests.

For the first few rounds of play, we were all separated, doing our duty at different tables. I soon became accustomed to shifting partners periodically, and to hiding my annoyance when my partner misplayed and lost us the hand. I was quite enjoying myself when, at the end of a particularly good round, James appeared to collect me for the next game.

Since a number of the guests had elected to trade positions, and several had abandoned the card tables entirely for the refreshments at the end of the parlor (thus totally confusing Lady Sylvia's careful arrangements), I was a little surprised to see him. We repaired to a table that had been set up in a rather cramped alcove in the library. Lady Sylvia and the Duke were already waiting, seated across from each other, so that James and I would play against them.

"Here you are at last," Lady Sylvia said. "James, will you deal?"

"My pleasure," James said as he took his seat. "Though there's hardly any point to it, with you two against us. We might as well concede right now."

"Concede?" His Grace said with mock horror. "My dear Tarleton! Surely you learned better than that on the Peninsula."

"I learned never to bet against you, Sir," James said as the cards flew through his fingers.

The Duke of Wellington gave a great neighing laugh, and we settled down to play. He and James quickly fell into military reminiscence, which occupied the first hand. James and I lost.

"Very good," Lady Sylvia said as she gathered up the cards and began shuffling them. "Now you must have a chance for revenge. Cecy, dear, will you cut?"

As my hand touched the cards, I felt the barest frisson of magic. I looked at Lady Sylvia. She nodded encouragingly, so I did as she had asked. She smiled and dealt the next hand, concentrating as she did. As each card landed, the steady rumble of the talk around us became more muffled, until the sound was as distant as if the crowded tables were in the next room with the door closed.

"There," Lady Sylvia said, setting the pack on the table and picking up her hand. She smiled at His Grace's intent expression. "It is so difficult to speak both privately and un-obtrusively at a gathering such as this. Much better to speak privately in public, I think."

Wellington's eyebrows rose. "You and I are not the only wizards here. The Comte de Villiers is no dabbler, nor is Lady Marchant, to name only two."

Lady Sylvia smiled. "That is why I gave James the first deal. I assure you, Your Grace, no one will notice this particular spell. I was quite careful; setting it up took the better part of the week."

"In that case, I should welcome a detailed description," the Duke said. "The usual cantrips are all far too obvious for the sort of diplomatic work I find myself doing these days."

"I shall send it to you tomorrow," Lady Sylvia promised. "On condition that you apprise me of any improvements that may occur to you."

"It is agreed," Lord Wellington said. "Now, I assume you did not go to all this trouble in order for us to make ourselves obvious, so we had better bid the hand. Then you can tell me what is behind all this."

We commenced play, and through the first several rounds Lady Sylvia described the arrival of the Sainte Ampoule, the failed attempt to steal it in Calais, and the successful theft on the road to Paris. The Duke looked more and more thoughtful as the tale went on, and played at least one card quite at random.

"I see," he said when Lady Sylvia finished. "I might have guessed that Captain Tarleton did not get himself shot engaging in senseless heroics. Reasonable heroics are much more his style. Even so, we'll have no more of that, if you please," he told James. "I can't be losing any more of my family now that we're at peace." For a moment, his eyes clouded, and I realized he must be thinking of all the officers who had died at Waterloo—James told me once that the Duke often referred to them as his family.

"Never fear, Sir," James replied. "I'm already under similar orders from my wife."

"Ah, then I need not worry." The Duke of Wellington smiled warmly at me. "You have found a pearl, James— wise as well as discreet. You've been in Paris more than three weeks, and I haven't heard a whisper of this business."

"You have reason to expect that you would have, had one of us been . . . talkative?" Lady Sylvia said. "Possibly you have already heard of this from another source?"

"But who else—" I paused. The only people Lady Sylvia had told of the Sainte Ampoule were the Bishop, whom I could not imagine informing anyone, and . . . "Not Mr. *Brummell*?"

The Duke did not answer, though he gave Lady Sylvia a quelling look (which appeared to have no effect whatsoever). He studied his cards, then played the nine of diamonds. He waited as the play went around the table. Then, as he collected the trick, he said, "I believe Captain Winters told you of the business at Sainte Chapelle?"

We all nodded.

Wellington frowned. "It's a much bigger business than you may realize. Someone is up to something."

"What sort of something?" James prompted. "Or do you know yet?"

"That's the trouble," the Duke said, half to himself. "It's a different sort of battlefield." He shook his head and looked at Lady Sylvia. "There have been other thefts," he said abruptly. "An ancient coronation robe in Spain—God knows why the French didn't cart it away when they had the chance, but they didn't. It was moldering in some fortress in Castile until a few months ago. And just this morning I received word that a royal ring has gone missing in Aachen that dates back to before the Holy Roman Emperors. Someone seems to be collecting royal regalia."

"But from different countries," Lady Sylvia said. "And is it a single item from each place? That seems unlikely for a mere collector. Also, you would not be so concerned if you thought that was all there was to it."

"Ah, there's the rub," said the Duke of Wellington. "I don't *know* anything. I suspect a good deal, but I can't look into things any further without causing all sorts of difficulties. There are already whispers—rumor includes at least one plot to assassinate or to enchant each member of the French royal family, and most of the members of the Estates-Generale as well, individually and collectively. And those are just the reasonably plausible ones."

"Well," I said, "if you don't *know* anything, what do you *suspect*?"

His Grace gave me a penetrating look. "I suspect someone of plotting to put Napoleon's empire back together. Possibly with Bonaparte himself at the head of it once more, though there has been enough activity in Austria lately that it may be the son they're considering."

I blinked. "How is stealing a lot of old coronation garb going to put Napoleon's empire back together? It's not as if anyone is going to be impressed because someone is wearing a moth-eaten robe and a secondhand ring."

The Duke gave another loud laugh, but he sobered quickly. "That is one of the questions for which I would very much like an answer," he said. "There's magic involved, of that I'm certain, but what sort of magic and who's behind it . . ." He shrugged. "At one time, I had hopes of learning something from Sir Hilary Bedrick—he was just the kind to get mixed up in that sort of experimental magic without thinking too much about what the consequences might be."

"Or without caring about them," James said.

"True. But when that business came out about his attempts to steal other wizards' magic—well, I didn't think he'd have had time to be involved in any other plots. And once the Royal College of Wizards stripped him of his magic, he would have been no use to them. And if he was no use to them, he'd have had no information for me."

"So you thought," Lady Sylvia said.

His Grace nodded. "So I thought. Then he was killed under . . . peculiar circumstances, and I wondered. Now you tell me that he was in possession of the Sainte Ampoule at the time of his death, and I've no way to discover whether it was by accident or design."

"Mr. Strangle might know," I said. His Grace looked at me inquiringly, so I explained about Mr. Strangle's previous association with Sir Hilary. Before I finished, James was shaking his head.

"Harry Strangle is a nasty piece of work, I grant you," he said. "But it's bad enough that Thomas has a bee in his brain about the man. There's no reason to think he's had anything to do with Sir Hilary since Sir Hilary's expulsion from the Royal College."

"Nevertheless, I'd welcome a chance to talk with him," the Duke said. "Unfortunately, that wouldn't be possible, even if he were still in Paris." He pinched the bridge of his nose and frowned unhappily. "There are still Bonapartists in Europe, you know, and not just in France. Also, some of our allies are not happy with the current state of affairs. They don't want France back on her feet—though it will take years to accomplish that—and they would welcome an excuse to arrange matters more to their liking. If I open any sort of official investigation, it will only encourage the lot of them."

"Are you perhaps hinting at the possibility of an *unofficial* investigation?" Lady Sylvia asked. "The sort of thing Thomas used to do?"

"Exactly." He looked from me to James.

James sat back with a look of resignation. "You want us to hunt up Harry Strangle and ask him your questions."

"And to keep an eye open for anything else that might have to do with the stolen regalia," His Grace said, nodding.

"You're on your wedding tour; you've the perfect excuse to travel wherever you like on a whim. And you've already stumbled across one part of the scheme—if it *is* a scheme."

"My wife has a knack for that sort of stumble," James murmured.

"The chrism was delivered to Lady Sylvia," I pointed out. "And if you hadn't made me stay behind, merely because I was indisposed during our passage to Calais—"

"Yes, I know," James said. "But if you'd come out with me, something else would have happened."

"Very likely," Lady Sylvia said. "But that only makes you a better choice for this." She looked back at the Duke of Wellington. "I assume you mean to include Thomas and his bride as well? They really should have been here, but unfortunately the numbers would not allow it."

"Yes, of course," the Duke said with only the barest hesitation. "Thomas has amply demonstrated his flair for finding things out."

"As has my daughter-at-law," Lady Sylvia said gently. "Is there any more you can tell us? There are rather a lot of ancient royal objects in Europe, one way and another. It would take months just to cross France, if one were to stop to look into all of them."

"Like Papa's antiquities," I said without thinking.

"Your father is interested in antiquities?" the Duke said, frowning once more. "Of what sort?"

"Illegible, mostly," James said. "But it might not be a bad idea to consult him. There may be some less obvious connection between these missing items that he could explain for us."

The Duke's frown deepened. "I can't have more rumors starting. If you are willing to begin this venture, you must manage it as you see fit—but there can be no mention of my name or anything remotely official."

"That does make it more difficult," James said.

I could not help myself. I sniffed. "That is because you do not know how Papa gets when something interests him," I said. "It is the simplest task imaginable. I will write him a letter, complaining that we could not visit Sainte Chapelle because of the break-in, and I will mention the other thefts in connection with that, as events that are public knowledge—they *are* public knowledge?" I said, looking at the Duke.

"All except the chrism," he said.

"So I will mention the thefts, and ask him what he makes of it," I went on. "And if I do not get a five-page response detailing the history of every item and its uses, with references going back to Ancient Greece—well, then I do not know Papa. I shall have to think of a tactful way to tell him not to cross his lines," I added thoughtfully. "His handwriting is hard enough to read as it is."

"I shall leave it to you, my dear," James said.

"I see the matter is in capable hands," His Grace said gallantly. "I'll send you a packet of information tomorrow. I need not tell you to take care with it."

"No," James agreed.

Our talk became more general, and Lady Sylvia let her muffling spell fade. Though James and I took the second hand, the Duke and Lady Sylvia won the third, and the game. I should have liked to go in search of Kate and Thomas directly, but upon reflection I thought it might attract just the sort of attention the Duke of Wellington wished to avoid, so I spent the remainder of the evening filling in wherever I was needed to make up the numbers.

The day after the card party, we all slept very late. I spent the early part of the afternoon writing my letter to Papa. Lady Sylvia explained the Duke of Wellington's request to Kate and Thomas, who agreed at once, and Thomas and James set about making preparations to leave Paris.

Later, Thomas took Lady Sylvia's spell over to the Duke of Wellington, and stayed only a little longer than might be expected of an old military acquaintance. I sent my letter off to Papa, with instructions to reply to the consulate in Milan. Reardon and Walker packed, while James made sure that the carriages we had hired would indeed be ready next day.

And so, on the second morning after Lady Sylvia's card party, we bade Lady Sylvia a fond farewell. Amid many promises to write—and to send any confidential information via the system of knitting she had shown us—we left Paris, heading toward the Alps.

From the commonplace book of Lady Schofield

18 September 1817
Paris
At Lady Sylvia's house

We leave Paris in two hours. Thomas and I said our farewells to Lady Sylvia last night, for we could not do them justice in this whirlwind of packing and hauling. I shall miss Lady Sylvia dreadfully, not least because she has a genius for comfortable travel. Thomas assures me that he has inherited her genius. I only hope it may be true.

Given the importance of our mission and the urgency of our journey, it is shameful for me to be so reluctant to leave Paris. I dare confess it only here in these pages, but my chief regret is *The Barber of Seville*. Thomas was to take me next Saturday and now I may never see it. I may never see true opera again. This is not the sort of thing I am willing to be seen to sulk over, so I will pretend I have forgotten about it as thoroughly as Thomas has. Indeed, I hope this will prove one of those occasions in which pretending to forget will lead to forgetfulness in truth. It was only Rossini, after all. We have had our Mozart, and that is what matters.

THE ALPS

25 September 1817
Martigny
At the Angel

Our journey has been blessedly uneventful so far. Lady
Sylvia took council with her friends, and it was determined
that our safest route will be south and east and through the
pass of Great Saint Bernard, then on to Milan via Aosta.
Many of the purchases we made in Paris were unnecessary
for the expedition (I do not mean the clothes, obviously.
Those are essential.) so they remained safely with Lady
Sylvia at her house. We have a great deal of baggage just the
same, but, fortunately, a great deal of baggage is necessary
to keep up the fiction that we are merely on our wedding
journey. This means that when we arrive anywhere, we do
so with great fuss and complete lack of speed, factors that
apply even more forcibly when we depart. I have grown
hardened to the staring and pointing that goes on, and try to
take comfort from the fact that to those who point and stare,
our progress may be the only entertainment provided in a
twelvemonth.

Tonight Thomas and James spent the entire evening telling us stories about their experiences with mules. If mules are truly as cunning and difficult as they say, I may never see the other side of the Alps at all.

29 September 1817
Aosta
At the Grapevine

When it comes to marveling at wonderful scenery, I am well able to do my part. I always knew home was flat, in the geographic sense of the word, not just socially. But I truly had no idea *how* flat until I'd seen the alternative. I have a fondness for rolling hills. They seem quite scenic enough for me, pretty to look at and no trouble to stroll about upon. But I had no notion how high a hill could get without becoming a mountain. By the time we came in view of true mountains, my respect for them was evenly divided between awe at their stark beauty and horror that we would be obliged to march through them.

These emotions were already sharp when the Alps were a dreamlike scrap of white in the extreme distance. At first it was possible to convince myself I was imagining that whiteness, misconstruing a cloud into a mountain. As our journey continued, it became impossible to miss the slopes and summits we neared. Then it became impossible to think of anything else. As the mountains grew ever nearer through the dogged haste we made, my trepidation only deepened.

The afflictions of travel are many, and vary by the season. So far, my least favorite affliction is mud. Cold feet are a given. Wet feet are almost inevitable. Cold, wet, muddy feet cause not only discomfort, but the spread of dirt and disorder as well. Worst of all, to deal with muddy boots requires someone get his hands dirty. I detest getting my hands dirty. So I am usually detestably cross in the coach, for I have mud on my cold, wet boots, mud on the hem of my skirt, mud on the hem of my petticoat, and mud on my hands. Yes, I do have gloves when I set out each morning, but one is soon soaked and by midafternoon the other has a tendency to vanish as completely as if it had melted. I do not know what becomes of my gloves. One would think there must be a mountain of them by now, wherever it is they go when they disappear.

At the end of each day's journey, our routine is the same. We descend upon the night's lodgings in force. Thomas and Piers deal with the host first, demanding adequate accommodation be provided, and then James and his man take over, all reason and toleration, to smooth the demands into requests and make sure all is bestowed securely. Only the necessary luggage is unloaded. Our rooms, such as they are, are rendered as comfortable as hasty application of firewood and hot water can make them. We sleep too many to a bed, but that just helps us endure the cold. With Reardon's help, I have been able to stay fairly clean and fairly presentable. I make no claim beyond that.

Cecy is in high spirits, now that James is back to full strength. If anything, the two of them spend even more time in one another's company than before. Some days she rides in the carriage, but most days she is on horseback. When inclement weather drives her to choose travel with me, she has with her a book Lady Sylvia gave her. When the carriage is stopped, she ignores the delay and reads attentively. From time to time, she shares a paragraph with us, from which I gathered that Napoleon's feat in crossing the Alps paled in comparison with the Romans', who had been up and down these mountain passes more often than I have been up and down the back stairs at home. At first I found that a comforting thought, but as we ascended into the heights, my respect for the Romans increased. Imagine marching through such terrain wearing sandals. It doesn't bear thinking of.

There is one advantage to traveling in the mountains. When one shares the carriage with others, what seems unacceptably crowded in more clement conditions becomes comfortingly cozy. On those rare days when even Thomas chooses the carriage, I grow quite fond of the way he warms me, even through his heaviest coat. Fortunately for me, done up to my eyebrows as I am in my own heavy wraps, the press in the coach not only keeps me warm, it keeps me from all but the worst of the jostling when the going grows rough. Reardon has a deft way with a hot brick, so my feet are often nearly warm, at least early in the day.

Given that Thomas is in charge of our party, I see less of him than I am used to, and when he comes up to what passes for my room, it is only to be sure I have everything I need, and to see for himself that the place is dry, if not warm.

One night he drew me aside as we were all waiting for dinner to be served. "Your hands are cold."

My feet were much worse, but I merely said, "I know. Yours, too."

For some time we stood in silence while he held my hands in his. "Two rooms for the lot of us." He looked disgusted. "I shall be glad when this is behind us. It isn't what I planned, lurching across bad roads all day and huddling en masse in a rabbit hutch all night."

"I'm grateful for two rooms. Isn't Piers sleeping in the stable?"

Thomas scowled. "He'd better not sleep. I put him there to keep an eye on the horses."

"Poor man."

My hands were warm by then, but Thomas still held them. He looked at me in a particular way. "You're too tired, and so am I," I said reluctantly, "even if we had any privacy."

Thomas looked deeply affronted, but his weariness was proven when he didn't *say* anything at all.

On 26 September we reached a village called Bourg-Saint-Pierre, where Thomas and James engaged mules for us. The next morning, it was still dark when, all arrangements made, we sallied forth from the inn as the procession of mules arrived. Harness bells are used most liberally in this part of the world, and even if was too dark for us to see it very well, the mules' arrival sounded as festive as Morris dancers.

"You haven't said much," Thomas observed, as we watched James give Cecy a leg up. Once she was in the saddle, James checked every detail of mule and tack for the second time. It was a dauntingly thorough performance. "You aren't worried, are you?"

"Me? No." *Yes.* I couldn't admit it, but I found the idea of riding along precipice after precipice, to the point of exhaustion and beyond, an alarming one. I kept quiet while Thomas helped me up on my allotted mule. Once my feet were safe in the stirrups, riding a mule is exactly like riding a horse. Except for the precipices.

"I'll lead your mule, if you like."

I accepted Thomas's offer gratefully. Not only would it make me feel more secure, it might keep him from doing something daft, should the mood strike.

Thomas called Piers over and explained the situation. At once, suitable equipment was found, and my mule was safely moored to Thomas's. There is something about mules. They look much less kindly than horses do, more critical, and something about the way they look down their noses reminds me of Aunt Charlotte.

"Don't laugh, Kate. This is a serious business," Thomas warned me.

"Yes, I know." When I am frightened, on occasion a silly streak comes over me, a useless impulse to laugh. Not only is this impulse utterly unhelpful, it is most unbecoming. I do try to fight it. But between my apprehension and the thought of Aunt Charlotte, I had to fight to keep a straight face. It wasn't just the mules that made me want to laugh. We all looked utterly absurd. By the time we were all mounted, the quantity of fabric in our coats and skirts made the mules look as if they'd been badly upholstered. Every move the mules made rang their festive harness bells. We might have been a band of tinkers, we had such a holiday air, waiting for the signal to begin our procession.

Before the hairy, glum-looking man in charge of our mules gave the signal to depart, he and his helpers busied themselves stuffing rags into the bells and tying the bits of cloth in place. The sound of bells dwindled and died.

"What are they doing that for?" I asked.

"We travel snow-covered mountains. The slopes are steep, and even at this season the snow is deep and treacherous up there," Thomas murmured. "Any sharp noise could trigger an avalanche. They are muffling the bells to make sure that we don't bring anything unpleasant down upon our heads."

"Oh, dear." Any desire to laugh was utterly quenched by the thought of such a disaster. Bad enough to be cold and wet. To be buried beneath a mountain's worth of snow would be horrid. Such a fate could only be made even more unpleasant by the reflection that one's own foolish noise had brought the catastrophe down upon oneself.

"Quite so." Thomas seemed pleased by the sobering effect this had on me.

I resolved to be as quiet as possible, no matter how alarming the journey ahead.

Once we left the village, I made it a point never to look down at the trail we followed. Just looking out and up made me quite dizzy enough. At times our path was so ridiculously narrow, I could not envision how my mule could proceed in safety. I must have looked quite terrified, for once when Thomas looked back to see how I did, he drew rein to come near enough to speak softly to me.

"If you lean outward, the mule leans in. It makes him less likely to slip over the edge."

I gasped at the audacity of this advice. "Truly?"

Incorrigibly honest, Thomas shrugged. "I don't know. It's what they told me in Spain. I never saw any of those mules go over, or even come close. Of course, the terrain is a bit steeper here."

No ice or snow in Spain, either. I thought it over. "I'll just carry on as I am."

"Good idea. You're doing wonderfully."

We were in the icy grip of the Pass of Great Saint Bernard by midday. Stone and shadows are what I remember of it. Even at the height of summer, I think the sun must never truly warm the depths of that pass. I never knew there were so many shades of blue and gray as those I found in the shadows on the snow, yet I found no beauty whatsoever in the sight. To me, it was a terrible place, bleak and ugly, where man was never meant to go. I was too frightened to perceive even a trace of that sublime beauty that finer souls drink in. Such heights are mere desolation to my eyes, and the only way I knew I had a soul was that I found myself praying for our delivery from danger, for a quiet spot by a decent fireside, and for a nice cup of tea.

By the end of the long day, we had gained the relative safety of the Hospice of the Great Saint Bernard. This sanctuary provided us with the simplest of food and drink, but it was a vital respite from the dangers of our journey. We were shown by one of the resident monks into one large chamber, heated by a fire that smoked persistently. I cared nothing for a bit of smoke. We were out of the wind and off the mules. I was so tired, I remember only the play of flickering light and shadow on the vaulted ceiling before I fell asleep.

From the deposition of Mrs. James Tarleton, &c.

Thanks to Lady Sylvia's generosity with her horses, the journey from Paris was extremely pleasant, for me, at least. Kate has never shared my love of riding, and chose to keep to the carriage, but so long as the weather remained fine, I much preferred traveling on horseback alongside the carriages with James to sitting mewed up inside studying the books on magic and history that Lady Sylvia had pressed upon me before we left. I did my best to make up for my neglect of my magical training in the evenings and on the occasional rainy day, but I did not make as much progress as I could have wished. Our accommodations were too cramped and too public.

"You have become very studious," James observed the night before we reached the base of the Alps.

"Lady Sylvia gave me a deal of advice before we left Paris," I said, closing my book with a sigh. "But I think I would have to be three people at least in order to accomplish all that she advises. Basic magic, warding and detection spells, royal and magical history—"

"Warding and detection spells?" James frowned. "I have the greatest respect for Lady Sylvia, but those are far more advanced magic than you can manage yet."

"I know," I said. "I don't think she means me to cast them myself; I think she expects Thomas to do that. But she felt that it would be wise to have more than one person who could tell if they were being tested or tampered with."

James's frown deepened. "Thomas hasn't been casting warding spells."

"Not yet," I said. "But I expect he will want to do so when we reach Milan and are settled in one place for a few weeks."

"I suppose she's thinking of that attempted theft in Calais," James said. "But wards hardly seem necessary now—it's not as if we still have the chrism."

I looked at him in fond exasperation. "No, but we may very well come upon something else that is just as important. And if we do, and Thomas suddenly starts putting up wards then, everyone will realize that we have it."

"Not everyone," James said. "Only wizards who bother to check on us. Though I do see your point. Those are exactly the sort of people we wouldn't want to notice anything out of the ordinary."

"Besides, I have been acquiring a good deal of theoretical information about magic, but I haven't had much chance for practical application," I said. "I think Lady Sylvia means it to be a chance for me to practice."

"And possibly a chance for Thomas to practice as well," James said thoughtfully. "He improvises brilliantly, and it's hard to find someone to touch him when he sets himself to working out the equations for a complex spell, but the trouble is, he doesn't get down to it often enough."

"I'll make sure to mention it to him when we reach Milan, then," I said.

"I'll do that," James said hastily. "I may not be able to contribute much directly to the magical end of things, but I think I can get Thomas moving."

"You can do more than that if you remember your Greek and Latin," I said. "The authors of Lady Sylvia's books don't seem to write spells in anything else, and the bits and pieces I've picked up listening to Papa are simply not adequate for this."

James grinned, and we spent the rest of the evening drilling Latin verbs. The following day, we arrived in

Bourg-Saint-Pierre, and I had to shift for myself while James and Thomas hired guides and mules to take us across the pass.

I was not much impressed by the mules, but one cannot deny that they are sure-footed. We were fortunate to begin the crossing on a clear, sunny day, which made the cold more bearable and allowed a clear view of the scenery. This last was a mixed blessing, as occasionally the trail was so narrow that if one looked down, one saw one's foot in the stirrup suspended over miles of empty air that ended in ice and jagged rocks. A little mist would at times have been welcome.

It was difficult to determine what time we arrived at the monastery hospice near the top of the pass. The mountains are so tall that the sun had been well behind them since shortly after noon, and we were all too tired to pay much attention in any case. As we rode through the gates onto the monastery grounds, I felt a jolt of energy, and I sat bolt upright on my mule with an exclamation.

"What is it?" James asked.

"I felt something," I said. "Magic, I think. Just as we entered."

The brown-robed monk who had come forward to take hold of my mule's halter said something. James responded; the only part that was comprehensible to me were the names Julius Caesar and Napoleon Bonaparte.

I dismounted carefully, as my legs were feeling decidedly wobbly. "What did he say?" I asked after a moment.

"Just a minute," James said, and he and the monk continued their incomprehensible discussion. Finally, James turned to me and took my arm. As we walked across the courtyard toward the visitors' quarters, he said, "This monastery is very old—parts of it go back to Roman times, and perhaps even earlier, though our friend was a bit cagey about that part. I suppose there's a problem with his religious sensibilities. Anyway, the place is a well-known stop—there's some legend about Julius Caesar and his legions staying here on their way to conquer Rome, though I doubt it's true. Bonaparte wanted the hospice as a base. The monks didn't like the idea, so they arranged for him not to find it."

"They arranged for him not to find it?"

"The spell you felt when we came through the gate," James said. "It's some sort of misdirection or illusion spell—the monk wasn't specific. Very powerful. And clearly very effective."

"It can't be all *that* effective, or we wouldn't have found the place ourselves," I pointed out.

"The monastery is only hidden when the monks wish it," James said. "Or possibly it's only hidden from people they don't want here, or only from people of evil intent. The fellow I was talking to speaks the most abominable dialect."

"I'm surprised he told you anything about the spell at all, if it's that important," I said.

"Well, they can't exactly keep it a secret when every wizard who comes through the gates can feel it."

We had come up with Kate and Thomas by this time, and Thomas heard the last of James's remark. "Feel what?" he asked. James explained, and Thomas nodded. "No, no, that monk was giving you a warning, as much as anything else."

"Warning?" Kate said, yawning. "Of what?"

"There are strong wards up to prevent casual visitors from studying the spells here too closely," Thomas replied. He looked at me. "If you pay careful attention, you can separate the feel of them from the main spell."

James looked a trifle alarmed, until I said, "I suppose it wouldn't be wise to do any magic while we're here, then. I can't say I'm sorry; all I really want right now is dinner and a bed."

The food we were served was plain, as one might expect from monks, but we devoured it and went to our beds. I confess to some misgivings, as at some of our earlier stops I had noticed Thomas carefully enchanting our quarters against fleas and other vermin. With the monastery's wards in place, such spells were, of course, not possible. However, the chamber proved quite clean and comfortable, if as plain as the food.

I expected to sleep soundly after the long ride, but instead I tossed and turned for most of the night. I could not escape the feeling of being watched. When we roused next morning, it was plain that Thomas, at least, had been similarly afflicted.

"Warding spells are all very well," he grumbled over the

breakfast breads, "but it's going too far when they interfere with everyone's sleep."

"Is *that* what the problem was?" I said.

Kate and James looked at each other and shrugged. Thomas continued muttering until finally James said, "If you're that annoyed, complain to the abbot. I'm not the one who interrupted your sleep, and I don't see why I should be the one to suffer for it."

"An excellent idea," Thomas said. He was quite cheerful for the remainder of the meal, and took himself off immediately afterward. We did not see him again until we gathered in the courtyard (rather later than we had anticipated) to begin the next stage of our journey. He turned up at the last minute, wearing an expression I would describe as somewhere between thoughtful and much too pleased with himself.

"Well?" James said as the muleteers led out the mules once more and began the long process of readying them for the trail.

"The abbot was appropriately apologetic," Thomas said. "At least, I'm fairly sure he was; his English wasn't much better than my Italian. We muddled through, nonetheless. Apparently there was a bit of a disturbance last week."

"A magical disturbance?" I asked.

Thomas nodded. "The monks added some extras to the warding spells to prevent a repeat, and we're the first magicians to come through since then. The abbot hadn't intended the improvements to be quite so obvious, or so unsettling."

"I'm sure he didn't," I said. "About that magical disturbance—you *did* ask, didn't you?"

"Of course he asked," James said. "He's only being provoking for the fun of it."

"There's very little to tell," Thomas said. All three of us gave him pointed looks, and he sighed theatrically. "Oh, very well. A group of travelers arrived last week, having crossed through the pass just as we did. In the night, one or more of them slipped down to the crypts under the monastery and . . . did something."

"'Did something'?" I said. "You mean, cast a spell?"

"More of a ritual with magical overtones, as far as I could tell," Thomas said. "The crypts are the most ancient part of the monastery. I suspect that if anything remains of the ancient Roman temple that was here before the monastery, that's where it is. They're forbidden to everyone but the monks, and the abbot was as upset by the trespass as by the peculiar goings-on that resulted from it."

"And?" Kate said. Thomas looked at her. "What else did you find out?" she asked him. "You're too pleased with yourself for that to be everything. Were there traces of chrism in the crypts, or did the abbot tell you where Mr. Strangle is off to?"

Thomas stared at her. "How do you keep *doing* that?" he said in a plaintive tone. "You're right, as usual—Harry Strangle and your young Mr. Daventer"—he nodded at me—"were among the travelers stopping here that night. Accompanied by an attractive young lady. The abbot did not approve."

"I should think not!" I said.

"It's a shame you couldn't get a look at the crypts," James said thoughtfully. "You might have learned even more."

"I doubt it," Thomas said. "The monks purified the place next day; if there were any lingering traces of enchantment, they were dispelled then."

"I had not realized that Mr. Strangle was that good a magician," I said.

"He's not," Thomas said. "He barely deserves the name. Still, he has enough skill to contribute a bit when a spell needs more than one magician, and he's perfectly capable of triggering a preset enchantment. That and his lack of scruples are what make him useful to people like Sir Hilary. He's a perpetual hanger-on of coattails."

"But whose coattail is he hanging on now that Sir Hilary is dead?" I asked. "And what do he and Theodore Daventer have to do with these peculiar rituals we keep running across?"

Everyone looked at me. "Oh, come," I said. "You can't all have missed noticing that Mr. Strangle and Theodore were in Paris when someone broke into Sainte Chapelle and did a not-exactly-magic ritual there. Or that the abbot's account of the disruption here also fits that incident quite well."

"And you said Mr. Strangle did something at that temple in Amiens," Kate said. "Though from your description it didn't sound as elaborate as the other two rituals."

"It wasn't as elaborate a temple," I pointed out. "At least—I'm quite sure the Temple of Minerva Victrix doesn't compare to Sainte Chapelle, but I don't know about the monastery crypts."

"If they're Roman, they're dark and narrow and low," Thomas said. "If they're earlier than that, they're even darker and narrower and lower."

"Very helpful," James said in a tone that meant the exact opposite.

Just at that point, the muleteers brought the mules forward at last, putting an end to the discussion for the time being. When we reached the accommodations on the far side of the Alps that evening, however, the discussion resumed. James seemed to think it his duty to remind everyone repeatedly that we did not actually *know* that Mr. Strangle was responsible for the break-in at Sainte Chapelle or the disturbance at the monastery. Despite this, he and Thomas agreed wholeheartedly that their first action on reaching Milan would be to track down Mr. Strangle.

Next day, when we boarded the coaches hired to take us to Aosta, the talk turned to various methods they might use to accomplish this. They returned to the subject several times during the journey, and as a result, our travel time passed far more quickly than usual.

MILAN

1 October 1817
Milan
At our lodgings in the Via Santa Sofia

My feet are warm again. It seems days since I could say as
much. Not coincidentally, we've been in Milan for an afternoon and a night and a morning, and it was only a moment
ago that I realized my feet were actually warm *and* dry. I
thought I would record this novelty, so that someday when
I am sweltering in the heat of summer, I can think back on
this day and indulge in a pleasurable shiver. I admit it seems
a remote possibility just at the moment.

It is raining. That is why we are all of us still indoors
this morning. When I use the word *raining*, it is because it is
the word everyone else uses. I confess it seems a pale, insubstantial word compared with the deluge that has been falling
since last night. This side of the mountains is much greener
than the barren slopes on the French side, and I suppose
these quantities of rain explain the difference in prospect.

Lady Sylvia has sent one of her knitted missives to say
that things are much as we left them in Paris. It took all four

of us to decipher it. Cecy is almost always the quickest to guess the significance of the objects incorporated into the stitches. She was first to realize Lady Sylvia represents Thomas with a bit of peacock feather. But it was Thomas who solved the question of what the fishhook meant. (The Duke of Wellington, as it is a reference to his soldierly nickname, Old Hookey.)

2 October 1817
Milan
At our lodgings in the Via Santa Sofia

Thomas has arranged for us to go to the opera tonight. We are to see *La Cenerentola,* which I understand to be as near to *Cinderella* as makes no difference. Lord knows, I have seen Thomas looking extremely pleased with himself upon occasion, but when I thanked him for his thoughtfulness, he surpassed all previous efforts.

3 October 1817
Milan
At our lodgings in the Via Santa Sofia

Last night was simply splendid. We attended the opera, the four of us, in our full Parisian finery. It was, if anything, more enjoyable than last time, because I was not in the least worried about my own appearance. I couldn't be bothered to care who was looking greenly at us. There was the music. More than that, I was far from the only one there who had come to *listen*.

As Paris is to pastry, La Scala is to opera. I cannot imagine that one could better La Scala and its audience. To behold those gilded boxes and the enormous stage fills me with joy, but alone they would make an empty paradise. It is the audience that makes it Heaven, all those people who know and care about the music. The throngs filling the seats are not invariably refined, and they are (I am told) almost never entirely respectful. Yet they know what they are hearing, and they appreciate it. Their criticisms can be unmistakable. I have been told sometimes they throw things to express their indignation at a poorly executed aria. What a world it would be if this level of critical appreciation were more widespread. If the chef sends up a badly cooked dinner, one could hurl a cabbage at his head by way of reply.

No, on the whole, far better not to let such exacting standards escape the confines of the opera house.

4 October 1817
Milan
At our lodgings in the Via Santa Sofia

I knew that there would be sociability in Paris. I never expected that we would find sociability in Milan, at least, not so readily. It seems that the British Consul had been alerted to our arrival so there were invitations waiting for us by the time we arrived. At the Consul's residence, we were introduced to some of the prominent residents of the city, and more invitations followed in short order.

Mail was waiting for us, too. It has been a pleasure to take paper and pen and ink pot to write a simple letter home. Much less arduous than the work I have been putting into my knitted replies to Lady Sylvia. I refuse to try to knit an account of going to the opera.

N.B. Where is my good left glove? I can't have lost it. I do seem to have lost the last of Aunt Charlotte's handkerchiefs. Luckily, I bought more in Paris.

5 October 1817
Milan
At our lodgings in the Via Santa Sofia

We now have been to *La Cenerentola* twice. There was also a work by Gritti, *Caterina Sforza,* but one performance of that was enough to convince Thomas that we did not need to see or hear or even think of it ever again. The La Scala audience was even more exacting than Thomas, and the Gritti production has closed, as preparations begin to replace it with an opera by Pacini.

My time at the opera was golden. Even the hours before and after seemed filled with music. Once the rain stopped, the weather warmed delightfully, so we could have the windows open in our rooms. Each morning bells and birdsong wake us. Every street vendor seems to make a song of his wares, and everyone who sings can carry a tune. Thomas does not seem as enchanted by this phenomenon as I am, but despite the occasional complaint, he never gets up to close the windows.

7 October 1817
Milan
At our lodgings in the Via Santa Sofia

Upon our arrival, Thomas and James did their utmost to locate Mr. Strangle through persistent inquiry. I am sure that they would have succeeded in time. They didn't have a fair chance to demonstrate the excellence of their methods, as pure luck forestalled them.

Fortunately, among the invitations we received after enjoying the hospitality of the British Consul was one from the Conte and Contessa di Monti to a garden party to be held in the grounds of a fine estate near the city. It was a fête to salute the generosity of the Conte di Capodoro, who had just announced the donation of his collection of Roman and Etruscan antiquities to the city of Milan for the enjoyment of her people. The Conte and his Contessa were honored guests, and we joined the local notables in congratulating them on their philanthropy.

It was a fine day, unseasonably warm, so there was no excuse to linger indoors. I was disappointed by this, as I'd hoped for more chance to admire the villa itself. Instead, we were escorted to the fine gardens, where we were greeted by our host, the Conte di Monti, who does something important for the Hapsburgs, and his Contessa, our hostess. They introduced us in turn to their guests, the Conte and Contessa di Capodoro among them. The Conte and Contessa di Monti were like a pair of Persian cats, both with flowing white hair and pleased expressions.

The man of the hour, the Conte di Capodoro, was no taller than Thomas, a very thin and bony man with a fine prow of a nose and hooded amber-brown eyes that reminded me of a falcon. His wife was even more distinguished in appearance and demeanor. She wore pure white silk in the most Grecian style imaginable, complete with a delicate gold fillet threaded through her dark curls. She had the small, remote smile of a classical statue of Venus. There was an air of stillness about her, and it seemed to me that her smile served to conceal her shyness, for she spoke scarcely a word. I wondered if the Conte di Capodoro had collected her because she resembled one of his antique beauties, or if she had adopted the classical style to please him.

The formalities began when we were conducted to little chairs ranked in rows before a lectern. Once we were seated and gazing attentively, our host welcomed us officially. He then described the excellence of the Conte di Capodoro's character, the width and depth of his erudition, and the excellence of his taste. He thanked the Conte on behalf of the citizens of Milan for the gift of his collection of classical antiquities. He congratulated the Conte on his immense generosity, and he foretold the gratitude of all civilized people would ensure his name lived down the centuries, renowned and respected.

After the Conte di Monti's address, the Conte di Capodoro rose and made a few gracious remarks expressing his gratitude. It was an excellent speech, short enough to leave us hoping for more, yet sufficiently grateful that all our host's courtesies were amply returned. We were then invited to make free with the refreshments and to stroll through the gardens.

Thomas spoke quietly with the British Consul. James, Cecy, and I chatted with our hostess and one or two others as we drifted through the garden. To be strictly honest, James and Cecy chatted with the Contessa di Monti, and I concentrated on keeping my skirts from catching on the rosebushes as we walked.

We came to a spot where the rosebushes met an avenue of topiary with a reflecting pool at the far end. It was as I bent to free myself from a particularly awkward thorn that my attention was drawn to a man and a woman standing by the reflecting pool. They were well out of earshot but close enough for me to see facial expressions.

The man was very tall and extremely thin, and there was something horridly familiar about the set of his head and shoulders. He was speaking intently, from what I could see, with scarcely a pause to permit his companion an opportunity for a response. The woman smiled shyly up at him. This surprised me considerably, for the woman was the Contessa di Capodoro and the man (I will not sully the word *gentleman*) was Mr. Strangle.

As I freed myself from the rosebush, I took an involuntary step back the way we'd come. I don't think I made any sound whatsoever, yet my awkwardness caught Cecy's attention. She could tell something out of the ordinary had happened. "Kate, what's wrong?" Everyone else turned to stare at me, mild-eyed and curious as a herd of dairy cattle.

"Nothing. Nothing at all," I said hastily. I smoothed my skirts and moved to rejoin the group. "Merely my usual clumsiness."

After a few moments, chat resumed and our party drifted on aimlessly. My reply had deceived Cecy not at all. She and James closed in, one on either side of me. Under her breath, Cecy asked again, "What's wrong?"

"Mr. Strangle is here," I murmured back.

With the greatest effort of will, the three of us maintained our lackadaisical progress. "Where?" James asked.

"Right there." I nodded toward the reflecting pool. The Contessa di Capodoro had retired, but Mr. Strangle still stood there, staring into the water like a heron waiting for its next fish.

Cecy was decisive. "Kate, go find Thomas. James and I will follow Mr. Strangle at a distance. We will keep an eye on him without letting him know we're interested."

James looked grim. "We'll follow him to kingdom come, if necessary."

"It will be such good practice for you." Cecy looked from James to me. "Do hurry, Kate."

I hurried.

Thomas was right where I'd left him, part of the circle listening to the British Consul. He took one look at me and extricated himself from the circle with almost as much courtesy as efficiency. "What's happened?"

I looked back the way I'd come. "Mr. Strangle is here. Cecy and James are keeping him in view without letting him know it. There is a most convenient topiary nearby, but if he walks far in any direction, I don't know how they will contrive to stay out of his sight."

Thomas took only a moment to register that. I knew he'd grasped the situation completely when he said briskly, "Then we must hurry."

He accompanied me through the gardens as quickly as we dared. It really would not have been wise to bustle noticeably. We did not wish to attract any unnecessary attention.

Mr. Strangle was still beside the pool when we rejoined Cecy and James. I wondered why. Was he admiring his reflection in the water? Or was he waiting for someone? No one seemed to be taking the least notice of him. More unusually, he seemed to be taking very little notice of his own surroundings, not even leering at the fashionably dressed ladies who drifted past.

"What's he doing here?" Thomas demanded under his breath. "He can't be an invited guest. Surely the Conte di Monti has better taste than that."

"Perhaps he accompanied Theodore Daventer," Cecy suggested. "Theodore mentioned an uncle they were to meet. Perhaps that is what Harry Strangle is doing here, bear-leading the young man until he can turn him over to his uncle."

"What is he doing now?" I asked.

Mr. Strangle had reached into the pocket of his coat and produced something that looked remarkably like the end of a loaf of bread. It must have been quite stale, for he seemed to have trouble breaking off the small bits he sprinkled into the pool.

James said, "It looks very much as though he's feeding the fish."

"The blackguard. Let's have a word with him." Thomas took a careful look around to be sure that our host and hostess were nowhere in view, then marched across with James. The two of them flanked Mr. Strangle so neatly that he dropped the whole bread crust into the water in his surprise. Cecy and I joined them, keeping a safe distance.

"I *beg* your pardon," Mr. Strangle exclaimed. He tried to retreat, but James and Thomas held his arms firmly. "What is the meaning of this?"

"You disappointed me in Paris, leaving so abruptly," said Thomas. "I wanted a word with you but you ran away from me."

"Can you wonder at it?" Mr. Strangle demanded. "You attacked me."

Thomas was grim. "I never touched you."

"I am uncommonly fleet of foot." Mr. Strangle looked as pleased with himself as usual. "That is the only reason you didn't."

If anything, Thomas's grimness increased. "Now that we're all here together, you won't mind answering a few questions, will you? For a start, why did you murder Sir Hilary Bedrick?"

I gazed at Thomas in surprise. This was quite a feat of illogic, even for Thomas. The effect it had on Mr. Strangle, however, was galvanic. He all but leapt into the air, and only the greatest effort from James and Thomas kept him securely in their grasp.

"Who said that?" Mr. Strangle's terror seemed to contain a great deal of anger. "He's lying! I never saw him— not since last summer. I never saw him at all after he lost his magic."

"He didn't lose his magic," said Cecy. "He had it taken from him by the Royal College of Wizards."

James added, "And richly he deserved the punishment."

"Someone thought he richly deserved to die. Were you the one who killed him?" Thomas put more pressure into his grip on Strangle's arm. "You knew he was dead. You know what happened to him."

"Of course I heard he was murdered." Strangle swallowed hard. "That kind of word travels fast. But I had nothing to do with it. I didn't even know he was in France. I had my own affairs to worry about."

Cecy looked severe. "That's something else we should discuss with you. But first things first."

"What was Bedrick up to?" Thomas demanded.

Mr. Strangle didn't answer the question. He eyed Thomas defiantly. "You will have to use force, won't you? Hardly the done thing at a garden party. You will have to use fisticuffs, as you did in London. You won't object to beating a helpless man, I know. But the civilized guests here deserve to know what they're confronted with, once you reveal your true colors."

"If anyone asks, it will be my pleasure to explain to them precisely what kind of fellow you are, you malignant swine." Thomas glanced over at James. "Can you hold him for me?"

James nodded and took a firm grip on both Strangle's arms, but he looked distinctly uneasy about it.

"Fine." Thomas stepped back and made a series of swift gestures, touching just a fingertip to Strangle's forehead, his chest, and finally his mouth. *"Dicemi veritatem."* I felt a soft throb from the ring on my left hand, which seemed to grow warm as he spoke. "What was Bedrick up to?"

Mr. Strangle's voice came out as a soft whine. "He

wanted revenge on you. More than that, I don't know. I had barely arrived in France myself."

"Who killed Bedrick?" Thomas demanded.

"I don't know." The whine trailed off uncertainly.

Thomas considered a moment, then changed his tack. "Why did you come to France?"

"I was engaged as a tutor for Theodore Daventer. The post became available unexpectedly. Thanks to you, I had no prospects in England, so I crossed the Channel and began my duties immediately."

"Who engaged you?" Thomas asked.

"The boy's uncle, William Mountjoy."

We all looked surprised. Cecy exclaimed, "Mountjoy is Theodore's uncle? What a small place the world is after all."

"Where did you cross the Channel?" Thomas asked. "And when?"

"I crossed from Dover to Calais. Everyone does. I took up my duties there, after I was introduced to young Theodore and given a final interview with Lord Mountjoy."

From a short distance away, the distinctive tones of the British Consul hailed us. "Schofield? What's the meaning of this? What are you doing?"

With a sound of pure exasperation, Thomas snapped his fingers. The sensation of warmth faded from my wedding ring.

"Let him go," Thomas told James.

James relaxed his hold on Mr. Strangle, who turned to

the British Consul as a drowning man welcomes his rescuer. "Thank you a thousand times for deliverance from this ruffian!"

The Consul gazed confusedly from Thomas to Mr. Strangle and back. "I *beg* your pardon?"

"This man attacked me. Not for the first time, either. He and his friend physically restrained me and then cast a spell of compulsion upon me. In front of ladies!" Mr. Strangle brushed imaginary dust off the lapels of his coat and squared his shoulders as if to reassure himself that he was truly free. "I demand retribution. I demand justice."

"Er. Yes." The British Consul thought this over. "What did this spell compel you to do?"

"I wanted the truth from him," Thomas said. "I've grown tired of his lies and evasions." Thomas gave the Consul an abridged account of Mr. Strangle's misdeeds. "I wanted answers to some questions. Honest answers."

The British Consul was unmoved. "Understandable, I suppose, Schofield. But you must know it is hardly polite to go around employing spells of compulsion at a social event. Damned bad form."

Thomas looked contrite. "I'm sorry, Sir."

The British Consul turned to Mr. Strangle. "I was fortunate enough to be consulted by the Conte and Contessa di Monti when this event was proposed. I count myself tolerably familiar with the names on the guest list. I must confess that your name, Sir, was not among them."

Mr. Strangle took an involuntary step backward. "Your memory is at fault then. For I am an invited guest."

"Are you? I'm so sorry to imply anything else. The matter will be a simple one to clear up. Let's go ask our hostess, shall we?"

"That's really not necessary—" Strangle took another step back and encountered a rosebush. "Ouch. Ow! Damn!" He turned and tore himself away from the thorns of the rose, then sprinted—there is no other word for it—down the lane of topiary and away.

"What an extraordinary fellow," said the British Consul. He turned a disapproving eye on Thomas. "You're not to do it again, do you understand? Whatever it was you did."

Thomas looked entirely chastened. "No, Sir. Under no circumstances. I'm sorry."

"Good. Apology accepted. Now I really must go smooth things over with the Contessa di Monti. She won't be pleased, either by your activities or by her uninvited guest." He took his leave of us all and marched back up the way he'd come.

We watched him go in silence.

"What a pity we didn't just follow Strangle home and accost him there." Cecy sighed a little. "Still, it shouldn't be hard to find Theodore Daventer in a city this size."

James looked more cheerful. "At any rate, it spares us the ordeal of slinking along in Strangle's wake."

"You were doing very well before Thomas joined us," Cecy assured him. "All you need is a bit more practice."

From the deposition of Mrs. James Tarleton, &c.

I continued to find Mr. Strangle's unexpected appearance at the garden party extremely puzzling. The Conte and Contessa di Monti were persons of considerable importance in Milan, and while it had become clear to me that Continental manners were a good deal more easy than those in England, it still seemed very odd for Mr. Strangle to sneak uninvited into their party. (No more than Thomas could I bring myself to believe that he had received an invitation.) There seemed no reason for him to have done so. For a time I considered the possibility that the castle grounds contained some ancient temple or monument that he wished to get into, but I could find no reference to such a thing in any of the books Lady Sylvia had so thoughtfully provided, so I was forced to abandon the idea.

Considering ancient temples, however, led me to think of other antiquities. A few of the most impressive pieces from the Conte di Capodoro's collection had been on display at the party, but amid the excitement attendant on Mr. Strangle's appearance, none of us had seen them. I determined to remedy this, on the triple grounds that something in the collection might have been Mr. Strangle's objective; that even if the articles had nothing to do with Mr. Strangle, my Papa would be greatly interested in hearing a report of them; and that, in any case, visiting the collection would be something to do besides listening to yet another opera.

Following the party, Mr. Strangle had vanished as thoroughly as ever. James and Thomas returned to their manhunt, and so could not join the expedition to see the collection the Conte had donated. Thomas therefore told Piers to accompany Kate on any outings that he, Thomas, could not join, pointing out that a bodyguard did little good if he was on the other side of town from the person he was supposed to be guarding. I was inclined to agree with James's assessment that Thomas had a bee in his brain, as there seemed no particular reason to think that Mr. Strangle would approach Kate, but Kate acquiesced with little objection. So we were five on the day we drove down to the building that now housed the antiquities: myself, Kate, our maids, and Piers.

The doorman examined our tickets with care before letting us join the crowd already inside. The building had evidently been hastily refurbished to suit its new function, for the rooms smelled of fresh whitewash and strong soap. The pieces of the collection had been laid out haphazardly on tables in a series of rather small rooms off a central hallway. Iron belt buckles and chipped pottery mixed indiscriminately with stones and small lead tablets bearing nearly illegible inscriptions. Very little had been labeled, none of it in English.

The curator, a rather harried-looking gentleman in a green-and-gold uniform, roamed from room to room, attempting to explain the fine points of the exhibits to the visitors. Unfortunately, his English was not good. After two unsuccessful attempts to enlighten us, he gave up and left us to our own devices.

We passed through the first few rooms with almost unseemly speed. "It is a pity your Papa isn't here," Kate said. She frowned doubtfully at a small bronze object that looked rather like a tiny bowl stuck to the side of a small gravy boat. "He could at least tell us what things are."

"I believe that particular piece is an oil lamp, my lady," Kate's maid, Reardon, said diffidently. "From the era of the Republic, if I am not mistaken."

"It certainly resembles the illustrations in Papa's manuscripts," I said. "Though it is far more battered. Have you seen such things before, then?"

"A few, though I am more familiar with Egyptian antiquities than those of Rome," Reardon said with some reluctance. "My father was in service to Monsieur Champollion, the Egyptologist, for many years, and one cannot help but absorb some information when one is raised in such an environment."

"Just so," I said, thinking of Papa. "What is your opinion of this?" I pointed at a triangular piece of clay, one side of which was covered in small tiles that made a picture of a head with two faces. "I thought it might be intended as the two-faced Roman god, Janus, but there is something odd about the style of the headdress."

Reardon allowed herself to be drawn into a discussion,

and her comments made the exhibits far more intriguing. Our progress slowed to a more leisurely pace, and other visitors began passing us by.

"Perhaps we should move faster," Kate said as a recent arrival walked past with a disapproving look. "Not that it isn't all very interesting."

"I suppose we might as well," I said. "Papa will be quite happy to hear about what we've seen so far, and I can't imagine that old coins and fragments of mosaics would have any attraction for Mr. Strangle— Oh, my!"

The next-to-last room, which we had just entered, was quite different from the others. A waist-high shelf had been built along one wall, and lined up along it were dozens of little statues and one or two pieces of bas-relief showing robed figures. The rest of the room was empty but for a table draped in green that had been pushed up against a window in the far wall. The air had just the barest hint of old magic in it, like the faint scent of roses that lingers in a room for a while after the flowers themselves have been taken away.

"Household gods," Reardon said. She frowned and added disapprovingly, "Some of them are Egyptian."

"Didn't the Romans conquer Egypt?" Kate said. "Perhaps those are some of the spoils they brought back with them."

I walked to the table at the far end. The feel of magic was stronger, though still very faint. The table contained several small lamps made of reddish pottery, two statuettes of a woman holding a torch, a gold ornament shaped like the branch of a tree, and a sword made of corroded bronze. The sword's blade was flat and almost rounded at the end, though I could not tell whether that was its original design or whether the point had corroded away. There was a small card in the corner of the table bearing a phrase in Italian.

"Reardon, do you know what these are?" I asked. "They don't look like anything I've heard of."

The others came over to join me. "I think the statues are of a goddess," Reardon said. "Possibly offerings of some sort. This"—she gestured at the gold ornament—"seems to be a cloak pin."

"But which goddess?" I asked. "Vesta was the Roman goddess associated with fire, but I don't think the Romans ever made statues of her, and I can't think of anyone else it could be."

"I am afraid I don't know either, Madam," Reardon said.

Behind me, Piers cleared his throat. "The card says, 'From the King of the Wood at Nemus Dianae.'"

"Piers!" Kate said. "Why didn't you tell us you spoke Italian?"

"Er," said Piers. "I, um, didn't want to distract you, my lady."

"You're sure it says the *King* of the Wood?" I said. Piers nodded. "That can't mean the statues, then." I glared at the card. "You would think that a label would say something more *useful*."

"It's an odd set of objects for a king to have," Kate commented. "That is, I suppose the sword is ordinary, but why the statues? And you'd expect a king to have a crown, certainly."

"Yes," I said thoughtfully. "You'd certainly expect that. I suppose they might not have found the crown with these other things, but if they did—"

"Then it's gone missing, like those other things the Duke of Wellington mentioned," Kate finished. We looked at each other.

"Thomas and James might be able to find out whether the Conte's collection used to include a crown," Kate said after a minute.

"And I expect Papa will know *something* about this goddess," I said. "I'll write him this afternoon. And one of us should send to Lady Sylvia."

"I'll do that, if you check my knitting," Kate said as we started toward the door. "It's so difficult, knowing that dropping a stitch may change the whole meaning of a message."

"I'll be glad to," I said. "Piers, what are you doing?"

Piers had come to a dead halt in the middle of the hallway, forcing the rest of us to pause likewise. "A moment, if you please, Madam," he said, his head cocked in an attitude of listening.

I was about to say something scathing, when I remembered that Piers was, after all, a professional bodyguard. So instead of distracting him, I listened for whatever had attracted his attention. At first all I heard was a murmur of Italian echoing down the hallway from the first display room, but after a moment, the voices began to rise. Unfortunately, they were still in Italian, but one was clearly a man's voice and the other a woman's. The argument seemed to reach a climax, then the man snapped something. I caught the names "Tarleton" and "Schofield," and then Piers came to life.

"In here, quickly," he said, and we all piled through the nearest doorway onto the landing of the back stairs.

"What is going on?" I whispered.

"I do not think we should be seen by the lady who was arguing with the gentleman at the end of the hall," Piers said. "And as they will be coming this way in another moment—"

"You are nearly as closemouthed as your employer," I said. "Move over."

Piers looked confused.

"Move over," I repeated. "I want a good look at this lady who is so cross about *Tarleton* and *Schofield*, and I think that if we open the door a crack, we can get one."

"I don't think your husband would approve of that, Madam," Piers said.

"He probably won't," I said. "What has that to do with anything? Move."

Reluctantly, he stepped aside, and I opened the door two finger-widths. The others crowded around the crack as well. A moment later the curator went past, still expostulating in Italian, into the room full of statues we had just quitted. Following him was a young woman in a neat cream morning dress, quite simple, in the Italian style. Her hair was a rich, dark brown, and her figure resembled that of some of the ancient statues Papa is so fond of—the sort of statues that Aunt Elizabeth considers most improper. Piers stiffened and Walker gasped.

I shut the door as hastily as I could without making a noise, though I did not think the woman had heard. "What is it?" I asked Walker softly.

"But that woman is the one I spoke of, the one who visited the Strangle in Paris!" Walker said. "I knew she was not *respectable*. How is it that she is here?"

"That is an exceedingly good question," I said. "Piers, you must follow her when she leaves, and find out where she is going."

"I fear I cannot oblige you, Madam," Piers said uncomfortably. "Er, my employer engaged me to act as bodyguard, and one cannot guard someone if one is elsewhere."

"If I promise to go straight back to our rooms with Cecy?" Kate said. "I don't see how anything could happen to us with both our maids along, in broad daylight, in such a short distance."

"I am sorry, my lady," Piers said, even more uncomfortably than before. "I cannot see my way to it."

I could tell that he was going to be stubborn, and I did not know how much time we had. "Walker! Can you follow her without being seen? And then come back and tell us whatever you find out, of course. I'd go myself, but Mr. Strangle has probably given her descriptions of all of us, if they're working together, and she might realize it was me."

Walker blinked at me in startlement. Then her eyes began to sparkle. "*Oui*, Madame!" she said. "She will never know I am there."

Piers looked appalled. "Madam—"

"Go, then," I said to Walker, and slipped her out the door. I frowned at Piers. "It would have been much better if you had gone, because you speak Italian and you could have told us what she said," I told him.

"I *could* not, Madam," Piers said miserably. "She would have recognized me at once."

"Recognized you?" I said. "Have you been flirting with Italian housemaids, now? I thought you learned your lesson in Calais. Though she doesn't look much like a housemaid, now I think on it."

"She didn't in Calais, either," Piers said. "That was Eve-Marie."

"What?" Kate and I said together. We looked at each other, and then Kate continued, "*That* was the Young Person who tied you up and locked you in the scullery the night someone tried to enter Lady Sylvia's rooms?"

Piers nodded.

Kate and I looked at each other again. "What a good thing we sent Walker," I said after a moment.

"*You* sent Walker," Kate pointed out. "I wish you'd told her to be careful."

"There wasn't time," I said. "Besides, she'll *have* to be careful if she's not to be seen. Have they gone?"

"Reardon, you're the only one of us she might not recognize," Kate said. "Would you look?"

Reardon opened the door and stepped calmly into the corridor. After what seemed an extremely long time, she returned. "I believe they have departed, my lady," she said. "And the curator has removed that last exhibit you were looking at. The one 'From the King of the Wood.'"

"That's curious," I said as we moved down the hallway toward the door.

"Was that what they were arguing about, Piers?" Kate asked. "Was she trying to make sure we wouldn't see it?"

"I believe that was the main part of their disagreement, my lady," Piers said.

"We had better get back," I said. "James and Thomas will want to know about this, and we ought to write down as much as we can about that exhibit before we forget any of it. If they didn't want us to see it, something about it must be important."

"But what?" Kate said.

None of us had a good answer, though we discussed the matter all the way back to the inn.

From the commonplace book of Lady Schofield

> *10 October 1817*
> *Milan*
> *At our lodgings in the Via Santa Sofia*

Thomas has thought of many questions he ought to have posed to Mr. Strangle when he had the chance. His annoyance with himself over the missed opportunity made his pursuit of Mr. Strangle more dogged than I would have thought possible. While he and James hunted for the Strangle, as Cecy's maid calls him, Cecy and I were left to our own devices.

Walker came up trumps in the matter of surveillance. She returned flushed with triumph and joined us in the parlor, where Cecy was studying a map of the city, and I was writing letters.

"I have followed that woman. She went straight to a private house. Waiting to see if she would emerge again has made me late, and I regret it most sincerely. However, she did not emerge. I have every confidence that the house to which I followed her is the place where she is staying."

"What house?" Cecy asked. "Where did she go?"

"That woman went directly to a fine house in the fashionable quarter off the Piazza Saint Basila. She was received as a visitor, no more, but she must be there as a guest of the house. No social call could have lasted so long." Walker's expression made her opinion of Eve-Marie perfectly plain. No better than she should be, that was evident.

"Show me on the map," Cecy said.

This proved difficult, as the mapmaker had been more intent upon portraying every glory of the city, from the Duomo to the Castello, than in representing side streets accurately.

"Here," said Walker at last, indicating a crowded spot on the city plan between the Duomo and the eastern gate. "Do you see, Madame?"

I held out my pen and a fresh sheet of writing paper. "Perhaps you could sketch a more detailed map for us?"

"But of course." Walker dipped the pen and, without a single spatter of ink, drew a diagram of a piazza and the streets angling off it. She put an X halfway along one street, on the north side. "It is unmistakable," said Walker, "for the facade of the house is of the same shade of yellow as the opera house." To me, she added, "That is a shade that would suit you to perfection, Madame la Marquise. I have thought so since I first saw it."

I must confess that her suggestion made my heart sink a little. I know I would miss it if Cecy ever left off suggesting colors that would suit me to perfection. She's always right. It is a great talent of hers. Yet when Walker does it, it piques me. Does the whole world know better than I do what suits me?

Thank goodness that Reardon is not prone to this helpfulness. I do not think I could bear it if she did it, too.

What makes me feel particularly foolish about my pique is that I had privately thought much the same thing about the dull golden yellow of La Scala's facade. It would look well on me. But since we have no need to order more gowns and, even if we did, no time in which to do so, I don't see what I can do about it.

11 October 1817
Milan
At our lodgings in the Via Santa Sofia

It is not possible to visit Milan without also visiting the *L'Ultima Cena,* which is what the Milanese call Leonardo's *The Last Supper.* To see the fresco, one visits the Convent of Santa Maria delle Grazie, a pleasant enough place. Pleasant enough, indeed, to make up for the grim dinginess of the room, once the convent's dining room, in which the fresco is located.

I found the famous masterpiece disappointing, for the painting is obscured by the filth of ages, its colors mere shadows in comparison to those of the gaudy Crucifixion on the opposite wall. Fortunately, I was not alone on the excursion. Cecy and I were accompanied by Walker, Reardon, and the ever-present Piers. Although I was a trifle put off by the faint smell of mold that haunted the place, Cecy was fascinated.

"Only think of it. Leonardo da Vinci worked here, Kate. Perhaps he stood on this very spot. Very likely he must have, in order to step back for a better look at his work."

I did my best to counterfeit enthusiasm, but the best I could do was, "I am thinking of it, and if the great painter actually stood on this very spot, I hope the mildew was not quite so advanced in his day."

"Oh, do cheer up, Kate." Cecy gave me one of her Looks. "Leonardo wasn't just a painter. He was a master of spell casting, a wizard of wizards."

"Then it's a pity he wasn't able to keep the paint from peeling off this wall."

"He experimented. This was one of his experiments, that's all. Not everything works perfectly straightaway." Cecy's enthusiasm for Leonardo and all his works was interrupted as another visitor joined us in the refectory. Cecy's eyes grew enormous. "Why, Mr. Daventer!"

The newcomer, a well-dressed, rather solemn youth, made a creditable bow. "Mrs. Tarleton, I'm pleased to meet you again."

"Lady Schofield, may I present Mr. Theodore Daventer?" Cecy completed the introductions. I was, as usual, mildly astonished by the use of my title, but I think I was able to greet Theodore Daventer without betraying the fact. To my disappointment, and I think to Cecy's as well, Theodore was not accompanied by Mr. Strangle, nor, indeed, by anyone else.

"Are you a fellow admirer of Leonardo da Vinci?" I asked Theodore. "Cecy was just explaining the nature of his genius."

Theodore gazed around the room entranced, as if it were lined with gold. "I longed to visit Amboise, where the great man lived out his last days in the service of the French king, but, alas, our travel arrangements did not permit it. This is the first chance I have had to visit any of Leonardo's masterworks, and I simply could not let it go by."

Cecy's face lit up. "I should think not." The pair of them indulged in a bit of admiring reminiscence concerning Leonardo's virtues, before she inquired, "Is your tutor also an admirer of Leonardo's genius?" She looked around as if Theodore's escort might materialize from thin air.

Theodore looked uneasy. "I don't have a tutor at the moment. My uncle has dismissed Mr. Strangle from his service. I don't know when he will engage another."

"Oh, dear." Cecy was sympathy itself. "How distressing that must have been. Did your uncle give a particular reason?"

"I complained to him of Mr. Strangle's lack of erudition," Theodore confessed, "yet that did not seem to concern my uncle nearly as much as Mr. Strangle's lack of discretion. Mr. Strangle had been discussing my uncle's private affairs with outsiders, so of course he had to be dismissed."

"I hope you do not blame yourself for that dismissal?" Cecy seemed to read the answer in Theodore's troubled expression. "Mr. Strangle has made his bed many times over, and now he must lie in it. You are not to be held responsible for his faults."

"His many faults," I echoed.

"Indeed, I know it." Theodore seemed to struggle inwardly a moment, then added, "I fear I am far happier today, free to view this masterpiece unhindered by Mr. Strangle's observations, than I have been since I arrived on the Continent."

With her customary social ingenuity, Cecy took the matter in hand. "You are well rid of Mr. Strangle, if I may be excused for saying so. Have you made plans for other excursions while you are here in Milan? I can recommend the museum of antiquities without reserve."

"What a delight it is to encounter ladies of such erudition," Theodore exclaimed. "I have visited the collection with my uncle and I found it fascinating, but I would hardly have expected you to share my interest."

"Cecy's father is a notable historian," I said, "so perhaps it runs in the family."

"May I ask his name?" Theodore was courtesy itself.

"Arthur Rushton of Rushton Manor," Cecy replied.

Theodore's eyes widened. "Not the Arthur Rushton whose distinguished paper upon the geographic origin of the first Etruscan tribes appeared in last year's proceedings of the Royal Society of Antiquaries?"

Cecy seemed taken aback, so I said, "Yes, that sounds very like Uncle Arthur. We had Etruscans for every meal while he was expounding his original theory."

This was pure slander, and not merely because I did not live under Uncle Arthur's roof and so did not take my meals there. Uncle Arthur loves his subject, but he debates his theories only with those of equal erudition, largely through correspondence, and he is the last man in the world to bore his family with table talk.

Theodore seemed to find this remark highly amusing. "Very good, Lady Schofield. Nothing would suit the Etruscans better than such convivial surroundings."

I simply regarded him in mute confusion, but fortunately Cecy was able to take up the conversation again. "Your uncle appreciated the splendid collection as much as you did, I hope?"

Theodore's regret was clear. "Only to the degree that any gentleman of breeding must admire the beauties of the classical world. My uncle is no scholar, though he appreciates the achievements of others." Despite the firmness of Theodore's words, something in his tone suggested to me that we were hearing Theodore's hopes for his uncle more clearly than his experience of the man. "He does not pretend to an erudition he does not possess."

"Unlike Mr. Strangle," I murmured.

Cecy forged onward. "You may be able to enlighten him as your travels continue. If you are here in Milan for some time, you will surely have a chance to discuss the splendors of the city with him at length."

"My uncle is less concerned with the splendors of the past than with the splendors of the present," said Theodore, with a trace of sadness. "The palaces of Vienna mean far more to him than the splendors of Rome. He has quite a different itinerary in mind from the one I would have liked."

"Vienna?" Cecy looked puzzled. "There aren't any antiquities there, are there?"

"Only the Dowager Empress, Mr. Strangle said," Theodore replied.

"That is precisely the sort of remark I should expect Mr. Strangle to make," said Cecy. "I cannot regret his dismissal. I am sure your uncle's influence will be far more salutary."

"My uncle shares your views," said Theodore. He gazed upon Cecy with such intensity that I was forcibly reminded of a sheepdog. Or possibly just a sheep.

"What a pity he did not accompany you," said Cecy. "I would be delighted to make his acquaintance."

"And he, yours, I am sure." Theodore made sheep's eyes at Cecy. No question, the young man was smitten. And Cecy would never notice, not in a hundred years. I felt a pang of sympathy for the youth. "If you would accompany me back to the house he has engaged, nothing could give me more pleasure than to introduce you."

"What a splendid notion," said Cecy, with as much candid delight as if she had not been angling for the invitation almost since the moment she laid eyes on Theodore. "But you won't wish to be hurried away from this masterpiece so soon, I am sure. Indeed, we are disposed to linger ourselves. Kate can never be satisfied with a brief visit to the work of the old masters, can you, Kate?"

"No, indeed. I dote upon them all," I assured Theodore with as much conviction as if I were indeed one of the *bas-bleu* he clearly took us to be. "Indeed, no matter how I wish to express my admiration, words fail me." I did my best to resemble a young lady with an unhealthy appreciation of such things.

Cecy drew Theodore away to point out a particularly exquisite patch of mold. Their perusal of the fresco was leisurely, but at the end of it, Theodore allowed us to accompany him home without a moment's suspicion.

To be honest, I had some preconceived notions about William Mountjoy. The description of his Venetian dressing gown went with what I had seen of his fashionable slipper. I was sure he would be a coxcomb, a vain young man of fashion. To my surprise, Mountjoy turned out to be a man of middle years, with a receding hairline and a paunch. He seemed as mild as milk. Once Theodore had introduced us, he offered us refreshments in the drawing room of the house he had hired for the duration of his stay.

Mountjoy said, "It is my loss that I did not meet you and your cousin weeks ago. I believe we were all guests at Dessein's the night they were visited by a robber."

"Indeed. A shocking occasion," I said.

"A shocking occasion, indeed. Dessein's can't expect to keep their reputation if they let that sort of thing go on. Not only thieves, but the ceiling fell in, yes, actually fell down upon a dinner party."

"Indeed?" I gave Mountjoy my stupidest look. If he

persisted in discussing the plaster that fell during our dinner party, I set myself to feign complete ignorance of the event. "They never found the culprit, I believe."

As Cecy and Theodore continued their discussion of the genius of Leonardo da Vinci, I thought boredom with my stupidity began to seep into Mountjoy's courteous demeanor.

"You are very kind to entertain your young nephew's friends," I said.

"I am delighted to do so," Mountjoy assured me. "We are just getting to know each other. Sometimes that is easier to do when there are others to smooth the way. I confess that I had no idea young Theodore's admiration for Leonardo da Vinci was so . . . consuming."

"His tutor seemed unaware of it as well. Theodore told us that Mr. Strangle would not permit him to visit Amboise, where Leonardo da Vinci spent his last days."

Mountjoy looked as stern as his round face allowed. "If I had known of Theodore's partiality for such things, I would have ordered Strangle to take him to Amboise."

"Indeed. It is a shame he missed such a treat. Theodore told us Mr. Strangle has been dismissed."

"Dismissed!" Mountjoy's indignation was clear. "He should have been horsewhipped. He may count himself lucky he was merely turned off without a character."

"I am sure you showed great restraint." I tried to make my tone an invitation to show no restraint in telling me the whole. Alas, I did not succeed.

"I did. I won't sully your ears with the details, Lady Schofield, but if you ever hear differently, you will know it for another falsehood told by that lying hound."

"We aren't likely to hear differently, are we?" I asked. "Mr. Strangle won't find honest employment here. I suppose he will return to England."

"I suppose he will go to the devil," said Mountjoy violently. "Not that I care where he goes or what he does."

"No, indeed," I said meekly. "So long as Theodore is safe from him."

"Oh, yes. Theodore." Mountjoy cleared his throat. "I must see about engaging a proper tutor for the boy. He can't run wild forever."

"He doesn't seem likely to run wild at all," I said. "He seems a very studious and responsible young man."

"No thanks to Strangle," said Mountjoy darkly.

Cecy could probably have done better, but Theodore monopolized her until it was time for us to go. Despite my best efforts, I was unable to coax any more information about Mr. Strangle from William Mountjoy. We took our leave of them and returned to our lodgings only moments after the arrival of Thomas and James. Both were in a state of great excitement.

"We found him," said James.

"Found who?" Cecy demanded.

"Strangle," Thomas answered. "He's dead. The authorities fished him out of the ornamental pool in the di Monti gardens."

From the deposition of Mrs. James Tarleton, &c.

Thomas's abrupt announcement startled us all. "Dead?" I said after a moment. "But who could have—"

"I'm sure we'd all like to discuss that," James said. "But not in the hall, I think."

We proceeded up to the sitting room. "When did they find him?" I asked as soon as everyone was settled.

"This morning," Thomas said. "And before you inquire, yes, it was foul play. Not, however, of a sorcerous nature. It was a straightforward knife in the back."

"Oh, dear," Kate said. "Then when we were talking to Lord Mountjoy, he was already— Oh, dear."

"I can't see that it would have made much difference if we'd known," I said. "One could hardly offer insincere condolences to an ex-employer, especially one so put out as Lord Mountjoy was."

"You spoke with Mountjoy?" Thomas said.

"Kate did, mostly; I was occupied with Theodore," I said, and explained the circumstances.

"I don't like it," James said. "The way this young man keeps popping up is beginning to seem a little too convenient."

"But convenient for whom?" I said, frowning. "And why? Nothing quite fits together."

Thomas started to say something, but Kate looked at him and he only cocked an eyebrow inquiringly. "What do you mean, nothing fits?" Kate asked.

"Well, first there's the chrism. The Lady in Blue had it all ready to hand on to Lady Sylvia the very day we arrived in Calais—but all our travel plans were so scrambled, how did she know Lady Sylvia was going to *be* in Calais that day? And how did Mountjoy know where to try to intercept it?"

"*Did* he try to intercept it?" James asked mildly.

"Someone certainly did so," I pointed out. "And Mountjoy was there. That story of a thief running off with one of his slippers always seemed unlikely to me. Furthermore, he lied about his reasons for being in Calais. He clearly hasn't left the Continent, after all." I sat up very straight. "Remember, Mr. Strangle said he came to Calais and took up his post as Theodore's tutor 'after a final interview with Theodore's uncle'? Mountjoy was in Calais to see Strangle, and he didn't want us to know about it."

"That fits with what Strangle told us," Thomas said. "But it doesn't have anything to do with the chrism. In fact, it is entirely unexceptionable. Much too entirely unexceptionable."

Behind me, Walker made a diffident noise. I turned and nodded encouragingly.

"The Lord Mountjoy we spoke to today, Madame," she said. "He is the small gentleman who visited Monsieur Strangle in Paris."

"No surprise there," Thomas said.

Kate and James gave Thomas identical reproving looks. I cleared my throat. "Then there is Sir Hilary's attack—those highwaymen who shot James."

"Sir Hilary may have proposed it, but I don't think he was behind it," James said. "Remember the letter Lady Sylvia's friends found."

"I was getting to that," I said. "Sir Hilary was after *us*— but those highwaymen stole the chrism. So Sir Hilary's mysterious friend, the wizard who assisted him with the ambush, must have been trying to get hold of the chrism."

"You think Mountjoy is Mother's X?" Thomas said thoughtfully. "An interesting idea. I said his excuse for being in Calais was too unexceptionable."

"You didn't say it very loudly," James put in. Thomas ignored him pointedly.

"I don't see how it can have been Lord Mountjoy," Kate said. "Those highwaymen came from Paris, and he was still in Calais. With Piers asking him things."

"He was, but Eve-Marie wasn't," I said. "If Mountjoy was the thief, she must have known him. She got Piers out of the way for him, after all. Mountjoy could have sent her off to Paris with instructions for the highwaymen as soon as he realized he couldn't steal the chrism from Lady Sylvia. Eve-Marie would have had plenty of time to get there while we were in Amiens visiting temples and bishops and so on. But it doesn't explain why Sir Hilary was killed."

"Hold on a minute," James said. "We know that Sir Hilary wanted revenge on us, but he could have been after the chrism as well."

"Someone would still have had to tell him we had it," I

pointed out. "And that is most likely to have been Eve-Marie. Unless you think the Lady in Blue would have gone straight to Paris to let him know."

"The highwaymen didn't seem to be looking for anything in particular," Kate objected. "They were taking everything." She glanced at Thomas. "It might have been a sort of accident that they stole the chrism."

"It seems most unlikely," I said. "And after what happened to Mr. Strangle, I don't believe that Sir Hilary's demise was merely a falling-out among thieves, either."

"But what does Strangle have to do with the chrism?" James said.

"That's just the trouble," I said. "Mr. Strangle and Theodore don't seem to have anything at all to do with the chrism and the rest of the missing regalia. It was quite by accident that we ran into them in Amiens."

"At that temple your father suggested visiting," James said.

Kate's eyes widened. "Cecy! All those places!"

"What do you mean?" I said.

"Wait." She practically flew out of the room, and returned a few moments later carrying her commonplace book. "The Temple of Minerva . . . Victrix, in Amiens," she read. "Sainte Chapelle on the Île de la Cité in Paris. The Etruscan crypts at the Hospice of the Great Saint Bernard." She looked up triumphantly. "All the places we've run across Mr. Daventer and Mr. Strangle—they're all on your father's list of antiquities to visit. I remembered because I copied it into my book a few days ago. I had spilt soup on the page your Papa gave me, and it was becoming illegible."

"Becoming?" Thomas murmured.

"Good heavens," I said. "But what could *Papa* have to do with Theodore and Mr. Strangle and Lord Mountjoy?"

"I doubt that he has anything to do with them," James said. "But I think you might write and ask him where he found his list of antiquities to recommend, Cecy."

"And what else is on it?" Thomas asked.

Kate consulted her book. "A great many places we haven't seen," she said. "Though I suppose Mr. Strangle and Theodore may have visited some of them; indeed, I think it likely. The royal crypts at St. Denis, the Mithraeum at Ville-franche, the—"

"Yes, but what comes *next?*"

"Oh." Kate frowned. "There are some Roman ruins in Westphalia, and a great many shrines and things in the north of Italy. There are dozens of places around Rome, of course." She looked up apologetically. "I am afraid I could not read all of them. And there's the Royal something in V-something. Venice, or Vienna, I think."

"Too many different possibilities. It's a pity we don't know where Strangle intended to take his charge from here," Thomas said. "It might be very informative."

"And it might not," James said. "This is all very inter-esting, but as Cecy said, Strangle and young Daventer don't seem to have any connection to the missing regalia. Which is what we are supposed to be looking into, if you recall."

"Yes," I said slowly. "And the reason the Duke of Wellington asked us to look into it is because being on our wedding journey gives us a marvelous reason to go anywhere we wish. And shepherding one's charge about the Continent on the Grand Tour is an equally marvelous excuse for that, don't you think?"

"That is true," James agreed with some reluctance. "But if so—"

"If so, these peculiar rituals that Mr. Strangle has been doing must have some connection with the missing regalia," I said. "I wonder if that's what Theodore meant when he spoke of 'practical applications' at that bookstore in Paris?"

"That, on the other hand, is leaping to a conclusion with a vengeance."

"Maybe," Thomas said. "I'm inclined to side with Cecy in this, however. If only because I doubt that whoever disposed of Strangle was merely concerned about the Daventer boy's morals."

"Theodore seemed to think his uncle dismissed Mr. Strangle for talking out of turn," I said. "If so, the obvious question is, who was he talking to? And just how much did he give away?"

"He was talking to the Contessa di Capodoro at the garden party," Kate commented.

"So he was," James said. "Just before we accosted him."

"And Eve-Marie showed up at the Conte's exhibit just after we saw it," I said. "Perhaps Mr. Strangle was trying to get information about the exhibit from the Contessa and let something slip."

Thomas frowned. "I believe I shall pay a visit to the Conte di Monti," he said. "Express my concern about this, er, unfortunate turn of events. I'm sure he'll understand my desire to be reassured that I don't have to spirit my wife straight back to England for safety's sake."

"You wouldn't!" I said.

"No, he wouldn't," James said. "You can't visit the Conte, Thomas. The man may be a bit woolly-headed, but he won't have forgotten that you and Strangle had a run-in at the garden party. If you show up asking questions, you'll have every authority in Milan down around our ears. I'll go."

"And I think Kate and I will send a card to the Contessa di Capodoro," I said. "We can invite her to tea. As an appreciation of her husband's generous donation. You'd better sign it, Kate; 'Lady Schofield' sounds so much more impressive than plain 'Mrs. Tarleton.'"

"All right," Kate said. "If you insist."

Thomas, having been thwarted in his desire to interrogate the Conte (for he had to admit the force of James's arguments), instead set himself to finding out who else Mr. Strangle might have spoken to indiscreetly during his time in Milan. James returned from the Conte with the expected reassurances and the surprising news that Mr. Strangle had indeed been invited to the garden party; his name had been on the special guest list of people the Conte di Capodoro particularly wished to be invited (in addition to the Conte di Monti's choice of guests). Applying his considerable address, James succeeded in seeing the list, and informed us that Mr. Strangle's name appeared to have been added to the end, in another hand.

This left us very little further along than we had been. For though we knew that *someone* had wanted Mr. Strangle at the garden party, we had no idea who or why. Thomas determined that Mr. Strangle had arrived very shortly before us, and, of course, he left immediately following our confrontation, so he had not had time to talk to many people. Indeed, the only person we *knew* him to have spoken with was the one we had seen ourselves, the Contessa di Capodoro. Kate and I were therefore exceedingly pleased when the Contessa accepted our invitation to tea quite promptly.

"So very English a custom," she said in a soft voice, studying the tea tray.

"Will you have milk or sugar?" Kate asked somewhat reluctantly. It had not occurred to either of us until the last minute that, as both Lady Schofield and the hostess, she would have to pour. This was a mixed blessing; on the one hand, it meant that she had not had time to work herself into a state over the potential for accidents and social embarrassments, but on the other, it also meant that she had had no time to practice.

"No, thank you," the Contessa replied.

Kate handed her a cup with evident relief, and poured for

herself and me without mishap. We settled back in our chairs
to sip and nibble and make polite remarks. The first few minutes passed in unexceptionable comments about the beauty of
the city. When Kate mentioned how much she had enjoyed
the performances at La Scala, it developed that the Contessa
was likewise a devotee of the opera. The Contessa's shyness
evaporated as they compared various performances; indeed,
for a time it appeared that the purpose of our meeting would
be totally forgotten. Kate was at something of a disadvantage,
as we had not been in Milan long enough for her to see many
different operas, but the Contessa graciously conceded that
one's first visit to La Scala must be memorable, no matter the
quality of the performance.

"And the present opera is very good," she added. "Now,
when I first came to Milan, Salieri's *Armida* was playing."
She shuddered expressively. "And yet, it was La Scala, and
so I treasure the memory."

"How long have you been in Milan?" I asked, hoping to
turn the subject.

"Some seven years," the Contessa replied. After a moment, she added quietly, "It is my husband's home."

"And where is yours?" Kate asked with ready sympathy.

"Rome," the Contessa answered. "Or it was. Now my
home must be here." She sighed. "At least there is La Scala."

"Does your husband share your enthusiasm for the
opera?" I asked. "Or is he entirely taken up with antiquities?"

"The latter, I am afraid," the Contessa said with a little
smile. "He is sometimes . . . very concentrated. We travel a

good deal, always to places where he hopes to find more of his Etruscan things. He speaks of Vienna soon."

"Vienna?" I said. "I thought the Etruscans lived around Rome."

The Contessa looked at me in surprise. "You know of the Etruscans?"

"My Papa is an antiquarian," I said. "He is quite... quite passionate about it at times. One cannot help but pick up a few things."

The Contessa laughed. "He sounds a twin to my husband. I am not sure why he hopes to visit Vienna; some new theory that he has recently learned of, I think. We have been many other places that were even less likely—Spain, Prussia, France."

Kate and I exchanged glances; I think we were both mentally comparing the Contessa's list of destinations with the Duke of Wellington's list of missing royal antiquities. "It must be pleasant to travel so much," I said. "I have never been outside England before, and I must own, I am vastly enjoying the experience."

"It would be more pleasant if it were not always in such a hurry," the Contessa confided, making a little face. "I think my husband is trying to make up for lost time. He was so busy, when Bonaparte was in France, and he did not have time for antiquities then. Now, it is all different."

"Was he in the army?" I asked.

"No, no," the Contessa said, shaking her head. "He would never have fought against Napoleon. Never! No, he was trying to prevent the Austrians from coming. It is a pity he did not succeed."

"Forgive me, Madame, if I have misunderstood," I said. "But are you saying that your husband worked *for* Napoleon Bonaparte?"

"Ah, you are English," the Contessa said with considerable vigor. "You do not understand how it was. Italy was in many little pieces before Bonaparte—as it is once again now that he is gone. The Emperor was a . . . a believer in unity. He was good for Italia."

I was unsure how best to respond without provoking an argument, especially when it seemed to me that very few of the other Italians we had met agreed with this position, but Kate nodded sympathetically. "If your husband was unable to pursue his interest in the Etruscans while Napoleon was in power, it was even more generous of him to donate his collection to the city," she said.

"He is very proud of his home," the Contessa said. "And . . . I think he hopes for some new and more dramatic finds soon. It is not so hard to let go of things of lesser value when one has the prospect of gaining those of greater worth."

"More dramatic?" I said. "That would be quite an achievement. Kate and I visited the collection a few days ago, and I found it very impressive. Though I suppose if he *does* find Etruscan ruins in Vienna . . ."

"He does not discuss it with me, you understand," the Contessa said earnestly. "But it is as you say: 'One cannot help but pick up a few things.' And I believe he has just such hopes. I beg you will not discuss it. It would be so embarrassing for him if he is wrong."

"You may rely on our discretion," I said.

"I believe it," the Contessa said. "But let us talk of something else. How long are you in Milan?"

"Thomas speaks of leaving soon," Kate said. "I don't believe he has decided where we will go next."

"You are leaving? You have hardly arrived!"

"The Marquis was most concerned about the recent news," I said. "You must have heard—an Englishman found dead in a fountain! My husband was nearly as worried; he talked of returning to England at once."

"I had heard of this; indeed, it would be difficult not to," the Contessa said. "The city is full of talk of it. But surely your husbands do not think it is common for Englishmen to drown themselves in our fountains! If it were an ordinary thing, it would not be so much talked of, you see."

"That seems a most sensible way of looking at it," Kate said, cocking her head as if she were much struck by the Contessa's words. "I must remember to mention it to Thomas."

"Besides, the Englishman who was found was a . . . a most unpleasant person." The Contessa ducked her head. "I should not say it, perhaps. But he . . . he spoke with me once, at a garden party, and I found him most distasteful."

"I'm not surprised," I muttered.

"Pardon?" the Contessa said.

"You actually talked with this person?" Kate put in. "What did he say?"

"Nothing that I wish to repeat," the Contessa replied, looking down. "He assumed— He was far too hasty, even if—"

"I understand," Kate said sympathetically. "I met him once, some time ago, in England."

"Then surely you can prevail upon your husband to remain in Milan!" the Contessa said. "It would be a shame for you to go so soon, when we have only just met."

"I thought you and your husband would be leaving for Vienna soon," I said.

The Contessa looked up, plainly startled. "Yes, I— It is not yet certain."

"Well, we have not determined to leave yet, either," Kate said. "And if we do, perhaps we could arrange to meet in Vienna."

The Contessa brightened. "I had not thought of that! Yes, that would be very pleasant."

She and Kate discussed the matter from several angles, and then returned to talk of opera until the tea went quite cold. At last the Contessa departed, with much cordiality on every side. Her carriage had hardly rolled away from the door when James and Thomas pounced on us.

"Well?" Thomas demanded. "What did he say?"

"Who?" Kate asked, widening her eyes innocently.

"You know perfectly well who," Thomas said. "Strangle."

"Nothing to the purpose," I said. "Only what we might have expected him to say to a pretty woman."

James frowned at the windows, in the direction the Contessa's carriage had taken. "That's a little odd. She doesn't seem like Strangle's usual fare. Too petite, and shy into the bargain."

"And if Strangle was in league with the Conte to steal all those royal antiquities, it would be the outside of enough for him to try to seduce the Conte's wife," I said.

Everyone turned to look at me. "Oh!" said Kate. "I hadn't thought of that, but you're right."

"Why?" Thomas said. "What other important information have you neglected to mention that leads the pair of you to this rather startling conclusion?"

"The rest of the Contessa's remarks," I said, and summarized it quickly for them.

"So the Conte's a Bonapartist," Thomas said thoughtfully when I finished.

"I think the travel itinerary is more indicative," James replied. "Especially if he's using Etruscans as an excuse. Only a complete cloth-head would look for Etruscans in Spain."

"But what ought we to do?" Kate said. "Shouldn't we stop him somehow?"

This time, everyone looked at her. She frowned at us. "Well, Mr. Brummell said, that very first night, that Vienna was the last place that Lady Sylvia ought to take the chrism. And if the Conte has it, and he is going to Vienna next—"

"We shall have to do something about him," I finished.

"Venice," Thomas said.

"Yes, that might do," James replied. "And if we set it about that we're taking ship for Greece next—"

"A ship?" I said. "You cannot mean to take a ship from Venice to Greece. I refuse. I'm not setting foot on a boat again until I've made a focus and had it long enough to be positive I won't be afflicted with that seasickness again."

"I don't think they mean for us actually to go to Greece," Kate said. "Only to say that we are, so that the Conte doesn't worry that we're following him."

"Oh," I said. "Of course."

James and Thomas left to begin making arrangements. Kate stayed where she was, frowning slightly. "Cecy, are you planning on creating a focus soon?"

"I've been planning on creating a focus for some time now," I said a little crossly, for I was beginning to think I would never have the opportunity.

"Oh." Kate squeezed her eyebrows together, the way she does when she is worried about something but is not quite sure how to put it for fear of annoying someone else.

"What is it?" I asked.

"It just seems a little . . . Aren't there an awful lot of things that could go wrong? Even without Lord Mountjoy and the Conte and whatever they're up to."

"You're thinking of Thomas's first try," I said. "But I won't be in a hurry, and I won't have Sir Hilary interfering. Everything went well for him this time, didn't it?"

Kate reddened and looked confused. "I, um——"

"It must have gone well, or Lady Sylvia would have noticed and made him mend matters before we left Paris," I said. "It's not really a complicated spell, after all; it hardly takes more ingredients than those charm-bags I made for you and Oliver last spring."

"Then those charm-bags were far more complicated than they looked," Kate said severely. "I, um, saw Thomas set things up this time."

"Well, it's not much more complicated," I said. "And I've had James coaching me on the Latin, and reams of advice from Lady Sylvia."

Kate had been about to say something, but she stopped short. "That's right," she said reluctantly after a minute. "Lady Sylvia did say that you ought to create a focus soon. I remember."

"The difficult part is deciding what it should be," I said. "Not something that's easy to lose or mislay, but not something that's difficult to keep nearby; not something too fragile, but probably not something too permanent, either——"

"Not permanent?" Kate looked alarmed. "Why not?"

"If the focus is something hard to destroy, then it is more difficult to change it to something else if one decides to do so," I explained. "If I were to, oh, use an emerald brooch as a focus, and then later discovered that it was inconvenient, it would take some complicated magic to transfer the focus to something else. But if I used something fragile, like one of those little glass ornaments we saw at the market yesterday, all I would have to do would be to smash it and start over with something else. Only, if one uses something *too* fragile, then one is very likely to drop it or sit on it or destroy it accidentally in some other way. Which would almost *certainly* happen at precisely the wrong moment. Things like that always do."

"Not always," Kate said. "It didn't with Thomas's chocolate pot."

"Well, it wasn't an accident that I smashed it," I said, "but you have to admit, it definitely broke at the wrong moment from Sir Hilary's point of view."

"Yes," Kate said. "Oh, Cecy, I know it is very wrong of me, especially with Thomas and James so worried about it, but try as I may, I *cannot* be sorry that Sir Hilary is dead."

"If he were alive, Thomas and James would be even more worried," I pointed out. "And they would probably have whisked us both back to England as soon as they realized."

"I expect so," Kate said, but she still looked unhappy.

"What *is* the matter with you today?" I said. "Except for when you and the Contessa were talking about opera, you've been cross as crabs all day—ever since Piers brought in the post. Were you expecting something?"

"No, but there was a letter from Aunt Charlotte," Kate admitted. "She wrote a good deal about my responsibilities and—"

"Stuff!" I interrupted. "The only one who has anything to say about your responsibilities now is Thomas. Go and talk to him about it."

Kate brightened up at once and went in search of her husband. I do not know how it is that Aunt Charlotte so often has such a dreadful effect on Kate's spirits, but it has been so for as long as I can remember. Fortunately, Thomas has proved a most effective antidote. I rang for Walker and told her that she and Reardon had best begin packing, and sat down to give a few minutes more thought to the question of my focus, magic in general, and what the Conte and Lord Mountjoy could possibly be up to.

From the commonplace book of Lady Schofield

14 October 1817
Milan
At our lodgings in the Via Santa Sofia

Today I answered Aunt Charlotte's letter. I wrote in a kind and diplomatic style for which I think I deserve any amount of congratulation and reward. She and Georgy are back at home, ready for a few months of peace and quiet. In Georgy's most recent letter, while mourning the utter flatness of Rushton, she alluded to an arrears in her allowance. I take this (together with a remark of Aunt Charlotte's) to mean that Georgy's gambling debts have been settled and she is paying Aunt Charlotte back out of her pin money. The matter will be straightened out eventually, but I'm sure Aunt Charlotte won't be paid in full until sometime in the next century.

Meanwhile, the only punishment that really means anything to Georgy is that Oliver has made it clear he is no longer enamored of her. Under that foppish streak of his, it seems there dwells a genuine prig. He has given Georgy to understand that, hardened gamester as she is, he cannot possibly return her affections. This enraged Georgy, as she has spent a good deal of time displaying her indifference to Oliver and demonstrating her social success. In her view, she had withdrawn her affections first. I think it is true, yet Oliver, quite typically, failed to notice.

The best thing to come out of the gaming imbroglio is that Georgy and Oliver have at last lost interest in seeing themselves as Romeo and Juliet. It was long past time for that bit of silliness to come to an end. Aunt Charlotte feels precisely as I do on this point. This should make me feel better. In fact, it fills me with chagrin.

Thomas says Georgy is sure to make a grand match next Season. To tease me, he lists the prospects, each of higher station than the last. I know Georgy too well to think she would choose a suitor for his title and fortune alone. At least, I hope I know her too well to think that. But Thomas says—

VENICE

20 October 1817
Padua
At the Sign of the Dovecote

This is the first opportunity I've had in days to sit down and write properly. Now I can't remember what I was going to say. Something about Thomas and his absurd list of dukes, eligible and ineligible. Piers came in just then. Thomas and I were alone in the private parlor. Thomas was mending the fire and I was at the writing desk with this commonplace book. Piers murmured something to Thomas, and Thomas put the poker back among the fireplace tools with such force that the rack fell over.

To Piers, Thomas said, "Find Mr. and Mrs. Tarleton and let them know." Piers took himself off at once. To me, Thomas said, "Lord Mountjoy's staff is under orders to prepare his carriage to depart at dawn."

"Lord Mountjoy is leaving Milan?" I hesitated. "Will he take Theodore with him?"

"I don't see why not. No matter who goes with it, his carriage is leaving." Thomas looked pleased with himself as he added, "Piers said the staff were told to prepare for the road to Venice."

I was surprised. "Venice—not Vienna?"

"It's on the way, isn't it?" Thomas capped my inkwell for me. "No time for your scandalous memoirs now, my ink-stained darling. If Mountjoy leaves Milan, we leave Milan, too."

I let the remark about scandalous memoirs go for the moment as I regarded Thomas narrowly. "At dawn, no doubt."

"No doubt whatsoever." Sometimes Thomas's good cheer is very nearly too much to bear.

"For Venice, no doubt?"

"Unless we change our minds," said Thomas. "You know how unpredictable we can be, careering about the countryside on our wedding journey."

"I do. There's always the chance we may need to break our journey and indulge in a ritual of some kind."

"I understand that's all the rage this season," Thomas assured me. "I wouldn't be at all surprised if Mountjoy stopped for a ritual or two himself."

"I'll have a look at Uncle Arthur's list, shall I?" I suggested.

"Excellent notion," said Thomas. "But first tell Reardon to pack."

I blush to confess it, but at first I found foreign travel excit-ing. Every detail fascinated me. I have grown weary of fascinating details. My feet are cold. I am tired of foreign food and foreign languages. To see a famous antiquity, be it renowned throughout the world, I would not trouble myself to do any more than rise from my chair, cross the room, and look out of a window.

I am not homesick. I do not long for the family I left behind. I'm just tired of traveling. I am heartily sick of Padua and I haven't been here above six hours.

The hour before dinner I spent knitting a letter to Lady Sylvia beside the parlor fire, listening to the industry of others. Even when we travel with maximum haste, our party requires attention. The brunt of the work is done by our servants. Despite that, the innkeepers invariably shout at their own unfortunate servants. I use the word *shout* to be polite. *Shriek* is more accurate. I take some comfort in my own ignorance. At least here the shrieking is incomprehensible to me. All foreign hostelries run according to the same scheme. Shrieking is indispensable, as is some kitchen mishap to spoil the meal we have ordered. Many doors must be slammed, before and after one shrieks. At all costs, one must mend the fire just as it is starting to do nicely. With luck, entire private parlors can be rendered uninhabitable by smoke, only by a deft application of green wood. These are not the only incidents to provoke the shrieking. There are others, some of which seem to originate from nothing but the pure desire to shriek. I think I begin to understand the impulse.

James joined me in the parlor before dinner. He knows how to make a fire behave itself, thank goodness. He used the fire tools to good effect and drew up a chair beside mine. "Tired?" was all he said.

I must have looked pretty bad for James to remark upon it. I admitted to some fatigue and asked after the plans for our journey to Venice.

"We're making an early start. Provided Thomas encounters no difficulty with his plan, that is."

"Thomas seems full of confidence." I thought better of the words the moment I'd uttered them. "Of course, he always does."

James looked amused. "He does. You must be accustomed to it, since Cecy always does, too."

Some of my traveler's sulk lifted as I remembered the occasion upon which Cecy persuaded the Reverend Fitzwilliam to venture out upon the dance floor with her, because she wanted to see him make good his boast of grace and agility in dancing the allemande. As thoughts of dancing often do, this made me think of Thomas. Dancing with Thomas is one of the finest pleasures in life. "There's much to be said for confidence, in the right place, at the right time," I said to James. I am sure I sounded stuffy, but he did not seem to notice.

"Our meal will be ready in a moment," James said. "I'll bring Cecy if you will go and pry Thomas away from his mad schemes."

"Our meal." I sighed. "If only it were going to be a proper meal. Even a bit of toasted cheese would make a nice change."

"You are tired," said James. "The sooner you get a good meal inside you, the brighter things will seem."

James went off to find Cecy. I went off to fetch Thomas. I am sure Cecy is very happy with James, and he with her, but I don't know what I would do if I were married to someone who reminds me that eating a hearty meal will improve my spirits.

If I had said the same thing to Thomas, he would have agreed with me. What's more, he would have offered to try his hand at making me toasted cheese over the parlor fire, too. There would have been more ordering of servants, more slamming of doors, and, in all likelihood, more shrieking. But it would have been worth it.

Later, I asked Reardon if she ever missed toasted cheese. "I don't care if I never see another bit of it," she told me. "I think some people are lucky to be so fond of a place they are going back to. But it's not lucky if they let that blind them to the place they find themselves. I have never had better food than these past few months, and I am never likely to again. I'd hate to miss a morsel."

As she put me in my place, she put my hair into its place.

So I came away from that exchange improved in two ways.

"How do armies do it?" I asked Thomas last night, and he laughed at me.

"Fear helps. Not of the enemy. Of the officers in command." All very well for him to joke. We left Milan five days and many miles ago. Thomas and James have spared no exertion, still less expense, to reach our destination in time to catch up with Lord Mountjoy and Theodore Daventer. We have made remarkably good time, given the inclement weather. I thought the word *rain* inadequate for the weather we had in Milan. The combination of rain and wind we have encountered since our departure has been worse.

I would not call our journey uncomfortable. After all, we are not riding mules. What slight hardships there are, we have grown accustomed to. James and Thomas manage the logistics of coaches and innkeepers, Reardon manages the luggage, Cecy follows our progress on the map, and I try not to lose any more gloves than I already have. Our chief enemy is boredom. Mile upon mile, change upon change. The road is not bad, but it is not good enough to permit a passenger to read or nap.

Piers has shown himself to be surprisingly adroit at questioning the staff at each place we stop. Thanks to his efforts, we had a good description of the carriages ahead of us on the Venice road. One equipage in particular riveted our attention.

Piers made his latest report before dinner tonight. "The stable boys here told me there is a carriage answering the description of Lord Mountjoy's not six hours ahead of us. The only passenger in the coach is a lady."

James looked at Thomas. Thomas just looked surprised.

"Not Lord Mountjoy, then," James said.

Piers said, "No, Sir. The lady—I should say woman, rather—fits the description of Eve-Marie."

"How gratifying," said Thomas. "Did they happen to hear the fair traveler mention a destination?"

"They heard only her demands for haste. Haste is her only consideration. The fastest horses at every change, no matter the expense. Also there is one trunk in particular that she is concerned with. Whatever it contains, it must be very important. She doesn't let it out of her sight."

"What does it look like?" asked Cecy.

"A trunk. An ordinary trunk. But she does not treat it as if it were at all ordinary. She treats it as if it contains something precious. Something delicate, even."

I looked from Piers to Thomas, to James, to Cecy, and I could feel the expression on my face was a match for theirs. Sheer curiosity. Wild speculation.

"Six hours ahead of us, and we've been here two hours," said James thoughtfully. "She could be in Venice by now."

"Or she could be on the road beyond, headed for Vienna," countered Thomas.

"Or she could be taking ship from Venice to somewhere else," said Cecy. "How provoking, if she takes to the water. She will give us the slip entirely."

"How will we find out which it is?" I asked. "And how will we find out where Lord Mountjoy and Theodore go if we are haring off after Eve-Marie?"

"Eve-Marie was the only passenger in the coach all along, wasn't she?" James said. "They've given us the slip."

Piers grimaced. "Sorry. It was foolish of me to assume that Lord Mountjoy's coach necessarily contained Lord Mountjoy."

"It can't be helped. You've done well," said Thomas to Piers. "Get something to eat and what rest you can. We'll be in Venice tomorrow. We can't make any final decisions until then, so there's no point in tormenting ourselves over it."

Dinner was welcome and bed afterward even more so. Traveling in haste is as uncomfortable as sitting a trot. One bounces along until one's teeth rattle, with no confidence that the discomfort will ever end. Inefficient and unpleasant, that's the disadvantage of foreign travel. Damp beds, bad food, and not enough hot water.

No mules, though.

23 October 1817
Venice
Palazzo Flangini

We arrived in Venice the day before yesterday, muddy and exhausted. If we looked like something the cat dragged in, it must have been a very undiscriminating cat, indeed. My bonnet was destroyed with the wet, the hem of my gown stiff with mud. I looked as if I had walked from Milan at the tail of a cart. I almost felt as if I had. My weariness had one benefit. I did not care how I looked or who I met. I could have been presented to Bonaparte himself and not turned a hair.

So tired was I—and so travel-soiled—that I did not care in the least how I clambered in and out of the gondola that bore us to our lodging. What harm would a ducking do me, in the event I did fall into the canal? It might help with the mud stains on my clothing.

As sometimes happens, indifference cured my usual clumsiness. I was almost nimble.

When we reached our lodging, I did not even bother to remark at the splendor of this place. *Magnificent* is not too strong a word. But I did not have the spirit to notice. The very floor seemed to rise and fall beneath my feet, I was so weary. Reardon brought me hot water and helped me out of my ruined clothes, I remember that. There was a meal on a tray, Reardon's doing again, I'm sure. A bite or two was all I could manage. Then I was in bed and asleep.

I woke in the small hours yesterday morning when Thomas joined me. He was chilled to the bone. By the time I'd done something about that, I was wide awake. Unfortunately, Thomas was too tired to do more than mutter a few answers to my questions.

Yes, Eve-Marie has been seen at a hostelry on the edge of the city, and has apparently arranged to stay for more than a mere change of horses.

No, Thomas doesn't know how long we are going to stay in Venice ourselves, but he had no intention of moving so much as a single muscle for the next twelve hours.

Yes, Thomas will see to it that we attend the opera at La Fenice at the earliest opportunity. But not for twelve hours or so.

I remembered Thomas's remark that last evening in Milan. "Scandalous memoirs," I said in his ear.

Thomas made a soft noise comprised of sleepiness and interest and murmured, "What about 'em?"

"Is that what you think I'm writing in my commonplace book?"

"Isn't it?" Thomas sounded hurt. "Lord knows I've given you enough material."

"There can be nothing scandalous between husband and wife," I reminded him.

"Not if they have a little good sense and are lucky enough to be married to each other, no," Thomas conceded. "All the same, you've been writing a devil of a lot. You'll be out of pages soon."

I had concerns of my own about that. "I suppose I should try to confine myself to the essentials."

Thomas snorted. "Nonsense. It won't be the essentials we'll be interested in fifty years from now. It will be the details that seem unimportant, the things we will have forgotten. That dish of mussels I ate. The way I tie my neckcloth. This conversation. Blaze away, my tea cake. I'll buy you another book tomorrow."

I had to ask. "Do you really think everything I write down is about you?"

Thomas said, "Well, this next bit had better be. I insist."

It is very bad for Thomas's character when he gets his own way all the time. That's why I'm going to omit the next bit. If he has forgotten it in fifty years or so, too bad for him. I won't have.

It was not twelve hours later when I awoke, but Thomas was gone just the same. Reardon brought me another tray. I consumed the contents with enthusiasm, pulled up the coverlet, and fell asleep again. Somehow, the entire day slipped away from me. It was not until this morning that I had a chance to explore our splendid new accommodations.

Thomas does nothing by halves. We have hired an entire palazzo on the Grand Canal. The terms seem ruinous to me, but perhaps we will not be here very long.

For, indeed, Thomas has hardly let me unpack, so certain is he that we will be off on our travels again at a moment's notice. He and James have worked with Piers to arrange a watch upon Eve-Marie's hostelry. When she departs—or, at least, when Mountjoy's carriage departs—we will know of it almost immediately.

Because Thomas isn't often wrong, and because he was kind enough to bring me a new bound book for when I fill the last pages of this one, I set down here a recipe for the dish of mussels he likes so much.

Zuppa di cozze:

Scrub a good supply of mussels and discard any that do not open when they should.

Heat some oil and add garlic. Just before it has cooked too long, put in some parsley and stir.

Squeeze in the juice of half a lemon; add a small glass of white wine, a small glass of water, and the broth made when you heated the mussels to see if they were good. You should have strained that broth before you added it.

Put in the mussels. Cook until done. Serve piping hot in a well-warmed tureen.

N.B. Where is my left best glove? It is not possible that I lost it. I packed them both with the greatest of care. I remember distinctly. I was thinking how lovely it will be to wear them when we go to the opera again.

25 October 1817
Venice
Palazzo Flangini

The inevitable has happened. I have fallen in the canal. Fortunately, we were not in any great haste. I was able to return here to repair my appearance without discommoding anyone else. Now that it has happened (I felt sure it would ever since the first time Thomas mentioned the possibility), I can stop worrying about it. It was extremely nasty, and I wouldn't like to go through it again, but I seem not to have sustained any ill effects.

It happened, as so many of my mishaps do, in the pursuit of pleasure. Thomas and James were off to the embassy to see if we had received any mail, so Cecy and I were left to our own devices. Everyone tells us that the fortunes of Venice are in eclipse, that the ruin of the Republic, the ill will of Bonaparte, and the machinations of Prince Metternich have made the city a mere chattel of Austria forevermore. I am sure the people we speak with know precisely what they are saying. All the same, if this is La Serenissima in eclipse, I can only marvel at what the city must have been in her glory. What wonders must have been taken for granted, to make this place a mere shell, a shroud for the ruined beauty that remains.

Rushton may be flat, but flat has its advantages. I grew up under a marvelous sky. London was wonderful, but sometimes I missed the sky of Rushton. Venice is, in its way, a city as wonderful as London yet possessed of a sky to rival Rushton.

Its many little flights of steps deceive one into forgetting that Venice is built on the flat. Yet it is, and it is accordingly possessed of its own marvelous sky—pearly, at times opalescent.

How glorious is Man, that his works can result, in a mere

thousand years, in this remarkable mix of stone and water, where jewels are as common as glass and the glass itself resembles jewels.

It was glass that caused my downfall, the quest for Venetian glass. Cecy and I were bent on a shopping expedition. Cecy had a list. There are times when her resemblance to her father is startling. Cecy with a list can be utterly relentless.

Cecy's list took us (and our maids, of course) into many, many shops. In and out of the gondola, in and out. Custom made me careless. For once I did not slip, nor trip. I simply stepped where I thought the gondola was. And it wasn't. I went down feetfirst into the filthy water of the canal.

My skirts buoyed me up long enough for me to catch at the gondola's side. In temperature, the water of the canal was not much different from the pond at Rushton. Very different, alas, in smell.

Cecy, as usual, was aplomb itself. She and the gondolier hauled me in before I could do more than utter a stifled shriek.

Reardon helped me wring out my skirts, assuring me all the while that someday I may be able to wear that gown again.

We went directly back to our palazzo. Reardon may or may not be right about salvaging the gown. Meanwhile, I have bathed and changed. As soon as my hair is dry enough to be presentable, I will leave off this entry and go see what Cecy is doing.

Later

For once my clumsiness may have been a good thing. While I was whiling away the time it took to dry off by writing in my commonplace book, Cecy was left to her own devices in the palazzo. I suspect her of planning something in connection with the construction of her focus. No matter her reasons, she had just emerged from one of the disused rooms at the back of the house when she surprised an unfamiliar figure in the corridor. Not unreasonably, she improvised a weapon, I believe a pair of fireplace tongs, before she asked the intruder his business.

The intruder said, "What are you doing back so soon?" in Thomas's most curmudgeonly tones.

When Cecy described the scene to me, she sounded almost awed. "I knew it was Thomas. Even if he hadn't spoken, I would have known. He didn't look the least like himself, but I could tell it was him. I think I am making progress with my studies."

At the time, she looked Thomas square in the eye and told him I had fallen into the canal.

"Why didn't you say so?" said Thomas, most unreasonably, and came to me at once, plucking his false beard as he went.

Cecy, always considerate of the servants, returned the fireplace tongs to their rightful spot before she followed. This was perfect, as it gave me a moment to assure Thomas of my safety before she joined us.

When he was sure I was unharmed, Thomas indulged in

a bit of scolding. "I've seen you fall in the duck pond at St. James's Park. I've done all mortal man can do to keep you from falling in the English Channel. I bring you all the way to Venice and this is how you thank me? You fall into a canal behind my back? Kate, you are a monster of inconsideration."

"Yes, I know." I continued to towel my hair dry. "It won't happen again."

"See that it doesn't." Thomas went to his room to remove the last traces of his disguise.

Cecy told me all about her encounter with Thomas while I toasted myself dry beside the fire.

When he rejoined us, Thomas was properly dressed. Cecy started in with questions. Thomas ignored her while he selected the plumpest cushion. He dropped it at my feet and sat on it so that he could lean against my chair as he basked at the fireside. After a few moments he tilted his head back to look up at me pleadingly. "Make her stop, Kate."

It is a wife's duty to be honest to her husband. "I can't, dear. No one can. Unless James is back from the embassy?"

"Not yet, worse luck," said Thomas.

"Just tell us about it in your own time. That way, Cecy won't need to ask any more questions. Will you, Cecy?" I gave Cecy a pointed look.

Cecy's eyes widened. "Of course not."

"Of course not. Oh, very well." Thomas sighed. But once he'd given in, he gave us a full account. This is what Thomas told us:

"Eve-Marie shows no signs of leaving Venice. On the

contrary, she has kept regular hours since her arrival. Each day she leaves her lodging at midmorning and returns at midafternoon. She doesn't always go to the same place, but she is always gone at the same time."

"She gives the servants a chance to turn out her room," Cecy ventured.

Thomas quelled her with a look, or tried.

"That wasn't a question," Cecy countered, undaunted.

"She goes out for luncheon," I said. "What then?"

"Then nothing. But today I made it my business to be among the visitors to the hostelry between the time Eve-Marie left her chamber and the time she returned."

"You disguised yourself and went there by yourself to spy on Eve-Marie." Cecy was careful to keep her words a declarative sentence, but the accusation in her words was plain. "Without telling anyone."

"James knew. He insisted Piers accompany me. We debated telling you, and before you start, James wanted to tell you. I overruled him."

Cecy didn't have to speak. Her expression made her low opinion of this high-handedness all too clear.

"If we hadn't come home early and surprised you, would you have mentioned any of this?" I asked.

Something in my tone made Thomas turn hastily and take my hands in his. "Of course I would. As soon as James is back, we must have a full council of war. I'm not sure of the significance of what I learned and I don't know what to do next."

"What happened?" Cecy asked. "What did you learn?"

Thomas kissed my hand and let it go. "I left Piers outside and went in the servants' entrance. I took the precaution of casting a spell to make myself difficult to see."

"An invisibility spell?" Cecy looked intrigued.

Thomas answered Cecy as one enthusiast to another. "Not exactly. I've never encountered an invisibility spell that didn't carry the unfortunate side effect of temporary blindness."

"Oh, that sounds most unpleasant," Cecy said.

"It is, so don't let yourself be taken in by any promises of easy invisibility," Thomas cautioned. "I arranged matters so that I was difficult to look at directly. Someone might see me out of the corner of his eye, but he would look away and take no notice. It's less showy but easier to sustain."

"I'll remember," said Cecy.

"I'm sure you will. Remember to tread lightly, for anyone can hear you coming, even if they'd prefer not to see you." Thomas abandoned the magic lesson to return to his story. "I found my way to Eve-Marie's room by trial and error. I think you must be right about the housekeeping, Cecy, for that is certainly what was going on when I found it. When the room was finished and the servants had moved on, I went through Eve-Marie's things."

"The trunk!" Cecy and I said in unison.

"You searched the trunk?" I asked Thomas. "What did you find?"

Thomas had turned back to look up at me, eyes bright with mischief. "Nothing."

Before we could begin to pepper Thomas with our questions, James came into the room carrying a substantial parcel of mail.

"There you are," he said. "Our luck is in. The mail has come."

From the deposition of Mrs. James Tarleton, &c.

While Thomas brought James current on his disappointing adventure at Eve-Marie's hostelry, Kate and I fell upon the mail. There was an assortment of rather late congratulatory notes on our weddings that had been sent on from London, a brace of letters each for Thomas and James from various acquaintances, a small package from Paris for Kate, and letters for me from Papa, both my aunts, and Oliver.

Having distributed the bounty, we each took a comfortable chair and settled in to read. I turned to Papa's letter first, as I felt it was most likely to be of interest. I must confess that I also considered it likely to consume the greatest amount of time in deciphering, for in addition to the difficulties normally posed by his handwriting, the letter was unusually fat.

Upon unsealing the letter, I was slightly disappointed to discover that although it was indeed three pages, the second sheet comprised a list of names and directions, and the third was a general letter of introduction. I glanced quickly at the list, then proceeded to the first sheet in hopes of discovering what Papa meant by this unexpected response.

"Cecy?" James said a few moments later. "What do you find so compelling?"

"It's a letter from Papa," I replied. "Why?"

"Nothing much—only that I'd twice asked whether you would care to visit the Basilica San Marco without getting a response."

"It can't possibly live up to the Duomo in Milan," I said, "but at least it will be finished. I suppose that we ought not to slight it. When did you have in mind? Tomorrow morning?"

"I'll have to do some checking," James replied. "I believe the tides are such that the piazza is currently accessible only for a few hours a day, so a visit to the cathedral requires careful planning. Hence my question."

"Why would anyone build a cathedral they can't get to most of the time?" Kate asked.

"Oh, you could get to it when it was built," James said. "And you can still get to it any time you like, if you're willing to wade knee-deep. The weight of the cathedral and the plaza together have sunk the islet it's built on a few feet. Enough that when the tide is high, it makes for damp walking."

"I think we've had enough wading for today," Thomas said with a glance at Kate. "What did your father have to say, Cecy? Anything to the point?"

"As much to the point as Papa ever is," I said. "Which is

to say, there is a good deal of useless history about Sainte Chapelle and the Île de la Cité, but—" I stopped, frowning at the letter.

"What is it?" Kate and James said together.

"Papa mentions a monograph about the Île de la Cité, by one Monsieur Montier," I said. "And I have just remembered—when I met Theodore in Paris, he mentioned the same monograph. He said it was the only thing Mr. Strangle had given him that was worth reading. And ... no, let me just read you what Papa says."

This suggestion proved acceptable to everyone, so I began.

"My dearest Cecy:

"Having received your letter from Paris, I am delighted with your report of the Temple of Minerva Victrix, which was all I could have hoped for and more. I am of course pleased by your great happiness, and pleased as well to have acquired so estimable a son-at-law as Mr. Tarleton, for it is to his benign influence that I must attribute your newly acquired interest in history, though it is clear from what your Aunt Elizabeth says of her correspondence with you that you have not lost your taste for Society in the process. I therefore trust hopefully in your husband's full and complete recovery by this time from the unfortunate indisposition you described, as well as in the entire likelihood of the remainder of your journey being without similar incident, highwaymen not being of such common occurrence even on the Continent as to trouble you twice.

"I entirely comprehend your frustration at the closure of Sainte Chapelle, which prevented your viewing it, but you need not repine too greatly. Though the chapel and the stained glass are reported very fine, they are relatively modern, dating only from the thirteenth century. It is the location itself that is ancient, having been the sacred site not only of the Frankish kings, but of the tribal chieftains of the Gauls before Rome conquered them, and possibly even of prehistorical barbarians, though the earliest traces have naturally been obliterated by the constant passage of the later occupants, so that the truth or falsehood of the matter must necessarily remain speculative.

"Monsieur Montier, in his otherwise enlightening and informative monograph on the subject, places great emphasis on the continuous nature of the site's occupation; too much, I feel, to support the weight of his argument. His remarks on the ceremonies of the Gauls, the Romans, and the early Franks are comprehensive and, so far as I can determine, accurate, but his contention that the Bourbons lost the throne of France due to their neglect of the preeminent importance of the Île de la Cité and

Sainte Chapelle in creating them true kings is, of course, nonsense. Such rituals may, perhaps, be enhanced and strengthened by being performed at a particular location, in the event there is some question as to the legitimacy of the claimant to the throne, but no such question has ever arisen about the rulers of France.

"Prehistory and superstition aside, however, there is no question that the Île de la Cité is an ancient and sacred royal area, and it is a pity you could not have visited it. By this time, however, you will no doubt have seen even more ancient and wonderful places. How I envy you! The crypts in the monastery at the pass of Great Saint Bernard, the ruined baths in Westphalia, the shrine of Jupiter Optimus Maximus, the temples of the Forum in Rome!

"I can tell from the tenor of your questions that such background as I can provide, being little and, by virtue of the distance these missives must travel, too late to give timely enlightenment, will very likely be unsatisfactory. I must therefore refer you to others, should you have additional queries to which you require prompt attention. As you must be all too well aware, I have maintained a regular correspondence with a number of like-minded colleagues in France and elsewhere, a list of whom I enclose, along with a suitable letter of introduction, in hopes that no matter where this letter finds you, you may discover a useful source of information and intelligent discourse nearby. I regret exceedingly that I did not think to suggest it before you left England, but perhaps this tardy amends will serve the purpose.

"Your affectionate Father."

When I finished reading the letter, there was a moment's silence. "He does have a fondness for flowing periods," Thomas commented at last.

"Are any of his correspondents close to Venice?" James asked. "I can think of several queries I'd like to put to one of them."

I looked at the list, blinked, and went over it again more slowly. I had indeed been well aware of Papa's voluminous correspondence with other antiquaries, but I had had no idea that Papa included two royal dukes (one of France, one of Austria) and a double handful of lesser nobility among his fusty colleagues. "Yes, there's a gentleman living just off the Rio San Giacomo Dell'Orio, one Cavalier Coducci."

"Never heard of him," Thomas said.

"I have," said James, to my surprise. "He's been a well-known expert in classical Rome for years. He must be getting on a bit."

"Then we'd best arrange to meet with him soon," Thomas said, peering over my shoulder at the letter of introduction Papa had sent.

"*All* of us," Kate said firmly.

Thomas looked wounded. "Would I even consider anything else?"

"Yes," Kate and James said together.

Thomas looked even more put out, but he did not argue. He did, however, leave the business of arranging our visit rather pointedly in James's hands.

Unfortunately, Cavalier Coducci was not currently in town, but his *maggiordomo* informed us that he would return any day. James rolled his eyes at this, and muttered something about the Italian sense of time. As there was nothing we could do to hurry Cavalier Coducci's return, James and Thomas went back to occasionally watching Eve-Marie, Kate and Reardon searched booksellers and libraries for a copy of Monsieur Montier's monograph, and I set about creating a focus for my magic.

I had been thinking about what to use for some time. At first I had planned on some piece of jewelry, but I soon saw that it would not do. For unless I chose some bit of mere trumpery, I would not wish to smash it if ever I decided to change my focus, and it would quickly become obvious to anyone if I wore the same cheap ring or brooch with everything (besides which, it is quite impossible to find *one* piece of jewelry that is suitable with *everything* one wishes to wear). On the other hand, I did not wish to have to pack something as bulky and inconvenient as Thomas's chocolate pot everywhere I went.

When we reached Venice, however, I found what

seemed the perfect solution. Venetian glass is quite lovely, and among the many unusual things they make from it are intricate paperweights of solid glass with colored patterns inside. Being made of glass, they are quite smashable; being solid, they are not at all easy to smash by accident. (I spent an afternoon experimenting with several samples that I had purchased while Kate and I were out shopping. I confess that I had a hard time forcing myself to destroy such lovely things, for although I had looked for the ugliest ones on purpose, I had been unable to find any that fit such a description.) The smallest of the paperweights fits quite comfortably in the palm of my hand, making it a convenient size for carrying in a reticule.

Having chosen an object for my focus and gathered the necessary ingredients for the spell, all that remained was to find a quiet time and place for the ritual. This was not as difficult as I had anticipated. I simply stayed behind one afternoon when Kate and Reardon went on their search, and sent Walker off in search of some embroidery silks. This left me with most of the palazzo to myself, as Italian servants are mostly inactive in the afternoon.

I read through Lady Sylvia's directions twice, to make certain I had committed them to memory, and also reviewed the incantations (though I had memorized them weeks before, with James's help). I closed the door of the sitting room and cleared all the miscellaneous objects—the candlesticks, my embroidery, Kate's inkwell, a penknife that someone, probably Thomas, had left lying near—into drawers or cupboards, and pulled the little writing desk I had been using for my sewing into the middle of the room. I set the basin in the center of the desk, with my chosen paperweight beside it and the candles, salt, water, and feather near to hand.

I took a deep breath and began the ritual. It is curious how sweeping out a room, which is the most ordinary of activities, becomes a matter of magic requiring serious concentration simply by virtue of muttering the proper Latin while doing it. Having cleaned the room, I laid a ring of salt on the desktop, enclosing the basin. I was *extremely* careful to be sure the ring was unbroken, and I was equally careful about positioning the candles along its edge, alternating one inside the ring and one outside it, so that I did not brush the salt out of line in the process.

Still chanting, I reached between the candles and placed the paperweight inside the basin. Then I lit the candles, working clockwise. As I did, I felt magic gathering around me. Carefully, I reached between the burning candles to pour water into the basin, to wash both my hands and the paperweight. The magic swirled through the air around me, then flowed along my arms like the water, into the circle and the basin.

When I could no longer feel magic anywhere outside the circle of salt, I picked up the feather and held it over the basin. "Candles, salt, water, feather," I said in Latin. "Fire, earth, water, air, be a binding link between me and this object. *Fiat, fiat, voluntas mea.*"

As I spoke, I felt the magic within the circle swirl and

intensify. Then, with my final words, it surged downward and outward at the same time. Suddenly everything seemed clearer, sharper, and more distinct, the way it sometimes does when the wind unexpectedly clears a smoky haze that one had not realized was there.

And then the writing desk exploded.

From the commonplace book of Lady Schofield

> *27 October 1817*
> *Venice*
> *Palazzo Flangini*

When catastrophe strikes, in the domestic sphere at least, it leaves behind a curious hush, a silence different from all other silences. That silence is no mere absence of sound. It is the hush that results when enormity sinks in.

This afternoon Reardon and I returned from our search for the Montier monograph to find the palazzo entirely silent. Not a servant was stirring. Reardon and I noticed the phenomenon at the same time. She and I looked at each other askance for a moment, but, really, we were listening. An unnatural silence held, precisely the sort of thunderous silence I know so well from Aunt Charlotte's lectures. I would not have thought it possible the effect could be so marked in an edifice (for call it a *house* I simply cannot) the size of the palazzo.

"I'll find out what has happened." Reardon helped me out of my muddy shoes and into a pair of dry slippers. "If you can manage, my lady?"

"Of course, of course." I sent Reardon on her way and went to the chamber we had been using as a sitting room. To my consternation, the door was closed and locked. I put my ear to the panel but could hear nothing. Then, when I held my breath to be sure, I thought I heard the rustle of fabric. I knocked on the door. "It's Kate," I said, quite unnecessarily. "Do let me in."

After an unintelligible grumble in Thomas's distinctive voice, the door opened. Thomas stood in the doorway, arms spread wide so I could not enter. The look in his eyes was pure relief. "Thank God you're back. Don't come in." With his neckcloth disarranged and his hair untidy, Thomas looked somewhat harried, but otherwise much as usual.

"Are you all right?" I looked past him into the room. "What on *earth*—" The pictures on the walls were intact, and the great windows looking out on the Grand Canal were undamaged. Everything else in the room looked as if a giant had come by and stirred it with a spoon.

"I'm not finished yet," said Thomas hurriedly. "I'll come out as soon as I can." Before I could ask my first question, he held up a hand to stop me. "Cecy has had a little mishap, that's all. James is with her now. We've sent for a physician, just to be perfectly sure she's all right."

I clutched at Thomas's lapels. "*Cecy!* What's happened to Cecy?"

"Don't be alarmed. It's all right. I promise." Thomas put his arms around me. "Cecy would be the first to reassure you. She's fine."

"Oh, Thomas. You know Cecy. She would claim to be fine if both her legs were cut off."

Thomas had the gall to chuckle. "Very true. But I promise you, she *is* fine. Truly. These things happen. Occasionally."

I looked back at the wreckage of the sitting room. "They do?"

"They do when you don't take pains to ground your focus spell." Thomas tightened his embrace. "Kate, you don't fancy yourself a magician, do you? You'd never try something like this on your own? You'd tell me if you were planning to, wouldn't you?"

I gave Thomas an impatient shake. "Are you mad? Of course not. I don't know anything about magic. Why would I try to perform any?"

Thomas gave me a small shake back, more gentle yet far more effective. "Promise me you'll never try anything like this."

"I promise. Anything like what? What did Cecy *do*?" Reluctantly, I turned my full attention from the expression in Thomas's eyes to the destruction in the room beyond.

"She created her focus. Unfortunately, there were one or two problems with the parameters, so the magic didn't enter the focus she'd chosen." Thomas looked distinctly grim. "Fortunately, her magic destroyed the object it entered into inadvertently. Just as well, because I don't think even Cecy could explain away taking a writing desk with her everywhere she went."

"A desk?" I looked around again. The gilt-legged, marble-topped writing desk I remembered was gone. Thomas had been sweeping something that looked remarkably like a heap of gold dust, or possibly sand, into a tidy heap on a sheet of newspaper.

"I've been cleansing the room and gathering the magical residue. The lion's share of it is back with Cecy again," Thomas explained. "But I'm taking no chances."

"Residue?" I echoed weakly, looking at the heap of golden dust.

"That's why you can't come in. No one can."

I regarded first the room and then Thomas with great misgiving. "Why? What happens when you have magical residue?"

"I don't intend to find out. But at the very least, no games of chance should be played in this room for the foreseeable future." Thomas added wryly, "I think the laws of probability may be on holiday at the moment."

I gazed at the heap of dust. Really, it looked much more like housekeeping than it did like magic. "What will you do with it?"

"I'll remove as much of the magic as I can before I clear up the residue. Get as much of it back to Cecy as possible."

"How long will it take you to do that?" I asked.

"I'm not entirely sure. Things are greatly improved

since James and I returned, but there are still traces of the ritual to be cleared away." Thomas took another look at me. "Why don't you go change out of that very muddy gown? I'll join you as soon as I can."

"You must on no condition hurry," I countered. "I'll just go see if Cecy needs anything."

"Don't look so stricken," Thomas said. "If nothing else, one good thing has come out of this."

"Oh?" I gazed at the ruin of the once lovely room and tried to think of a single good thing about it.

"Now that she knows firsthand that there's more to focusing one's magic than meets the eye, Cecy can never again make slighting remarks about my chocolate pot." With that, Thomas kissed me, locked himself in the sitting room and, I surmised from the muffled sounds I heard through the door, went back to work.

At Cecy's door, I met Walker coming out with a tray. Upon it she carried a decanter of brandy and a pair of empty glasses. Apparently James and Thomas subscribe to similar beliefs concerning the medicinal powers of strong drink. "May I see Mrs. Tarleton?" I asked Walker softly.

Before she could answer, Cecy's clear voice came from her room. "Oh, Kate! You're back. Come in!"

I entered the bedchamber to find Cecy reclining on the grand gilt bed, with James in attendance. Cecy looked at least as healthy as James. In fact, the pair of them shared a certain high color. I wondered if brandy alone were responsible.

"Cecy, are you all right?"

"I'm fine," Cecy assured me, "only I must perform the ritual again. I was particularly careful about the parameters, no matter what Thomas thinks."

"I'm quite sure you were," I said. "James, is she really all right?"

"We'll let the physician have the last word on that subject," said James.

At precisely the same time, Cecy said, "I'm fine."

"She seems fine," James conceded. He made a minute adjustment to the shawl around Cecy's shoulders, and I thought I detected a faint tremor in his hands. I felt a rush of gratitude toward him for taking good care of Cecy.

"Thank heavens for that." I found a chair and sank into it. "What precisely have you done, Cecy? The sitting room looks as though you'd been at it with a sledgehammer."

"I was creating a focus for my magic." Cecy sat up straighter, her eyes bright with enthusiasm. "Only there seemed to be quite a lot more magic than I expected. It was so unfortunate, for in the moment before the magic destroyed the desk, I was truly *focused*. I've never experienced anything quite like it. Oh, Kate, it was simply *splendid*."

I remembered helping Thomas to create his focus. Splendid was not too strong a word, I judged from his reactions at the time.

"It was rash," stated James. "You could have been seriously hurt, perhaps even killed."

"But I wasn't." Cecy's happiness dimmed for a moment.

"I'm sorry about the writing desk. Although it was quite spectacular to see the marble dissolve as if it were made of sand. Golden sand, when the gilt mixed in. I suppose we will have to find a replacement for it, or pay damages."

"Worth every penny," said James.

"Do let me conduct the ritual again before we try to replace any of the damaged furniture," said Cecy. "I believe it might help to perform the spell in an empty room. Easier to sweep, for one thing."

The physician arrived before Cecy could persuade James that she should conduct the ritual again. At Cecy's request, I remained, but the examination did not take long. I could see why the physician was considered a favorite among the English visitors to Venice, for his manners were even more excellent than his English.

"A light diet and no excitement," was his recommendation. "Mrs. Tarleton will not leave her room for a day or two. When she does, she must take only mild exercise for another day or two. Then, if there is no relapse, she may resume her ordinary routine."

"But I'm fine," Cecy declared, for approximately the one hundredth time.

"Of course you are," agreed the physician. "But for now you will humor those who love you and rest."

"Oh, very well." Cecy looked up at James. "You'll stay, won't you?"

James agreed very readily to stay with her, and the

physician and I left them in peace, with Walker to see to anything they needed.

When I had seen the physician on his way, I went back to the sitting room. Thomas was still not finished there. I did not wish to distract him, so I came back here to our chamber to write this.

Cecy does seem to be largely unharmed by her experience. I know Thomas has a great deal of experience in dealing with spells that refuse to be cast as they should. But when I think of the remains of that writing desk, reduced to a few pounds of dust upon a sheet of newspaper, it makes me wonder what else might have gone wrong. What a good thing it is Cecy who has the aptitude for magic and the interest to gain the skill to use it. If it were me, I might have blown myself to atoms by now.

28 October 1817
Venice
Palazzo Flangini

Among the many letters and packages that we have received since our arrival here in Venice was a parcel for me from Lady Sylvia. Most mysteriously, the parcel contained no letter, not even a note. I can think of no particular reason for Lady Sylvia to send me a gift, but only she would have chosen something so perfect. It is a shawl. At first I thought there must be some message either embroidered or woven into the very fabric, but I can detect none. It is made of soft wool, not too heavy, the very thing for these cooler days, and it is a most pleasing shade of pink. I love it immoderately. I'm only sorry the note that she must have sent with it has been lost, but I have already posted my letter of thanks.

29 October 1817
Venice
Palazzo Flangini

The mystery of the vanishing gloves has been solved. I don't know what is to be done about it, but at least I know I have not been imagining things.

Chilly as the city can be at this season, Venice is not without beauty. I find it remarkable that I am beginning to feel accustomed to living in such grandeur, where the streets are, for all intents and purposes, liquid. Thomas and I were out admiring the splendor of it all, eating roasted chestnuts Thomas bought from a vendor as if we knew no better than to eat in public. Thomas peeled mine for me, a childish bit of chivalry I found absurdly touching.

"I'll let you," I told him, "because if anything happens to this pair of gloves, Reardon will be so cross." I was joking. It is true that I have only two good pairs left, but Reardon would never be really cross with me about it. I find her

tranquil acceptance of my wretched clumsiness quite soothing. She has a remarkable way with mud stains, too.

"You tremble in your boots at the prospect, I see."
Thomas handed me a peeled chestnut and started on one for
himself. "There's a simple solution. Order more gloves."

"You are a good, kind husband," I said.

Thomas looked very pleased with himself. "I know."

"But shouldn't there be some sort of mathematical limit
to the number of gloves I can lose? Some upper theoretical
boundary? Given the laws of probability?"

Thomas ate his chestnut and started to peel me another.
"They make excellent gloves here. If by some wild chance
you are asking me for my opinion, I say, order more and
perhaps we'll find the sum of an infinite series."

I looked deep into Thomas's eyes. Very wonderful eyes
he has. Sometimes, when the light is at a particular angle,
they are the exact color of brandy. That particular gray October day, they were merely brown. But to me they looked
wonderful just the same. "I don't deserve you."

Thomas beamed at me. "Ah, that's where you're wrong.
You do." He broke off, but the emotion in his words was still
there in the silence.

After a moment he changed the subject by offering me
the latest in peeled chestnuts. The mood dissipated. Yet
when we moved on, I might as well have been floating in
the air.

Perfect happiness is good for one's soul. It is wonderful

for one's temper. However, in my experience, it tends to impair one's wits.

On my return to the palazzo, I floated into my bedchamber with a smile on my face and not a thought in my head. Only the talk I'd had with Thomas made me look twice at Reardon, who seemed to be doing something to the fire in the hearth.

"The glover will be sending another dozen pairs." With care, I removed the as-yet-unstained gloves I was wearing. "Thomas wanted me to order even more. What do you think? Will a dozen be enough?"

I looked up from fussing with my gloves. Reardon was standing at attention before the fireplace, her hands behind her back. Her eyes were fixed on a point some six inches over my head. To judge by her expression, I might have been a firing squad, so grim she looked.

"Is something wrong, Reardon?" It was the happiness still clouding my wits that made me ask the question. The meanest intelligence could tell something was wrong. Something was very wrong. "Are you all right?"

Reardon gave a despairing sigh. "Oh, Lady Schofield, please don't turn me off here in Venice. I shall never get home to Stroud from here."

I could only stare. "Why on earth would I turn you off?"

"I haven't been stealing your gloves," Reardon declared, but when she brought her hands from behind her back, I saw that she held one of my gloves. Mrs. Siddons in character as

Lady Macbeth could have regarded her hands with no more horror. "I *swear* it."

Every tenet of Aunt Charlotte's I'd ever heard concerning the proper approach to tyrannizing one's servants came crashing back to me. I ignored them all. "Who said you have?"

"You." Reardon was having a hard time keeping her voice steady. "You ordered more gloves. You asked me if I thought a dozen pairs would be enough."

"I didn't mean that. It was just a question. You know how often I lose a glove."

"I wouldn't steal." Reardon had her firing-squad expression back.

"Of course you wouldn't. My gloves haven't been stolen. I just lose them. Usually the left. No one steals just one glove. They steal the pair." I saw I was making no headway against Reardon's obvious distress and tried another tack. "I've been losing things for years. I drop things, too. What is there in that to trouble you so?"

Reardon looked as if she might be ill. "I haven't been stealing them. I have been burning them." She offered me the glove she held. It was a left.

Alerted by the intensity of her regard, I examined the glove as Reardon looked on. Almost unstained but sadly crumpled, the glove was undoubtedly one of mine. But there was an area of faint discoloration at the base of the ring finger, as if I'd spilt tea on it. I smoothed the soft leather between my fingers as I looked at it more closely. The stain was visible on both sides of the glove. I turned the glove inside out and saw that the discoloration was even darker within. "What on earth is that?"

Reardon looked grimmer than ever. "Some of the gloves, the ring finger was all but burnt off inside. I couldn't risk throwing the glove away. What if a stranger noticed? I had to burn it."

I tugged at the finger of the glove. With only the slightest resistance, it came away. I felt a twist of sympathy for it, poor mangled thing. "Why did you never tell me?"

"I thought you didn't care." Reardon met my eyes and her own rounded with astonishment. "You mean you didn't *know*?"

"No, of course I didn't know. I still don't—" I broke off, because I had a sudden very good notion I *did* know. This was my wedding ring at work. I have been losing things for years, but never had I lost one thing more than another. Never had I lost anything with such frequency as I had lost gloves since Thomas focused his magic.

"Is that what happened to my good long gloves?" I gazed searchingly at Reardon. "The pair I wore to the opera?"

Reardon nodded.

I felt my heart sink a little, but reminded myself that gloves could be replaced. There were more important things to worry about. "Is there anything else you've noticed? Anything odd?"

"About your wardrobe?" Reardon looked thoughtful. "You know the pearl eardrops don't like it if they can't see each other?"

"Er, yes. I know about those," I said. "Anything else?"

"There's something a bit strange about that pink shawl," Reardon said. "Nothing sinister. Just—it's been charmed somehow."

"Has it?" I thought that over. "How do you know? Are you a magician?"

Reardon almost smiled. "Not I, my lady. But I have picked up a bit of knowledge here and there. I know the signs."

"Well, bring Lady Sylvia's shawl along. I want to see what Cecy makes of it."

"Mrs. Tarleton?" Reardon looked surprised. "Not Lord Schofield?"

"No, not Thomas. Not yet. He and Mr. Tarleton are paying a call at the moment. We'll discuss it with them when they return. For now, you and I will have a discussion with Cecy."

Cecy, despite her frequent claims of perfect health, was still confined to her room, although she was up and dressed. She had a writing desk placed to get the best light from the windows. Enough correspondence for our entire journey was being written during her enforced rest. Venice is as renowned for its stationers as it is for its glovers. She was alone except for Walker, who was sitting by the fire, doing something deft to the trim on a pelisse of Cecy's.

"Cecy, I'm sorry to interrupt, but I need to show you something. I've found out why I'm always losing gloves." I put the pieces of my poor maimed glove down on the blotter before her.

"Have you?" Cecy looked up from the letter she was writing. "I always knew there was something peculiar about that talent of yours."

I felt a surge of embarrassment. "It's hardly a talent. In any case, Lady Sylvia gave me that test with her tea tray last summer. If I had any magical aptitude to speak of, I'm sure she would have mentioned it."

Cecy sanded her letter with great attention to detail. Without taking her eyes off the letter, she asked, "Are you?"

Embarrassment yielded to impatience. "Am I what?"

"Are you quite sure she would have mentioned it? Because I'm not." Cecy's expression, when she finally looked up at me, was grave. "Lady Sylvia knows a lot about teaching magic."

I caught myself frowning at my cousin. Quite silly of me, for there was no reason for me to be out of patience with her. "Anything Lady Sylvia knows about me, Thomas knows, too. He would tell me."

Cecy didn't answer immediately. All her attention was focused on the glove I'd given her.

"He would," I said. "Thomas would tell me anything I ought to know."

"Yes, of course he would." If I hadn't known better, I would have said Cecy was humoring me. She studied the glove in minute detail.

I waited as long as I could before demanding, "What do you think?"

Cecy pointed to the detached finger of the glove. I could almost see her choose her words. "I think *that* explains Thomas's reaction to the highwaymen."

I kept my tone brisk and businesslike. "Exactly."

For a moment, Cecy looked quite fierce. Then she seemed to relent. "Cockle-headed," she said, half to herself, and I knew she was referring to Thomas.

"Reardon has been disposing of the damaged gloves for me." I considered it wiser to return to the subject at hand than to dwell on the incident of James's shooting. "I should have noticed much sooner. It was always the left glove. I used to lose both with equal regularity."

Cecy said, "It's a great pity you lost so many gloves, but it is certainly fortunate that Reardon took proper care of them for you." To Walker, Cecy said, "Will you be so good as to take Reardon with you to purchase those skeins of yarn we discussed? Thank you."

I felt a moment's surprise at the non sequitur, but a glance from Cecy explained much. It was one thing for me to trust the nature of Thomas's focus to Cecy. Better not to risk Reardon or Walker knowing any more about the matter than they already did. "Yes, by all means. Thank you, Reardon."

When we were quite certain we were alone, Cecy spoke softly. "Thomas didn't tell you anything about this?"

"I don't think he knows," I said. "What causes the stain? It looks as if I burned it, but I didn't."

Cecy was very grave. "Let me see the ring. No, don't take it off. Just let me look at it."

After a full minute of careful scrutiny, Cecy released my hand. "Thomas focused his magic in the ring."

"I know that," I reminded her.

Undisturbed by my interruption, Cecy continued. "One's magical focus does not work precisely the way a pair of spectacles works, but it is not at all a bad analogy. One can perform magic without one's focus nearby, but it is all a great deal more comfortable if one has it at hand."

I was starting to feel impatient again. "I know that, too."

"When Thomas uses his focus, do you feel it?" Cecy asked.

"No." I hesitated. "That is, I don't think so."

"Kate." Cecy regarded me with something like reproach. "*Tell* me."

I spoke haltingly at first, but soon the words were tumbling out. I told Cecy about the sense of shared experience I felt when Thomas created the focus. I told her how sick I'd felt in the carriage at the start of the highway robbery. I told her everything I could think of.

When I finished, Cecy studied my glove again. "If you took the ring off, Thomas could still use it as his focus, and I am sure your gloves would go undamaged."

"Very possibly," I replied. "I don't care about gloves. I'm not taking this ring off."

"That's the only solution to *this* problem I can think of," said Cecy. Before I could protest, she forestalled me. "But I'm much more interested in another problem that we don't have enough information to solve. If Lady Sylvia were here, we could simply ask her about the results of your magical aptitude test. As it is . . ." Cecy let her words trail off.

"As it is, I must ask Thomas."

"Yes, you must." Cecy was firm as only Cecy can be.

I took back my glove and remembered Lady Sylvia's shawl. Reardon had left it on my chair. I handed it to Cecy with care. "There's this, too."

"Your new shawl?" Cecy fingered the soft fabric. "Lovely."

"Reardon says it has a charm on it."

Cecy's interest sharpened. "Oh, does she?" After another close inspection had been carried out, Cecy looked up, obviously speculating. "She's right. Does Reardon have magical training as well as expertise in hairdressing and classical antiquity?"

"I don't think so. She says she doesn't. But she recognized there was a charm on my pearl eardrops. Whatever her educational background, I do trust her."

"Very well. Are you quite certain this shawl came from Lady Sylvia?"

"Am I—? The parcel came from Paris. The color is perfect. I thought—" I broke off, bewildered. "If it wasn't Lady Sylvia, who sent it?"

Cecy smoothed the soft fabric on her lap. "Thomas may be able to get more from this than I can. I don't think it is a malicious charm of any kind. It's wholesome enough." She paused for a moment, her entire attention focused on the shawl. "It's a bit . . . stern," she said at last. "It's for . . . truth. I think it has something to do with seeing things as they truly are. Not letting the vain and worldly people of Society turn one's head."

"How odd." I took the shawl back and held it at arm's length. "If it is Lady Sylvia's doing, Thomas will recognize the charm, won't he?"

"I should think so," said Cecy. "But in the meantime, be careful."

Thomas had his chance to inspect the pink shawl that night after dinner. With Reardon standing vigilantly near us in case of an emergency, he sat with me by the fire in our bedchamber and examined every thread of the shawl.

"Cecy was right," he said at last. "Nothing to do with Mother. Are you sure it came from Paris?"

"It certainly looked as if it did. I wish I'd saved the wrapping paper it came in, but it went to kindle the fire." I ran a cautious finger along the edge of the fabric. "What sort of charm is it?"

Thomas looked disgruntled. "It's a protective charm, the sort of thing one might use to protect the simplicity of the young."

"Cecy said it had to do with truth. Seeing things as they are."

"Yes, that's right. And that makes no sense whatever. Who would bother to send you an anonymous parcel containing a gift meant to protect you from the cheats and liars of this world?"

"There must be more to it," I said. "Perhaps the protective spell is concealing something else?"

"I suppose anything is possible." Thomas picked the shawl up and handed it to Reardon as if it smelt bad. "Keep that somewhere safe, please. I don't want to destroy it just yet. There's a chance it might prove useful, if we once find out who sent it and why."

"I'll put it away," said Reardon.

When she had left us alone, I handed my damaged glove over and made a full confession to Thomas, up to and including the fact that Cecy now knew about his focus.

"It can't be helped," said Thomas. "She's never going to forgive me for contriving to get James shot, is she?"

"Never," I was forced to agree. "But as matters stand, I think she's willing to overlook it for now."

Thomas sighed a little. "That's lucky, I suppose. I'll just

have to make it up to her somehow. And to James, of course," Thomas added, plainly as an afterthought.

"Is it something I'm doing?" I asked. "Is there something about the focus that I'm not doing properly?"

Thomas traced the burnt mark in the leather. "I need to do a bit of research first, but I think there's a spell that will put a stop to this. It should be quite straightforward. Still, I'm taking no chances. It's nothing you are doing or not doing, Kate. Just double that order of gloves and soldier on."

I fixed Thomas with my best glare. "You aren't going to tell me, are you?"

Thomas winced but said nothing.

I kept up the glare. "Just as you never told me the result of the test Lady Sylvia gave me. But you would tell me, wouldn't you, if it were something important?"

I saw the exact moment Thomas surrendered. His eyes dropped and he took my hand. "Kate——"

I waited for him to go on. Patience was easy now that I knew he saw things from my point of view.

"There are two things you must understand. The first is that talent runs in families," Thomas said, meeting my eyes again at last. "You know that."

I nodded.

Thomas chose his words with evident care. "It's like blood horses. Sometimes a horse can win a dozen races and sire a dozen runners that win high stakes in their turn. But

sometimes the speed doesn't come out in the next generation. Sometimes it waits for the generation after that."

"Like Eclipse," I said. "His sire, Marske, was nothing
like as fast as he was."

Thomas stared at me.

"Grandfather's library was my favorite spot on rainy
days," I explained. "He had every volume of the Stud
Book."

"Of course he did," said Thomas dryly. "I might have
known he would."

"Yes, he did far better gambling at the racetrack than he
ever did at the tables. So you believe that our children will
inherit talent from both sides of the family," I said. I have
given our children a great deal of thought, at least the idea
of our children, but this aspect of the situation had never occurred to me.

"That may well be, but I—"

Much struck by this novel idea, I didn't let Thomas finish. "I suppose we must take great pains to engage a nurse
who is prepared for such an eventuality."

"Excellent notion," said Thomas, "but that's not—"

"I'd better mention it to James and Cecy, too," I went
on. "Only think what their nursery will be like."

"I'd rather not," said Thomas. "Do come back to race-
horses, Kate, just for a moment. What I'm trying to say is,
sometimes the speed doesn't show at first."

"Eclipse was never trained at all until he was five," I

said, "but I don't believe it was because they didn't think he was fast."

"I take it back," said Thomas. "Forget Eclipse. Forget horses. What I'm trying to tell you is that we don't know whether your talent has fully developed yet or not."

"But I don't have any talent," I reminded him.

"You don't have any interest in cultivating your talent," Thomas countered. "That's a different matter, and one Mother and I have tried quite hard to leave in your hands. But talent runs in your family."

"Perhaps," I said, "but it doesn't run in me."

"Talent without cultivation is useless. It is without form and void. There is no pattern to it. Like the spark one sometimes strikes, sometimes not, when one touches a metal doorknob after walking on a wool carpet." Thomas took my hand. At the gentle concern in his expression, I felt a rising tide of dismay.

"It can be a great inconvenience." Thomas's voice was hushed, as if he were delivering very bad news indeed. "Like spilling things."

"That's my talent?" I cried, pulling away. *"Clumsiness?"*

"That can be a sign you *have* talent," Thomas answered. "It isn't the talent itself. But it's a good sign."

"Good?" I regarded Thomas with something near dislike. "What's good about it?"

"Bouncers, Kate." Thomas reminded me. "You are able to make people accept some of the remarkable things you say as truth, in defiance of all laws of probability and common sense."

"I do lie rather well," I conceded.

"I regret to inform you that you're nothing out of the ordinary as a storyteller," Thomas stated. "But you have a useful way of winning the confidence of those who listen to you. You make them willing to believe you."

"Lying? I have a talent for falsehood?" I was good at being clumsy and at telling lies. Things grew worse and worse. No wonder Lady Sylvia kept it from me.

Thomas tugged at his neckcloth. "Forget your talent. I'm sorry I ever mentioned it. I'm trying to say that it is too soon to be sure of anything concerning your talent, and we'll *never* know if you don't cultivate it. Neglected talent can cause strange things to happen. What you call your clumsiness may very well have such an explanation. Now, for the second thing."

I had almost forgotten there was a second thing. "There's more?"

Thomas patted my hand. "Don't look so stricken. It isn't you. It's me. And I think it explains what happens with your ring."

"It's you?"

Thomas nodded. "I think so. You see, there is a connection between us. On all sorts of levels. But in this case, it is a dangerous one. You remember Sir Hilary and his epicyclical elaborations?"

I remembered what Cecy had told me of Sir Hilary's attempts (some successful) to drain others of their magical ability to enhance his own power. "Yes."

Thomas had gone very gentle again. "It is possible for a magician to use power that belongs to someone else. Whether you choose to use it or not, Kate, you have power. With the connection that exists between us, it would be perilously easy for me to draw on your power as well as my own. I never want that to happen. I have taken steps to prevent that from happening. But I think there must be times when my magic strikes a kind of spark with your inborn talent. It is my hypothesis that one outward sign of such an occasion is the scorching and discoloration you've detected."

I tried to rephrase what he was telling me. "You use your focus and it burns my glove. So were you using magic at the opera?"

"Nothing was further from my mind. It is not necessarily when I am using my magic. It is when my power meets yours. Think of a duck pond. Toss a stone into it and what do you get?"

"A wet stone," I replied promptly.

Thomas scowled at me. "Oh, very droll. You get a wet stone and you get ripples, Kate. Concentric rings as the ripples move outward from the stone. Now, then. What do you get when you toss in two stones at the same time?"

"More ripples?"

Thomas looked delighted. "Exactly. Two sets of concentric rings—where my set of ripples meets your set of ripples is the point—in my hypothesis, at least—where your glove comes into it."

I searched for words. At last, I managed, "Why can't I feel it, then? I felt it when you created the focus. I felt it when you were sick in the coach. Why don't I feel it when the ring burns my glove?"

Thomas took my hand. "I don't know. Perhaps because it happens when we cancel one another out? I'm glad you don't feel it, though. What if it caused you pain?" He traced the shape of our wedding band with the tip of his finger.

We sat together in silence for a long time. The only sound in the room was the fire in the hearth.

Eventually I brought my thoughts back to the subject. "If being clumsy is a sign of magical potential, why wasn't Cecy ever clumsy? What about you? How did your talent manifest itself?"

"I believed I could fly." Thomas looked embarrassed. "Fortunately, I had an extremely vigilant nurse. Beyond the very minimum of broken bones, there was no harm done. But it wasn't clumsiness that broke my leg. It was over-weening pride."

His humble expression was so out of character it was all I could do not to laugh aloud. "You, Thomas? Proud? Never!"

"It's still a failing of mine," Thomas confessed. "It comes on me sometimes." He looked deep into my eyes.

"Does it?" I was ready for Thomas to make a joke of it, the way he stared at me so intently.

"Just now and then. When I think of you." There was not a trace of mockery in Thomas's eyes, and his voice grew just a little ragged. "You make me proud."

30 October 1817
Venice
Palazzo Flangini

What a relief to be safely back home at our hired edifice. I have just changed into dry clothes. By the time I finish roasting my toes by the fire, I may feel comfortable again. By that time, however, dinner will surely be served, so I will catch up writing this journal in the interim, and wriggle my toes luxuriously between paragraphs.

The use of Uncle Arthur's name during James's unsuccessful call upon Cavalier Leo Coducci has borne fruit, for we received a formal invitation to visit Mr. Coducci this afternoon, only a day after his return to Venice. The rain has been relentless, but we splashed our way there with great promptitude.

Mr. Coducci received us in a grand salon that gave the impression of being crowded, even though he was the only person in the room. The furniture was fine, although sparse, but most of the marble floor was taken up with statuary, a few authentically Greek, more Roman, and the rest modern copies. Mr. Coducci's collection of antiquities is very fine, I'm sure. Nevertheless, I found it a trifle disturbing. Imagine

Medusa with a voucher for Almack's Assembly. Once she turned everyone she beheld to stone, the effect would be very like Mr. Coducci's grand salon.

It is clear that Mr. Coducci thinks very highly of Uncle Arthur. His hospitality was as remarkable as his erudition. Before long he and James were on easy terms, and their discussion left the rest of us in the dust. Fortunately, the dust featured excellent refreshments. I had a chance to look around the room as I sipped my glass of ratafia. One wall of the salon was all windows that looked out over the Grand Canal. The other walls were hung with mirrors. Not only did this enhance the amount of light in the room, even on a rainy autumn day, it also multiplied the apparent number of statues.

While Cecy and I admired the view from the windows, Thomas seemed to be fascinated by the veining of the marble on the floor. I wondered why. It was a perfectly good floor, but I could see nothing to merit Thomas's particular interest.

Belatedly, I noticed the flush of embarrassment on Thomas's cheeks. It takes a good deal to embarrass Thomas in public. I took a closer look at the statuary, to see if I'd missed anything. At last it occurred to me to look up at the ceiling.

It was a high ceiling, but not so high that anyone with normal eyesight could mistake the goings-on painted among the billowing clouds of the fresco. It was a pagan holiday up there, with no convenient bits of drapery to conceal the details, no sprays of foliage, not even a fig leaf. I trust it was all exceedingly authentic. I really couldn't say. I only know my cheeks grew hot with my blushes. After the first moment of disbelief, I kept my eyes on the floor as assiduously as Thomas did. I only hoped Cecy wouldn't notice and ask me what was wrong. I didn't think I could answer suitably in such mixed company.

Now I come to think of it, I find that a curious reaction on my part. If I had been alone with Thomas, I would not have been so terribly embarrassed by the painting. If I had been alone with Cecy, very likely I would have giggled at it. Even if it had been Thomas and me viewing the fresco with Cecy and James, I would have been less abashed. It was the presence of Mr. Coducci, as amiable as he was venerable, that made me so uncomfortable. Yet it was Mr. Coducci's fresco. How strange we are, or, rather, how peculiar manners make us.

From the deposition of Mrs. James Tarleton, &c.

Fortunately, Cavalier Coducci did not return to Venice before I was allowed to resume my usual routine. I would have been most put out had I been forced to miss talking with him when I did not feel the least bit indisposed. His prompt invitation to visit did much to restore my spirits, which were sadly cast down by the failure of my attempt to create a focus. I went over and over the attempt in my mind, and I was quite positive that I had performed every step correctly.

Nonetheless, it had plainly not worked. I even wondered whether I was, after all, truly suited to be a magician.

Thomas was no help, though I admit he was more than usually forbearing when it came to commenting on the matter. The first thing he did when I was at last allowed to rise from my bed was to present me with a pouch containing, he said, the dust that was all that remained of the writing desk.

"It's safer with you," he told me when I protested. "It's your magic that made it, after all."

"Safer?" I said. "What do you mean?"

"In the hands of anyone else, it will affect the laws of probability," Thomas said. "Rather drastically, I suspect, given how much effort it took to clear it all out. It shouldn't bother you at all, because it's still attuned to you."

"Am I going to have to cart this around forever?" I said, eyeing the bag with disfavor. I did not add, "The way you had to cart that chocolate pot?" because I did not wish to give him more of an opening.

"I'll work out some way of reducing it," Thomas assured me. "But we can't do anything until we're out of this palazzo. We'll want an area for the spell casting that's completely clear on the arcane levels, and this place won't be magically clear for months."

I found his use of "we" reassuring. Nevertheless, I was pleased to have our visit to Cavalier Coducci to distract me from my thoughts.

At first glance, Cavalier Coducci seemed nearly as much

an antiquity as his collection. He had a thick shock of white hair and a mustache that, while neatly trimmed, was equally thick. Most of his energy seemed to have gone into producing hair; the rest of him was thin and slightly stooped. (He also quite clearly had no more notion than Papa of which antiquities are suitable for public display. Though I must add that I had never before seen quite so *many* entirely unsuitable antiquities in one place. Their existence in such numbers gives one a very *odd* impression of the ancients, if one stops to think.)

He and James hit it off at once, and they seemed quite happy to go through the whole crowded salon one piece at a time, comparing the execution and history of each and every statue (in English, though I was not certain whether or not to be thankful for that, as it meant that I could not justify ignoring the discussion on the grounds of unintelligibility). I was about to abandon them in favor of the thoughtfully provided refreshments, when James particularly complimented one of the statues.

Cavalier Coducci smiled and shrugged. "It is fine, yes, but please do not be too generous with your praise. These are only the most ordinary of my collection."

James gave him a look of polite incredulity. "If these are ordinary, the main part must be impressive indeed."

"Only if you have a curiosity about the arcane," Cavalier Coducci said a little uncomfortably. "It is not an area that interests many antiquarians, I fear, and there are many disagreements among those few of us who concentrate our efforts on it."

"I shouldn't think you'd find much to work with," James commented. "The Romans abandoned magic quite early in favor of engineering, which, if I recall correctly, they considered more reliable. And the few Greek texts make it quite clear that what little magic they succeeded in doing was based primarily on word rituals rather than on objects. That wouldn't seem to leave you much to collect."

Cavalier Coducci's face lit with a fervor that I recognized all too easily, having seen it often in Papa's expression. "The Greeks and the Romans are not the only ancient peoples of interest. It is a limitation, a most unwise and unnecessary limitation, to look no further back than Greece or Rome."

"I suppose the Egyptians were in many ways as civilized as either," James acknowledged. "Likewise the Babylonians."

"Egyptians? Babylonians? Bah!" Cavalier Coducci waved his hand, dismissing them. "In arcane matters, the Egyptians had some awareness, I grant you. But the true ancient magics were not *civilized*."

"Do you mean the Etruscans, then?" I said. "Or the Gaulish tribes or . . . or . . ." I struggled to remember one of the other groups Papa had mentioned.

James came to my rescue. "Germanic tribes," he murmured softly. "Goths and Visigoths."

"Or the Goths, or the Germanic tribes?" I finished.

Cavalier Coducci beamed at me. "Yes, yes, exactly!" he said. "Not civilized, and of course with no knowledge of the modern techniques that have made magic reliable, but practitioners of a sort nevertheless."

"Practitioners, perhaps, but so little of their writing has been preserved—and so little was written down to begin with—that it is practically impossible to know what they actually did," James said. "Like the Druids; all we know of them is from Roman writings, and some of those were plainly unreliable."

"Ah, one must know where to look!" Cavalier Coducci rubbed his hands together. "Come, I will show you. Come, come!" He beckoned to Kate and Thomas, then led the four of us down a marble-floored hall and up a flight of stairs at the back of the palazzo. A chain of rooms stuffed with books and more antiquities brought us finally to a large, high-windowed room lined with glass-fronted cabinets and filled with lavishly carved tables. Most of the tables were covered with polished rocks and bits of wood; the nearest cabinets held chunks of clay and an occasional lumpy object like a child's attempt at a statue.

"Here, you see?" Cavalier Coducci said proudly. "This, these are the true record of the old magic."

I leaned closer to one of the tables. "They don't feel magical," I said doubtfully. "I can't sense anything."

"Cecy," James said in a warning tone. He was developing an alarming tendency to become overprotective regarding my magic ever since my little difficulty in creating a focus. Not wishing to encourage this, I ignored him.

Cavalier Coducci looked at me warily. "You are a magician?"

"A dabbler only," I said with some regret.

He gave me a relieved smile. "Ah, that is the difficulty. Venice is not kind to magicians. It is because of all the canals—the water disturbs the system of the beginner, and disrupts his attempts at spells, and so progress becomes impossible. It is why our great city has produced great sailors and merchants instead of great wizards and magicians. To become a Venetian magician, one must go elsewhere to learn and to create a focus, and only then return."

I stared at him. All that I could think was, *That's what went wrong with my focusing spell! I knew I didn't get the parameters mixed up.* I glanced at James, and saw by his expression that the same thing had occurred to him.

Thomas coughed. "Do you mean that a properly focused magician would sense some magic in these items?" He leaned casually toward the table.

"But of course!" Cavalier Coducci spread his hands wide. "That is how I found them. Spells of the old magic left a residue, a strong residue, and each use increased the resonance. All of these objects were part of repeated rituals, so that the residual magic became very strong. Strong enough to last centuries, though of course it has faded in that time. Still, if you were a magician, you would feel it yourself."

"Even from this?" Kate asked. She had walked a little farther into the room and was looking at a corroded knife on one of the tables. I joined her, and as I studied the knife I felt a faint, unpleasant tingle.

"Especially from that," Cavalier Coducci said. "I have said before, the old magic was not civilized. They had no science of magic; they did not have the theory to construct new spells that need but a small amount of magic. They had the most rudimentary forms and rituals, which could only have worked by applying vast amounts of power. Yet even in the writings we have there are tales of great spell castings—the raising of storms, the leveling of hills and mountains, the healing of diseases, even the calming of waves. Think of the power they must have had!"

"I believe the consensus among wizards is that such tales are on a level with those of Atlas lifting the mountain," James said slowly. "That is, mere tales."

Cavalier Coducci frowned. Before he could take offense, I said, "But, James, what if they weren't? If these things"— I waved at the collection—"still have enough magic power for a wizard to sense after thousands of years, they must have been used for something major." Despite myself, my eyes returned to the knife, and I felt a shiver down my back. I knew a little, from experience, about the unpleasant ways an unscrupulous modern wizard could go about accumulating magic power. A wizard who was both unscrupulous and uncivilized . . .

"Yes, yes!" Cavalier Coducci nodded vigorously. "That

is precisely my theory. A sensitive and skilled wizard can tell not only which objects have been used for magical rituals, but which have been used in the *same* ritual. By bringing them together, and with careful study, one can begin to reconstruct portions of the spell."

"I see," James said.

Thomas was less tactful. "Guesswork," he said. "And no way to prove any of it, even if you do stumble across something that works."

Cavalier Coducci seemed less put out by Thomas's skepticism than he had been by James's. "Ah, but if one were to reconstruct an entire ritual, and then cast the spell again using the same objects, with their original residual power! That, I believe, would not only demonstrate the correctness of the spell reconstruction; it would also reawaken the residual magic that has faded from the ritual objects so that the success would be clear." He sighed. "Unfortunately, the spells that are easiest to reconstruct are not . . . suitable for such a test."

"Not suitable?" Kate said. "What do you mean?"

"Ah . . ." Cavalier Coducci glanced at Kate, then at me. "They require difficult ingredients and so on."

"Difficult ingredients?"

"A human heart, for instance," Thomas said. "Not necessarily difficult to obtain, if one isn't scrupulous, but extremely difficult to explain to the authorities if one hopes to publish a paper on the subject."

Kate shuddered. "Not suitable, indeed."

"You are, I take it, attempting to reconstruct more, ah, suitable spells in order to test your theories?" James said to Cavalier Coducci.

"Yes, yes, you have it," Cavalier Coducci said with some relief. "The primary problem is in recovering the ritual objects, for, of course, they are much more difficult to detect."

"Because those spells weren't used as often?" Kate said. "Or because the unsuitable spells were more powerful and left more traces?"

Cavalier Coducci looked at her with mingled surprise and caution. "Both, I believe. Are you also a magician then, Lady Schofield?"

"Er, no," Kate said.

"What sorts of spells have you been trying to reconstruct?" I asked. "And if Venice is so difficult a place for magicians, how can you work here?"

"Oh, I do not work here," Cavalier Coducci said. "The testing is much too delicate a process. I have a laboratory in Firenze, and another in Milano. But Venezia is my home." There was a moment of pensive silence, then he shook his head. "Enough, enough. Your father's letter said you might have questions regarding the antiquities you have seen. What is it you wish to know?"

Since he had asked in so straightforward a manner, I replied in the same way. "There are two things. First, during our travels, we have visited a number of different antiquities, and it has seemed to me that some of them are similar, perhaps even related. Yet they were constructed at different times by completely different peoples. I was hoping you could explain the puzzle." From my reticule, I took the list of places where we suspected that magical rituals had been performed and handed it to him.

Cavalier Coducci glanced at it and smiled. "You are perceptive, Signora Tarleton. But then, I would expect no less of the daughter of the Signor Rushton. These are all places where royal rituals took place."

"Royal rituals?" James asked in a bored tone that belied his interest.

"The rituals that made a man of royal blood truly the ruler of his people," Cavalier Coducci replied. "Among ancient tribes, it was not enough merely to be the son of the ruler. Rituals were required to confirm the authority of the chieftain or king."

"Like a coronation?" Kate said.

"Very like," Cavalier Coducci said, giving her a sharp look. His voice took on a lecturing quality. "Most coronation ceremonies are, in fact, derived from the most effective of those ancient rituals. Oddly, the modern versions are seldom as effective as the older rituals purport to be, despite the application of the most current magical theories. There are, of course, various theories as to why this should be. Monsieur Montier avers that the primary reason is the lack of continuity of place—few modern-day monarchs wish to be crowned in the caves and crypts that our ancestors so often used. Herr Rüstach maintains that the fundamental nature of magic has changed and developed over time, and that this is necessarily reflected in the progress we have made in other areas. He feels that the coronation rituals are less effective because monarchs and emperors are outdated, in other words. Of course, he is considered quite radical.

"I myself feel that the problem is twofold, and not subject to simple correction. On the one hand, continuity is of great importance for the royal rituals—continuity not merely of place but of blood, of process, and of implements. As Monsieur Montier pointed out, few modern coronations take place in the locations the ancients used. Fewer still make use of the old instruments our ancestors used; indeed, it is not possible for them to do so in many cases, as the ancient crowns and swords and cloaks and so on have been lost or melted down or rotted away. Bloodlines, too, are not as continuous as one might like in many cases. Of course, that is precisely what the rituals were intended to remedy, so I deem it a minor difficulty compared to the others.

"But most important, in my opinion, is the change in process, which I believe began with the rise of the Roman Empire. When they outlawed human sacrifice throughout their Empire, they disrupted a great many of the oldest royal rituals and spells. Their conquests also obviously caused breaks in the continuity of bloodlines, as the chieftains and rulers led their armies against Rome and were killed or taken as slaves. And, naturally, quite a lot of the more valuable ritual items were looted." Cavalier Coducci shook his head. "The Romans have a great deal to answer for."

"Indeed," Thomas said in a noncommittal tone.

"You must not think I am advocating a return to that sort of magic," Cavalier Coducci said quickly. "I regret the loss of knowledge, that is all. Only think what wonders we might accomplish if we could apply modern theories of magic to the old rituals!"

"It all sounds utterly fascinating," I said. "Have you any duplicates of your work that you could share? I am sure Papa would be very interested, if you have not already sent them to him."

James gave me a Look, but did not say anything. Cavalier Coducci was very willing to provide us with all of his published monographs, and even promised to send over some of his notes on the spells he had tried to re-create, as soon as he copied them.

That settled, he said, "And what was your other question? I believe you said there were two."

I handed him my second list, the one of missing regalia that the Duke of Wellington had given James. "We were wondering about—" I broke off. Cavalier Coducci had gone as white as his hair. "What is wrong?" I said.

"What game are you playing?" Cavalier Coducci demanded.

"What do you mean?" I said, a little startled.

"This . . . this . . ." He thrust the list at me. It was shaking visibly.

"Obviously, it has great significance to you," James said. "I trust you will explain it to the rest of us in due time."

"You mock me, Sir!"

"I do not," James said gravely. "The things on the list you hold have been stolen from their respective owners, and we are trying to discover anything that would lead us to the thief."

I looked at James with surprise, for we had agreed in advance to be circumspect, and while he had not told Cavalier Coducci quite *everything*, his statement was hardly as indirect as I would have liked. James's bluntness, however, had an extraordinary effect on Cavalier Coducci. The paper trembled in his hand as he looked at James. "Stolen?" he said in a hoarse whisper.

James nodded.

"I had nothing to do with it!" Cavalier Coducci said, thrusting the list at James. "Nothing! I would never— It is unthinkable!"

"Somebody's thinking it, whatever it is," Thomas said in a tone that was a little too firm for politeness. "If you—"

"Oh, Thomas, not just now," said Kate, of all people. "Cavalier Coducci has clearly had a shock; give him a moment to collect himself. Pray, sit down, Cavalier, and—and rest a moment. Would you like me to ring for a glass of water?"

And in very little time at all, she had him settled in a large, heavily carved chair, with the rest of us arrayed around him. Thomas half sat on one of the tables, his left foot on the floor and his right dangling casually. James stood close behind me, while Kate fussed over our host. In a short while, he had regained some color, and Kate smiled at him and said, "Do you feel well enough to tell us about it now?" And Cavalier Coducci did.

He had, apparently, been working on his reconstructions of ancient spells for many years. In fact, despite his modesty on the subject, it was quite clear that he was known as an expert in the area. Though his theories were not altogether popular, other antiquarians often sent him ancient objects they suspected of being magical in nature, for him to test or identify.

A few years previously, shortly before Napoleon Bonaparte's first defeat, he had been asked to evaluate an extensive collection amassed by one of his countrymen. The collection—

"In Milan?" Thomas interrupted.

"No, in Rome," Cavalier Coducci said.

"Ah. Carry on."

The collection had taken several months to work through, and Cavalier Coducci had become quite familiar with its owner. They had a number of "stimulating discussions" on a wide range of subjects, including both politics and the reconstruction of ancient spells. Finding themselves in agreement—they both despised Napoleon Bonaparte, and they both felt that it would be possible to apply modern magical theory to fill in gaps of knowledge in ancient spells—they "reconstructed" a spell that had never existed. An imperial coronation spell.

"There *was* no ancient Emperor of all Europe," Cavalier Coducci said earnestly. "The Romans came nearest, but they were later and did not use magic in the ways the ancients did to reinforce the right and power of a ruler. And some of the items I chose for the ritual were . . . known to be much too recent in origin to have been part of any real spell, if there had been a real spell of that kind."

"Items like the Sainte Ampoule?" Thomas murmured.

"No, that one is quite old enough to have been used in pre-Roman rulership rites," Cavalier Coducci said. "The Spanish coronation robe, however, dates only to the twelfth century, though Señora La Sola has theorized that it incorporates pieces of older—" He broke off, shaking his head. "I don't suppose it matters much, now."

"You mean to say that this ritual you designed would magically make someone *Emperor of Europe?*" James said carefully.

"Oh, not just anyone," Cavalier Coducci said. "He would have to be of noble birth, to begin with, probably even of royal blood, though there are innumerable descendants of forgotten kings and chieftains about. And the candidate would have to meet certain other requirements—it was really quite complicated. But it would have worked."

"How?" Thomas demanded. "You can't just wave a hand or dab some oil on someone's forehead and get everyone to acknowledge him Emperor!"

"Not in the political realm, not all at once," Cavalier Coducci said. "But if—*if* someone, or his deputy, were to complete the ritual, he would have . . . a certain advantage in convincing people. Or conquering them. As we saw with Napoleon Bonaparte."

"*Napoleon* used this ritual of yours?" I said. "I thought you didn't invent it until after he was defeated!"

Cavalier Coducci shook his head. "He did not use *my* ritual; if he had, I doubt that he would have been so easily defeated." James and Thomas looked at him in disbelief. Cavalier Coducci did not appear to notice. "But Bonaparte did *something*," he continued. "Not as effective as my ritual would have been, but I saw the man once, years ago when his armies marched through Italy, and the traces were unmistakable. It is why we created our ritual—we thought that the only way to be rid of Bonaparte would be to create someone with a stronger spell to defeat him."

Cavalier Coducci sighed. "Before we had quite finished, Napoleon had been defeated after all. So we did not publish our ritual. With Napoleon gone at last, there seemed no need."

"But now someone appears to be collecting the objects necessary to complete your spell," James said.

Cavalier Coducci nodded. "And if someone is serious enough to attempt the ritual—" He sagged in his chair. "It will be a second Bonaparte, rampaging across all Europe. And I am too old to see more wars."

We all looked at him for a moment, appalled. "I think you had better give us a copy of that ritual," Thomas said at last. "Including *all* the details. And the name of your antiquarian friend in Rome."

"I will be happy to provide you with the ritual," Cavalier Coducci said, "but I fear the Cavalier Pescara died two years ago. If he kept a copy in his papers, I do not know who would have inherited it. I can give you the name of the agent who handled his affairs, however—a very respectable Roman firm."

Thomas frowned. "Very useful, I'm sure, but since we will undoubtedly be on our way to Vienna shortly—"

"No! You must stop this madman," Cavalier Coducci said.

"Of course," James said. "That's why we're going to Vienna. That's where Napoleon's son is."

Cavalier Coducci stared at him in bewilderment. "Bonaparte's son? What has he to do with the matter? You cannot stop the ritual in Vienna! Vienna is not old enough. The imperial ritual can only be completed in Rome."

We had a quiet journey home from Cavalier Coducci's palazzo. This was in part due to the weather; the annoying drizzle that had dampened everything on the way there had become a downpour that showed no sign of letting up. The rain was heavy enough to make me wonder if the gondola we had to take for part of the way might be swamped, but in the event, we reached our lodgings safely. Thomas and James were most solicitous of Kate and me as we climbed in and out of the boat, though there was no real need. Kate only repeats her minor mishaps; her major ones are invariably unique. Besides, we were all of us soaked through from the rain already.

Kate and I retired to dry out our garments, which took some time. The four of us did not meet again until dinner. Thomas arrived a bit late, carrying a thick sheaf of papers. "Cavalier Coducci is prompt," he said. "Also thorough. He appears to have sent along the latest copies of all of his research on spell reconstruction, not merely that imperial ritual he invented and the monographs Cecy asked for."

"Appears to?" James said.

"It's all in Italian," Thomas said. "I can make out the sense of it, but the sense of it isn't enough for spell casting. Not that I'd want to cast some of these. Difficult ingredients, indeed!" He looked rather grim. No one asked for specifics.

James reached for the handful of papers.

"Not over dinner," Kate and I said simultaneously. We looked at each other, and I continued, "You'll get crumbs on them, and there won't be room for you to spread out, and you'll be unhappy because you can't give them your full attention and eat at the same time, and you'll make mistakes."

"And I'm sure to spill something on the most crucial page," Kate added. "Wait until later."

James and Thomas exchanged glances. "You sound quite positive," James said in a mild tone.

"It's experience," I told him. "Papa used to try to go over manuscripts at dinner sometimes, no matter what Aunt

Elizabeth said. It never worked, and he was always in a bad mood for *weeks* afterward."

"Ah," said Thomas, and he tucked the papers inside his jacket. They made an unsightly bulge, but there was no more talk of immediate translation.

I expected dinner to be more hurried than usual as a result of all this, but it is impossible to hurry Italians, particularly where food is concerned, even if they are not eating it themselves. The servants brought in each course in due time, no matter what. I think Thomas would have bolted after the *antipasti* if James had not given him a stern look.

Between courses, we talked. None of us had the least doubt that the thefts the Duke of Wellington had asked us about were related to Cavalier Coducci's ill-advised imperial spell, but beyond that, our opinions varied. Thomas thought that Eve-Marie was waiting for some final artifact that would be necessary to the spell, and that we should stay in Venice to intercept it. James thought that Eve-Marie was a decoy, and that we should proceed to Vienna with haste, as the Conte di Capodoro and Lord Mountjoy had likely taken the northern road there already. Kate and I thought that we should go to Rome; Kate, because in Rome we might learn more from the agent who had handled the estate of Cavalier Coducci's deceased friend, and I, because Cavalier Coducci had said the spell could only be finished in Rome, so the conspirators would have to go there at some point, and it seemed to me more useful for us to be in Rome waiting for them than to continue chasing after them and perhaps arrive too late.

James was much struck by this argument, but Thomas frowned. "We have only Cavalier Coducci's opinion that the ritual must be completed in Rome," he said. "That's why I want a look at these papers before we make any decisions. I've no doubt that he's quite expert when it comes to ancient spells, but modern magic has improved a good deal in the past few years, and I suspect he hasn't kept up with the latest developments."

"Good point," James said. "The spell was already an adaptation; if someone found a way to adapt it a little more, so that it could just as well be completed in, say, Vienna . . ."

"But how could Lord Mountjoy or the Conte di Capodoro have discovered the ritual?" Kate said.

"The Conte is a collector of antiquities," I pointed out. "Perhaps he purchased some of the collection Cavalier Coducci evaluated." A thought struck me, and I looked at James. "Some of them may have been part of the exhibit Kate and I saw in Milan! We must send to Cavalier Coducci in the morning, to see if he remembers any particular pieces."

"I don't think that's likely, but I can't see that it would hurt anything to ask," James said. "It will take us more than an evening to decipher all that Cavalier Coducci sent us, in any case. There's plenty of time for it."

The next course arrived, a savory fish in wine sauce, and

we were silent for a few moments as it was dished up. Then Kate said, "What puzzles me is Mr. Strangle."

"He would puzzle anyone," Thomas said. "Don't think of him."

"I don't mean his . . . his death," Kate said. "I mean what he was up to. He can't have been simply collecting stolen goods for Lord Mountjoy, you know."

Everyone looked at her. "Why not?" Thomas said in a careful tone.

"Because it doesn't explain all those magical rituals he and Theodore were doing," Kate said. "Or who could have taught him how to do them. You said yourself that he was only enough of a magician to follow directions."

"Or why all the magic he's done seems to have been in places where old royal rituals were performed," I said. "There must be some connection."

"Practice?" James said.

Thomas looked thoughtful. "It's not a completely out-landish idea, if the spell is as complex as Cavalier Coducci indicated. They wouldn't have all the artifacts and they weren't in quite the right places, but they might get some idea how the spell was working from the resonance of the older rituals. Fine-tuning, so to speak."

"I can't quite picture Theodore plotting to overthrow Europe," I said.

"I can't quite picture Lord Mountjoy as a Bonapartist," Kate said. "He's too . . . too . . ."

"Thickheaded?" I suggested.

"No," Kate said. "I just can't see him trying so hard to help someone who might very well disagree with him. About anything."

"Well, perhaps these"—Thomas touched the bulge of papers under his coat—"will shed some light on the matter."

So Thomas and James retired to one of the lower rooms immediately after we finished eating. They spent much of the night there, and returned to it again the following morning after breakfast. I was beginning to wonder whether it would be better to call them out or to send lunch in to them, when I heard an angry roar from the room where they were working.

"Diddled, by Heaven!" Thomas's bellow was clear even through the floor. I rushed down the stairs and met Kate coming from the other direction. Together we pushed open the door and went in.

Thomas and James were bent over the table, scooping spread-out papers into an untidy pile. "You'd better go pack," Thomas said. "We're leaving immediately."

"I've never been unpacked," Kate informed him. "Reardon has been complaining about living out of a trunk ever since we arrived, and I can't say I blame her. What is it?"

"We've been following a red herring," James said grimly. "The imperial spell can be cast on a stand-in—a sort of proxy for the actual candidate. They don't need young Bonaparte at all, as long as they have a suitably prepared substitute. That's what Strangle was doing with young Theodore. Not practicing—preparing."

"And the journey Mountjoy will be taking from Milan to Rome is straightforward, even at this time of year," Thomas said. "Whereas we'll have to get through the Apennines or else take a boat all the way around Italy."

"No boats," I said firmly. "And how can you be sure they'll head for Rome next? Theodore said quite clearly that his uncle planned for them to go to Vienna."

"Because Coducci was right; they *have* to finish the spell in Rome," Thomas said, and then he explained.

The ritual that Cavalier Coducci and Cavalier Pescara had designed was both elaborate and elegantly flexible. Because Napoleon had been rampaging across Europe at the time they worked it out, they had chosen to avoid creating an intense three- or four-day coronation ritual that would draw together all of the countries under their imperial candidate (and attract an enormous amount of unwanted attention from other wizards and Napoleonic authorities). Instead, they had developed a series of much shorter and simpler ceremonies based on the most ancient kingship rites and locations they could find.

Each ceremony was designed to activate the residual magic of the old places, re-creating the rites that had reinforced the ruling power of centuries' worth of ancient kings and tribal chieftains. Although most of the kingdoms and peoples and tribes no longer existed, their descendants made up the modern nations of Europe. When the same person performed all the rituals, he became "king" of a great many bits and pieces—and eventually the bits and pieces added up to all of Europe.

In this way, the candidate could travel quietly from one obscure ancient site to another, activating spells and accumulating ritual kingships. Even so, the two magicians felt that it might be difficult for one man to reach all the various sites, since it was impossible to predict where Napoleon might choose to send his armies next. So they designed a way for someone else to activate spells on behalf of the candidate. A simple linking spell would allow a deputy to perform distant rituals to benefit the intended Emperor instead of himself.

"Coronation by proxy," James put in. "There's some precedent for it, though not recently."

"Not on such a scale, though," Thomas said, and went on with his explanation.

Once the kingship rituals had been performed, only the imperial ritual itself was required to activate the spell. Here Cavalier Coducci and his friend had been forced to improvise, and, according to Thomas, they had done a brilliant job of it. Each piece of ancient coronation regalia had been carefully chosen for both its symbolism and its power; each came from a different country so that all would be drawn together in the final spell, to be completed on the night of the full moon in November in Rome.

And nowhere but Rome would do. The Roman Empire had, at its height, united Europe from Britain to Persia; after the Empire broke apart, the spiritual authority of Rome remained strong for centuries. Throughout Europe, Rome was still symbolic of her ancient imperial glory, and symbolism is extremely important in working complex and ambitious enchantments.

"I haven't had time to work out all the equations," Thomas said, "but that one was easy enough. Mountjoy won't go to Vienna. The stolen regalia and all the minor kingship rituals won't do him a particle of good there. He has to take Theodore to Rome to finish the ritual, or there's no point to any of this."

"Sending Eve-Marie to Venice was a very good decoy, then," Kate said thoughtfully. "It seemed most plausible, since Venice is very nearly on the way from Milan to Vienna."

"Just so." Thomas beamed at her.

I sighed. "I'd better tell Walker to start packing," I said. "How soon do we leave?"

THE ROMAN
ROAD

It wasn't that simple, of course. Making travel arrangements is not a speedy business at the best of times; in Italy in early winter, it takes forever. Not the least of the difficulties was convincing people that we meant to cross the Apennine Mountains, which run down the center of Italy, at such a time. In the end, I am sure we convinced everyone that all English persons are quite mad, but we succeeded in hiring two travel coaches and departing Venice in less than three days.

Just outside the city, we turned southwest onto an old Roman road heading for the Apennines. I suppose it is a great accomplishment for the Roman roads to continue in use after nearly two thousand years, but having ridden on them, I am inclined to think it reflects more poorly on the state of modern road building—and repair—in the Italian kingdoms. The cobblestones were not merely uneven; a good many were missing altogether (James said because local people had been carting them away for building material for centuries). The coach lurched along in a way that made talking quite impossible.

On the second night out, when we reached Bologna, I persuaded James to hire an extra parlor when we stopped for the night, so that I could recast my focusing spell. I had purchased several more of the glass paperweights in anticipation of using one as my focus (and the others as gifts for family members when we returned to England), and I had plenty of the other necessary ingredients. James was dubious, but he could not pretend that we had not come far enough inland to prevent any interference from all the Venetian canals.

This time, the spell went perfectly. I am afraid I stayed up most of the night afterward, however, as the excitement of being fully focused for the first time gave me far too much energy to allow for sleep.

In the morning we were told that the pass through the mountains was undoubtedly closed by snow. Thomas had been in something of a brown study for most of the day; when he heard this, he shut himself in the inn's parlor with Cavalier Coducci's notes and did not emerge for several hours. Once he did, he sent Piers off to market with a most peculiar shopping list—two pounds of fresh pig's liver and six feet of sky blue ribbon were the most ordinary items on it. He also ordered some small modifications to the harness of the lead carriage horses.

"Thomas, what are you up to?" James demanded as soon as Piers had left. "You aren't thinking of trying to get us through the mountains by magic, are you? Because if you are, I shall have to begin making inquiries about the local provision for Bedlamites, and I'm not sure my Italian is up to it."

"Nonsense," Thomas said. "It's quite clear from Cavalier Coducci's notes. He's really done quite a remarkable job reconstructing some of these ancient weather-working spells; if he were more of a wizard or less single-minded in pursuit of his theories, he'd have seen the implications for himself. The Royal College of Wizards will have a field day with these when we get back to England."

"Specifics, Thomas," Kate said firmly. "You are not going to distract us with Cavalier Coducci and the Royal College. We want to know what your intentions are."

"Everything that is honorable, I assure you," Thomas said, looking wounded. "I thought I had proved that when I married you."

"Thomas . . ."

"Oh, very well. I've been studying Coducci's weather spells. They're all partials, and no one in his right mind would dream of using them—they all require rather a lot of, er, 'difficult ingredients.' But if you look at them closely, there are some extremely suggestive patterns that I think can be profitably applied to Caswell and Barnett's cantrip for—"

"Thomas, you can't mean to change the weather that much!" I said, appalled. "It would take a tremendous amount of power—the pass must be miles long. And even if you could warm things up enough to melt the snow in a day or two, the river would probably flood and block the road."

"Oh, the *weather*," Thomas said. "I wasn't planning on meddling with the *weather*. Not exactly."

"Then exactly what *were* you planning?" Kate demanded.

"I'm going to clear the road so we can get through," Thomas said as if it were the most obvious thing in the world. "Snow is just weather that's sitting around on the ground, if you look at it correctly, and changing *that* shouldn't take nearly so much power, especially with Coducci's work to base it on. Even without the 'difficult ingredients.' The equations were actually quite simple, once I saw how to translate Coducci's work into modern terms." He paused and looked at me. "There is just one thing."

"And that is?" I said warily.

"You're going to have to do the warding spells tonight, before we reach the pass. I don't want to be even slightly drained when I start work on this, but I don't want to be eaten alive by fleas in the night, either."

The discussion did not end there, of course, but in the end Thomas had his way. We stayed in Bologna barely long enough for him to make his preparations, then lurched off toward the southwest once more. We reached the small town of Passo di Porretta at the north end of the pass without incident, and spent the night quite comfortably. The following morning we all crammed into two carriages and set out again, amid much head shaking and eye rolling by our Italian hosts.

The road grew quickly snowier and slipperier as it climbed, though it was nothing like as steep as the trail—I cannot in conscience call it a road—over the Alps had been. Barely an hour from town, it became clear that further progress would soon be impossible, and Thomas called a halt. Then he took the large bag of ingredients Piers had procured for him and walked forward until he stood in a bank of slushy snow.

Bending over, he drew a diagram in the snow. With great precision, he laid out a mirror and surrounded it with other objects—a bare tree branch, an empty flowerpot, a small fish, and several similar items. He wound the blue ribbon between them in a complex pattern, muttering under his breath, and I could feel power gathering.

He straightened, looking down at his handiwork, then squinted up at the sun. He shifted his position slightly. Still muttering, he took up the pig's liver and smeared it over the surface of the mirror. Then he put a hand in his pocket and drew out a glass paperweight, very like the ones I had purchased in Venice: clear, with a pattern of green and yellow swirls inside. He held it over the mirror, and his voice grew louder. The sense of gathering magic grew stronger, then stronger still. Suddenly, he shouted, *"Fiat!"* and threw the paperweight down on the mirror.

The mirror shattered, and as it did there was a sort of quiet explosion. Snow flew soundlessly in all directions, and there was a great deal of intense light. The horses shied; it was all Piers could do to hold them. When the dazzle cleared from our eyes, Thomas was picking himself up several feet away. He walked back toward the spot where he had cast the spell. The paperweight rested on bare ground where the mirror had been, glowing with a warm, golden light. There was no sign of any of the other ingredients.

Thomas bent and picked up the glowing paperweight. Kate made a small noise of protest. Though he could not possibly have heard it, Thomas glanced back and nodded reassuringly. Holding the paperweight out before him, he marched up the road.

The snow parted in front of him, evaporating under the light from the paperweight. Along the edges of the road, the snowbanks remained, steaming slightly, but the road itself was clear and dry. Thomas nodded again, this time with evident satisfaction, and walked back to the carriage. He placed the paperweight in a fishnet bag that Piers had attached to the front harness; it swung like a pendulum, but the netting hardly obscured the light at all. Swinging himself up beside Piers, he said, "Well, man, let's be off. That spell won't last forever."

Piers set the horses moving at a steady walk. They were plainly nervous at first, but they soon became accustomed to the way the snow quietly vanished as they approached it. I sat back, calculating. It seemed that we would have no trouble with the pass after all, and would probably reach Florence, on the other side, by nightfall. There, we could take our choice of routes to Rome.

From the commonplace book of Lady Schofield

5 November 1817
Florence
At yet another inn, as drafty and dirty as all the rest, yet, mercifully enough, a bit less noisy

I am an idiot. It was a stupid idea to focus Thomas's magic in my wedding ring. I regret it extremely.

The connection between us proves most inconvenient at the moment, for Thomas is exhausted. I fear he overreached his power when he won our way over the mountains. I do not have the force of will to be much use to him at the moment, for the connection seems to be working the way it did during the highway robbery, and I feel utterly wretched.

It is tiresome, having scarcely the ability to do what must be done, with no spirit left to do more. Whatever ails Thomas, I must steel myself to do better. We cannot both be stricken. Thank goodness Cecy and James are with us. Someone with a bit of common sense.

6 November 1817
Florence
At the Golden Lion

I feel much better this morning. My indisposition was certainly caused by the link with Thomas. I am sure he feels much worse than I ever did, poor fellow. I will say, in my own defense, that my concern for Thomas lay heavy on my spirits. By the time our carriage made it down from the pass, he was perfectly gray with fatigue. He fell over soon afterward and spent the rest of the journey to Florence lying with his head in my lap. Given the cramped dimensions of our carriage, this was nothing like as picturesque as a novel might make it sound, and both my legs fell asleep beneath his weight. I never wish to spend another moment that remotely resembles those dragging hours on the road, dashed half to pieces by the lurching of the carriage, and worrying over the poor darling fool with every yard we traveled.

Later

Thomas is himself again! He ate a portion of beefsteak with his dinner. What is more, he washed it down with half a bottle of claret and pronounced himself completely recovered. I think porter would have done him more good than claret, but we are in a strange land and porter is not something they understand here. Even the claret was difficult to come by.

The important thing is that Thomas is feeling himself again. I had feared he would sleep himself into a coma. This afternoon when the maid came to mend the fire, Thomas woke quite naturally and even swore a little at the noise she made when the coal scuttle knocked over the fire irons.

I am feeling much more the thing myself. Such relief!

ROME

From the commonplace book of Lady Schofield

10 November 1817
Rome!
At our lodging off the Piazza di Spagna

Thomas is indeed himself again. There is not a hostler left uncursed between here and Florence. One would expect that Thomas's return to form would weary me a little, but one would be wrong. I am so happy to have him back in his usual frame of mind, energetic, sure of himself, and even surer of me, that I can hardly express my delight and relief. Truly, all my prayers have been answered. Reverend Fitz-william used to make some extravagant claims for the power of true devotion. I may have to revise my opinion of his wisdom.

I did not pay much attention to the weather while I was concerned for Thomas, so I don't know when it improved. We have had fair weather for a few days now. The drier roads make a delightful change.

Yesterday I saw a barefoot boy with a herd of sheep. I cannot think how many times I have seen boys with sheep back home, but never before did they seem remotely Biblical.

As I beheld the boy, I was able to understand the ease with which one might envision scenes of an antique age. He might have stepped from a painting of Arcadia, he was so striking. Glossy dark curls and snapping dark eyes aside, however, I feel sure he smells just as the shepherds back home do. Sheep are still sheep, after all.

11 November 1817
Rome
At our lodging off the Piazza di Spagna

James and Thomas have already spoken to the British embassy about Theodore and Mountjoy. Thomas is convinced they must be around the city somewhere. Piers has very obligingly vanished into the Roman underworld in search of gossip. While Thomas and James hunt, Cecy and I have been paying such social calls as are appropriate. We have been invited to tea with the ambassador's wife tomorrow. There was a time when the very idea of taking tea with the wife of the British ambassador in Rome would have sent me into strong convulsions. Now it is merely a matter of deciding what gown to wear. There may be an element of truth in all the twaddle people talk about the importance of a Season. Perhaps my experiences in London have given me some address. No, on second thought, any polish I possess is entirely due to the efforts of Cecy, Lady Sylvia, and Reardon. Any poise I demonstrate, I owe to Thomas, who considers himself a connoisseur of sangfroid. Connoisseur he may or may not be, but he does make an excellent tutor.

From the deposition of Mrs. James Tarleton, &c.

By the time we reached Rome, I was quite familiar with the spells for removing fleas and other vermin from our rooms, for of course Thomas was in no condition to cast them himself for several days after his dramatic performance in the pass. Even after he was fully rested, we alternated casting the spells. For it was quite obvious that if any confrontation of a magical nature occurred, Thomas must bear the brunt of it, since he was the most experienced wizard we had available; therefore, it only made sense for him to be as well rested and prepared as we could arrange. It was also quite obviously a good idea for me to practice my own spell casting as much as possible, so as to take the more routine magical chores and preparations off his hands, should it become necessary.

Finding the time for study and practice became unreasonably difficult once we reached Rome. Social engagements closed over us almost at once—in particular over Kate and me, for of course Thomas and James had no scruples about declining invitations when they felt they had more pressing business. Every English person in Rome wanted to have us to lunch, tea, dinner, or some sort of party. Those who had been abroad longer than we had were eager for news of home; those who were less traveled wanted the stories of our adventures and advice on what to see and what to avoid in the places we had already been.

In addition, everyone was curious about our sudden arrival. Society abroad is quite as gossip-ridden as Society at home, I find; everyone knew that we had been, to all appearances, settled in Venice for the winter, and everyone was, as a result, impossibly curious about our change in plans. Those who were familiar with the Italies also wondered how we had managed to cross the Apennines at this time of year.

After the briefest of consideration, I referred all inquiries to Kate. Her ability to concoct convincing tales out of whole cloth seemed the most likely solution to the problem, and this indeed proved to be the case. Once presented with Kate's explanation (which leaned heavily on Thomas's reputation as the Mysterious Marquis, as well as upon more mundane matters such as the unreliability of Venetian servants and the inedibility of the food there), Rome lost interest in our doings. Invitations remained as frequent, but they became less pressing, and we at last had the leisure to pursue our own concerns.

First on our list was to interview Signor Moltacchi, the estate agent to whom Cavalier Coducci had referred us. This was accomplished by the simple expedient of having James send him a message asking him to present himself at our rented palazzo on a matter of business.

Signor Moltacchi responded with flattering promptness, and we arranged an appointment a few days later. He arrived, late but apologetic, carrying a handsome vase about a foot high, which he begged we would accept as his gift. After a great many more compliments and a round of current gossip, we at last got down to business.

"My father-at-law is an antiquary of some note," James began. "He has expressed considerable interest in some documents that he believes formed part of the estate of the late Cavalier Pescara. I should like to obtain them for him. Cavalier Leo Coducci of Venice informed us that you handled the sale and might therefore be in a position to track down and obtain the papers."

"Tracking down the documents will not be difficult," Signor Moltacchi said confidently. "There were not many different buyers." He hesitated, as if something had just occurred to him. "I must tell you, though, that securing the things you wish may not be so easy." He paused again.

"Why?" asked Kate when he showed no sign of resuming.

"The person who purchased the bulk of the estate, and in especial the papers, is a collector who seldom relinquishes the things he acquires," Signor Moltacchi said reluctantly. "And there are other possible complications. I fear I cannot guarantee to obtain your documents. I can only promise to try."

"Papa will be so happy if you can find them for him," I put in.

"Perhaps I might do something to, er, persuade this unwilling collector to sell," Thomas said idly.

"Because you are a British Marquis?" Signor Moltacchi said, raising his eyebrows. "I do not think so. The gentleman in question is himself a Conte, and not easy to impress."

"Indeed." Thomas contrived to look unutterably bored, though he must have been as deeply interested as the rest of us. "Who is this paragon?"

"The Conte di Capodoro," Signor Moltacchi snapped. Thomas made a small sound of satisfaction or possibly surprise. Signor Moltacchi frowned, as if he regretted having spoken.

"What a pity!" I said quickly. Whether the Conte di Capodoro had obtained the coronation spell when he purchased the estate or not, I did not want Signor Moltacchi carrying tales of our interest to him. Nor did I wish Moltacchi to think too carefully about what he had told us. "I fear Papa will have to be content with something else. Have you anything that might interest him, Signore? He is particularly interested in the Roman Republic."

The Signor was quite happy to discuss all of the items he had for sale, and he and James soon settled on a selection of ancient documents—none of them having to do with magic or coronations—which he offered to bring back the following day for James's inspection. He left in a cloud of anticipation, and we all looked at one another.

"The Conte di Capodoro," James said thoughtfully.

"That's unexpected. Even though we talked about him, I didn't really think he had anything to do with Mountjoy."

"From what the Contessa said, her husband is very much a Bonapartist," I pointed out. "If this is indeed an attempt to restore Napoleon's empire—and, really, I do not see what else it can be—he is just the sort to be in favor of it."

"And there is Eve-Marie," Kate said.

Thomas looked at her. "Tell us about Eve-Marie," he said in a fascinated tone.

"Oh, Thomas. It's quite plain from her actions that she is mixed up with Lord Mountjoy, yet when we encountered her in Milan, it was at the Conte's museum exhibit. And she was giving orders as if she expected to be obeyed, and in quite good Italian, Reardon says. The curator wouldn't take orders from a mere maid, nor from someone who was simply conveying the wishes of an Englishman. So he must have known she was speaking for someone else, and the Conte seems by far the most likely candidate. And there's that whole business of her visiting Mr. Strangle in Paris. Lord Mountjoy wouldn't need to send someone; there's no reason he shouldn't be seen with his nephew and his nephew's tutor. It makes far more sense if she was relaying information from the Conte."

"Yes," I said slowly. "That makes nearly everything fit. Though I must say, Lord Mountjoy looks a most unlikely plotter."

"People in real life don't *have* to look like villains in order to be so," Kate said. "It's only in the theater that you can be sure the stuffy, middle-aged gentleman isn't behind all the plotting."

"Just so," James said. "Still, we haven't proof of any of this yet. We can't very well go to the authorities with this farrago of coincidence and conjecture and ask them to do anything."

"Assuming they would," Thomas put in. "Rome isn't Paris, and it's less than two weeks until the day Coducci's final ritual can be performed. No, I think that if anything is to be done about this, we'll have to do it ourselves."

"Thomas, what are you thinking?" Kate said with some alarm.

"This time, thanks to Coducci, we know when the ritual has to take place, and we know where," Thomas said. "It shouldn't be difficult to catch them in the act."

James pursed his lips. "It shouldn't be difficult, but somehow with you it always is," he said. "Not that I'm objecting to the general outline of the plan, you understand; I'd simply prefer a bit more . . . planning. If something went wrong and they managed to complete the ritual, we'd have one Bonaparte or the other rampaging all over Europe again, and from what Coducci said, there'd be very little chance of stopping him."

"Thomas!" I said. "Can you design a spell to interfere with the ritual? We could arrive early and set up the spell before they get there, so that even if something goes wrong it won't be as bad as James fears."

"Yes," Thomas said after a moment's consideration. "I believe I can do that."

"But not more than that," Kate said, at the same time as James said, "And no frills, Thomas. This isn't a good time to show off."

Thomas gave them both a wounded look. "I had no intention of going beyond the basic requirements," he said in a tone even I could tell was mendacious.

"Good," James said. "Keep it that way. And while you are designing the spell, I'll write to Wellington. He should know what we've found out."

"And I'll write Lady Sylvia," Kate said.

Designing the spell proved more difficult than we had anticipated. While Kate and I visited antiquities (of which Rome has an unreasonable number), Thomas pored over Cavalier Coducci's neatly written pages (and James's translation of them) and scribbled arcane equations, which he then crumpled up and threw at the wastebasket. (At least, that was where he claimed he had intended to throw them, when Kate just mentioned how very many wads seemed to be decorating the floor.)

Three nights before Cavalier Coducci's ritual was due, Thomas emerged from the study triumphant while Kate and James and I were attempting to play three-handed whist. "I have it!" he said, waving a piece of paper that was densely covered with writing.

"It's about time," James said, looking up from his cards. "Does this mean you can go over to the Forum tomorrow and set everything up?"

"It will take a day or two to collect all the ingredients," Thomas said. "Even though none of them is at all unsuitable."

James chuckled. I frowned at him and said, "Won't that be cutting it a little close? If anything turns out to be difficult to come by—"

"The difficult things I already have," Thomas said. "The real problem was the timing. Coducci is no modern master, I'm afraid. Once I got the details converted to modern equations, it became obvious that there are several weaknesses in his design. He stuck too close to his beloved ancients, I'm afraid."

"What does that have to do with the timing?" Kate asked.

"Coducci had his final ritual planned for midnight," Thomas said. "But moonrise would work far better, because of the way the correspondences line up in the fourth pair of equations. That's just a little after sunset. And if either Mountjoy or di Capodoro has enough training to notice, they're sure to move things up to take advantage."

"That just means we have to be finished with our spell by sunset," I said. "Doesn't it?"

"Not quite," Thomas said, sounding a bit cross. "Not if we want 'our spell' to have the maximum effect. The timing affects everything."

Kate looked at him in dismay. "Does that mean you're going to have to cast two spells?" she said. "One to interfere with the ritual if they cast it at midnight and another for if they cast it at moonrise?"

"No," Thomas said, sounding quite pleased with himself. "I worked out a spell that will cover both possibilities. But I'm glad there wasn't a third potential time to cover. There's just one small difficulty." He paused and looked at me. "It will take two people to cast."

"Here!" James straightened abruptly. "Cecy hasn't the training for the sort of thing you pulled off in the pass and you know it."

"She won't need it," Thomas assured him. "I don't need expertise. I need an extra pair of hands with some basic magical competence. And you can't claim she doesn't have that, not when she's been spelling the fleas out of your bed ever since we left Venice."

"Not that long," I said. "Just since we crossed the mountains. James, what *is* the matter? You're not going to object every time I want to do any real magic, are you?"

James frowned. "I'm talking about this cantrip of Thomas's, nothing more."

"If you're concerned about safety, you can look over the equations yourself," Thomas put in rather quickly.

"Thank you. I will," James said, and before I could say anything further, the two of them retreated to the study once more.

Kate looked after them with a worried expression. "Oh,

dear. I do hope——" She broke off and looked at me. "Cecy, you won't let Thomas do anything . . . too dangerous, will you?"

"I like that!" I said. "James is the one of the pair who keeps getting himself shot. And you have far more influence with Thomas than I do."

"I know," she said, still sounding troubled. "But he was so very tired after that last spell. It reminded me of the time when Sir Hilary was trying to leach all the magic out of him."

"Oh, Kate, I never thought of that," I said remorsefully. "No wonder you're worried. But this spell won't be anything like that—it won't have to be sustained for hours, for one thing. And, anyway, you'll be there yourself, to keep an eye on things. It will be all right, you'll see."

But when Thomas and James emerged, it soon became clear that Thomas wanted no one but himself and me to be present during the spell casting. Setting up the spell was too delicate a matter, he said. I did not think he was telling the whole truth, and I could see that James did not think so, either, but Thomas would not budge from his assertion. By the time we parted that evening, nearly everyone was cross with everyone else. The only thing we all agreed on was that the Conte and Lord Mountjoy had to be stopped.

Matters did not improve over the next few days. Thomas was out most of the time, collecting ingredients. When he wasn't out, he was in the study mixing them and casting preliminary spells. I spent most of my time studying my part, which was quite small and not dangerous in the least, no matter what James said. Kate did not say much, but the worry wrinkle between her eyebrows grew deeper every day. James stayed away from the palazzo as much as possible.

By the morning of the twenty-third, I was extremely tense, even though I was quite confident that I had my part letter-perfect. I could not help but think of what might happen if we somehow did not succeed in disrupting the ritual. Cavalier Coducci had said that Napoleon Bonaparte had had some magical glamour about him, and Bonaparte's rampage over Europe had been dreadful. The ritual Cavalier Coducci had created was stronger and more elaborate, as it needed to be to counter Napoleon—if it now, instead, made a new Napoleon possible, things would be worse than before.

Thomas and I left for the Forum at three in the afternoon, carrying several bags of materials. The Roman Forum is a half-mile-long tumble of ruined walls and broken pillars. Slipping into the area was quite easy, as there were plenty of trees and bushes growing between the ruined buildings despite the paving stones that once had been roads. We planned to finish our spell well before sunset and then return to the palazzo to meet James and Kate. The four of us would come back to the Forum together to make sure that the ritual was not completed.

The Basilica Julia, where the final ritual of Coducci's spell would take place, is on the south side of the main square of the Forum. He had chosen this site for his spell because it was built in honor of Julius Caesar. Since the Roman Empire had ruled most of Europe, and since Coducci intended to create a new Emperor (at least in spirit), setting the final ritual in the temple of the first of the Roman Emperors was just the sort of symbolism he wanted.

I do not think that Cavalier Coducci could have seen the Basilica Julia recently, or he might have thought twice about the symbolism involved. To call it a ruined building would be an exaggeration: Several long, cracked steps, part of a brick wall, and two long rows of circular stumps where columns had once stood comprised the whole. There were no other walls and of course no roof.

Thomas marched out into the center of the former building and set down his sack. "You take that side," he said, gesturing at one of the rows of column stumps. "I'll do this one." As I set down my own sack, he added (most unnecessarily), "Mind the color sequence; if you get it wrong, I won't answer for the consequences."

We each went down one of the rows, marking every stump with precise symbols in different colored chalk. Some of them were so deteriorated that it took me some time to find a place to make the diagrams. We finished at about the same time. After inspecting my work, Thomas circled the temple to mark the boundaries of our spell. Then we settled down to work in earnest.

The spell Thomas had invented was extremely complex, and I admit that I did not fully comprehend the reasons behind all the things he had chosen to do. At several points things had to be done simultaneously at opposite ends of the area—lighting and snuffing candles, sprinkling herbal mixtures, and so on—and that was my part. It all took quite a lot of time and concentration.

"There," Thomas said with considerable satisfaction when we finally finished. "That should take care of things. Let's go collect James and Kate before he decides I've turned you into a toad by accident."

"We should clear up before we go," I pointed out. "If Mountjoy and the Conte notice sacks of colored chalk and puddles of wax and parrot feathers all over, they are bound to become suspicious."

Thomas agreed, though rather reluctantly, and we started working our way around the Basilica, clearing away all obvious traces of our spell. As we came to the rear of the Basilica, I heard voices behind the wall. "Thomas!" I hissed.

Thomas nodded to indicate that he had heard me and gestured to me to hide. We slipped around the crumbling rear wall to a convenient clump of bushes. Thomas melted in among them with admirable ease. I followed, feeling thankful that I had had the forethought to wear a forest green walking-dress. A moment later we saw a group of people emerging from among the much more complete columns of the temple just behind the Basilica Julia. They started along the verge beside the Basilica, heading for the edge of the Forum, so that we could see and hear them all quite clearly as they passed by.

The first to appear were two dark, stocky men in somewhat rough clothes. Theodore came next. He was dressed in a most peculiar fashion, in a robe heavy with tarnished gold embroidery. There was a wreath of stiff green leaves on his head and his forehead was shiny with oil. In one hand he carried a rusty sword, the same one we had seen in the museum in Milan; on the other was a heavy gold ring. His expression was rather blank, and he evinced no interest whatever in the antiquities around him but marched along as if he were in the middle of London. Behind Theodore came Lord Mountjoy, talking over his shoulder. It was his voice I had heard, and as he came through the columns I was able to make out the words.

"—never liked the idea of such drastic changes," Lord Mountjoy complained. "We had every reason to think the original spell would work perfectly. Now ... Well, just look at the boy. He's no different at all. If your alterations have spoiled the ritual, we've wasted six months of work."

"Patience," said a woman's voice, and, to my utter astonishment, the Contessa di Capodoro emerged from the shadows behind Lord Mountjoy. "It will take a little time for him to absorb his new role completely, especially since he was not expecting it. It would have gone better if you had prepared him more."

"It's not as if I could *explain*," Lord Mountjoy grumbled. "Heaven only knows what he'd have done if he'd understood properly."

A horrible feeling was growing on me. Lord Mountjoy and the Contessa were speaking as if the final ritual had already been completed. I glanced over at Thomas. He was frowning fiercely at the little group and did not notice.

"Patience," the Contessa said again. "We do not seek a mere Napoleon, remember. Our purposes require these changes. Unless you would prefer to shepherd your nephew through a decade of war before he rules all Europe unopposed?"

"It will certainly be much simpler if people bow to him at once," Lord Mountjoy admitted. "But I dabble a bit in magic myself, and there's no reason I can see for changing the ritual from midnight to noon, let alone from the Basilica Julia to the Temple of Saturn. The Basilica is more suitable, to my thinking."

"That is because you do not know the Roman history so well," the Contessa replied. I thought that she was annoyed, despite her outward appearance of calm.

Lord Mountjoy did not notice. "Enlighten me."

"The Temple of Saturn is the oldest temple in Rome," the Contessa said. "It is dedicated to the ancient god-king who ruled before Rome had an Empire, a god-king who ruled not by conquest, as Julius Caesar came to do, but by right. Since we—" She broke off suddenly, and her head came up as if she had heard something.

"Yes?" Lord Mountjoy said.

Theodore was by this time well ahead of the others, and was still marching steadily toward the edge of the Forum. The Contessa and Lord Mountjoy had reached the nearest end of the Basilica Julia, where they would have passed only a few feet from where Thomas and I were hiding if the Contessa had not stopped. I held my breath, but she was looking toward the Basilica and not the bushes.

"What is it?" Lord Mountjoy asked.

The Contessa waved him to silence. Frowning slightly, she began muttering under her breath. She made a sweeping gesture, and abruptly I felt quite ill. Beside me, Thomas gagged. It was very like the illness I had felt in the carriage outside St. Denis, just before the highwaymen stopped us and James was shot, but much stronger and more sudden.

"Ah," said the Contessa. She waved toward the bushes and said something in Italian to the two stocky men who accompanied her. They came up the steps and dragged Thomas and me out into the open. Neither of us was in any condition to resist.

"What, what?" said Lord Mountjoy. "It's that dratted Tarleton woman that Theodore keeps going on about. What's she doing here?"

"She and the Marquis have been attempting to interfere," the Contessa said. "That is what I conclude from the aura lingering over the Basilica Julia. How fortunate that they chose the wrong place and the wrong time."

"Yes," Lord Mountjoy said, rocking back on his heels. "Quite fortunate. But why did you drag them out? They haven't done any harm, and now we have to decide what to do with them."

"We will bring them with us," the Contessa said. "We cannot let them loose until the last spell is finished, or they may try to interfere again. Besides, they may be useful when we come to Nemi."

Though I did not have the strength to struggle, I did manage to wonder where Nemi was and what it had to do with their plans. Cavalier Coducci's ritual had made no mention of that place, though it had specified a great many others. Naturally, the Contessa did not stop to explain to us. She spoke again to her two henchmen, then started after the rapidly vanishing Theodore. The men followed, dragging us along, and Lord Mountjoy brought up the rear, sputtering.

From the commonplace book of Lady Schofield

> *23 November 1817*
> *Rome*
> *At our lodging off the Piazza di Spagna*

This is speculation. Mere speculation. What I know for certain: Thomas and Cecy have not returned from their spell casting. No sign of them remains at the place chosen to set the spell. James and I searched it thoroughly.

James returned to search again after he brought me back here. I wished to stay with him, but he insists one of us must be here to receive a message, should one be sent. That is good, sound, practical thinking. I'm glad that James is here to provide it. I find myself incapable. With every hour that passes, I find it more difficult to discipline my thoughts.

This book has given me a place to record my reflections. I don't wish to record the reflections I'm having now.

If Thomas were here, he would tell me to stop being such a watering pot.

Later

It is after midnight, and still no sign of Thomas or Cecy. James sent me a message. Under the circumstances, he has notified the authorities of Thomas and Cecy's disappearance. He is on his way to Lord Sutton to enlist all the help our embassy can provide. No word yet of Mountjoy's whereabouts, still less the young Theodore. No doubt when we find one, we will find the other.

Later

I must be calm. I must remain collected. Yielding to my natural impulses will do nothing to help anyone, least of all Thomas. Therefore, I will remain collected. I will be calm. Unless I cannot control myself. In which case I must admit that I am succumbing to the vapors and take to my bed like the poor useless creature that would make me. I do not wish to take to my bed. I do not intend to succumb to the vapors. Therefore I am calm.

Later

Reardon has just brought me a plate of toasted cheese. Given the difference between Roman bread and bread at home, given the difference between the cheeses, she could not have done more to duplicate the toasted cheese of my wistful thoughts of home. It was her intention to soothe and comfort me. It is not her fault that the kindness of her gesture overset me. I do feel better for having indulged in a few tears. In truth, it was my foolish distress over the sight of a flea that sent me up into the boughs. Nothing could have brought Thomas's absence home to me more directly than the sight of a flea. I had almost forgotten fleas existed.

If Cecy were here, she would tell me we must *do* something.

I agree wholeheartedly. Yet I seem unable to do anything at all. If I were in an opera, I would have an aria to sing. That would be some comfort. Even if it wasn't a very good aria, it would at least prove a distraction. As it is, I sit here in the dark and long for morning, even as I dread it. I think the same numb thoughts over and over. Thomas, where are you? You can't be dead. Surely you cannot be dead. I would know it if he were dead. But if something terrible has happened to him, what am I to do? How can I possibly tell Lady Sylvia that her only remaining son has gone? It is too dreadful, simply beyond contemplation.

When I find out what happened, when we know who is responsible for this, I shall insist upon a reckoning. James may carry out every threat he has made. He has my permission to beat anyone he pleases insensible. But I insist upon a reckoning.

24 November 1817

Thomas is still missing and Cecy with him. James returned a few hours ago looking perfectly haggard. He spent the small hours of the morning with Piers and the men they've enlisted to help in the search. He only returned here to shave and change clothes.

With deep reluctance, James described last night's interview with Lord Sutton to me. Our esteemed ambassador, who I gather was well flown with wine at the time, is inclined to treat the entire matter as a joke. The obvious explanation, according to Lord Sutton, is that Thomas and Cecy have run away together—an elopement of sorts—and that Mountjoy has nothing to do with anything. The embarrassment is unfortunate, of course, but the sooner one learns to live with it, the better.

Poor James. It must have taxed his social ingenuity, as well as his temper, to the utmost. Then, after enduring such treatment, he had to return here and describe it all to me.

Now I think of it, James might not have described it all to me. It might have been a good deal worse. It would be just like him to spare my feelings. What he told me was quite sufficiently dreadful. I won't press him for more.

Thomas would never try to spare my feelings.

This really will not do. Watering pot, watering pot, watering pot!

Why did I not insist that Thomas teach me to use magic? Without that skill, I am surrounded by tools and I cannot use them. All I need is the simplest location spell. Thomas travels with a staggering amount of luggage. Any article of his clothing would do—if I had the skill. Cecy's pearl earrings have a spell ready cast upon them. So do mine. Alas, there is no way to make my pearl earrings take the slightest interest in hers. My own wedding ring, so inconveniently tuned to Thomas in the matter of nausea and faintness, could surely be of use—had I any skill whatsoever. But I don't. If I get Thomas back, I swear I'll make him teach me.

I have gone through every article of our luggage—even Cecy's things—and the only item that seems of any use whatever is the coarse powder Thomas swept up after Cecy blew up the desk at the Palazzo Flangini. Magical residue, he called it. The laws of probability on holiday, he said. What application the laws of probability will have, I do not know. It is not as if *I* know anything about them. But Thomas handled it with such care that I will be careful of it, too.

Later

With Reardon's help, I intend to take steps. We have enlisted Walker as our chief ally. The moment the hour has advanced sufficiently to make a social call possible, I mean to visit Lord Sutton's residence.

It is hours until then. In the ordinary way of things, I would pass the time by writing in this journal. But now I find it difficult to form my thoughts into words fit for the page. I don't wish to remember this.

Last night was the first night Thomas and I have spent entirely apart since we were married.

Later

It is in the lap of the gods now. Or perhaps I ought to say goddesses. For the moment I have done what I can. Reardon has brought me another plate of toasted cheese, and this time I was able to eat every morsel. From that, and her general air of celebration as she told Walker about our call, I gather that I have acquitted myself well.

From James's description of Lord Sutton's misapprehension, I knew it was vital I make it clear that Thomas and Cecy could not possibly have disappeared for the motive ascribed to them by common gossip. Therefore, I was determined that I would change the ambassador's mind. No amount of common sense from James would do it, and no mere words of mine would succeed, either. It was incumbent upon me to present myself as a woman no man in his right senses would leave for another.

As soon as it was light, I attempted to explain my intention to Reardon. I had not gone beyond the first halting words when her eyes lit up and she asked, "May Walker help?"

"Of course. I shall need all possible assistance," I said.

Reardon said, "Chin up, my lady. I think you'll be surprised at the difference a few touches can make."

"I'm willing to try anything," I said. "Even gilding my toenails."

Reardon looked as if she'd tasted something sour. "There will be no need for that sort of thing, my lady."

Within the hour, I scarcely knew whether I was on my head or on my heels. Walker and Reardon between them had dressed me in the best of the Parisian gowns suitable for day, a pink morning dress, had done my hair in a style utterly foreign to me, and had applied themselves to those touches of immaculate grooming that I generally despair of.

"This is Thomas's favorite gown," I said as Walker made slight adjustments to the bodice.

"Of course it is," said Walker. "In this gown, you in no way resemble a woman whose husband would leave her for another."

Reardon made a small sound of pure disapproval. "She is a lady, not a woman."

"No, no." Walker was firm. "In this gown, milady is entirely a woman. Wait and see. It is the coiffure that renders the effect. Lord Sutton will not understand why he regards her as a lady, for all his attention will be upon the gown. Yet the coiffure will influence him without his knowledge, and he will treat her as the lady she is."

"I just want him to realize he's made a foolish mistake," I said tartly.

"Hold still just one more moment," said Reardon. "There. That does it." Under her direction, I turned slowly in a circle so my two critics could survey their handiwork.

"Head up, back straight," said Reardon. "Shoulders back."

"The slippers are perfect," said Walker. "No eye could fail to note the workmanship."

"With the right shoes, gloves, stockings, and hat," said Reardon, "Lady Schofield would always be known for a true lady, no matter what gown she wore."

"But this gown makes it simple for the world to see with one glance that Madame la Marquise is a *young* lady." Walker settled my mysterious pink shawl on my shoulders with precision. It was reckless to trust an unknown charm, but in my situation, the chance it could help me detect a lie was worth the risk.

"Now keep your shoulders back, do not hold your chin too high, and all will be perfection." Walker clasped her hands. "Just so."

"Thank you for your help." I turned to Reardon. "Is the carriage ready?"

Reardon handed me my muff and reticule. "Everything is ready, my lady."

Reardon and I did not exchange a word on the ride to the ambassador's residence. I was ready for any of my usual domestic troubles, from a snagged stocking to a torn hem, but nothing untoward occurred. I had one moment of panic as I waited for the response when I sent in my card. What if my talent for telling lies would not extend so far as my need to tell the truth? What if Lady Sutton was not at home? What if she were not at home to me? What if my reputation was already insufficient to gain entry anywhere? How would Lady Sylvia deal with this situation?

Lady Sylvia would demand entry, I decided, as I tightened my shawl around my shoulders. Its warmth and softness comforted me. If it turned into some kind of trap, I would tear it off and go without. Whoever sent that shawl, it reminded me of Lady Sylvia just the same. Just the thought of her steeled my resolve. When the butler returned to show me in to Lady Sutton's presence, I did as I'd been told. Head high, shoulders back, chin up, but not too far.

Lady Sutton was not, as I had hoped, alone. An elderly lady, with sharp features so like Lady Sutton's that she must surely be her mother, was knitting by the fire. Lady Sutton was at a writing desk nearby. Both regarded me with the keenest of eyes as I stood in the doorway.

Now I think of it, in the days of my London Season, I would have found their scrutiny disturbing. I would have wished myself miles away. Every step into the room would have been an adventure, for I would have worried that I would trip over the edge of the carpet or somehow contrive to slip and lose my balance for no reason at all.

Nothing of the kind occurred. I met their scrutiny and returned it. Indeed, I felt a pang of triumph when I saw the way Lady Sutton's eyes widened and then narrowed to study me.

Yes, I told myself, that was exactly the effect I had hoped to achieve when I asked Reardon and Walker for their help. Just that look on Lady Sutton's face. I let myself draw courage from my success.

I suppose any fencing match begins the same way. We were all three of us extremely polite as we took one another's measure. I apologized for intruding so unexpectedly. Lady Sutton introduced me to her mother, Mrs. Montgomery, and had me share the settee opposite. I let the exchange of pleasantries go on until I could see Lady Sutton's curiosity agleam in her sharp eyes. When I judged the time was right, I asked the question that had brought me there.

"I've come to ask your opinion, Lady Sutton, Mrs. Montgomery." With what I devoutly hoped was a stately nod, I indicated my intention to consult both ladies. I schooled my countenance to convey my respect for their wisdom, my regard for their position, and the possibility that butter wouldn't melt in my mouth. "Would you advise me to seek an interview with Lord Sutton on my own behalf? There has been a grave misunderstanding."

Neither Lady Sutton nor Mrs. Montgomery moved a muscle. Neither altered her expression of kindly interest. Yet I could feel it as their attention sharpened. They came on point, as a good hunting dog does when it scents its quarry.

"Indeed?" Lady Sutton was all puzzlement. Diplomatic life must demand considerable theatrical skill. One would never have guessed that she knew precisely what I meant. I could not be sure if it was the shawl or my imagination, but

I had no doubt that she was dissembling. "What is the nature of the misunderstanding?"

This is no opera. But if I have ever had an aria, it was the performance I gave there by the fire. In halting phrases, I told them the truth, or as much of our mission as I dared confide. My husband and my cousin had been abducted in circumstances as alarming as could well be conceived. And base rumor—I did not name the source of the base rumor—held that my husband had eloped with my cousin. The authorities would not take matters seriously unless they were made to do so—and who could possibly perform such a miracle but the most influential representative the British Crown possessed?

Lady Sutton and Mrs. Montgomery were the ideal audience. At first I could not tell if they shared a natural reserve or if they were prepared to give me enough rope to hang myself. Accordingly, I delivered my account as concisely as I could. I did it with all the stoicism I could muster, ending with the broadest hints that the Duke of Wellington had a keen interest in Mountjoy's precise whereabouts.

Once I finished, a silence fell, but it was not an uncompanionable one. Lady Sutton and Mrs. Montgomery exchanged meaningful glances. I composed myself and waited for the verdict.

Mrs. Montgomery spoke first. "You are on your wedding journey, I think?" When I nodded, she went on. "We have friends in common in Paris, I believe. You and Lord Schofield have many well-wishers there."

"We——" I cleared my throat lest my voice break. "Paris is lovely."

"Indeed it is," said Lady Sutton with vigor. "Rome can rival it, I promise. Don't trouble yourself with the gossips. I will see to it that everything possible is done to alert the local authorities to the true state of affairs."

To do everything is difficult, indeed, impossible. To do everything possible is a very different thing. I dared to press Lady Sutton. "May I hope Lord Sutton will use his authority on behalf of my husband and cousin? Their safety is my one concern."

Lady Sutton looked disappointed in me. "I cannot promise anything on Lord Sutton's behalf. That is not my place. Only rest assured that he will be informed."

"Informed," said Mrs. Montgomery with a touch of dryness, "and perhaps enlightened."

I could see I had won them over. The promise of help was genuine.

I thanked Lady Sutton profusely and rose to take my leave. As I made my good-byes, at the moment my attention was most closely fixed upon Mrs. Montgomery, she lifted her hands a little so that I could see the piece of work she held in her lap. I had known since my first glance at her that she had been knitting. Now I could see the nature of that knitting. Crafted of undyed wool, it was patternless, almost shapeless. A twig had been worked into the stitches, one end of it tied with a bit of gold thread.

I met Mrs. Montgomery's sharp eyes. She smiled at me

and gave me a little nod, as if of encouragement. As if to say, take heart.

I took my leave then, and I think I swept out of the room with some dignity. I am at my least clumsy when I am most distracted, and the suspicion—or, rather, certainty—that Mrs. Montgomery is one of Lady Sylvia's old conspirators is enough to distract anyone.

Later

As it is after midnight, and still no word from the authorities, I count this as the second night Thomas and I have been parted.

Mountjoy can't have disappeared without a trace. James sends word that the authorities—*all* the authorities—are cooperating in the search. I think it is inevitable that word will come. But when?

I have put on Thomas's dressing gown over my nightgown. It smells like him. If I am careful to pick up my skirts, I don't trip over the hem, or at least not often, no matter how I pace. Just touching it helps comfort me a little.

25 November 1817
Rome
My room

How provoking! Just as James and Piers found where Mountjoy had been staying and could persuade one of

Mountjoy's servants to tell them the man's current where-abouts, word comes from Lord Sutton at last with the same news. Mountjoy is a guest at a country house in the vicinity of Nemi. Fortunately, the house is not terribly deep in the country. Nemi is hardly more than twenty miles from here. James is composing a message for the runner to return to Lord Sutton, and I wait only for him as Reardon has finished with my final preparations. Walker stays here in case a message should come.

At last, at last—we can Do Something!

NEMI

Lord Mountjoy and the Contessa had two coaches waiting at the edge of the Forum. At the Contessa's orders, her men bundled Thomas and me into one of them, then joined us. The Contessa, Lord Mountjoy, and Theodore took the other coach, and we set off.

I had a brief hope that the spell the Contessa used to make Thomas and me ill would be less effective if the distance between the coaches became long enough, but either her coachmen were skilled enough to prevent a gap opening or the spell itself had a long range, for I did not notice any variation in how dreadful I felt. The coach rattled steadily along as the shadows grew outside the window.

It soon became clear that wherever we were going, it was not within the bounds of Rome. I think Thomas realized this first; it would explain why he tried to fling himself out of the carriage. He was more thoroughly affected by the spell than I was, however, and our guards had no difficulty in preventing him from leaping. On the whole, I think this was probably a good thing, as the coach was traveling rapidly enough that I doubt he could have escaped serious injury had he succeeded.

The twilight deepened, but the coach slowed only slightly. The pace at which we were traveling would have made me a trifle nervous during broad daylight, as our experience of Italian roads had not left me with a favorable impression. At night, even with the full moon, it added even more to my discomfort, though it did occur to me that a minor accident might provide one of us with an opportunity to escape. No such event occurred, however.

Hours later, the coach slowed at last. The wheels clattered over some sort of pavement, and we stopped. Thomas and I were dragged out. I had a confused impression of a long, lumpy building with pale stone columns shining in the moonlight; we stood in a sort of courtyard at the front.

The Contessa came to join us. Even by moonlight her face showed signs of strain. She snapped more orders at her men, and they stripped Thomas of his coat (which proved an unexpectedly difficult task for them, as Thomas favors the same sort of close tailoring Mr. Brummell brought into fashion). They then proceeded to search us both.

When she was satisfied that neither of us carried anything that might be useful, the Contessa waved her men toward the left wing of the building. They dragged us off and locked us in an exceedingly dark room. Almost as soon as the lock turned in the door, I began to feel better. A moment later, Thomas grunted.

"I was wondering when she was going to run down," he said a bit breathlessly.

"The Contessa?" I said.

I sensed, more than saw, Thomas's nod. "Keeping that spell going for so long has to have drained her. She won't be in any condition to repeat the performance for a day or two."

"So if we can escape, she won't be able to stop us. Not with that spell, anyway," I said, and yawned. "That's another good thing, then."

"Another?"

"It's obvious now that the Conte and Contessa *were* in league with Sir Hilary, right from the start. Unless you think it was some other spell that someone used on us when Sir Hilary held us up outside St. Denis and took the Sainte Ampoule."

"No, it was the same spell all right. And she won't have a chance to use it on me again, if I have anything to say about it." Thomas's voice was grim. "Stay where you are for a minute, so I don't have to worry about tripping over you."

Thomas moved away from me in the darkness, and I heard him fumbling his way around the walls. From the sounds, the room was much larger than I had expected. After a moment, I heard a crash.

"What was that?" I said.

"I barked my shins on a box," Thomas replied. "There are a dozen of them over here; we seem to be in a storeroom of sorts."

I yawned again. "Is there anything you can do about the door?"

"As soon as it's light, I can try to—"

"In that case, I'm going to sleep," I said firmly. "I don't suppose there's anywhere in here that's likely to be more comfortable than anywhere else?"

"If they stored any bedding or blankets, I haven't found them," Thomas replied. "Try over here next to the wall."

I staggered toward his voice without any major mishap, and curled up beside one of the crates Thomas had stumbled over. It was cold and hard, but I was extremely tired. I barely had time to wonder whether I would be able to fall asleep under such conditions, when I had done so.

When I woke, I thought at first that it was very early in the morning, for though there was light, it was quite dim. Once I was fully alive to my surroundings, I realized that I had mistaken the situation. The room we were in had but a single window, hardly more than a slot high up on the wall and deeply set, which barely let in enough light to examine our surroundings.

The room was quite large and long. There were two doors along the wall where we had entered; the window was in the center of the wall opposite. Above were the beams that held up the roof. An occasional soft cooing made it clear that doves or pigeons had built a nest there. A stack of ancient wooden boxes leaned against the shorter wall. In one place, the lowest box appeared to have rotted through, causing several others to collapse in a tumble across the floor.

Thomas was curled up next to the door, but he came awake as soon as I stirred. He brushed at his rumpled coat briefly, before giving it up as a hopeless task. "No one has been by since they dumped us in here," he said. "Not even to offer a bit of breakfast. Though it's nearer to lunch now, I think."

"No wonder I'm hungry," I said. "Do you think they mean to starve us?"

"I doubt it," Thomas replied. "The Contessa, Mountjoy, and young Daventer had the same late night we did, remember. And they have better beds. They're probably all still asleep. The servants won't make a move until someone gives them orders, and the Conte isn't likely to give any until he's heard the full story from his wife and Mountjoy. Which he won't get until they wake up."

"You are probably right," I admitted. "Though I wish you weren't. The question is, how soon will they get here?"

Thomas frowned at me, opened his mouth to say something, then closed it. He stared a moment longer, his expression fading from irritation into thoughtfulness, before he said, "Do you get it from Kate, or does she get it from you?"

"What? Oh, don't waste time. If you can't manage a guess when our captors will be back, just say so. I thought perhaps your experience in these matters would make you a better judge of what was likely."

"What *has* James been telling you?"

"Very little, in the way of actual information," I said absently. I squinted up at the window. It looked as if it might be just possible to wiggle through it, if I could get up to it in the first place. "Mostly it's been hints. Do you think you can lift me up to that window, or had we better move some of those crates and try climbing on them?"

"I'll lift," Thomas said.

"If you hear someone at the door while I'm up there, don't be chivalrous," I said. "We don't want them to suspect anything. Just drop me."

"It will be my very great pleasure," Thomas said politely.

"I rather thought it might," I said.

We arranged ourselves under the window. Our first attempt was awkward and unproductive. Then Thomas had the happy idea of tossing me up as if I were mounting a horse. He made a stirrup of his hands, and as I stepped in it, he pushed me up until I could grasp the window ledge.

That was the theory. In the event, Thomas lifted with enough enthusiasm that my entire head cleared the ledge, giving me a clear view of the entire opening. The ledge narrowed toward the outside of the wall; a three-year-old child might perhaps have wriggled out, but no one of adult size could possibly manage it. I sighed and stepped down.

"Nothing to grab hold of?" Thomas said.

"No point in grabbing," I replied, and explained.

"Then it'll have to be the door. I was hoping for another solution. If we do manage to get out that way, anyone looking out of the villa will see us immediately."

"I know, but it can't be helped," I said. "Can you do anything with the lock?"

"Credit me with some sense," Thomas said. "I looked at

it before you woke up. It's old and rusty; I'm amazed they can manage it with a key. I'm not sure I could pick it even with the best tools from the heart of the London rookeries."

"I meant magically," I said.

Thomas shook his head. "Not a hope. It's iron—not amenable to minor spell casting. And even if I could work up something major without any ingredients, the Contessa at least would surely sense it."

"Well, let's see if there's anything useful in these boxes," I said.

Half of the boxes were empty; the rest contained moldering sacks of grain that fell apart at a touch. Even the wood was damp and soft with rot. "This is disgraceful," I said. "It's clearly been years since anyone even *looked* in this storeroom."

Thomas looked amused. "It's as well for us that you're right. The wings of these villas were meant for keeping animals. I'm just as glad none of them has been in residence lately."

"Do you suppose the Conte—"

Just then a rattle of keys at the door announced someone's arrival. As we turned, it swung open, and Theodore Daventer entered, with the Contessa's burly footmen on either side. "Mrs. Tarleton, Lord Schofield, I am so very, so very sorry!" he stammered. "There's been some dreadful mistake."

"You're right about that, my boy," Thomas said.

Theodore's eyes were on me, all apologetic. "My uncle

didn't understand. As soon as I found out, I told him . . . You *will* come and see him now, so he can explain?"

"Have we a choice?" I said. "Besides being locked up again in this stable?"

"It isn't a stable," Theodore said. "Not for fifty years or more, the Contessa said. And it really is all a mistake, I promise. Just come and talk to Uncle William, and we'll get everything straightened out."

I was tired, stiff, and cold; my hair and gown were in a dreadful state; I had had little sleep and no breakfast. I ought to have been able to deliver a blistering retort, but I found myself feeling rather sorry for Theodore. Surely, I thought, it would do no harm to do as he asked. And it would at least get us out of the storeroom for a while. I opened my mouth, but Thomas beat me to it.

"Very well," he said in a bored tone. "Let's see what excuse your uncle has for kidnapping us."

"Thank you," Theodore said in a relieved tone. "Come this way."

We followed him outside, along the covered walk, back into a tiled courtyard with a small fountain, and up the stairs. Above, we moved along a long hallway lined with crudely designed frescoes depicting a queue of people in more and more peculiar dress. As we walked, I considered the exchange we had just had, and the more I considered it, the odder it seemed. I did not think it wise to comment on it at the moment, however.

At the end of the hall, Theodore stopped and knocked at

a white-painted door. Almost at once the door opened to reveal Lord Mountjoy. He was frowning and seemed a bit distracted. "There you are, Theodore!" he said in a tone of false heartiness. "And our guests. I'll just, er, consult with them now. You can run along."

"I'm not a child, Uncle," Theodore said.

"No, no, I didn't mean—" Lord Mountjoy began hastily. With visible effort, he pulled himself together. "Never mind. If you will come in, my lord, Mrs. Tarleton. I'll talk to you later, Theodore."

"Don't forget what I said about explaining," Theodore said as he turned to leave.

"I won't," Lord Mountjoy said with unexpected sincerity.

We went into the room, which seemed to be a sort of study. At first glance everything seemed in order, but a closer look revealed that the expensive brocade of the curtains had been carefully darned along the folds, the bookcase was loosely shelved to give the impression of fullness from an inferior number of volumes, and several large potted plants had been placed in peculiar locations, probably to hide worn spots in the carpet. The desk, though sturdy, was black with age, and while the chairs were similar enough to a casual glance, they did not actually match.

Lord Mountjoy seated himself behind the desk and gestured Thomas and me to chairs in front. "I must begin by apologizing for this . . . unpleasantness," he said. "I had nothing to do with it, I promise you."

"No?" Thomas said with considerable skepticism. "Yet I

swear you were right there when the Contessa's bullyboys dragged us to that coach and shoved us in."

"I couldn't do anything about it!" Lord Mountjoy said. "There were circumstances . . . You don't understand!"

I nudged Thomas's ankle with my foot. Much as it might relieve his feelings to say annoying things to Lord Mountjoy, I thought it would be better to learn as much as we could. "Perhaps you could explain, then, Lord Mountjoy," I said sweetly. "For you know, it all seems very odd to me as well."

"Yes, Theodore said you'd listen," he replied, half to himself.

I stared at him for a moment, feeling very odd. Theodore had persuaded us to talk to his uncle, and he had apparently persuaded his uncle to talk to us. His arguments, now that I thought of it, had not been strong—indeed, he had scarcely offered any. Yet here we all were. I had not sensed anything magical about him, but it seemed extremely odd.

Lord Mountjoy shook himself and leaned forward. In an earnest tone, he said, "It's like this—," and began his explanation.

Cavalier Coducci and his Roman friend had not been moved to create their plot against Napoleon Bonaparte until late in his reign. They had still been polishing up the rough edges of their imperial ritual when Bonaparte was defeated and exiled, first to Elba and then to St. Helena. Since there seemed no further need for it, and since Cavalier Pescara was ill, they had abandoned their efforts, though neither of them destroyed their records.

When Cavalier Pescara died, the Conte di Capodoro had purchased most of his movable estate. Lord Mountjoy had been staying in Milan with the Conte and his wife then, and he had made no secret of his peculiar views. He felt that England had been foolish not to take advantage of what he saw as Napoleon's work toward unifying Europe.

"Unifying!" Thomas said. "Is that what you call—" He broke off, because I nudged his ankle again.

"Do continue, Lord Mountjoy," I said.

"When the Contessa discovered that spell among Pescara's papers, she naturally approached me for advice," Lord Mountjoy said. "I saw the potential at once, and—"

"The *Contessa*?" I said. "But, surely, the Conte . . ."

"Oh, the Conte," Lord Mountjoy said with a sniff. "He's just like Theodore's father—no head for anything but old statues and moldering ruins. He'd sorted out all the old manuscripts from Cavalier Pescara's papers and was prepared to burn the rest. It was the Contessa who insisted on going through them. And, of course, when she found the ritual, she knew it would be no good going to him. She needed a man of action, not a woolly-brained scholar." He puffed up his chest in remembered pride.

Thomas opened his mouth. I drew my foot back in preparation. He glanced at me and closed his mouth again. Lord Mountjoy, oblivious, continued.

It was quite plain to me, from everything he said, that it

was the Contessa who had been behind the entire plot that evolved. She had questioned him about suitable candidates for the ritual, pointing out the need for someone young and malleable so that she and Mountjoy could continue to control him, and so run all of Europe once it had been united. It had been her idea to enlist the help of the remaining Bonapartists in acquiring the necessary ingredients—the chrism, the ring, the robes, and the rest of the coronation regalia that had been reported stolen from all over Europe—while Theodore's tutor shepherded the boy from one ancient site to another, activating each of them so as to link them in the final ritual.

Things had gone very well for some time, right up until the conspirators located the chrism. One of the Bonapartists had absconded with this vital ingredient, and Lord Mountjoy had hurried off to France to track it down. He had experienced some difficulty in doing this, and I wondered if it was not because the supposed "Bonapartist" had actually been one of Lady Sylvia's mysterious network. It would explain how the chrism came into the hands of the Lady in Blue, and why she took such pains to deliver it to Lady Sylvia at the earliest opportunity.

Lord Mountjoy's inability to recover the chrism in Calais led the Contessa to take a hand directly. She had been waiting for him in Paris. When Eve-Marie reported Mountjoy's failure, the Contessa arranged the holdup on the road to Paris—Sir Hilary Bedrick was indeed another of her unsavory connections, and he made a perfect stalking horse.

When Sir Hilary became too importunate, she arranged to have him disposed of and so obtained the chrism. She departed immediately for Milan, leaving Lord Mountjoy and her assistant (the woman we knew as Eve-Marie) to keep an eye on things in Paris.

I think it was at that point that Lord Mountjoy began to be a little nervous about his situation. It must have occurred to even the meanest intelligence that if the Contessa was capable of arranging Sir Hilary's demise, she would be equally capable of disposing of Lord Mountjoy. He chose, however, to believe that all would continue according to their agreement.

Our appearance in Milan, and our subsequent encounter with Mr. Strangle at the garden party, worried the conspirators not a little. Lord Mountjoy had been pleased to see us decoyed to Venice. He had been less pleased with the Contessa's growing tendency to take the reins of the plot into her own hands.

"I take it you think she was responsible for the unspeakable Strangle's, er, mishap," Thomas said.

"Well, if she was, I must say I can't blame her much in that instance," I said. "Though drowning people in fishponds is a bit extreme."

"He didn't drown," Thomas reminded me. "He was stabbed to death before he was left in the fishpond. Unnecessarily dramatic, that. Under the circumstances."

Lord Mountjoy stared at us as if he did not quite understand what we were saying, then continued as if neither of us had spoken. It was as if, now that he had begun, he felt he *had* to finish, no matter the interruptions or possible digressions.

In Milan, or shortly after, Theodore had completed the last of the preparatory rituals. Only Cavalier Coducci's final ritual, the one in Rome, remained. Lord Mountjoy and Theodore departed for Rome; the Contessa followed shortly after, leaving the Conte, still oblivious to the conspiracy in his household, in Milan.

At the Contessa's advice, Lord Mountjoy and Theodore had taken up residence in a small inn in Rome, while she had come to the villa in Nemi. It was only a day or two before the final ritual that she had told Lord Mountjoy that certain changes would be necessary to Cavalier Coducci's design.

Thomas leaned forward intently, and this time I did not stop him. "What changes?" he demanded.

"You already know most of them," Lord Mountjoy said, frowning. "Ritual at the Temple of Saturn instead of the Basilica Julia, noon instead of midnight, some minor changes to the wording. The main thing, though, is that she claims that wasn't the end of the matter. I'd thought we were finished, but she says, no, we need one more ceremony. Here at Nemi, at the old grove, the day after tomorrow."

"The old grove?" I said.

"She says it's another one of these blasted ancient ritual sites," Lord Mountjoy said. "Some goddess or other this time, and her Sacred King. The Conte dug up a batch of his old pottery there." He shook his head. "The Roman ritual was the last of Coducci's; it's made Theodore dashed persuasive. She says this one will make him irresistible—anything he tells people, they'll do. I don't know if that's a good idea, though. The boy is already getting out of hand with the way he keeps talking people into doing things."

"The Sacred King at Nemi," I said, trying to think what it reminded me of, and then I recalled the museum exhibit. "The King of the Wood at Nemus Dianae?"

"You are much too clever, Signora Tarleton," said a voice behind us, and we turned to see the Contessa standing in the doorway. She wore an old walking-dress with stained sleeves, the sort of thing one wears in the country when one has a messy chore to attend to. Her color was high; she did not look tired or drained at all, and there was no trace of the shyness she had aped at that long-ago tea in Milan. She glared at us coldly, then transferred her gaze to Lord Mountjoy. "I might have guessed you would do something this foolish. Did you not think that these two are wizards?"

"Theodore said it would be all right," Lord Mountjoy muttered.

"Ah, yes, Theodore." The Contessa's eyes narrowed. "I had not anticipated how much nuisance his new abilities would be. I have dealt with that, however; the sleeping draught I gave him will keep him from causing any further upset before the final ritual is complete, and I have the power to restore the ancient glories of my family."

"Ancient glories?" Thomas said. "You mean this drafty pile? It's Palladian, and a bad imitation of the style at that—can't be any more ancient than the sixteenth century."

The Contessa stiffened. "My family has lived here for centuries," she said. Her voice took on greater depth of emotion. "Before the Borgias and the Medicis ruled, before the Goths plundered Rome, before Rome itself ever rose, we were here. First as priestesses, then hidden among the lesser folk, until we rose again to fortune. Yet not to glory— that is to be my task, when I wake the old power once more. Then my ancestors' images will smile from their places in the gallery once more."

"Oh, is *that* what all those bad frescoes in the hall are supposed to be," I said. "Your ancestors! I took them for visitors waiting to get into a costume ball. Really, paintings would be far more the thing. You would at least have some chance that one of the artists would be good."

The Contessa flushed but remained outwardly calm. Only her high color betrayed her anger. "Signora Tarleton, you do not know of what you speak. My ancestors were great; I shall make my house great again." She smiled coldly. "And you shall be of much help, unwilling as you are."

She gestured over her shoulder and spoke in Italian. Her two large henchmen appeared behind her. "These gentlemen will escort you back to your quarters. And just to be sure that you do not attempt anything foolish—" She gestured, and spoke, and once again I felt too ill to resist.

The two guards took Thomas and me back to our storeroom. Again, the illness evaporated as soon as the door locked behind us. I took several deep breaths, then said, "I thought you told me she would be too drained to work that spell again for at least a day."

"I did," Thomas said. "And so she should have been. I don't know where she got the strength to do that, but this time she's been too clever by half."

"What do you mean?"

"I heard the whole spell this time," he said with considerable satisfaction. "And it's not at all difficult to do. Or to guard against."

"Show me how to do both," I said immediately. "If either one of us can turn the tables on her, we'll have a better chance of actually doing so."

"It's a pity it only works on wizards," Thomas commented. "I wouldn't mind sickening those two bullyboys of hers as well."

Learning the spells served to pass the time, and to distract me from my growing hunger. I was starting to wonder whether the Contessa meant to starve us when the door rattled. The two footmen appeared, flanking a maid carrying a tray. The meal she offered was spartan—day-old bread, water, and a bit of cheese—but Thomas and I disposed of it with as much relish as if it had been a French chef's finest offering.

When the servants left, I settled back against the wall. The light was fading, and we had already exhausted the possibilities for escaping from the storeroom. All that was left to us to do was to think or to talk. My thoughts continually turned to James and Kate and how dreadfully worried they must be. Despite all my efforts, I could not force them into more productive channels, and so I chose to talk, instead.

"What *can* the Contessa mean to do with us?" I said. "And why did she make those changes in Cavalier Coducci's ritual?"

Thomas had been staring at his hands, his face drawn and unhappy. When I spoke, he looked up. "I don't know."

"Well, *think*, then," I said sharply. I quite understood that he was as worried about Kate as I was about James, but I did not see how falling into a brown study would help matters. "You worked with Cavalier Coducci's ritual for days, designing that counterspell. Surely you must remember some of it. Can't you at least guess at what effect her changes would have?"

Thomas blinked; then his eyes narrowed. "She changed the time and the location," he said slowly. He frowned in concentration. "The time was theta, multiplied by the sum of the energy derived from alpha-one through..." His voice trailed off, and he stared into the gloom, muttering equations to himself. I held my breath. After a moment he looked over at me.

"Changing the time creates the linkages but leaves the spell unresolved," he said. "It needs something more to finish it off and make it permanent."

"Then there's still a chance to stop them," I said. "What about the location? What would moving the ritual from the Basilica Julia to the Temple of Saturn do?"

"That's more difficult to fathom," Thomas said. "The Basilica Julia was chiefly of symbolic importance. Julius Caesar was not merely the first of the Roman Emperors; he *made himself* Emperor. Just what you'd want to carry into a spell to make someone Emperor of Europe." He said the last words as if they left a bad taste in his mouth.

"But Saturn was a Roman god, not a ruler," I said. "Surely the Contessa can't be silly enough to think that a coronation ritual can make someone into a god!"

"No, and I'll wager that if she were, it's she who'd be the candidate for goddesshood and no one else," Thomas said. A strange expression came over his face.

"What is it?" I demanded.

"Saturn became a Roman god, yes," Thomas said slowly. "But before that he was both god and king of Latium. He founded the first city on the Capitol, where Rome was eventually built. And he was sometimes called the god of the Underworld."

"It sounds very ominous," I said. "But I still don't see the point of using his temple for the spell instead of Caesar's." I considered. "The Contessa changed the spell so that it isn't finished yet, and changed the symbolism to do something else that we aren't sure of. She's going to finish the spell the day after tomorrow in the grove of the King of the Wood at Nemus Dianae." I sighed. "I still can't make anything of it. I wish we'd had time to examine that exhibit in the museum in Milan more closely. I'm sure it was important."

Thomas shrugged. "Mountjoy said the Conte dug up a lot of old pottery there. The Contessa undoubtedly didn't want us to know she had any connection to Nemi, that's all."

"No, I'm sure it was more—" I broke off suddenly. "Thomas, what does *Nemus Dianae* mean?"

"It's Latin for 'Diana's Wood,'" he replied.

"Oh," I said. "Oh, dear."

"Oh dear *what*?" Thomas demanded in tones of exasperation.

"Papa translated some papers a few years ago about Diana of the Woods," I said. "He went on about them for some time over dinner, until Aunt Elizabeth made him stop. He said Diana of the Woods encouraged human sacrifice. And that she was the foster daughter of Hecate, who was the goddess of magic and the Underworld."

"Hecate is a Greek goddess," Thomas observed.

"The Romans borrowed gods and goddesses from all over," I said impatiently. "The important point is that Diana of the Woods is a bloodthirsty, ancient goddess, and the Contessa has some reason for connecting her to this ritual."

"Priestesses," Thomas said slowly. "Ancient glories. But what good will it do her?"

"Power," I said. "She spoke about power." I was starting to feel ill, and this time it wasn't because of the Contessa's spell. "Thomas, I think I know what she's planning. I know why she didn't seem drained by all that spell casting last night."

Thomas looked at me, waiting.

"She *was* drained, but she killed something to replace her power," I said. "Some animal, probably. That's why there were stains on her sleeves when she came to the study. All that talk about ancient glories and ancestors—and Cavalier Coducci's ritual was based on his work re-creating ancient spells. She must have found more extensive notes in those papers the Conte purchased, not just a copy of the ritual itself. She's going to re-create the ritual of Diana of the Woods. The one that included human sacrifice. She wants to bring back the old magic; that's what she meant by 'waking the old power.'"

"Bring it back and use it. It hangs together," Thomas said after a moment. "Perhaps I wasn't so far off when I said she wanted to be a goddess. But why would she go through Coducci's ritual before—" He broke off. "The king was always the most powerful sacrifice the ancients could make," he said in an altered tone.

"Theodore!" I said. "He can't know. But Lord Mountjoy—"

"He probably doesn't know, either. He's too much of a cloth-head to conceal it if he did."

We were both silent for a time. Finally I said, "Thomas, what can we do to stop it?"

"Let me think on it," Thomas replied.

I did my best not to disturb him, all that long night and the next day. The servants came twice more with our scanty meal, but we saw no one else. Neither the Contessa nor Lord Mountjoy appeared (after the Contessa's comments about sleeping draughts, I had no expectation of seeing Theodore). I felt helpless, for it was clear that the Contessa was a wizard of considerable power, quite beyond reach of my meager training. The only way I might possibly be of use would be as a distraction at some crucial moment. The thought was very lowering, and several times I came near demanding that Thomas teach me some spell that I could use against the Contessa, or at least against her henchmen.

Good sense kept me silent. Thomas was a far more experienced wizard than I. It would have been the height of folly to waste his time teaching me minor spells when he was our best hope for stopping the Contessa.

My restraint was rewarded shortly after the servants removed the remnant of our evening meal. "I think I have it," Thomas said. "We'll have two chances. The Contessa can't work two spells at once. She'll have to have Theodore resolve the imperial ritual first. Once that is done, she'll have to perform whatever ritual she has concocted for her sacrifice. Murder out of hand won't be any good to her. If we can disrupt either spell, her plans won't work."

"I see," I said. "I do hope that blocking the spells also involves preventing the murder? Or murders—I can't think what other 'use' she could be planning for us."

"The Contessa isn't likely to waste her sacrifices, once she realizes they won't do her any good," Thomas said confidently.

I cannot say that I shared his confidence, but I held my tongue. I did not see what other choice we had. For though

I was sure that James and Kate would be doing their best to find us, I was equally sure that to depend on their arrival would be the height of folly.

"Blocking the imperial ritual is a complicated process," Thomas went on. "We haven't the resources to do it magically. Interrupting it should serve quite as well and should be much easier to do."

"And if we don't get a chance?"

"Then I'll try to block the final spell," Thomas said. "I can't do much without supplies, but my old tutor used to claim that applied concentration would do, if one had the time. I have the rest of the night to find out how right he was." He looked at me. "Distraction will work, in a pinch— the timing has to be important, or she wouldn't be waiting like this. Even a short delay ought to invalidate her spell."

I did not like the sound of "delay." I wanted something closer to "prevent entirely." Delay was, however, all I was going to get. There really was no more to say; I understood Thomas tolerably well. If his spells did not serve the purpose, I might be able to slow the Contessa down by more mundane means. I think he intended me to have a fit of hysterics or raise some similar row, but I did not see that it would serve with a woman like the Contessa. I had in mind something more direct, possibly involving a large rock.

We spent an even more miserable night than before. Shortly before dawn, the door rattled. Much to my surprise, it admitted not only the two hulking footmen, but Eve-Marie, who I had thought was still in Venice. She snapped directions at the footmen and watched from the doorway as they carried out her orders. Thomas and I both struggled when we realized they meant to bind and gag us, but to no avail.

Under Eve-Marie's direction, the footmen dragged us ignominiously out of the storeroom and loaded us into a donkey cart. There was a pause while Eve-Marie disappeared through another door. She emerged with a goat, which she tied to the rear of the cart, and we set off.

One of the footmen drove, while Eve-Marie and the other footman walked on either side. It was quite uncomfortable. Thomas and I were securely bound back-to-back, so we had the greatest difficulty in shifting position, and we appeared to be lying atop a quantity of jars and sticks and other paraphernalia.

It was just past dawn by this time, so we could see the beauty of the woods as we passed through them. After some time, we lurched down a hill and arrived at the edge of a ring of enormous oaks. On the far side was the lake, mirror-dark and smooth.

The footmen unloaded Thomas and me and dragged us to the far side of the clearing, where they took turns standing guard while Eve-Marie and the remaining footman unloaded the donkey cart. Eve-Marie tethered the goat next to us and sent the spare footman off with the cart. Then she began her work.

It took her at least two hours to set the stage—and setting the stage is what it was, as much as ritual preparation; I had learned enough of magic to know that much. She swept the entire clearing three times with a broom made of twigs (doing considerable damage to the grass in the process) and tied back the bushes along the trail where we had entered, so that they would not interfere with someone walking. She disappeared briefly into the woods, returning with several freshly clipped laurel branches, which she (after some struggle) bent into a wreath and tied together. She laid this at the edge of the clearing, along with a torch; flint and tinder; several small bowls, which she filled with herbs; and one large, shallow bowl.

All this while Thomas and I struggled with our ropes, but the footmen had a deal of unfootman-like skill with knots, and we could not win free.

Eve-Marie stood back at last and looked over her efforts. She squinted at the sun, said something else to the guard in Italian, and sat down under a tree to wait. Perforce, we waited with her.

A little before noon the second footman returned. Eve-Marie rose and, with his help, bound the goat and laid it in the center of the clearing. As they finished, I heard someone approaching down the path. Eve-Marie took a last look at her preparations then melted into the bushes—to keep watch, I assumed, for I could not imagine that the Contessa would want any interruptions to her rituals.

On the heels of Eve-Marie's departure, the Contessa appeared, wearing a pure white robe in the style of Ancient Greece and carrying a gold sickle. I could not speak, but I snorted. Even I know that it was the Celtic Druids who used sickles, and not the Greeks or Romans. Behind her came Theodore, his eyes glazed, wearing an even more outlandish outfit—a Roman-style toga with a border stripe of imperial purple. Hanging at his side was the rusty, leaf-bladed sword.

Last of all came Lord Mountjoy. He looked uncomfortable and decidedly out of place in his morning coat and cravat, and he kept glancing uncertainly from the Contessa to Theodore and back.

In a honey-sweet voice, the Contessa directed Theodore toward the largest of the ancient oaks. He moved toward it docilely, his eyes still glazed and empty. I could feel the spell she was using to control him, but of course neither I nor Thomas could do anything about it, bound and gagged as we were. The Contessa raised her arms and chanted a long invocation in Latin. Then, in English, she said, "Now, Theodore Daventer! Claim your throne!"

Theodore drew the leaf-shaped blade, and I felt the shock in my bones. Cavalier Coducci's theories had been right in this much, at least: Putting this ancient ritual object to use once more certainly woke its old residual magic.

Reaching up, Theodore grasped the end of a low-hanging branch and swung the sword. The oak branch parted, again with a shock I could feel. Power rushed into Theodore, and I knew that the first ritual was complete at last.

Lord Mountjoy started forward, but the Contessa shook her head. She spoke again in Latin, in tones of triumph, then said, "You are now the King of the Wood. The sacred grove is yours to protect and defend, until you go to the goddess."

"I will defend it," Theodore said. He sounded as if he were a long way away, or underwater.

"Good, good," Lord Mountjoy said briskly. He stepped forward as he spoke. "That's finished, then. Shall we—" He broke off, eyes widening, as Theodore spun and raised the sword. "What—what are you doing?"

"I will defend the grove," Theodore repeated in the same blank tone. He started toward his uncle, plainly intent on mayhem.

Lord Mountjoy paled and backed away. "Theodore? Theodore! Gently, my boy."

"He is the King of the Wood," the Contessa said with fierce joy. "He will kill any man who enters the grove."

"I—I—" Lord Mountjoy backed up again. As soon as he crossed the edge of the circle, leaving the grove, Theodore lost interest in him and turned back to stare at the giant oak. "I'll just be going, then."

"Theodore!" the Contessa commanded. "Tell him to stay where he is."

"Stand still, Uncle," Theodore said.

Lord Mountjoy stopped in his tracks. He goggled at his nephew, then at the Contessa. "Here now! What is this? I can't move a step!"

"This is the power of the Emperor of the Soul of the World," the Contessa intoned. "All who hear him shall obey." She bent and set down her sickle, then lit the torch with the flint that Eve-Marie had left ready. It took her several tries, which I do not think she had anticipated, and her cheeks were red with anger by the time it caught. She took a pinch of herbs from one of the bowls and sprinkled it over the flame, then waved the torch at Theodore and cooed, "Stay and commune with the grove, O King of the Wood and Emperor of the Soul of the World, whilst I perform the final rite, the ultimate ritual that will renew at last the ancient powers that you should command."

Theodore's gaze did not waver from the oak. Satisfied, the Contessa picked up the largest of the bowls and set it by Theodore's feet. She returned to her supplies and picked up the laurel wreath, which she set upon her own head. Then she took up the sickle once more.

I felt a wave of despair as she began circling the clearing, chanting in an impassioned voice. She had completed the first of her rituals without our being able to interfere in any way, and it looked very much as if she was about to complete the second. The very atmosphere in the grove seemed to become more dense and more quiet as she circled it, slowly spiraling inward toward Theodore.

And then I saw something moving in the bushes behind our guards. An instant later James emerged from the shrubbery, intent on taking the footmen from behind. I had not thought that I could be any more terrified, but I was wrong. For it occurred to me instantly that if Theodore or the Contessa were to see James, they would attack immediately— and there was no way in which he could resist Theodore's new ability to command obedience. I looked away, hoping that no one had noticed him yet, and saw Kate march into the grove from the opposite direction.

She was, as my brother, Oliver, puts it, done up to the nines. Not a hair was out of place; not a ruffle drooped. Her eyes blazed, but her face was an icy mask—as cold and reptilian as Aunt Charlotte at her worst. *Oh, dear,* I thought. *I haven't seen her this angry since Oliver tied the sleigh bells to the dog's tail to make it run, back when we were eleven. Somebody is in for it now.*

From the commonplace book of Lady Schofield

> *26 November 1817*
> *At the Villa delle Colombe, near Nemi*

Our journey to the villa where Mountjoy was hiding seemed interminable to me. I had expected it to be cold and damp—journeys nearly always are—but my rose-colored shawl was ample warmth, even over the pink morning dress. I was wearing Thomas's favorite again, for luck as much as the impression I hoped to make.

Piers drove and Reardon sat beside me, so I spent hours face-to-face with James, who only rarely looked up from the map he was studying. When he thought of it, James would grumble about the folly of permitting me to accompany him, so it was as well he was silent much of the time. I did not find his grumbles worth a reply, so I maintained my own silence.

By the time we reached Nemi, we found ourselves amid steep wooded hills. The town of Nemi overlooks a singularly beautiful small lake, and to judge purely by appearances, Nemi is a peaceful place. James produced a compass and telescope and put both to good use in his map study. The villa was well situated overlooking the lake and executed in the Palladian style, so that it looked a good deal more like a Roman temple than a Roman temple itself does.

At a prudent distance from the villa, Piers drew up and turned the reins of the carriage over to James. James and I waited with the horses while Piers reconnoitered the villa under the guise of delivering a message for Mountjoy.

James shut his telescope with a snap. "A brigade of horse, that's what I should have insisted upon. These villains did for Bedrick and Strangle. I'm sure of it. Somehow they got the better of Thomas and Cecy. Clearly, they stick at nothing. It's madness to proceed without reinforcements."

"Sheer madness," I agreed. Given James's grumpiness, I thought it best to be as soothing as possible.

James took another look through the telescope. "There's no alternative. Even if Lord Sutton persuades the authorities to send something resembling sufficient force to help us, Lord knows how long they will take to get here."

"Lord knows," I agreed.

James lowered his telescope. "Piers has gone inside."

"What shall we do if he doesn't come out again?" I asked.

"*We* won't do anything." James went back to squinting through the telescope. "I will move in, and *you* will stay here."

All James's attention was fixed upon the view through his telescope so I felt free to roll my eyes. Before he noticed my silence, James straightened.

"Here's Piers again."

"Won't it make them wonder, Piers walking all the way to their villa?" I asked.

"Not half as much as they'd wonder at Piers rolling up to the door with this carriage," James answered me absently. "I don't see any sign of pursuit. I half expected them to send someone to follow him."

When Piers rejoined us, he was scarcely out of breath. "Mountjoy is here. Honored guest of the Contessa. Daventer is with him."

"Only the Contessa?" James asked, puzzled.

"Not the Conte?" I echoed.

"Not a whiff of the Conte," said Piers.

"That's odd," said James. "Did you see Mountjoy or Daventer?" James moved aside to let Piers back on the box. "Did they see you?"

"I didn't see anyone but the maid." Piers took the reins. "At first she was cross because she had to answer the door, but I turned her up sweet."

Beside me, Reardon broke her habitual silence to ask, "How sweet?"

Piers adjusted his hat to a jauntier angle. "She told me that the Contessa has taken the English gentlemen for a walk in the woods. She even pointed, so I know which way they went."

"Isn't that rather peculiar?" I clutched my reticule more tightly. "A walk in the middle of the day?"

"Deuced suspicious," James agreed. "At this hour, I think we can safely assume that Mountjoy is not merely botanizing."

"They took the footmen with them," Piers added, "or my maid would never have had to put down what she was doing to see to the door."

"Let's go see what they're doing, shall we?" I spoke with all the firmness I could muster, for I knew this was the point at which James would be most likely to attempt to leave me behind. Indeed, I think he considered the matter carefully, but something in my demeanor must have convinced him not to try.

"Yes, let's," was all James said.

Piers drove on. We were in a wooded lane when the horses balked and refused to go further. "Down there, I think." Piers pointed in the direction of what looked to me like a bramble thicket. "Near the lake, if the maid was right."

"Right." James climbed down. "I'll reconnoiter this time." To Piers, he said, "If anyone comes along, you'll be inspecting the harness." To me, and by extension Reardon, he said, "Stay here. I'll be right back." With a rustle of bare branches, he set off through the undergrowth.

James was as good as his word. Within fifteen minutes he emerged from the shrubbery and rejoined us. He looked, if anything, more haggard than before, but there was new light in his eyes and a truly mulish set to his jaw. "I've found them."

As Reardon and I descended from the carriage, Piers dealt with the horses and carriage while James gave us a brief description of what he'd found.

"The underbrush grows thicker for about a hundred yards as you go downhill. Good cover. Bear to the right as you go, Piers. Kate, keep as straight as you can. The slope eases just before the cover thins. There's a clearing in a grove of oak trees before you come to the lake. That's where they are."

"Who?" I demanded. "Mountjoy and Theodore or Thomas and Cecy?"

"All of them." James looked grim. "The Contessa di Capodoro must have curious tastes in entertainment, for she's wearing some sort of fancy dress. Cecy and Thomas are tied up, unharmed, I judge, and, from all appearances, Daventer has wrapped himself in a bedsheet. Mountjoy, thank God, is fully dressed."

"So, two of them for the two of us." Piers, finished with the horses, produced a small but efficient-looking pistol and set about preparing it.

"Not quite." James produced a firearm of his own and checked it over. "There are two servants guarding Cecy and Thomas."

"Four, then." Piers didn't seem alarmed at the change in odds.

"Five, if you count the Contessa, and I do," James said. "From the way they all dance to her measure, I won't be surprised to learn the Contessa considers herself to be in charge."

"Oh, dear." I remembered the comfortable chat we'd had over tea, Cecy and the Contessa and I. It had been so nice to meet someone who truly knew about the opera. "What sort of fancy dress is she wearing?"

James thought about it. "I think she means to be an ancient Greek. Flowing white draperies, that sort of thing."

That didn't help. "I do hope she is just being Greek in general and not thinking of some particular Greek. Medea, say. Greeks can be very drastic."

"Ask her," James suggested. "Or do anything else you can think of to distract her. Because Mountjoy looks sick as a sheep. From all appearances, it's the Contessa who is responsible for what they've done to Cecy and Thomas."

I thought hard about what it would mean, walking in on four men and a woman who knew enough magic to capture Thomas and Cecy. "If I distract the Contessa, can you and Piers free Thomas and Cecy?"

James nodded. "Give us time to get into position before you show yourself."

"If the Contessa does something drastic to me, you will help Thomas set it right as soon as possible?" Try as I might, I could not help pleading for a bit of reassurance.

"Trust me," said James as he and Piers headed for the shrubbery.

It felt wrong just to walk away and leave the carriage unattended.

I turned to Reardon. "Perhaps someone ought to stay with the horses."

Reardon was having none of it. "Nonsense. The horses will do very well by themselves. I will accompany you."

"It will be safer with the horses. In all likelihood, I will be turned into a frog at once."

"Then you will need me to look after you," said Reardon.

"If you are with me, you will be turned into a frog, too," I pointed out. "With luck, though, Thomas will be able to turn us back as soon as James frees him."

"I am sure Lord Schofield will do his best." Reardon was dauntless. "I will stay with you."

"Very well." I opened my reticule. "Hold out your hands." I showed her the powder Thomas had swept up so carefully after Cecy's first effort to focus her magic. "It won't protect us from spells, but it may disrupt them. I intend to be a distraction, nothing more, but you must have some of this, too."

I divided the powder between my reticule and Reardon's. At Reardon's suggestion, we sifted a bit of the powder over each other so that when we set off for the grove, I not only carried half a reticule of the stuff, I had it sprinkled over my hair and in my shoes, as well as liberally scattered over my gown.

We set forth again, as stealthily as possible under the circumstances, and I remember wondering how anyone could truly enjoy gambling. The gamble I took was unavoidable. How could anyone take such risks just for fun? My grandfather must have been mad.

On the other hand, I thought, remembering Lady Sylvia and the League of the Pimpernel, perhaps my father had taken his risks for fun, too. Perhaps in my way I am as big a gambler as anyone in my family. I just take after my father instead of my grandfather.

The undergrowth was thick indeed, but, mercifully, the footing was not treacherous. If it had been a wood back home in Rushton, there would have been leaves and twigs underfoot, as well as a good deal of mud to contend with. We were fortunate, given the time of year, that so many of the trees were oaks, for although oak leaves wither they do not fall from the branch until much later in winter. Good cover, as Cecy would say. Reardon and I were able to catch our breath and, incidentally, to restore order to our appearance at the foot of the slope. There, as James had described, the shrubbery yielded to a clearing in a grove. Reardon and I crouched in the bushes to give James and Piers the time they had asked for.

If we had been back home in Rushton, there would certainly have been birds singing. With the slightest breeze, leaves would have rustled. Very likely a dog would bark in the distance, or one might hear the lowing of a discontented cow. In an ordinary wood, there would have been some kind of friendly noise. In that place, at that moment, there was no sound at all. The quiet, the utter stillness, seemed uncanny. The very air conspired to create an oppressive mood, for there was not the slightest of breezes. Never before have I understood so well why we say "dead calm."

I peered through the branches of the particular bush I'd settled behind. From my vantage point, I could see Mountjoy quite well. James had not exaggerated. He did look as sick as a sheep. Theodore, if anything, looked worse. He was wearing fancy dress of a sort, white robes draped toga-fashion. His countenance was waxen, he was so pale, and his gaze seemed fixed as he regarded one of the oak trees in fascination. There was the scent of vegetation burning, for at intervals around the clearing stood braziers in which fresh greenery wilted and smoldered over coals.

If I craned my neck, it was difficult yet possible to see Thomas and Cecy, tied back-to-back, hand and foot, and gagged, but I made myself ignore the distressing sight. A pair of footmen stood guard over them. The footmen seemed very ill at ease.

Given the behavior of the Contessa di Capodoro, I could see why. She held center stage in the grove as much by her demeanor as her extraordinary costume. I could not

decide who, if anyone, her fancy dress was intended to por-
tray, but the effect was certainly striking. She was all antique
grandeur, with gauzy white draperies in the finest Grecian
style. The Contessa's hair was loose down her back and
she wore a circlet of laurel leaves with all the majesty of a
golden crown. In one hand she held a torch. In the other she
brandished a small sickle, the kind one uses to harvest bar-
ley, both handle and blade bright with gilt. The Contessa
was moving methodically about the clearing, intoning a soft
chant as she danced. It ought to have been absurd. It wasn't.
Every step she took deepened the silence in the grove.
Every syllable of her chant increased the sense of forebod-
ing in that place. Every eye was upon her. Even Thomas
watched, apparently fascinated.

I made myself take a few steps forward. I caught a whiff
of the strange smoke. It caught in the back of my throat and
made my eyes burn. There was a substantial oak nearby and
I found myself leaning against it with my eyes closed. Only
when Reardon poked me in the ribs did I recover my sense
of urgency. I moved toward the spectacle with reluctance.
Who was I, after all, to intrude on such mysteries?

From my new vantage point, I could see better. For the
first time I noticed that the Contessa was circling an object—something grayish, something about the size of a
large dog—in the center of the clearing. It was a goat. Apparently the creature was intended as a votive sacrifice, for it
was not tethered but tied fetlock-to-fetlock, fore and aft, so

that it lay helpless on its side. Despite its discomfort, the goat made not a bleat of protest, nor did it struggle against the cords that bound it.

The uncanniness of it, that goat's meek, most ungoatlike behavior, made the power the Contessa wielded real to me. If she could do that—render a goat docile—what couldn't she do? I felt despair.

Although the Contessa's dance circled the sacrificial goat, all her attention seemed focused on Theodore. Theodore, whose draperies were as picturesque in their way as the Contessa's, stood nearby, apparently leaning for support upon the largest oak tree of all. He, alone of us all, took no notice of the Contessa's extraordinary behavior. Instead, he seemed engrossed in studying the pattern of the bark on the tree trunk.

I reached into my reticule, took out a handful of powdered writing desk, and scattered it before me. To be honest, I could not think of anything else to do. I took a few steps farther into the grove. It was my duty to provide a distraction so that Thomas and Cecy could be rescued. Yet I could not think of a suitable speech with which to distract the Contessa. I knew her taste for opera. From the circumstances, I could deduce her taste for drama. What I ought to do was stalk in like a Fury, demanding revenge. Not for the first time, I regretted the lack of my imaginary aria.

I might have stood there indefinitely, a prisoner of my own self-regarding thought, but James emerged from the shrubbery, slinking toward Thomas and Cecy. Desperate to distract the footmen, if only by asking the Contessa for directions, I started forward.

I was perhaps twenty feet from the Contessa, still wondering what on earth to say, when I came near enough to see that the sacrificial goat was a nanny goat. And not merely a nanny goat, I saw, but a nanny goat in desperate need of milking. Cruel as it is to restrain an animal in such a fashion, it is crueler still to restrain a creature that needs milking. Oh, it surpasses cruelty. Even to think of it now makes me indignant.

At the time, I was not myself. I had not slept well, or indeed at all, for three nights. My dear husband was in mortal danger, as were my cousin and her husband. There was no shortage of danger to any of us. Therefore, it may seem strange that I grew so angry at the way the Contessa treated a nanny goat. All I know is that my initial sight of the goat's situation had filled me with fear for the Contessa's uncanny powers. When I saw the true state of affairs, the nanny goat's pitiful condition filled me with indignant rage. There can be no earthly excuse to treat an animal with such cruelty.

I shouted as I approached the Contessa. It was hardly the stuff of arias. To the best of my recollection, I said, "Contessa, release that goat!"

The Contessa stopped in her tracks, stared, and turned to confront me. She said nothing. Her eyes were blazing. I expected to be transformed into a frog on the spot.

From the corner of my eye, I saw that James paid no attention to my efforts at distraction. On the contrary, he carried on expertly, slipping between the footmen and crouching over Thomas. Mountjoy moved toward me, protesting. All Theodore's attention was fixed on his tree. The footmen goggled at me.

Glaring at the Contessa, I pointed at the nanny goat. "I said, release that animal at once! You should be ashamed of yourself."

To my consternation, the Contessa dismissed me with a sneer. Instead of transforming me into a frog, she returned to her dance. With unspeakable grace, she raised the golden sickle high and stepped behind Theodore, arm poised for a killing blow.

I screamed. I know that. I'm not sure what. Something along the lines of, "Theodore, look out!" Desperate to distract the Contessa, I threw my reticule and it struck her between the shoulder blades, puffing out powdered desk, and fell to the ground, spilling more.

Stirred from his reverie at last, Theodore turned to find himself nose-to-nose with the Contessa. He caught at her wrist at the last possible instant, foiling her blow, and cried, "Contessa!" Theodore sounded as if he might burst into tears.

The Contessa twisted free, snarling words I could not understand. She tripped over the goat, which uttered a bleat of protest. Balance lost, the Contessa dropped her sickle and her torch and fell headlong at Theodore's feet.

Reardon and I moved forward together, intent on catching her while she was down. For a moment, I was so close to the Contessa that I could see the bits of desk sparkling golden in the mud on her hands.

Then the Contessa made an economical gesture and spat out a word. I fell one way and Reardon another. By the time I picked myself up and looked around, the Contessa had regained her sickle and was coaxing the torch back to flame. I looked around.

A few yards from me, Reardon was back on her feet. She looked very angry. Beside her, the goat began to chew at the cords that tied its forelegs even as it kicked to loosen the cords that bound its hind legs.

Mountjoy was crossing toward Theodore, calling his name. He looked frightened. So did Theodore, who was staring around wildly as if he'd been wakened from a dream to find himself in a nightmare.

Across the clearing, James had freed Thomas from his bonds and turned to do the same for Cecy. As I watched, Thomas stood up and sat down again immediately. I deduced that the time he'd spent tied up had impaired his usual speed and grace. From his vantage point seated on the ground, Thomas intoned and gestured in a way that told me that whatever else was impaired, his magical powers were fine.

The Contessa, now satisfied with her torch, turned her attention to Thomas. Spell and counterspell flew faster than my senses could perceive. Deadlocked, the pair of them glared at each other across the clearing.

Cecy shook free of her bonds as James cut them and for a moment let James support her. Their embrace was brief, but I found it a touching sight.

The footmen seized James and pulled him away. Enraged, Cecy threw herself upon them. One footman held James and the other turned his attention to Cecy, actually lifting her from her feet. She struggled violently in his grasp.

Theodore, clutching his antique robes to preserve his modesty, eluded Mountjoy's grasp and started across the clearing toward Cecy. "Unhand that lady!"

The footman did so at once and stood over Cecy where she sprawled. I don't know which of them looked more astonished. James took advantage of the distraction to land a punishing blow square on his footman's nose. The footman staggered back and fell to his knees, swearing.

Thomas and the Contessa continued their unseen battle of magical will across the clearing. I could see nothing, and I understood nothing of what little I heard, but I could almost smell the intensity of their conflict. It hung in the air like the smoke from gunpowder when cannons are fired.

"Cecelia!" cried Theodore, and something in the deep emotion that throbbed beneath his words made me very sure indeed that Theodore had a taste for opera. "Are you hurt?"

Cecy glared at him. I waved to attract her attention and put the back of my hand to my forehead. Unerringly, Cecy understood my hint and acted upon it, falling limp, as if about to swoon. She pantomimed helplessness as Theodore bent over her. No one on a stage could have done better. I was proud of her quickness and pleased that our methods of schoolroom signaling to each other worked as well as ever.

All indignation, James protested. "Unhand my wife, Sir."

Mountjoy seized my wrist and hauled me to my feet. "You've ruined everything, you little goose." He brushed Reardon aside as she came to my aid.

I resisted Mountjoy vigorously and called him many names. The goat, free at last, sprang up almost under our feet, intent upon escape. Thomas and the Contessa continued their duel, shouting in Latin and Greek and what might have been Babylonian for all I understood of it.

Theodore shouted, "Be quiet, all of you! Just stop it. Stop everything."

We stopped everything, held motionless where we stood.

Thomas, caught between one word and the next, looked astounded. The Contessa glared daggers at Thomas but was as helpless to move or speak as any of the rest of us.

Motionless, Cecy was sprawled on the ground in a most becoming attitude. Theodore caught her in his arms. If looks really could kill, James, hardly an arm's length away, would have done for Theodore then and there.

Cecy's footman was looking more surprised than before. James's footman, nose bloodied, was halted in the very act of rising to his feet. Reardon, at Mountjoy's elbow, was frozen in her attempt to pull him away from me. I found myself curiously calm, despite the fact I was held as motionless as any marble statue.

Only the goat was unaffected. Distracted by the Contessa's fallen wreath of laurel—it had ended up in the mud as a result of our struggle—the goat sampled a few leaves. It looked around with interest as it chewed.

I am sure we presented a quaint tableau.

Theodore, the only one among us not struck motionless, was oblivious. All his attention was focused upon Cecy. "Are you hurt? Oh, Cecelia, speak to me."

The picture they made, Theodore cradling Cecy to his bosom, was as touching as it was ridiculous. I don't think any gentleman, no matter how passionate, could overcome the supreme disadvantage of finding himself in such a situation whilst wearing a bedsheet.

When Cecy obeyed Theodore's command and spoke to him, it was with admirable restraint. "Mr. Daventer, what are you doing?"

The crispness of Cecy's tone seemed to remind Theodore of the proprieties. He loosened his grip upon her with commendable speed. "I thought you were— I thought you might be hurt. Please forgive my forwardness, er, Mrs. Tarleton."

Calm despite the situation in which she found herself, Cecy said, "I'm fine, I assure you. Do help me up, Mr. Daventer." When she was on her feet, Cecy brushed a lock of hair out of her eyes, took a keen look about her, and said something I could not catch. Then, dusting her hands together with an air of a job well done, she addressed

Theodore in her most compelling tone. "You must tell James that he can move, Theodore." After a moment's reflection, she added, "Thomas, Kate, and Reardon, as well, if you please."

"I don't understand—" Theodore's confusion was almost painful to behold.

"You will," Cecy assured him. "I'll explain everything in a moment. But for now, please do as I ask."

"Very well," said Theodore, abashed. "Mr. Tarleton, Lord and Lady Schofield, Reardon, please do as you wish."

Theodore seemed about to add something more, but Cecy put her hand to his lips. "That will do to be going on with. Thank you, Theodore."

"Yes, thank you," I called. I found I was able to move as well as speak, and I pulled free from Mountjoy's grip with alacrity.

"You are entirely welcome," said Theodore. He really is a most amiable young man, despite everything.

The goat finished the Contessa's laurel wreath, apparently finding it quite tasty. Across the clearing, Thomas's first act, now that speech and motion were restored, was to tug his clothing into better order. Needless to say, Thomas denies this. He claims his first act was to kiss me. Despite my mock indignation when we discussed the matter later, in all honesty, at the time I found his unthinking vanity deeply reassuring. Nothing could have told me more clearly that Thomas was entirely himself. As he tugged at his neckcloth,

I stepped past Mountjoy, Reardon, and the goat. Yielding to my most heartfelt inclination, I ran into Thomas's arms.

The relief of feeling his embrace again, of knowing him to be safe—well, some things truly are beyond words.

From the deposition of Mrs. James Tarleton, &c.

I did not at once realize why it was that I felt so . . . *clear* from the moment Kate entered the grove, but when I saw the glittering dust she threw on the Contessa, I knew. Strong magic leaves a residue in the objects used for a ritual; turning the desk in the Palazzo Flangini into powder had been strong magic indeed, however uncontrolled. And it was *my* magic. I could feel it in the back of my mind—and I could sense the Contessa's magic, too, for just that brief moment.

A moment was long enough. As she raised her sickle to kill Theodore, I cut off the power she was feeding to the spell that was keeping him dazed and helpless. It was all I could think of, but, fortunately, it answered very well. He turned in time to keep the Contessa from stabbing him in the back. He did not, however, seem to have the least notion what was going on, and as I was still bound and gagged, I could not tell him. (James had most sensibly begun untying Thomas first.)

I tried to use my unexpected magical ability to interfere further with the Contessa, but manipulating raw magical power is nothing whatever like casting a proper spell. On the one hand, one does not require words or symbols, so that it is possible to use magic even while gagged; on the other, one has no way of shaping the power into exactly the sort of spell one needs. Despite my best efforts, I could only manage to inflict the Contessa with a general clumsiness. Between this and Kate's advance, however, she was sufficiently distracted to prevent any additional magical efforts for a moment. By then James had finished releasing Thomas, who immediately occupied her full attention with a duel arcane.

James released me next, and took a moment to assure himself that I was uninjured. The moment was too long— the two footmen who had been guarding us had by this time recovered their sense of duty and grabbed his arms. I could not use the loose magic of the powdered desk on them, for they had not been near enough to the Contessa to be sprinkled with the dust, and it was imperative to keep them from finishing with James and turning to Thomas. So I slapped the one nearest me.

This attracted his attention, and a brisk scuffle followed. James engaged in fisticuffs with the one footman, while I kept the other occupied. Then Theodore's voice rang across the grove in fine dramatic style: "Unhand that lady!"

The footman released me so quickly that I went sprawling. I am not sure which of us was most startled: me, the footman, or Theodore. As I struggled to my feet, Kate pantomimed for me to faint. Her instinct for such things has always been excellent, so I complied at once.

I could hear—and feel—the continuing magical struggle between the Contessa and Thomas. The Contessa seemed to be getting the best of him; I could sense depths of power in her that she had scarcely begun to draw on, while Thomas was tired and hungry. So, naturally, I attempted to feed Thomas some of the unexpected extra power I had available.

The attempt was a grave mistake. I very nearly overset Thomas's concentration entirely. I pulled back just in time, considered for a moment, and then tried, even harder than before, to feed extra power to the Contessa, instead.

This time, the effect was all I could have hoped for. The Contessa's spell backfired, shaking her severely and allowing Thomas just the opening he needed. And then Theodore's voice rang out once more: "Be quiet, all of you! Just stop it. Stop everything."

Perforce, we all stopped. The sudden silence was astonishing and intense. I am not sure how long we might all have stood like waxworks if Theodore had not demanded that I speak to him.

Once I was allowed to speak, I persuaded Theodore to release Kate, James, Thomas, and Reardon from the effects of his command. I used the lingering residue of the powdered desk to unravel the spell the Contessa had begun weaving about the grove, then reabsorbed the remaining power. I did not think it wise to leave loose magic lying around, no matter how useless it might be to anyone save myself.

While I was busy with the magic, James used the ropes that had bound Thomas and me to tie up the two footmen. Just as he finished, there was a commotion in the bushes, and a moment later Eve-Marie appeared, being marched along by none other than Thomas's valet-cum-bodyguard, Piers. She seemed most put out by her situation, and called Piers a great many vulgar names in the French language. At least, I assumed they were vulgar from the reactions James and Thomas had.

Theodore stared at them and opened his mouth to say something, and I held my hand up gently. "Mr. Daventer, please don't say anything yet. It's quite dangerous. The Contessa has . . . has cast a spell that makes everyone obey you, and you might cause all sorts of difficulties by saying the wrong thing by accident."

Theodore's eyes widened, and he nodded. Eve-Marie continued spitting incomprehensible French at the top of her lungs. I sighed. "Perhaps you could just tell Eve-Marie to be quiet and stand still," I said.

"Eve-Marie, be quiet and stand still," Theodore repeated, and she froze where she was. Piers gingerly let go of her arms, and she continued to stand as she had been told. Theodore's eyes grew wider, and he looked at me. "I did that?"

"You did indeed," I said. "But I don't recommend that you continue. We don't know yet how this spell is powered; you may be taking a year off your life every time you issue a command, or something similar. It would be wisest if you didn't say anything at all until Lord Schofield or some other competent wizard has examined the spell. Perhaps even *several* competent wizards."

This left us with the problem of what to do with Eve-Marie, Lord Mountjoy, and the Contessa. We did not have enough rope to tie them up the way we had the footmen, and it seemed most unwise to have Theodore issue more orders so as to get them to do what we wanted. Quite apart from the possibility of damaging Theodore himself, there was always the chance that some misphrasing would leave a loophole that the Contessa could use against us.

In the end we discovered that although they would not move of their own accord, they could be pushed or dragged along. So Piers took Eve-Marie, James hauled Lord Mountjoy, and Thomas shoved the Contessa down the path toward where James and Kate had left their coach. We had to leave the footmen, as neither Kate nor I was strong enough to make them move, and James and Thomas insisted on handling the more important prisoners themselves. Reardon came last, leading the goat.

When we reached the carriage, there was another argument, for even if James and Piers and Thomas all sat outside, there was not room for the rest of us—and neither James nor Thomas would allow Kate and me inside with the Contessa and Lord Mountjoy without, as they put it, some protection in case Theodore's orders began to wear off. Yet no one wanted to be left behind.

Luckily, just before the argument became heated, we

heard the rattle of another vehicle approaching rapidly. It was an extremely elegant light coach, making good time even over the rough ground. The coachman pulled up just in time, and the doors flew open, disgorging two gentlemen and a lady in a brocade-trimmed spencer and a full-skirted walking dress.

The first gentleman made a rapid assessment of us all, then bowed to Kate. "Milady Schofield!" he said. "The Signora Montgomery's complements, and we are here to provide any assistance you may require. Though it appears you have matters well in hand."

"Transportation," James said. "And a lockup for these three." He glared at the Contessa, Eve-Marie, and Lord Mountjoy.

"There are also two footmen tied up in the clearing back there," I said, indicating the direction. I had no idea who these people were, but Kate and James seemed prepared to accept them, and that was good enough for me. "And if any of you are wizards, it might be as well for you to examine the place carefully. I think we disposed of most of the Contessa's spell, but it would be best to make certain."

"I should like a shave," Thomas said around an immense yawn. "And someone should take a look at young Daventer here, and see if there's a way he can be made safe to talk again." Theodore gave him a grateful look.

"We should all like to go somewhere to rest," Kate said firmly. "Somewhere *close by*."

Which was what we did. Our reinforcements arranged

everything with great efficiency, and within half an hour we were installed in a local villa. I suspect that they turned several people out of their bedchambers to make room for us, but at the time I was past caring. The moment I saw the feather bed, I collapsed onto it and did not stir again for many hours.

By the time I awoke, matters were well in hand. James had been up talking to Mrs. Montgomery's friends for some time—apparently, a career as A.D.C. to the Iron Duke accustoms one to peculiar hours and little sleep—and had even been to the Contessa's palazzo to retrieve the stolen regalia. The wizards had spent hours examining Theodore Daventer, and had succeeded in reducing the effect of the Contessa's warped imperial ritual; no longer was everyone forced to obey him instantly. Despite their best efforts, however, the wizards had been unable to cancel the effect of the ritual entirely with the resources at their disposal, and recommended an immediate return to Rome.

The carriage ride from Nemi to Rome took considerably longer than the one we had made from Rome to Nemi, but it was far more comfortable, and gave all of us time to hear one another's stories. I was most impressed by Kate's daring and determination, and I assured her that she had my retroactive and permanent permission to search every one of my belongings for anything useful whenever I happened to have been abducted.

When we reached Rome, we handed the Contessa and Eve-Marie over to the Roman authorities, together with the stolen regalia. I was not altogether sanguine about this, as I was not sure that the Roman authorities were capable of dealing with so powerful and unscrupulous a wizard, but Kate's friends assured us that she would be properly guarded.

"The Conte da Monteferro and the Signor Sette will see to it," one of them told us as the Contessa and her henchmen were hustled away. "You will not know them, but they are excellent wizards, and friends of the Signora Montgomery." He winked and pantomimed knitting. "It is not possible that the Contessa will be let go after abducting two English citizens."

With that settled, we moved on to the English ambassador. Lord Sutton was every bit as stuffy as Kate's account of him made him sound, but once Thomas and James finally managed to convince him of the Contessa's crimes, he readily agreed to make the strongest possible representations to those same Roman authorities regarding the eventual punishment of the Contessa. He also took temporary custody of Lord Mountjoy and Theodore.

"The Duke of Wellington will want to speak with them both," James warned him. "I have already sent him an account of the entire matter, by the fastest ship I could find."

"You are on terms with His Grace?" Lord Sutton said uncertainly.

"I was A.D.C. to him during the war," James said, managing to look extremely military despite wearing an ordinary, somewhat rumpled morning coat that he had not changed in two days. "It was at his request that we looked into this affair. I expect you will be hearing from him shortly."

"Very well, Mr. Tarleton," Lord Sutton said. "I shall hold these two until then."

Despite his agreement, I do not think Lord Sutton really believed James until the Duke of Wellington's response arrived a week and a half later by the same route James's letter had taken (at a gallop from Paris to Toulon, by fast ship from Toulon to Rome). His Grace had clearly begun applying his superior knowledge of tactics to his "new battlefield," for he did not merely send a letter; he sent a Special Envoy with a stack of memoranda and a set of credentials that must have taken up half a trunk.

The Envoy's first action was to take charge of Lord Mountjoy and Theodore, much to Lord Sutton's relief. (I understand they will be returning to France with him, and from there to England, where arrangements have already been made for Theodore to be examined by an emergency gathering of the Royal College of Wizards.) His second was to extract the stolen regalia from the Roman authorities in some manner unknown to me and then to give it to Thomas for temporary safekeeping; and his third was to ask each of us to write out an account of the entire matter for the benefit of the authorities at home.

I have done as he asked, to the best of my ability and recollection. I do hope that no one will be too hard on young Mr. Daventer. As can be seen from my account, I am convinced that he was in no way willingly involved in the

Contessa's plots and, in fact, was the intended victim of one of them. It is not his fault that he is now in some sense the True Emperor of All Europe, and he has certainly not evinced the slightest desire to rule anyone.

Written this eleventh day of December, 1817, by Mrs. James Tarleton, Rome, Italy

From the commonplace book of Lady Schofield

> *28 November 1817*
> *Rome*
> *At our lodging off the Piazza di Spagna*

If I have anything to say in the matter, and I fully expect to, I will not ever spend another night away from Thomas. It is all very well to be reunited after such turmoil. I don't expect anything short of Heaven to measure up to the joy of getting him back again. But I will not willingly experience even such a splendid reunion if it means we must be separated first. Well, not unless the separation is for an extremely good reason.

As I was fully distracted by Thomas, I'm afraid I paid very little attention to the disposal of Mountjoy, the Contessa, and Eve-Marie. I do know that Piers helped Reardon milk the goat. It was base ingratitude on the nanny goat's part not to submit gracefully to this act of kindness. Yet goats are nothing if not ungrateful. It put up a stiff resistance, but between Piers and Reardon, they contrived to squeeze out enough milk to alleviate the nanny's discomfort. When they finished, it twisted away and they let it go with every sign of relief. On all three parts.

Thomas, Cecy, and James dealt with the most urgent demands of our situation, ably relieved by the wizards Mrs. Montgomery dispatched to our aid. Before long, we were in the carriage again—far more comfortably than when we had villains to deal with—this time headed I knew not where. James, fortunately, did. The night we spent at the Villa delle Colombe near Nemi was not uncomfortable. Indeed, I could have slept sitting up. Probably with my eyes open. For all I know, I might have done so.

Alors! That's what Walker said when we returned and Reardon told her of all our doings. Well, first she said something else, something I suspect is a bit too rude to record here. But the feeling in her voice summed things up exactly. *Alors,* indeed.

Our journey here from Nemi was blessedly uneventful. Mrs. Montgomery's wizards seem to have matters well in hand. Their adroit questioning has established that it was Eve-Marie, dissembling even in her grammar, who wrote the letter that lured Sir Hilary Bedrick to his doom. She was X, and she met Sir Hilary with the henchmen who carried out her will. So when Cecy wondered why Mr. Reardon and Mr. Lennox were so quick to assume Sir Hilary's murderer must have been a man, she had the stray thread of the matter. We just didn't have enough information to allow us to follow that thread.

Mr. Strangle's murder has been laid at the Contessa's door. Indeed, a stab in the back seems to be quite her style, given her plans for Theodore.

It is a great relief to be done with all these murders.

When we returned to our lodgings here, it was to find all was well under Walker's expert command. A day of peace and quiet and a few creature comforts sufficed to renew our sense of interest in the outside world, and this morning I felt curious enough to ask for any letters that have arrived in the past few days.

There were two, one from Lady Sylvia and one from Aunt Charlotte. If I have learned nothing else from Thomas, I now know that it is sometimes beneficial to take the sweet before the sour, so I read Lady Sylvia's first.

Dear Kate,

Thank you for your graceful letter of thanks for the shawl you like so much. I am only sorry that I am not the proper recipient of your gratitude. The parcel arrived for you here and I forwarded it un-opened. I suppose those black chamber people are up to their tricks again, reading foreign mail. If you do not know who sent you the shawl, I urge the utmost caution. Let Thomas have a good look at it before you wear it again. If necessary, burn it.

Lady Sylvia had signed with her usual flourish, and the rest of the sheet was taken up with her customary postscripts, some of them longer than the body of the letter itself.

I was glad Reardon had put the rose-colored shawl safely out of my reach the moment we returned to our lodging. I would be sorry to burn it, but if we could not find out who had sent it and why, it would probably be best.

Next I opened Aunt Charlotte's letter, forwarded from Paris.

Dear Kate,

I thought I had taught you the rudiments of courtesy, but once again I perceive I was mistaken. If you recall the elements of etiquette, you will remember it is customary to thank one who bestows a gift. I suppose the shawl I sent you is not fine enough for the most honorable the Marchioness of Schofield. I feared as much. Do not discard it lightly, I pray you, for I have had Elizabeth put one of her best spells on it. Who wears that shawl will have her eyes opened to the true merit of those around her. I would have done the charm myself, but I think you have more confidence in your Aunt Elizabeth than in me. It mattered more to me that the spell protect you than that you value the gift properly.

It occurs to me the gift may have gone astray, and that is why you never thanked me for it. I send this note to the same address to be forwarded to you, wherever you are on your journeying. If you receive it, you must have received the shawl itself. Let your conscience be your guide, Kate, but know that ingratitude breeds ingratitude.

Your loving aunt,
Charlotte

It goes without saying that Aunt Charlotte's letter vexed me greatly. But it was with mixed feelings that I retrieved the shawl from exile in its drawer. Had I known Aunt Charlotte was the giver, I would have received the gift with wariness that had nothing to do with any charm she asked Aunt Elizabeth to cast upon it. I had not known. I had assumed that a gift so thoughtfully chosen must be from Lady Sylvia, so I had loved it on her account. My affection toward the shawl should hardly change now that I know who the giver truly is. Though it comes from Aunt Charlotte, it is still the perfect color, the perfect texture.

As I put the shawl on, I could not help but wonder if the spell had played any part in my adventures. Had I been a little braver with Aunt Elizabeth's spell to clear my eyes? Had it been Aunt Charlotte's intent to brace me up, to stiffen my spine? Or had it been Aunt Charlotte herself who stiffened me, who taught me how to play the dragon when a dragon was who one needed to be? Or was it just me?

It seems strange that I can show more courage on a goat's behalf than on my own. It doesn't seem a bit strange that I can show more courage on Thomas's behalf than my own.

I suppose, somewhere down deep inside, everyone has her own goat. We know it when we see it.

I'll ask Thomas to inspect the spell on the shawl again when he returns, but I won't tell him why unless he asks. Once he knows Aunt Charlotte gave it to me, this will always be "Aunt Charlotte's shawl" to him. I think I shall keep my own counsel on this matter, at least for a little while.

Soon it will be time to dress for dinner. If I start writing now, I can have my letter of apology to Aunt Charlotte written, sanded, and sealed by the time Reardon comes to help me change.

11 December 1817
Rome
At our lodging off the Piazza di Spagna

All the stolen regalia has now been tenderly gathered up and stowed in a trunk, a case of all one's eggs going into one sturdy basket. I found the spectacle of the regalia, set out in the parlor as if they were so many ordinary household objects, quite astonishing.

Thomas gave us all a chance to examine them closely, then James and I looked on as Thomas and Cecy prepared to stow each item safely. The robe, the Sainte Ampoule, the sword, the ring—individually they spoke of the romance of history and the battering of time, but together they made a breathtaking assembly. I tried not to think what Theodore must have looked like wearing them. They could do him no more credit than his bedsheet had.

It is true that the coronation robe was falling to pieces. The cloth of gold was so grimy it was dark brown, almost black in places. The linen undercoat that lined it, sturdy in its day, was rotting away. Yet even so, the garment held a faint scent, a spiciness like the best beeswax candles—if I may be fanciful, a last whiff of fragrance from a lost world.

The alabaster flask of the Sainte Ampoule was well preserved, quite lovely in its way. The ring was curiously made, adorned with little knobs of gold like grains of rice. "Granulation, they call the technique," James told us. "The Etruscans were quite good at it."

"Is it *that* old?" Cecy exclaimed, turning the ring in the palm of her hand so it glowed in the firelight. Given the size of the thing, it could almost have served as a small doorknob.

"It's far from likely." James took the ring from Cecy and gave it back to Thomas.

"But not impossible?" I asked.

"Not quite impossible," said Thomas, as he put the ring safely away.

At first glance, the sword was almost as unprepossessing as the robe. A rusty bit of metal, I would have said. Upon consideration, however, the sword looked the oldest of all the regalia. Held at the proper angle, the dull surface gave back a gleam of blue gray, a hint of what the metal beneath must have been in its day. The curve of the blade was graceful, the balance perfect, making it seem deceptively light for its size.

Thomas let me hold the sword only for a moment, but when he took it back, it was to angle the blade for me so that I could see, so faint I would have missed it without his help, a pattern of flowing curves etched on either side of the thickened rib in the center of the leaf-shaped blade.

"Oh, like ocean waves," I said. "How lovely."

"Geometric," said Thomas. "I wonder what they used to draw the pattern? It's as regular as if they used a pair of compasses."

"It doesn't look old, does it?" I meant the pattern. The clean line of the curving design was simplicity itself, as pure as the first leaves in the spring.

With great care, Thomas took the sword back. "It must be very old indeed. Perhaps even older than the ring. A true treasure."

Working together as James and I looked on, Thomas and Cecy prepared the trunk for their spell. Then they wrapped each piece of the regalia in white linen and stowed it away, locked the trunk, and set a spell to secure it.

"It mustn't be permitted to fall into the wrong hands again," said Cecy, when they were finished.

"Indeed not," James agreed.

Thomas cleared his throat. "I'm delighted to hear you voice those sentiments."

Something in the way he devoted his attention to the lock on the chest, which was already quite thoroughly locked, made me suspicious. "Thomas. What have you done?"

Thomas regarded me with the most perfect expression of injured innocence it has yet been my pleasure to see. "Kate. Don't you trust me?"

"With my life," I answered honestly, "but in smaller matters, I have occasional reservations."

Thomas cleared his throat again. "I suppose I really ought to have consulted you all before I agreed to it."

"Oh, Thomas." James was looking pained. "What are we in for this time?"

"Now that we've dealt with young Daventer and the rest, I've replied to Wellington's letter. I've promised him I will see each of these items safely back where it belongs." Thomas corrected himself. "At least, safely back to where Wellington deems they belong."

A small silence fell as we took in the implications of this.

"Very sensible precaution," said Cecy. "We're bound to return to Paris eventually, so the Sainte Ampoule will be no trouble. The ring came from Aachen, and the robe is from Castile. Do we take the sword back to Milan?"

"No, oddly enough, Lord Wellington believes it belongs in Vienna," Thomas said.

"After all the planning we've done, it would be a shame to miss Vienna," I conceded.

"All on dry land," said Cecy, with great satisfaction.

"Although now that I've created a focus, it shouldn't be out of the question for me to travel by ship."

"Fortunate," said James, fondly, "given that we will have to cross the Channel to go home eventually."

"Not for months yet," Thomas reminded him. "We'll have to wait until spring for the mountain passes to reopen. I'm not melting my way over the Apennines twice."

"No, indeed." I did my best to conceal my shudder as I recalled the toll that journey had taken on Thomas. "We can make ourselves comfortable in Rome until it is quite safe to brave the passes again. I daresay we shall amuse ourselves very well."

"Remember," Thomas said, "at the next full moon, your lessons begin."

"I remember," I said. Thomas has promised to start me off with the most basic lesson possible, the magical equivalent of a musical scale. Still, I view the prospect with mild alarm.

"And no doubt there will be an opera performed somewhere." Cecy sounded most unenthusiastic at the prospect.

If I am any judge of expression, James wholeheartedly shared her views. "No doubt," he agreed, gloomily.

I could not resist saying, "But surely you and James will be far too busy for the opera, Cecy."

Cecy knows me well enough to catch my every tone of voice, so she looked a little wary as she asked, "Will we, Kate? Why is that, I wonder?"

"Oh, you'll be simply besieged with invitations. All the world will want to meet Mr. and Mrs. Tarleton, to see for themselves that you haven't absconded with Thomas after all."

Cecy, bless her, looked quite put out at the reminder. From the liveliness of her annoyance, I had no doubt James had given her a full account of his experience with Lord Sutton. "What a ridiculous notion. I've a good mind to box the ambassador's ears for him."

"I know precisely what you mean," said James, with feeling, "but I beg you to resist the impulse."

"Truly, I would never box Lord Sutton's ears." Cecy's statement was not as comforting as it might have been, despite its transparent honesty, for she was getting that gleam of speculation that those of us who love her have learned to view with alarm.

In haste, I added my counsel to James's. "Don't do anything irrevocable to Lord Sutton, I pray you. It would not endear us to Lady Sutton or her mother, Mrs. Montgomery, and I have every intention of learning as much as possible about Mrs. Montgomery's connection with Lady Sylvia. Another member of the League, no doubt. She was knitting in the Bishop's best style. I really must practice. When I write of all this to Lady Sylvia, it will require skeins and skeins of yarn. Enough to make a coverlet."

As I had hoped it would, this distracted Cecy. "Lady Sylvia knows half the world, doesn't she? And Papa knows the other half."

"Never fear," said Thomas. "By the time we return home, we will have met half the world ourselves, and we can practice our knitting as we keep up our extensive correspondence. In ten years, if nothing else, we will excel at all sorts of letter writing."

Ten years. I tried to imagine it and failed. In ten years I will be twenty-eight, which is very nearly thirty years of age, which is quite ancient. "It does not seem possible."

Thomas was looking as pleased with himself as I've ever seen him. "It's far from likely, I agree, but not impossible."

"Not *quite* impossible?" I asked fondly.

Thomas gave me a fond look back. "Not quite. We'll just have to wait ten years and see."